Laura turned towards the ballroom and, a moment later, felt the blood drain from her face. The hall between her and that particular doorway was thronged with earlier arrivals, standing in little groups, talking, laughing, twisting this way and that to see who else had accepted this unthinkable invitation. Every now and then their movements opened a random sight-line between her and . . . well, it was without doubt Maurice Petifer.

She closed her eyes briefly and then opened them again, praying it wasn't – and then just as vehemently praying that it was.

It still was.

The same shortish, trim-figured man who somehow held one's attention . . . the same dark, straight hair . . . the same full beard, as beautifully groomed as ever . . . the same way of throwing back his head and laughing . . . the same infectious laugh, bass and sonorous.

And – the moment he glanced in her direction and saw her standing there – the same compelling eyes. Their eyes met and locked in each other's for a moment.

Also by Malcolm Ross

On A Far Wild Shore
A Notorious Woman
An Innocent Woman
A Woman Alone

and writing as M. R. O'Donnell

Hell Hath No Fury
A Woman Scorned

A Woman Possessed

Malcolm Ross

KNIGHT

First published in 1992
by Judy Piatkus (Publishers) Ltd

First published in paperback in 1993
by HEADLINE BOOK PUBLISHING PLC

This edition published 2000 by
Knight an imprint of Caxton Publishing Group

10 9 8 7 6 5 4 3 2 1

ISBN 1 84067 197 1

Typeset by
Letterpart Limited, Reigate, Surrey

Printed and bound in Great Britain by
Mackays of Chatham PLC, Chatham, Kent

Caxton Publishing Group
20 Bloomsbury Street
London
WC1B 3QA

For
Katarina Ågren

Le ciel était très-prèt . . .

PART ONE

Nets and Cages

The reason why so few marriages are happy
is because young ladies spend their time
in making nets, not in making cages

Jonathan Swift

The carriage rocked slightly when Laura stepped in and a little more heavily when Giles followed her; there was even a suspicion of a leathery creak. Giles made a mental note to have a word with Hinks about it. 'Nip trouble in the bud,' was his motto.

'Blanche is such a funny little creature,' Laura said. 'I wonder if she knows it. D'you remember that ghastly children's book I picked up on the penny stall last month?'

'D'you mean *The Intelligent Child's Guide to Pestering its Parents to Death*?' Giles asked.

Laura laughed. 'Yes. She's reading it avidly. And she remembers it, too. She can't remember where she left her socks in the garden this morning but she can remember that Australia was once called van Diemen's Land – though she hasn't the faintest notion where it is, of course. She really is a most extraordinary child for a six year old.'

'She's a case for benign neglect, I feel. Why is Hinks taking us along Clodgey Lane?'

'Because they're digging holes all the way up Meneage Street.'

'Again?'

'The gas people this time,' she told him. 'I've forgotten whose turn it is next. The telephones, probably. We had electricity and water in the spring, didn't we? If the telephone men could manage to rupture the water pipes, they could keep it going until Christmas –

and then it would be time for next year's round to start all over again. Actually I had a brain-wave about that. Why don't you get up at the next council meeting and propose selling off the entire street? The four undertakings could buy it between them. Then you could wall off the two ends and they could dig away all year to their hearts' content. And the council could lay new streets for people along the backs of the shops.'

Giles grunted.

Am I talking too much? she wondered. It was nervousness, of course, because of the ball at Liston House. Because it was being given by Mr and Mrs Troy. She was more nervous on Mrs Troy's behalf than for herself. In fact, had this been any other ball, given by any other of Helston's leading hostesses, Laura would not have felt the slightest qualm; she'd be looking forward to meeting all her friends, dancing the hours away, setting the world to rights . . . and all the other things one did at such affairs. But a ball given by Mrs Troy – the first since all the scandals and the two-year-long round-the-world voyage she and Troy undertook in the wake of them – was quite another thing.

'You realize we may be the only guests there?' she remarked.

'You said that before,' he told her.

'It's still true. I couldn't actually name a single one of our friends who told me they are positively accepting the invitation. That's why it didn't say RSVP. Elizabeth Troy must *love* the suspense!'

They arrived at the turnpike and had to yield to a string of carriages from both the Wendron and Falmouth roads. 'There's your answer,' Giles commented. 'And we're among the *early* birds! They'll have to open the market square to park us all.'

'I suppose everyone's fascinated by the sheer effrontery of her invitation.'

He chuckled. 'But *we* aren't, of course – perish the thought!'

'Well, you have to admit, it is brave to the point of recklessness. Not just buying Liston House from the Kittos but throwing it open in the very first week for a grand summer ball. That takes some nerve – when you think of all the muck that came out during her divorce.'

He made a dubious face. 'I thought it was a very quiet divorce, as these things go. If anything, the general sympathy was with her, not him. He's a cad. Always was. And everyone knew it. The only job that man was ever fitted for was member of parliament. I never understood why she married him in the first place.'

'Oh, but he's such a very handsome cad!' Laura grinned.

'You mean the ladies were all on his side?' If it was true, he'd forgotten it; he leaned forward with interest.

'But of course we were,' she replied. 'Not just because he's handsome, mind. It was mainly because of *her* history. I mean, what was she to start with? A nurse! Her father sold insurance or something. Then to marry poor Bill Troy and have him die on their wedding day and then to inherit the entire Pallas estate. It's hardly calculated to endear her to the rest the town, is it!'

He shrugged. 'Certainly not to the grand ladies who actually run it! It took them generations to go from rags to where they are now.' He grinned provocatively at her. 'You and me included!'

'And then there was all that gossip about her and Courtenay Rodda when she lived at . . .'

'Tittle tattle!' he scoffed.

'They were actually seen *in flagrante delicto* on the rocks at Trequean Zawn. And you've only got to look at Trevanion and Zelah to see they're Courtenay Rodda's and not David Troy's.'

'The man's a cad,' Giles repeated. 'Troy, I mean. Not Rodda. Well, actually, they both are – but Courtenay Rodda's rather a jolly sort of cad, don't you think?'

'And anyway, those were the grounds for her divorce from David Troy – her admitted adultery. You can't get away from that.'

He shook his head. His glance conveyed that he thought she was being tendentiously naive. 'The *real* grounds for that divorce – even if they were never allowed to emerge in court – were, one, the marriage was a disaster and ought never to have happened in the first place. Two, he refused to consummate it – or, rather, to continue marital relations with her after their honeymoon – although he went at it like a stoat with her maid – whatsername? Oenone Beckerleg? That girl who used to live up by the church.'

'It's Oenone Troy, now!' Laura put in.

'Quite. But Elizabeth Troy – quite nobly, in my view – agreed to make no mention of all that in court. She agreed to take all the blame and admit to adultery – just to preserve his official reputation so that he could go on sitting in parliament. No cross-petition at all. Don't you call that noble?'

Laura shrugged a tiny and reluctant concession. 'She was rich enough not to have to bother about opinion. She just wanted to get rid of him. And it wasn't *her* money, either. It was all left her by *Bill* Troy.'

Giles clamped tight his jaw; for a moment his lips vanished in a thin line. 'It would be absurd for you and me to fall out, my dearest, over people as unimportant in our lives as the Troys. But I have to say I think you are being decidedly unfair to her. Bill Troy left her an estate that was bankrupt and run-down and on its last legs. I well recall a journey you and I made to Penzance once, when you pointed out that one could tell at a glance any farm belonging to the Pallas estate, just from its general dilapidation. But all changed for the better after *she* assumed the management of it. *She* was the one who took it by the scruff of its neck and shook it back into some sort of life. Whatever profit she got out of its sale was the profit of her own labour.' He stopped and drew a deep breath to cool himself down.

'Anyway,' Laura went on, neither arguing the point nor conceding it (though she knew it was true), 'what I was saying, if you recall, my precious, was that she was rich enough not to bother *what* people said or thought about her. And then – to pile cream upon pilchards – she goes and marries *Jimmy* Troy, who must be worth several millions by now.'

Giles laughed. 'That's what sticks in the gullets of the good ladies of Helston, isn't it! This nobody-nurse whose father sold insurance "or something" came down here and did what three generations of Troys had been incapable of doing with the Pallas estate. Then she took the profit she'd earned. And *then* she had the temerity to marry yet another wealthy Troy! I don't think "several millions" is correct, by the way; one million, perhaps. But that's what you and Mesdames Knox and Curwen and Treloar and Scawen can't abide – the fact that Elizabeth always lands on her feet.'

After a brief, frosty silence Laura said, 'I think what we really can't abide is the way the gentlemen of Helston are on a hair trigger to leap to her defence. A self-confessed adulteress who returns to the scene of her iniquity after an extravagant voyage around the world. And then, instead of lying low and living modestly and earning back the respect of her equals, she immediately buys the most prominent house in town and invites several hundred people to a grand ball – as if she had something to celebrate!'

He smiled, with a superior sort of amusement that always annoyed her. 'Perhaps she has,' he murmured.

'What?'

He waved toward the windows on either hand, where the view was hedged in by the sides of other carriages, all jostling their way round the corner into Church Street. 'The fact that, loathing her as they do, they nonetheless come! Every man-jack of them – or woman-jill.'

She gave an angry toss of her head. 'I wish we hadn't come now.'

He laughed again. 'And I'll bet ours is not the only carriage in which *that* sentiment is being voiced – and at this very minute.'

After a silence, during which they began their descent of Church Street to a chorus of screeching brakes and coachmen's curses, she said, in a voice deliberately reasonable, 'I really don't understand why the man-jacks, if you want to call them that – why they are so complacent about the fact of her adultery.'

He heaved himself across the carriage and sat facing her. Taking her gloved hands in his, he stared solemnly into her eyes and said, 'Is that a vague warning of some kind?'

'No!' She pursed her lips in would-be annoyance – though really to suppress a smile. 'Of course not. But adultery is the most poisonous and corrosive of all the social transgressions. It eats out the very heart of marriage, which is, in turn, the very heart of society.'

'Oh come!' he chided. 'This is the twentieth century now, not eighteen fifty.'

Her wide, astonished eyes stared into his, finding no

hint that he might be provoking her deliberately. 'Giles?' she asked in a tone both questioning and alarmed.

He shrugged. 'I can't speak for society, but I can voice my own view – which is that I wouldn't give much credit to a marriage that wasn't robust enough to withstand one or two small brushes with this red-eyed demon of infidelity.'

'Giles!' Now it was pure alarm.

'What, my dear?' he asked with every appearance of surprise at the strength of her emotion.

'Are *you* giving *me* a vague warning of some kind?'

'Of course not!' His hands squeezed hers. 'You are still the sun and moon to me. My life is still adorned by the stars you scatter. They light a world that, without you, would be nothing but darkness and despair. You are the first and last of all my wishes and desires.' He made a brief, comic face to show that he, too, was slightly embarrassed at this effusion. 'That's what I mean by robust.'

He did not repeat the sentiments that had accompanied his earlier use of that word, but they echoed in her mind nonetheless. His reaffirmation of his love was, naturally, comforting to her; but those echoes were less so. She would almost have preferred him to say that the slightest infidelity on her part would destroy everything he felt for her, and leave it shattered beyond all repair.

But the more she thought about it, the less could she explain why that would be more agreeable than his complaisance. He wanted her to feel free to love him in perfect freedom. Why could she not accept that? Why should she need the lash of his disapproval to keep her from straying – especially as she had not the slightest desire to 'go astray'? She thought fleetingly of Maurice Petifer and realized it was the first time for months –

for a whole year, perhaps. That proved it.

They turned into Cross Street, which meant they were only a few paces from the entrance to Liston House. She shrugged all uncomfortable thoughts aside and prepared herself for the immediate ordeal of exchanging greetings with their host and hostess. 'We shall be cool,' she said.

'Cool,' he repeated.

'Formal, you know.'

'Formal.'

'Correct I mean.'

'Correct.'

'Giles?'

'What, my angel?'

'If you don't stop that I'll kick your shins!'

Beaming broadly, her arms held open and wide, Laura advanced down the spacious hall at Liston House to the foot of the grand staircase, where Elizabeth and Jimmy Troy were waiting to greet their guests; Giles walked half a pace behind her, searching in vain for one shred of behaviour that might be described as even remotely cool or formal or correct. Laura would be annoyed with herself later, of course, yet her conduct filled him with a tender upwelling of love – to know that her heart would always overrule her head in matters of this kind.

As they drew closer he transferred his attention to Elizabeth Troy. They had never moved in the same circles before she and Jimmy Troy went off around the world, two or three years ago; in fact, she had not 'moved' in any circles at all, being far too busy either rescuing the Pallas estate or coping with that scoundrel

David Troy, or managing their divorce. Giles had met her first in the aftermath of the great fire that destroyed Pallas House in the autumn of 1894. The servants and farm workers had managed to save most of the furniture and art treasures and he had gone over there to buy some of them, since she had no house to move them back into. He recalled how she had led him around the frost-crisp lawns, pointing to the pieces she wished to get rid of and reeling off their prices as if she had an entire catalogue photographed in her head – an impressive performance that had commended her to him at once. He admired competence of that kind more than anything.

He had forgotten how pale were her light-brown eyes, how fine her auburn hair. It was not a face of great beauty yet there was something strangely compelling about it, especially to men – and perhaps to women, too, he thought, when one considered how strongly they reacted to her, whether as friends or as enemies. She always had plenty of both; no one was ever neutral about Elizabeth Troy. Merely to look at her was to come under some strange compulsion to adopt an attitude. You could actually feel your sinews gathering for a response.

Gathering or being gathered? That was something he could never quite decide. Was that magnetic, almost animal beguilement of hers an accident? Did she arouse these feelings within him quite unconsciously; or did she know it and revel in it – accept it as part of that universal tribute Adam cannot help but pay to Eve?

'Dear Mr and Mrs Troy,' Laura exclaimed. 'It was so good of you to include us in your little soirée!' A casual waft of her hand indicated the hundred or so who had already arrived.

'Mrs Curnow!' Elizabeth Troy was delighted. 'With

that wicked sense of humour – how we've missed it!'

'And how glad we are you decided to come,' Troy himself added. 'You, too, Curnow. Good to see you both again.' He had not lost his American accent – though here in Cornwall it might pass as local to the careless ear.

'D'you still have that little Regency whatnot I sold you that day after the . . .?' Elizabeth asked.

Giles chuckled. 'We do, indeed. Funnily enough, I was thinking about that dreadful morning only a moment ago.' He turned to her husband. 'And I remember something you told me later, Troy, when I said your wife had somehow induced me to part with something like double its true price.'

'Oh?' He raised a wary eyebrow.

'Yes, you said, "Never do business with a female. If her position's weak, she'll add in her sex and beat you. If it's strong, she'll subtract it and whip you to the deal anyway." D'you recall?'

'Of course he doesn't,' Elizabeth said vehemently. 'He says that to everyone.'

Laura, still holding her husband's arm, squeezed it rather fiercely and asked, in the sweetest voice, 'And which gambit did Mrs Troy use on that occasion, my dear?'

The lady herself took the question as humorous and replied languidly in the same vein: 'Both, as a matter of fact, but don't ever tell my husband. He believes it to be impossible.' Then, in a much more lively tone: 'Actually, I'm especially glad *you've* come tonight, Mrs Curnow. There's an old friend of yours here somewhere.'

'Of mine?' she asked in a mixture of delight and trepidation.

'Yes. A Cornishman Jimmy and I met on our travels in South Africa last year. He did very well in diamonds and – what with all this trouble with the Boers – he's decided to come back to settle in Cornwall. In fact, he's buying Yeol Parc – Courtenay Rodda's old place out near Wendron.' All the while she spoke she searched Laura's face for some sign of understanding. But every boat from the Cape brought hundreds of Cornishmen home – 'uitlanders,' they called them, sneering at their cowardice for running from the Boer. Laura merely shrugged. Her hostess turned and said, 'Trevanion, dear?'

A youngster of about nine stepped forward. Until then they had taken him to be some sort of hired page-boy. 'Yes, Mama?'

He was a solemn little fellow but with a hint of roguishness behind the mask; Giles, who hadn't seen him since he was about five, was forcefully reminded of Laura's remark that one only had to look at them to know their father was Courtenay Rodda.

'You remember Mr and Mrs Curnow, I'm sure. You certainly remember Henry and Gillian and Maurice. Go with them and see if you can find Uncle Maurice, there's a good boy.' She smiled at her two guests. 'He'll introduce you.'

'*Uncle* Maurice?' Giles murmured to Laura as he followed the young lad – only to discover that Laura was no longer at his side. She had lingered momentarily to ask Elizabeth Troy, 'Maurice Petifer? Is that who you mean?'

Elizabeth's eyes sparkled with pleasure as she nodded in confirmation.

Laura gasped and fanned her cheeks with her fingers. 'Whew! Thanks for the warning. It's not the sort of meeting one wants to come out of the blue.'

Elizabeth continued to nod. 'I did wonder. Actually, there he is over there – just inside the ballroom door, see? Oh dear, Trevanion and your husband have gone toward the buffet.' She had to break off and greet the next arrival.

Laura turned toward the ballroom and, a moment later, felt the blood drain from her face. The hall between her and that particular doorway was thronged with earlier arrivals, standing in little groups, talking, laughing, twisting this way and that to see who else had accepted this unthinkable invitation. Every now and then their movements opened a random sight-line between her and . . . well, it was without doubt Maurice Petifer.

She closed her eyes briefly and then opened them again, praying it wasn't – and then just as vehemently praying that it was.

It still was.

The same shortish, trim-figured man who somehow held one's attention . . . the same dark, straight hair . . . the same full beard, as beautifully groomed as ever . . . the same way of throwing back his head and laughing . . . the same infectious laugh, bass and sonorous.

And – the moment he glanced in her direction and saw her standing there – the same compelling eyes. Their eyes met and locked in each other's for a moment.

And there, unseen by her, not three paces away, stood Giles. He had halted on his return from the buffet room, transfixed at the sight of his wife's face. He had no need to glance toward the ballroom to see what affected her so powerfully. It was all there, plain for one who knew and loved her to read. It was in her eyes – he saw it in the trapped expression in her eyes.

He glanced back toward Elizabeth Troy and found her watching these exchanges; she smiled at him – a brief, unreadable smile – and turned to greet yet another band of arrivals.

'Can Henry and Maurice come over and play tomorrow, sir?' Trevanion asked.

'Eh?' He looked down at the boy. It was several moments before his mind returned to the immediate here and now. 'Henry and Maurice?' he echoed mechanically. Laura had chosen the name Maurice for their younger boy, he now remembered. Laying a ghost, she had called it – but that was when they all thought Maurice Petifer was dead.

'And Gillian, too, if she wants to play with Zelah.'

'Yes. Yes, of course,' he replied vaguely. 'They'd love that.' His eyes sought Laura once more and found her just before she passed through the ballroom door.

'Hallo, Maurice,' she said, in a voice that sounded amazingly flat and expressionless – compared, that is, to the turmoil within.

Yet why? Why any turmoil at all? If she'd met Elizabeth Troy yesterday and the woman had warned her of this meeting then, she'd have come in the calmest of spirits tonight, simply looking forward to renewing a friendship with someone who – fourteen years ago – had been so much more than a mere friend to her.

It was just the surprise, she decided. Sheer surprise. That was all. Those old feelings were quite dead. She was sure of that.

'Hallo, Laura,' he replied with an easy smile. When had anything not been easy to him!

Despite the turmoil, a part of her mind continued to function as coolly as ever. She knew there must be a dozen or more people in this room who would remember Maurice as her sweetheart. They would be highly intrigued to see how she coped with this moment of awkwardness. So, since her motto was 'Never meet troubles half-way when you can ambush them before they set out,' she leaned forward and kissed him warmly but briefly on each cheek and added, 'What a surprise, eh! How long have you been back?'

She had forgotten how sleekly silken his beard was; Giles had no beard at all, just stubble in the mornings.

He inhaled as they drew apart; she heard the faintest shiver on the rush of it and realized that he, too, was nowhere near as calm as he seemed. 'Only last week, as a matter of fact.'

'You should have called. Where are you putting up?'

'In Penzance.' He sounded a little surprised that she should ask such an obvious question.

'Your uncle's. Of course. I don't believe I've met him since . . .' She left the time unspecified; they both knew when she meant. 'You did well in South Africa, so Mrs Troy says?'

He nodded. 'Had a stroke of luck.'

'If I know you, luck had nothing to do with it. D'you remember buying a copy of the *Western Morning News* with me once?'

He looked at her questioningly. 'No?'

'You must do. It was the issue that contained the announcement of your membership of the institute.'

He smiled. 'I remember the issue all right. I have it still.'

'Of course you have – after all the trouble you took to get it! You drove the poor newsagent mad. You made him slit open three bundles, the whole delivery, and you inspected every single copy before you chose the one you wanted. I almost *died* with shame.'

While she reminded him of the occasion, her hand recalled a gesture it had almost forgotten: It reached up and placed a finger lightly on his forearm, and then rubbed it gently, persuasively, from side to side. And her eyes stared into his – not upward, for they were much the same height – now into his right eye, now his left. And her lips smiled.

Such was the attitude in which Giles found them as he entered the room. Despite the turmoil within, a part of his mind continued to function as coolly as ever. He knew there must be a dozen or more people in this room who would remember Maurice as Laura's sweetheart. They would be highly intrigued to see how he coped with this moment of awkwardness.

He fought down an almost overwhelming impulse to turn on his heel and, instead, came toward them, holding out his hand in greeting. 'Petifer! What a pleasant surprise! How long have you been back?'

And why am I doing this? he asked himself. He and this fellow had known each other since their schooldays, though, with almost six years between them, they had hardly been school friends. Indeed, they had hardly been friends of any kind, at any time in their lives – and especially not at that most delicate time of all, when he, taking advantage of those six years, had proposed to Laura while poor Maurice was still having a struggle to support himself.

'Last week,' came the reply. 'I'm at my uncle's in Penzance.'

'But negotiating to buy Yeol Parc, we hear?' Laura put in.

She did not need to sound *quite* so delighted, Giles thought.

'Or Culdrose,' he said. 'I hear talk that old Mrs Mullard might want to sell up there.'

Laura suddenly discovered what her finger was doing on his arm. With a short jab she disengaged herself, pushing him an inch or two away. 'Careful!' she warned him. 'We have our eyes on that place. You know we bought Chynoweth?'

'Oh, well, in that case . . .' He began making noises and gestures of disengagement from the very idea of buying Culdrose.

But Giles, much to his own amazement, heard himself saying, 'No, no, dear fellow. It was the merest whim. If you're seriously interested . . .'

The other two stared at him in amazement.

'I wouldn't dream of it,' Maurice assured him. 'Culdrose is a natural addition to Chynoweth. They march together. And Yeol Parc will suit me very well.'

Laura breathed out a most heartfelt sigh of relief.

Laura sank back into the upholstery of the carriage and gave a hearty yawn. 'Oh, do excuse me!' she said, lightly patting her lips with the backs of her knuckles. 'But what a wonderful evening it turned out to be.'

'Yes,' Giles said after the barest pause. He tapped on the ceiling with the knob of his cane and settled himself at her side.

She took his arm and hugged it tight. 'You don't sound terribly convinced about it.'

'At least I talked old Dewhurst into taking our Cornish butter in future instead of that Empire muck he's always insisted on.'

'Well then,' she said gaily, 'it ought to have been one of the best evenings ever. How long have you been trying to persuade him?'

'Years,' he agreed.

She regretted saying 'ought to have been.' It begged the very question they were both avoiding. 'Did you count the number of people there?' she asked hurriedly. 'It must have been over four hundred.'

'Even the merry widow herself condescended to appear.'

Laura chuckled. 'Tamara Dawson? I hope she

didn't overhear my opening words to Elizabeth Troy – about inviting us to her 'little soiree.' That was *her* joke originally, when Mrs Kitto gave one of her vast entertainments at Liston House. How does a woman of her age manage to look no older than me?'

'As *young* as you, you mean,' he corrected her. 'Why? What is she?'

'She's well over fifty. In fact, I can tell you exactly. They bought Montpelier from the Morvahs in 'seventy-five. I remember the first children's party they gave, which was the same year, and I was only six. And this evening Roseanne Morvah told me Tamara was only twenty-eight then. So she must be . . .' He smiled as he felt her fingers go pitapat on his arm. How could anyone need to *calculate* the addition of twenty-eight and twenty-seven? 'Fifty-three,' she announced confidently.

'At least,' he murmured.

She collapsed in a heap of giggles on his arm. 'Have I done it again?'

'You've done it again. What's eight and seven?'

'Fifteen. Ah! Well, then, she's fifty-*five*. You see, I knew seven and seven is fourteen and I knew it went one side of that or the other. I just plumped for the wrong side, that's all.'

Experience steered him half a mile round that one.

Laura added, 'And actually, that's right, because I remember now. Roseanne Morvah is fifty-three and she told me Tamara is two years her senior. Anyway, fifty-three . . . fifty-five . . . what's the odds? She still looks twenty years younger.'

'Talking of which, I thought a journey round the world had done little harm to our hostess, either,' he remarked. 'And Troy himself is still pretty *chipper*, as he'd put it, no doubt.' He laughed abruptly. 'D'you know what he said? We were talking about their voyage – staying at all the best hotels and so on – "living high off the hog," as he expressed it. "You know, Curnow," he said to me, "eating sweet ham for two years, you get to hanker now and then for just one plate of cold crow or a slice of pickled dog." There's a lot of wisdom in those casual remarks of his if you think about it.'

She thought about it – about Maurice Petifer telling her of his high life on the Rand and how it made him hanker for the simple existence of a Cornish gentleman-farmer. Now it suddenly struck her that there wasn't much land with Yeol Parc.

'Of course,' he went on, 'this evening was her great triumph. She had every right to look so radiant.'

'I wonder,' Laura mused.

'Don't you agree?'

'No, I didn't mean that. I was thinking – you remember all that talk there was in eighteen ninety-nine, about the new century dawning and how it was going to . . .'

'You mean about whether it should dawn in nineteen hundred or nineteen oh-one?'

'No. About whether it would cause a revolution in people's attitudes. And everyone said of course it wouldn't, because the difference between ninety-nine and a hundred was just the same as between ninety-eight and ninety-nine. But I wonder now. Half the ladies who were there tonight definitely wouldn't have come if all this had happened five years ago. It makes one think.'

'Mmm.' He, too, stifled a yawn and apologized.

She cradled his arm tighter, pressing it against the side of her breast. 'And I know what *you'd* have been doing five years ago – in a situation like this,' she said archly. 'And there'd have been very little talking involved, I can tell you!'

'Ah!' He laughed uncomfortably. 'Yes.'

When he said no more she shook his arm and said, 'Not to worry!'

'No,' he agreed. 'It'll blow over.'

Storms blow over, she thought. *The last thing you could call this is a storm! I remember storms with you, my man.*

For a while each stared out of the nearest window. Then, abruptly, he said, 'Fancy meeting young Petifer there, eh!'

Her grip tightened involuntarily and then she let go of his arm, apparently to wipe the corner of her eye. 'Indeed! It was very kind of Elizabeth to let fall the warning.'

'And to get Trevanion to lead me astray for a vital few minutes.' He chuckled. 'She's a woman of infinite resource.'

Laura laughed and took his arm again. 'Silly! That wasn't planned. How could she have planned it? It just happened. Why *should* anyone bother to plan such a trivial thing, anyway?'

But he remembered the look in her eyes when they first located Maurice Petifer; trivial was not the word that came readily to mind. He went on, 'And fancy him making a fortune like that! It's taken us Curnows three generations.'

The remark surprised her. It did not seem possible that Giles would fish for compliments – and certainly not with her; they fairly leaped out of the water of their own accord when she was around, straight into his net. Yet why else would he add that last remark? Anyway, it hadn't taken three generations. He'd practically done it himself in the last ten years. His grandfather had started a small Italian warehouse in Falmouth; his father had done little to increase the business in his day. It was Giles who had turned it into the largest wholesale grocery and warehouse undertaking west of Plymouth.

'But all he's come back with is money,' she remarked disparagingly. 'He hasn't built anything or created anything.'

'Yet.'

She laughed dismissively. 'You're thinking of this absurd ambition to become a gentleman-farmer?' she sneered. 'A fat lot of land there is with Yeol Parc!'

'Aha!' His tone suggested he had been waiting for her to arrive at that discovery.

'In which case,' she said, leaping several questions and answers – as well-matched couples often do – 'why on earth did you make that extraordinary offer – allowing him to understand we'd step back from the purchase of Culdrose?'

'I thought it might please you,' he said, though he knew it was not true – that is, it might well please her but that was not his reason. The truth was he could not say why he had done it. Bravado, perhaps? It was like assuring Petifer that his return to the district offered no possible threat. It was the equivalent of young Maurice's favourite phrase: 'See if *I* care!'

Young Maurice. Is that what they'd have to start calling him now? Agreeing to the name at all had been another bit of bravado.

'It obviously doesn't please you,' he added when she made no reply.

The response that had occurred to her was that he only ever did things to please her when it pleased him, too. At once the mental censor who sat over all her utterances stepped in and said that was unfair. After all, when had she ever done anything that pleased him but displeased her? In fact she was sure there had been many such occasions over the years; the trouble was she couldn't remember them. She always found it impossible to retain things like that in her mind. She lived too much from moment to moment. The passing hour was too rich. Anyway, she did not wish to be that sort of carping woman who could give chapter and verse for every tiny complaint. She'd prefer to let an argument – no, a contretemps – go by default than stock such a poisons cupboard in her mind. She did so now.

'Well, I'm sure you had your reasons, dear.' She injected a humorous acidity into the words. 'I'm sure I feel indifferent as to whether Maurice Petifer is our neighbour by half a mile or a mile and a half – but I should prefer to look out over the fields of Culdrose and to know that we exercised *some* form of control over the man who farms them.'

He laughed, but so briefly it was hard for her to tell how much warmth there was behind it. Nor could she say how much jesting there was in his reply: 'If it's a question of your exercising "some form of control" over Petifer or our telling a tenant with a ten-year lease what he may and may not do with his land – I'd back the first.'

He did not stress that it would be *she* who would curb Maurice but *they* who would dictate to a tenant. Nor did he need to. She sidestepped the point by going directly for the nuisances she had in mind, no matter who might be their neighbour. 'Suppose he wanted to graze several hundred pigs – just beyond our garden fence? Or if there was a bad slump in agriculture and he let the fields go fallow for several years? We'd be plagued with cleavers and thistles for evermore. One year's seeds, seven years' weeds.'

Several other nuisances occurred to her, but two would suffice. However, as they accumulated in her mind, she realized that it might be a stroke of genius on Giles's part to get Maurice into Culdrose – since he was to become part of local society, anyway. There was no such thing as a perfect neighbour; strong friendships could wither in an acre of uncut nettles; it would be hard to keep an ancient warmth alive for a man addicted to dungspreading on the second Monday of every month.

The thought that familiarity of that kind might breed if not contempt then at least indifference was comforting to her. 'Actually – and since you ask – it does please me,' she said.

Now it was his turn not to reply.

But she knew precisely what he had been thinking when, at last, he said: 'People will despise Petifer for cutting and running from the Boers. But I don't. It's a wise man who knows himself – and Petifer obviously does.' He gave a contented sigh. 'He never was a fighter.'

'Dare I ask you to help loosen these corsets?' Elizabeth asked with demure provocation.

Her husband chuckled. 'And dare I presume to wonder why you told your maid she could go off to her bed?' His fingers tugged the ends of the drawstrings out of the criss-cross where the maid in question had tucked them seven hours earlier.

'Because I want her up bright and early tomorrow,' she replied.

'Oh?'

'Big day. Maurice Petifer has invited me to look over Yeol Parc. He's thinking of buying it – at least, I *hope* he's thinking of buying it. I shall certainly do all I can to encourage him.'

He raised his eyebrows and then, realizing she could

not see his expression, thrust his face into the lamplight over her shoulder.

'Well,' she explained, 'it might cross his mind to buy Culdrose from old Mrs Mullard instead. And do you happen to remember where Culdrose is?'

'Right next door to Chynoweth. Ah, I get you now – you don't think that would be wise?'

Her eyes sparkled. 'I think it would be very amusing. Not to say just.'

'How's that?'

'Women who marry for reasons other than love deserve all the spanners we can throw in their works, don't you think?'

He rested his hands, though the knot was still tied, and gave a judicious tilt to his head. 'It didn't strike me that Laura Curnow isn't in love with her husband.'

'Perhaps she is now. She certainly wasn't when they married. She was lost, head over heels, calf-sick – whatever you want to call it – in love with Maurice Petifer. But, of course, he hadn't a bean and her parents more or less forced her to choose Giles instead. Maurice went to the Cape to drink himself to death and instead found he had rather more character than anybody ever gave him credit for. He's twice the man he was. I wonder how Laura is going to feel when she realizes that – if she hasn't done so already. However, none of this has any bearing on why I don't wish him to buy Culdrose. The fact is, I want it. I don't think the home farm at Pallas is big enough for us.'

'Us?'

'All right – big enough for me. Another fifty acres would just about suit me. Anyway, perhaps the Curnows want it, too. I know I would if I lived at Chynoweth.'

He shrugged and went back to his unlacing, which he was deliberately spinning out to tease her. 'Lucky

Mrs Mullard, then,' he remarked. 'There can't be that many farms for sale in Cornwall with three millionaires vying to purchase – each for a different reason, too.'

'Millionaires!' she said contemptuously. 'I'll bet Petifer's not worth more than a quarter of that. Oh!' She breathed in and felt the constraints of whalebone and steel yield at last to the pressure of her ribs. 'That is delicious! And as for the Curnows, d'you really think they're worth *even* a quarter of that?'

'Half a million, anyway,' he conceded, slipping his fingers inside the loosened garment, under her arms, where he began a gentle massage. 'Curnow's a close one. He knows money's for using, not spending. Don't ever judge that man by his carriage horses.'

She sighed and leaned back into him. 'Oh,' she murmured with interest. 'At last I seem to have caught you with your pants down!'

He leaned over and kissed her on the brow. 'You waited long enough.' His hands gathered up the full softness of her breasts. As she sank to the carpet beneath him, he said, 'You know, this is an absurd way for people like us to behave.'

Fifteen minutes later she turned out the light and slipped into bed beside him. 'What d'you mean,' she asked, as if nothing had happened in between, '*people like us?*'

'Unh?' He opened one bleary eye.

She reminded him of what he had said.

'Oh.' He cleared his throat. 'People who've been married five years.'

'Seven.'

He opened both eyes at that.

'I believe we were truly married – in all but legal formality – that August in Falmouth.'

'Falmouth!' He smiled in pleasure at the memory. 'Was that seven years ago?' He lay back and draped his arm loosely about her as she settled her head upon his shoulder. After a longish pause he said, 'Are you falling asleep there?'

'No.' She sighed. 'I was thinking.'

'About Petifer and Laura Curnow?'

She pressed her head against his shoulder. 'It's hopeless to try and keep things from you. How did you know I was thinking about them?'

'I saw you watching them – most of the evening, in fact. So tell me . . . there was something between them once upon a time, eh?'

'Let's hope so. I mean let's hope it is "once upon a time" – or was. Otherwise people will blame me, as usual. But how was I to know? When I invited Maurice's uncle I had no idea the young fellow himself was back in Cornwall. And when the uncle couldn't come . . .' She shrugged helplessly. 'But who's going to believe that – especially with my reputation!'

'With your thoroughly *deserved* reputation,' he said mildly.

She chuckled. 'You're right – did the world but know me as well as you do! Talking of which, it's going to be funny visiting Yeol Parc again. I haven't been there since Courtenay sold up.' After a pause she added. 'I lost my virginity there, you know – New Year's Eve, eighteen ninety. Already it seems a lifetime ago. In fact, it's almost as if it happened to another person.'

'What were Laura Curnow's parents like?' he asked.

'Why?'

'I can't imagine anyone forcing that young lady to marry against her will. How old was she?'

'Well now. Henry, their eldest, is thirteen. So they were married in 'eighty-eight. So she was . . . nineteen.'

'Then she can't have been more than eighteen when

there was all that business with Petifer. So that was just puppy love. It's no threat now.'

'Oh Jimmy!' She turned and kissed him briefly. 'You're such a *nice* man. You *want* it to be no threat, don't you. But I think you're wrong, all the same. The point is, it never *finished* properly. It didn't wither and die naturally, even if it was just puppy love. It was ended for them – harshly. And things like that leave wounds. And wounds don't always heal inside. I wish Sibylla Johnson hadn't gone away.'

'She'll be back in a week or two.'

'Yes, but she should be here now. This is when it counts. She's Laura's first cousin, I guess you know.'

'I didn't, actually.'

'Well, she knows her better than anyone. She helped her over having to part with Maurice, or so I'm told.' After a pause she added, 'Of course, it helped that she herself couldn't stand the man.'

'You didn't tell me about Laura Curnow's parents. Are they Cornish? Or were they, perhaps?'

'Her father was. Enoch Nisbet. There were three brothers: Drogo, Enoch, and Jethro.'

He laughed. 'My God, I can just see them, can't you – Drogo, Enoch, and Jethro!'

'You could still see Drogo – if you went to London. But the other two are "upalong," as Oenone used to say. In their boxes. Jethro was Sibylla's – father. A bit of a nonentity, they say. But Enoch was a dreadful man. No – he was more than just dreadful. He was an *impossible* man. I only saw him once, the year he died, about six years ago. But I knew him immediately, from everything I'd heard about him. I saw him go marching across the street – Coinagehall Street, it was, outside Buckett's the ironmongers. There was a gang of labourers on outdoor relief and he just stood there and harangued them on the virtue of *not* leaning on their shovels. He said things like, "From the slope of your brow, young man, and the mulish projection of your jaw, I perceive you to be a person of low intellect who can probably aspire to no higher avocation than that in which you are now engaged – or, to be precise, *not* engaged, which is, indeed, the point I wish to make to you." He could go on like that for ever and a day.'

'That was the year he died, you say. You're sure you don't mean the *hour* he died.'

She laughed. 'No – though how he escaped being murdered, I cannot imagine. He did a lot of that sort of public haranguing. But people just stood there and took it on the chin. He had that maddening ability to convince you – while he was there and actually talking – he could somehow convince you he was absolutely right. It was only later that you sort of shook your head and asked yourself how you could possibly have been taken in by him. But he'd do it again next time. Time after time.'

Jimmy made no response.

'Next question?' she prompted.

'I was thinking that Giles Curnow must have come as a pleasant surprise to Laura after a father like that. Can you imagine *him* laying down the law in such a fashion?'

'I wouldn't say he's a weak man.'

'Unh-*unh*! Far from it. Her father sounds weak to me – unsure of himself, anyway. But I have a lot of time for Curnow. Most men, you ask them how sweet the ham is and they'll start telling you the pedigree of the hog farmer. But not him. And Laura Curnow steps up a rung or two in my estimation, I may say. If she can go from a father like Enoch Nisbet to a husband who'd give her enough rope to hang herself ten times over – and *not* hang herself even once . . . well!'

'Not once . . . yet,' Elizabeth said.

Yeol Parc, a modestly imposing granite house, stood just under two miles northwest of Helston in arable country that was neither one thing nor t'other; it was neither the rich sort of farmland you find around the Helford River, nor was it the meagre, unyielding soil of the uplands between Helston and Redruth. The house itself was of an intermediate character, too. When Courtenay Rodda had bought it back in the 'eighties, people said it was too good for the likes of him, for the Roddas had never been anything more than tradespeople in a small way of business – and all of it retail, too. But now, Elizabeth reflected as she walked across the moor that Sunday evening, if Maurice Petifer bought the place, people would say it was far and away too modest for a man of his means – or his *rumoured* means, at least. Tongues would surely wag along those lines.

She rounded the flank of Little Tregathennan Hill, where the house at last came into view, and paused a moment to survey it. She was glad of a small pause for, though the heat of the day had been tempered by a stiff breeze, it had died almost as soon as she had set off, leaving her overdressed for what was now a calm, warm evening; late already, she had not felt able to turn back and change. Furze popped crisply all about her and skylarks held their final, manic auctions of their summer territories. It had rained briefly around mid-afternoon and a mighty fragrance, hot and soporific, rose off moorland and pasture all about her as she stood there and ran her eyes over the old house.

Oh, so many memories!

New Year's Eve, twelve years ago – the day she finally crossed the Rubicon. Courtenay had given a great party at Yeol Parc and had then escorted her back to Lavender Cottage – mainly to show off the new pressure lantern he'd been given for Christmas. Then he'd sneaked round the back, got out a ladder, and tried to climb in by her bedroom window. And so, to make him go away, she'd had to promise him she'd steal back to Yeol Parc when she was sure Oenone, her maid, was asleep. 'To make him go away!' She could smile now at the little fiction that had saved her face at the time. What a night that had been! As one very diplomatic adjudicator had said of the choir over to Germoe – 'I've heard sweeter, but never louder!' She had known sweeter nights since but never one more tempestuous than that.

Her eyes sought out the bedroom window. 'That's where it happened,' she told herself – and was disappointed to realize it meant nothing very special to her now. Her heart beat no faster; no sudden flush of remembered pleasure passed through her. It was just a memory – one among so many others.

The same sort of graying had happened with Bill's grave in Helston churchyard. Once, it had been the most fraught and moving place in all her world; now, although she still went to tend it every week and still told him all her news as she worked away, it had no more power to move her than any other grave in the place. Like them, it was a general reminder of her own mortality, but its specialness had departed, washed out by so many tears; all that remained was its very ordinariness.

There was a movement at the window; her eyesight was not good enough to let her identify Maurice Petifer for certain, but who else could it be? As she set off again, stepping out briskly to show him she knew she was late, she reflected how sad it was that all emotions – of love, sorrow, and passion of every kind – sooner or later grayed out to nothing, to be remembered only as a fact. But then, thinking of the man she was about to meet and the reunion he had enjoyed (or undergone?)

at Liston House last night . . . perhaps it was just as well.

He was waiting at the door to greet her. 'Sorry, am I late?' she asked brazenly.

'Not in the least,' he lied with equal ease. 'I got here early.'

'Keen to gloat over your good fortune in finding the place on the market, eh?' she commented.

As she walked toward him she tried to imagine how Laura Curnow must have felt on seeing him again. Their love had been broken up and Maurice had departed for the Rand a year or two before she, Elizabeth, had first come down to Cornwall; so she only had the word of others to go on – and she knew, from bitter experience, how they could exaggerate. It would be hard, however, to exaggerate the look she had seen in this man's eye last night, when he and Laura came face to face for the first time in . . . what? Something like fifteen years.

He had a great deal of magnetic charm, she had to allow – of a kind often possessed by short, powerfully built men. And a wary eye, too – the sort of eye she had come to associate with men who had gone out to make their own way in the empire; she had met her share of them during her travels with Jimmy. She had described him to George Ivey, an artist friend of hers who had formerly been a lawyer and who had known Petifer quite well. According to him, the fellow had been rather nondescript as a young man. 'I wouldn't have let them push me aside like that,' he had said. Now she couldn't imagine anyone pushing Maurice Petifer aside. How, she wondered, did *he* look upon his former self?

'I hope you haven't had second thoughts, Elizabeth?' he remarked.

She looked at him in surprise, which he misinterpreted. 'Or would you prefer me to call you Mrs Troy here in Cornwall?'

'Oh no, Maurice, that would be absurd.'

'Well, that's good of you. But I do realize that those informalities which come so naturally out on the veldt are not necessarily . . . I mean, they may not survive transplantation to these cooler climes.'

'What were you saying about second thoughts? What might I have had second thoughts about?'

'Oh, this visit, you know. I was standing at one of the upstairs windows and saw you hesitate the moment the place came into view.'

Two possible replies occurred to her, both true. One was about feeling hot, the other concerned the memories that can hang around old houses; the second suited her purpose best so she gave it him.

'Ah!' He stood aside to usher her in. 'Memories.'

'Yes, of course,' she replied, as if the thought had not previously struck her. 'You must know what I mean – you better than most. I lived all the early part of my life in Malvern, but I've never been back there since I went to train in London. I was a nurse, you know.'

He nodded. 'You told me – when you took that kaffir thorn out of my finger. Remember that night?'

'Oh yes!'

A night on the Great Karroo, when there had been more stars than you might hope to see anywhere else on earth; a breathless night, smelling of bittersweet aloes and nameless succulents whose flesh was still hot from the pitiless sun – a curiously stirring odour, which still had power to stir her a little now. 'I wonder how I'd feel if by chance I returned to Malvern tomorrow,' she concluded. 'Shall we start in the attics and work down?'

Side by side they ascended the broad staircase. 'It

really is very good of you to give up part of your Sunday like this,' he remarked.

'Oh, I enjoy looking over old houses, Maurice. Builders are the cunningest, slyest creatures on the face of this earth. In fact, I believe "serpent" in the Garden of Eden story is a mistranslation of "builder." He was building a house for Adam and Eve, I'm sure – I mean, isn't that the first thing *every* married couple needs? And he didn't tempt them with anything so simple as fruit off a tree – no, he showed them plans for extra conservatories . . . a new wing . . . a tennis court . . . don't you think?'

He laughed at her charming fancy and then moved behind her to ascend the narrower stair to the attics. Immediately she became conscious of moving more gracefully – showing off to him. 'But after a number of years,' she went on, 'their sins find them out – builders. You'd never believe the things I discovered at Liston House before we bought it. Also I especially adore looking over houses where friends of mine once lived.'

'Yes, I gather you know Courtenay Rodda quite well.'

Having reached the stairhead she turned to face him, to see if he were being facetious. But if he was, nothing in his expression revealed it. 'You might put it that way, Maurice. Didn't you know he and I jointly own the *Helston Vindicator?*'

He arched his eyebrows and dipped his head. 'That I didn't. You have an excellent farming section, if I may say so.'

'Ah yes,' she said vaguely. 'Farming.'

She clambered onto a rather rickety chair and poked her head up into the minuscule roof space above the attic ceilings. 'You can see everything,' she announced with surprise, 'there's a window in the wall at the end.

This roof's been treated recently.'

She jumped lightly down to let him see for himself; his eyes barely cleared the rim of the trapdoor. 'Courtenay told me he had it redone back in 'eighty-eight sometime,' he said. If the date stirred any memories in him, he gave no sign of it. 'Looks pretty good, anyway,' he added, leaping down, too.

They returned to the corridor again, where he merely glanced up the passage and said, 'The numbers of servants they must have kept to run the place in those times!'

She realized then that he had already decided not to buy the house – before he even came here today. So why had he brought her here? An uncomfortable premonition seized her.

'Where would one get so many now!' he added. 'How do you manage at Liston House, if I may ask?'

'We keep a permanent rump of about six – which we augment with casual hirings for occasions like last night.' He had already taken several steps back toward the floor below. 'Aren't you going to look at the other attics?' she asked.

He shrugged. 'D'you think there'd be much point in it? I imagine they're no different from that one.'

'Well, I'll just have a quick peep, if you don't mind. I'll catch up with you down there.'

The remaining attics were, indeed, no different from the one they had seen – not even the smallest damp patch or telltale crack in the plaster to justify a little homily from her on the subject of caution. She found him in Courtenay's old bedroom – the same room where she had earlier seen him standing at the window. He was staring out of it again now, his back to her, his hands spread on the sill – a dark, brooding shape against the summer evening.

'I have a confession,' he said with a sigh, not turning

to face her. 'I am in such a quandary, Elizabeth . . .'

'I think I can guess, Maurice: You've already made up your mind not to buy this place, and you're wondering how to tell me so without offending me.'

He swivelled round and stared at her. 'In fact, you're more than half right,' he said in a tone that suggested he was surprised she had read even that much of his mind. 'But that's not the cause of my difficulty, merely one of its effects.' He cleared his throat awkwardly. 'You know Culdrose is also on the market?'

Smiling, she nodded. 'And if you wish to go in for a little spot of gentlemanly farming, Yeol Parc has hardly enough . . .'

He shook his head. 'Again, that's not the real dilemma.'

She decided to risk all. Drawing a deep breath, she said, 'You mean the owners of Chynoweth.'

He closed his eyes briefly. 'You've heard, then. Oh, I suppose the whole of West Penwith is buzzing with it. That and my cowardice at running from the Boers.'

'Does that worry you?'

He shrugged. 'Not really. But gossip connecting me and her is quite another thing.'

'Well, Maurice, having been the victim of similar gossip in my time, I may tell you I pay very little attention to it.'

'You don't mind if I talk about it then? Perhaps you can help?'

She made a brief offering of her hands. 'If you think I can.'

'D'you like chocolate?'

She laughed. 'Yes.'

'Let's go out into the garden, then. All these dead flies depress me.'

'Look on the bright side. They're better than living ones.'

Courtenay had given her chocolate once, on just such a hot evening as this – her first evening in Cornwall – when she'd come across him accidentally in the back yard at Lavender Cottage, standing naked under the pump, washing himself down.

Unlike Courtenay, however, Maurice let her break off her own piece. 'You see . . .' he began. 'The thing is . . .' He sighed. 'I mean, the only reason I felt it would be safe to come back to Cornwall after all this time is that I was quite sure it was all in the past. Over and done with. You know what I'm talking about?'

'Laura Curnow.'

'Née Nisbet.'

'Yes, of course.' She settled back in the seat and stared up into the tree – some variety of apple with a fair load of fruit already set. Who'd get it this year? she wondered.

'In fact,' he went on, 'I was actually looking forward to a *friendship* with her. Some people say there's no such thing as a pure, disinterested friendship between a man and a woman. There's always a little frisson of . . . you know . . .'

'The builder in Eden,' she suggested.

He chuckled. 'But I don't hold with that. I think a pure, platonic friendship is possible.'

She noticed he did not cite their friendship as a case in point; she wondered why, when it so obviously fitted.

'And, as I say, I was looking forward to such a companionship with – Laura. I mean a friendly companionship, you know.'

'Why d'you say you *were* looking forward to it?'

'Because the moment our eyes met . . . it's absurd, I know. I realize I must sound quite absurd to you.

Things like that don't happen in the lives of sensible, mature people who've knocked around the world a bit, do they. I've never felt so *juvenile* in my life. Well, yes, I have – when I was sixteen and fell in love with Laura Nisbet for the first time . . . what I now realize was the first and only time. Can you imagine how awful it is to feel only sixteen again when you're more than twice that age!'

After a brief silence she said, 'Go on.'

'That's it. What more can I say? I think of her and I go all hollow. I think of her all the time. I'm sure my pulse is a hundred. But these are just endless variations on the same theme.'

'If you were sixteen in reality,' she said, 'that would probably be all you needed to say. But, Maurice, as you yourself pointed out, you're . . . what? Thirty-four? Thirty-five?'

He pulled a face. 'Thirty-four.'

'And Laura's married. And has five children. So you can't really leave it where an adolescent might, can you.'

For a while he said nothing; she let the silence grow, until it forced some reply from him. 'You didn't see her face when we met again last night,' he murmured. 'Her eyes!'

'I was watching you, though.' She chased the crumbs of chocolate among her teeth and tantalized herself with a glance at her only remaining lump of it.

He turned to her abruptly. 'Why d'you say it in that tone?'

'Because you had the look of a man who'd swear a marble statue loved him back.'

He gave a single, almost despairing laugh. 'You're probably right. I'm in such turmoil . . . how can I tell? I wish Sibylla Johnson were here. Do you by any chance know her?'

'Laura's great friend?'

'Yes – and no friend of mine, either.'

'Then I'm surprised you wish she were here.'

'Well the thing is, she more than anyone would know how Laura is really feeling.'

'But she'd hardly tell you – if what you say is true about her. Why does she dislike you?'

'I never could fathom it. She just doesn't.' Studiously he avoided her eye as he added, 'She might tell . . . other people, though. And then other people could tell me.'

'I see!' Elizabeth stared at her last piece of chocolate, wondering whether, in all conscience, she could now accept it. Then, before conscience could answer, she popped it in her mouth anyway.

He saw the gesture and chuckled. 'I'll give you *all* my chocolate if you do,' he said.

Laura had met enough trains at Helston during the past few years to know what subtle changes of sound each made as it traversed the last couple of furlongs – especially when, as today, the breeze was behind it: the thunderous roar as it crossed the viaduct, followed by a more brilliant note as it pulled onto the final, rising curve, and then the sharpened clamour when it entered the cutting beyond, framed by the arch of the road bridge at the western end of the station. Now, as the train bearing her cousin Sibylla approached, she pointed out these changes to Maurice and Blanche – chiefly to distract them from their eternal squabbling.

A brave sight it made, too, as it came into view at last, a saddle-tanker in green livery, panting for home on billowing skirts of steam.

'Loose stuffing glands!' Maurice said knowingly. 'They could save a million tons of coal a year if they dealt with all the loose stuffing glands in all the engines in England.'

'An engine driver's time is worth a thousand pounds a minute,' Blanche added.

Maurice, forgetting *Through the Looking Glass*, drew breath to challenge this absurdity, but their mother stepped in with: 'I wonder what adventures Martin, Agnes, and Meredith got up to in London? You'll be able to ask them yourselves in a moment.'

London! The very name struck terror into poor Blanche, for she had lately learned that the city was home to a certain foul ogress who was armed with two swords and lived in a chamber of horrors. She put her hands over her ears. She didn't want to hear a word about Madame Two Swords, who, in her imagination, was a latter-day incarnation of that Fiery Angel set to guard the gates of Paradise against the return of Adam and Eve. That particular illustration in her Bible had frightened her from the moment she first saw it. She closed her eyes now to stop herself from trying to recall its horrors.

Laura touched her arm gently. 'It's only a teeny little train, darling. If you stand back here by me, it can't possibly harm you – and look, it's such a pretty sight!'

Maurice found it hard to decide which was the more contemptible – a baby sister who was frightened of a bit of bustle and steam or a mother who *would* persist in calling an engine a train. A moment later, however, he abandoned himself to the heady reek of oil and steam, with their strong overtones of fish and porridge, the ear-splitting clank of rod and piston – to say nothing of the piercing hiss of defective stuffing glands. In ecstasy he renewed his vows to the sacred vocation of engineer, one fine day.

Sibylla stepped down from the first-class carriage. Sibylla the shrewd, Sibylla the practical, always bought a second-class ticket. On the main line she actually travelled second, too; but the moment she arrived at Gwinear Road, to catch the branch-line train to Helston, she would step boldly into a first and dare poor Frank Churchill at Nancegollan to charge her the excess. It was an easy enough challenge for the man to refuse. From his point of view a Christmas box of half-a-crown was more personally welcome, while she found it cheaper than half a dozen excess charges. 'That seems in order, Mrs Johnson,' he would say as he palmed her ticket and waved the train onward to its terminus at Helston. And 'that seems in order, Mr Churchill,' she would say when each Boxing Day came around.

'Sibylla!' Laura advanced upon her cousin with arms held high and wide. 'You look so well. Was it a tedious journey?'

They hugged each other warmly.

'I had the top bunk,' Martin told Maurice with all the grandeur of a ten-year-old who condescends to speak to a mere stripling of nine. 'You could peep out through the ventilator. I saw a Monarch at Swindon.'

Meredith, dark, stocky, pugnacious, smiled at Blanche and wondered what he might say that would show her once and for all that he was her superior in every possible way – even though she was three hours older than him. 'I was sick at Swindon,' was all he could produce. Slightly desperately he added, 'But it was worth it.'

'The land around here,' Blanche informed him calmly, 'is worth a thousand pounds an inch.'

Agnes, who, like Maurice, was nine, paid no heed to

either of her siblings, or to her second-cousins; she observed her mother keenly – how she laughed, how she smiled, how she shook her dark, luxuriant hair and embraced Aunt Laura (who wasn't a real aunt, in fact, but a first-cousin 'once removed,' whatever that might mean). And she could feel her own muscles twitching in barely perceptible mimicry.

'Haven't you grown!' Laura exclaimed when it was her turn for a hug. 'Quite the little lady now.'

People, Agnes realized, go to heaven for saying less. 'How's Gillian?' she asked and then dutifully added Henry's name.

'She has a slight chill, otherwise wild horses wouldn't have kept her away today,' Laura assured her.

The children were put in the dogcart with the luggage. Agnes wished to sit with the two grown-ups but Laura mollified their refusal by pointing out that Martin and Maurice weren't nearly sensible enough to look after the two young ones on their own.

'Well!' she exclaimed to Sibylla when they were alone in the gig at last. 'And how was Uncle Drogo? Did he deign to talk to you this time?'

'Once! He said, "Good morning, my dear"!'

'My my!'

'All those weeks in his house and just four words spoken! What an extraordinary family we are! But – my dear, you'll never guess!' Her eyes checked briefly that no one else was in earshot. 'I have met the Scarlet Woman herself at last! Not just glimpsed her on the stair. I mean actually talked with her.'

'No!' Laura's startled jerk on the reins checked the pony for a moment. 'What's her name? What's she like?'

'Such a story! Don't breathe a word to Uncle Drogo, mind. He knows nothing of our meeting.'

Behind her own eagerness to hear the tale, Laura was aware of a certain disappointment. The Scarlet Woman was Drogo Nisbet's mistress – or his 'mysterious,' as she and Sibylla had always jokingly pronounced it. He had a house in Fitzroy Square, on the northern fringe of Soho in London, and on the rare occasions when one or other of the cousins had visited him there they had, even more rarely, caught glimpses of a female who flitted briefly from shadow to shadow on one of the upper landings. Many years ago, after their first few sightings, the cousins had assumed she was his ward, though he never referred to her as such – indeed, he never referred to her at all. Perhaps, they further assumed, she was a simpleton; they had both read enough novels to know that unmentioned females occasionally glimpsed about the house usually are either feebleminded or raving mad.

But then a maid had dropped a couple of incautious remarks and the two women were onto the truth like terriers; by then they had both been married long enough to know that novelists, perforce, omit a great deal of what goes on in the everyday lives of real men and women. And thus the 'feebleminded ward' of one type of fiction had instantly become the 'Scarlet Woman' of another. Her dimly lighted figure had swelled overnight from consumptive to voluptuous; her lank hair acquired both body and lustre; her linen gown (for females always go mad in white linen) turned to silk even as its cold, white folds developed a seductive shade of peach; and there was a sudden aroma of musk and attar of roses on the air, where before had been the chill reek of the sickroom.

'How old is she?' Laura asked, choosing a ground where the truth might take up a decent opening stance.

Sibylla grinned merrily. 'Forty if she's a day.'

'Oh!' Laura knew her premonition of disappointment

had been right. From now on there would be two females in the house in Fitzroy Square – the Scarlet Woman of their incandescent imaginings and the drabber, older creature whom Sibylla was now about to reveal. 'Did you find out her name?'

'Oh yes, we spent almost the whole day together. We did the RSA exhibition, had luncheon, and strolled all around Hyde Park and Kensington Gardens. We met by accident, actually at the RSA. Of course, I didn't recognize her, but she knew me at once, naturally. Uncle Drogo thought I was with Haskins and Haskins . . .'

'The lawyers Elizabeth Troy recommended?'

Sibylla nodded. 'Anyway, they had some sort of crisis at the High Court and couldn't see me . . .'

'It doesn't matter – all that,' Laura said avidly. 'Tell me about *her*. What's her name?'

Sibylla giggled in anticipation. 'I know what she *calls* herself. You won't believe it: Aureole de Verity! Even a third-row danseuse would think twice about choosing such a *cognomen*, don't you agree? But that's what she calls herself.' A softer light stole into her eyes. 'Funnily enough, I think she's actually in love with Uncle Drogo.'

'Stop!' Laura pretended to tear out her hair in anguish. 'You're ruining everything! I want her to go on being young, devastatingly beautiful, hard as nails, heartless, tough, single-minded . . . all that – and you're turning her into a powdered, middle-aged ex-danseuse with a heart of gold.'

Sibylla laughed. 'Actually, she's all of that and more. You'll love her. She wants to meet you next time you go to London. Twenty years ago she was all those things you say – and she still is a remarkable beauty. Powder and rouge have no part in it, either.'

Laura frowned. 'Then why does she throw herself

away on an old ogre like Uncle Drogo?'

Sibylla shrugged. 'She doesn't see it like that, of course. There's no doubt that her first . . . I mean, in the beginning, her first relations with him were quite mercenary and cold. But now . . .'

'Oh!' This time Laura warded off the conclusion with her hands. 'You're going to say she's a reformed character. I can't *bear* reform. Especially not when it wrecks my own favourite daydreams.' Then, serious again, she added, 'But she must see something in our esteemed uncle that has escaped our closest scrutiny all these years – beginning, most obviously, with his appearance.'

They turned the corner into Clodgey Lane and Laura explained briefly that they were digging up Meneage Street yet again.

'She did point out one of his sterling qualities,' Sibylla admitted, returning to her cousin's earlier remark. 'She says he'd never interfere. If you were determined on some course of action, something that couldn't possibly result in any good for you or anyone else, and he knew it – he still wouldn't stop you. He wouldn't step in and burden you with sound advice to the contrary. He'd let you go ahead and do it.'

'And that's a *good* thing?' Laura stared at her in amazement.

'Miss de Verity thinks it is – and she's a great deal more experienced and worldly-wise than either you or me.'

'Well . . .' Laura's tone offered a provisional concession of the point. 'It's something neither of us has ever put to the test.'

'Yet,' Sibylla murmured.

Laura stared at her sharply but her expression was devoid of any special significance.

'Tell me what's been happening here,' Sibylla said.

'You haven't finished telling me about Aureole de Verity,' Laura pointed out. 'In fact, you've hardly begun.'

'It would take too long. Besides, we've got all summer. It'll keep. But I'm dying to know what's been happening here while I've been gone. Is it true that Elizabeth Troy asked four thousand people to a ball at Liston House and they *all* came?'

Laura laughed. 'Very nearly. I mean, the few who didn't come have since been heard to offer explanations for their absence – rather than justifications, if you follow.'

'Did you and Giles go?'

'Naturally. Why d'you even ask?'

'Oh . . .' Sibylla's tone was too offhanded. 'I've heard things about that occasion.'

'Ah!' Understanding dawned on Laura. 'Yes, well, it's all true, dear. The gentleman you love best in all the world has, indeed, come back to Cornwall and, yes, he was also there that night. *And* we danced together! Twice! And the tongues didn't stop wagging all evening. Nor did the pens stop waggling for days after, I suppose. Who wrote to tell *you*, as a matter of interest?'

'At least half a dozen.' Sibylla grinned tantalizingly. 'Though, as a matter of fact, I believe they were less interested in *your* response to this sudden reappearance of old Lazarus than in mine.'

'Lazarus?' Laura echoed dubiously.

'Didn't you suppose he had died?' Sibylla asked. 'That was his whole purpose in going out to the Cape, wasn't it? I certainly thought he'd succeeded at it. But obviously it was just wishful thinking. He's destined to fail at everything he tries.'

'Except finding diamonds.'

'I'll bet that was an accident.'

A sudden bellow of anger from the dogcart behind forced them to stop and dismount.

'What's all this?' Laura asked menacingly as they strode back down the lane. Poor Hinks, at the reins, just shrugged his shoulders and looked at her rather gratefully.

Little Meredith, his lips trembling on the point of unmanly tears, complained shrilly: 'Blanche says that words are worth a thousand pounds each and I say she's a liar!'

'Oh no you don't!' Sibylla warned him.

'Some words *are* worth a thousand pounds each,' Laura said grimly as she drew level with them. 'Shall I tell you five that I know of?'

Five pairs of eyes went wide at the promise of such a costly revelation.

'I'll have to charge you for them,' she warned.

They nodded eagerly – anything to hear these precious syllables.

'Very well.' She drew a deep breath and made a sentence of each word: 'Shut. Up. Both. Of. You!' She smiled savagely. 'Now that's five thousand pounds you owe me between the pair of you. So you just sit tight and cogitate how you're ever going to earn enough pocket money to repay me.'

Sibylla rose, took her coffee in her hand, and wandered across the terrace to the swing seat. She did not immediately settle in it, however, but rested her knee on its very edge and swung it idly, a mere inch or two, while she sipped at her cup and stared across the lawns. The first hints of twilight were stealing into the eastern sky. Giles raised an inquiring eyebrow at Laura, who merely shrugged in reply. 'Penny for 'em?' he challenged their guest.

She came out of her reverie with a little start. 'Oh . . . I was just thinking how very kind it is of you to put up with me and my horde.'

'Nonsense,' he said, meaning he knew very well that that was not what had been on her mind.

Sibylla, however, assumed he was merely dismissing her scruples, by way of being polite. 'It is kind, and you know it,' she insisted. 'I really thought they'd have put my roof back on again by now.'

Giles laughed. 'You're welcome here as long as you like, Sibylla, my dear. Don't make such a fuss.'

'Let's hope we get a spell of fine weather now.' She finished her cup and, setting it on a little bamboo table beside her, plumped herself down in the seat at last. With one vigorous kick she set herself swinging; she caught Giles's eye and gave him a brief, brilliant smile.

Laura saw her husband nod, equally briefly, and then stare away into the distance. Was he attracted to Sibylla? she wondered. And she to him? Then she realized that was not really the question. Most men and women were attracted to one another in a shallow sort of way – otherwise who would ever embark on the fraught and often disagreeable business of marriage! She herself could admit to being attracted to dozens of men . . . well, a good dozen, anyway. Jimmy Troy, for instance, Reverend Whicker, Arthur Trebilcock, her husband's general manager, even old Daniel Jago, who was Sibylla's partner in the Ponsharden Shipyard at Falmouth (having been her husband Adam's partner before his death, of course) . . . to name but some. Also the man whose name she didn't know who worked the weighbridge down by the market – a man whose name she didn't even want to know, because, as with all these other fleeting attractions, where would be the point of it?

Her mind, however, flinched from asking the real question, for it touched too closely on her present situation.

'I must see if Gilbert's have a replacement for that Staffordshire dog tomorrow,' Sibylla added.

'Honestly!' Laura exclaimed. 'You're not even to *think* of replacing it. Neither of us particularly liked it – and anyway, it was every bit as much Blanche's fault as Meredith's. She's just more artful at withdrawing from the fight at the last minute.' She laughed. 'I'm sure those two will marry each other one day – the way they fight!'

Sibylla shook her head, pretending to take the prediction seriously. 'He'll never overcome his chagrin that Blanche was born three hours before he was.'

'Three hours and twenty minutes,' Giles pointed out.

She looked at him in horror. 'Don't for heaven's sake ever tell him *that!*' When the laughter died down she added, 'How he manages to break so many things around him but never one of his own bones I cannot imagine. He leads a charmed life.'

Giles pulled out his watch and sighed.

'Oh no,' Laura complained. 'Not more business tonight! Sibylla's first evening with us!'

He nodded reluctantly. 'A meeting of the Ratepayers' Association, I'm afraid. It won't wait.'

'Quite right,' Sibylla put in, then, to her cousin, 'See! That's exactly what I was afraid of in accepting your hospitality – that you'd treat me like some kind of honoured guest and disrupt the ordinary course of your lives for *my* sake.' She turned again to Giles. 'You go, my dear – for my sake, if for no other. Reassure me that I'm not imposing.' She concluded with a peremptory nod at Laura, much as to say, 'put that in your pipe and smoke it!'

Laura, miffed that her cousin was laying down the law like this – and even more annoyed at having to admit she had a point, too – made a game of it. 'You still don't have *my* leave to withdraw, my dearest,' she told her husband frostily. 'Some people are easily satisfied, but I require an explanation.'

Giles grinned. 'For you, light of my life, nothing is too much. You ask for one explanation and I shall give you three.' He held aloft three fingers, felling them one by one as he spoke the names: 'Mr Eddy, Mr Gilbert, and Mr Jake Morvah – our Three Terrible Tories.'

Laura's shrug conceded his point. 'What's the trouble this time?'

'They want to call a public meeting to protest at the town's inadequate lighting system.'

'And why not?' Sibylla asked. 'It *is* a disgrace. The things that go on in the dark on the far side of the Grylls Memorial don't bear thinking about. Certainly not in mixed company.'

He smiled, as people do at the naïveté of others. 'Those three don't give a hoot about how well or badly Helston is lighted after dark.' He rose and put on his jacket. 'But with the local elections in the offing, they'll use any stick to beat a dog. Well, this old dog will head them off yet.' He patted the inside breast pocket and then added as an afterthought: 'Also, their only interest in what goes on in the dark behind the Grylls Memorial is that, if it leads to a marriage, Mr Eddy will supply the trousseau; and if it doesn't, Jake Morvah will draw up the paternity summons; and – either way – Mr Gilbert will furnish the medical *requisites* for the *accouchement*.'

'Shall I ask Cook to put out some sandwiches for when you get back?' Laura asked. Meetings involving

Jake Morvah had a way of going on and on until the opposition was worn to a frazzle.

'I've no intention of seeing any of them,' he replied. 'I'm off to meet Mrs Troy, which I think will prove far more agreeable.'

'What can she do?'

'I hope she'll agree to insert a harmless-looking little item in next week's *Vindicator* – to the effect that a subcommittee of the Ratepayers' Association will be meeting the borough engineer, er, "in the near future".' He chuckled. 'By which I mean "after the elections" of course.'

'Jake Morvah won't let you off with that!' Laura warned.

'It'll buy us another week,' he said over his shoulder as he strode back indoors. 'And where that young fellow's concerned, any delay counts as a victory. Shan't be late back.'

When he had gone, Sibylla said, 'I thought Giles was a Tory, too. Why is he going against them?'

Laura waved her hand about, implying that the man was a law unto himself. 'Because, I suppose, he is so innately fair. The Ratepayers' belongs to the entire town, not to any one political party. Giles is as stout a Tory as any of them but he'd never allow the young hotheads of the party to kidnap the Association, even if it means losing the election – which it probably will. He'd rather lose an argument by reason than win it by force.'

'I wish he'd have a word with Meredith, then!' Sibylla rose to refill her coffee cup and then thought better of it. 'I'm feeling restless. Care for a stroll?'

'Good-oh.' Laura rose eagerly. 'Anywhere except down by the Loe. The midges are terrible this summer.' The Loe was the large and now sandlocked estuary of the River Cober, which runs through St

John's at the foot of Helston.

Not pausing even to put on their bonnets, they sauntered arm-in-arm across the lawn, making for the thin fringe of woodland that separated Chynoweth from Culdrose Farm.

'How long have you and Giles been married?' Sibylla asked.

'Fourteen years.' After a moment's calculation she revised it to, 'Fourteen years and twenty days. Why?'

'You've grown together very well. You're good company . . . both for each other and for an interloper like me.'

Laura shook her arm. 'Interloper!' she exclaimed. 'You're just trying to butter me up, I know.'

Sibylla patted her arm and let the matter drop.

'Actually,' Laura began, 'when you say you wish Giles would have a word with Meredith . . .'

'It was a joke.'

'I know. But to be serious about it for a moment – d'you think the children miss a father's hand?'

'They miss Adam,' Sibylla replied, not quite to the point.

'D'you mind my asking?'

'Of course not.' After a pause she added, 'I suppose they do. I mean, they must. Why? Have you noticed anything? You'd probably see it before me.'

'Giles thinks children don't really need a father until they get up to Henry's age . . . twelve, thirteen, sort of time. We have no idea, really, what's going on in their minds, do we.'

'That's certainly true of Blanche's mind,' Sibylla said tendentiously, as if that were the most she'd agree to. 'But I think my three are like an open book – and with precious little written on any particular page, too! Martin and Meredith, especially. I'm sure all they think of is devilment – looking round for things to climb or steal. Or break.'

'Agnes has changed a lot, though. Since I last saw her, anyway. She hardly takes her eyes off you. Haven't you noticed?'

'Yes.' Sibylla sighed. 'Perhaps she's the one who's missing a father. I mean, really missing one.'

'And what about her mother, then?' Laura asked delicately.

Sibylla laughed and squeezed her arm. 'Come on! Who do you have in mind for me? You might as well spit it out.'

'Nobody!' Laura protested. 'I wasn't thinking along those lines at all – honestly.'

'Well, you must be the only woman in the whole of West Penwith who isn't.' Sibylla was glum again. 'I loved Adam. We had a wonderful time together, brief as it was. When he died so suddenly I thought my life had come to an end. I really did. If it hadn't been for the children . . . well, I don't know what.' After a pause she added, 'And Daniel Jago, of course. It would be churlish to omit him.' Jago had been her husband Adam's partner in the Ponsharden boatyard, over near Falmouth.

They arrived at the woodland verge. Many years ago a gardener had lopped off several branches that had overhung the lawn, too low for Giles's liking. Sibylla paused by one and fingered the scar of new bark, which had now almost entirely healed over the cut. She glanced briefly at Laura, who smiled back to show she took the point. Then she went on, 'But if what you're really asking is do I miss a *man* . . . just a man – you know – in my life . . .'

'Yes?' Laura prompted after a pause.

'Well, of course I do.'

To her own great surprise, Laura felt a strong

intuition that her cousin was not telling the truth. Or perhaps not the whole of it. Something – the most important part of it – was being withheld.

Perhaps Sibylla was aware of it, too, for she now started talking rapidly, as if to fill a gap. 'But that only makes me all the more cautious,' she said. 'I mean it would be the worst of all reasons for tying the knot again, don't you think?'

'Would it?' Laura interrupted sharply. 'Why?'

The other looked at her in surprise. 'Of course it would.'

'Why?' Laura insisted.

Sibylla gave a weak laugh. 'You mean you think it would be perfectly in order to marry again – just because one simply could not manage one's own life without a man?'

Laura took her by the arm again and gave it a warm hug as she led her among the trees toward the boundary fence. 'Don't twist my meaning,' she scolded. 'You know very well I wasn't referring to anything so vague or universal as that. Nothing so airy-fairy. I was talking about something very particular.'

'Oh *that!*' The words were fairly dismissive but no actual argument followed them.

Laura glanced at her and found her staring across the fields, up the slope to the now empty farmhouse on the darkening skyline; her expression was calm but the muscles at her temple were twitching. A brief, knowing smile flickered at the corners of her mouth but was quickly suppressed. 'I wonder why they never built a proper Cornish hedge here?' she mused. 'I think it's an omen that you and Giles are destined to buy the place.'

But Laura could not forget that smile, which was made all the more significant by its brevity and by the thoroughness with which Sibylla had suppressed it. What had passed through her mind at that moment?

What had she been about to say – which she had at once thought better of, hiding it behind this jest about Cornish hedges and buying the place?

'You could run the children's ponies there if nothing else,' Sibylla went on. 'It would give them a change from that field by the hospital. Anyway, you surely don't want *that* man for a neighbour?'

'I don't want *that* man for anything,' Laura replied.

Sibylla turned her large, hazel eyes full upon her. 'Good,' she said. 'Especially if true.'

Now it was Laura who stared up the rise to the dark monolith of the old granite farmhouse.

'*Is* it true?' Sibylla pressed her.

Twice Laura drew breath to answer; twice the words died in her throat. Her very silence turned into an accusation.

Then there was a little commotion inside the darkness at the hillcrest, a stirring of a shade within a shadow; for a fleeting instant Laura was reminded of the first intimations of a migraine hallucination. 'Oh, my God!' she murmured a moment later.

Sibylla, who had been watching her intently, tore her eyes away to see what might have caused this outburst. A sombre shape, detestably familiar, detached itself from the general darkness of the skyline and moved down into the green of the hayfield. 'My God!' The words echoed those of her cousin but her tone was contemptuous where Laura's had been aghast. 'Does he think he owns it already?'

'Saw you from the farmhouse,' Maurice Petifer shouted when he was still barely within earshot. 'I could hardly believe my luck.' He began a lazy trot down the knee-high meadow, which was almost ready for its second cut.

Laura took her cousin's arm yet again, this time for more than moral support. But to her surprise she felt

Sibylla's arm as tense as spring steel. And she was shivering like a coursing greyhound a second before being slipped. 'Don't do anything rash, now,' she murmured.

'Rash?' Sibylla asked belligerently.

'Yes. And don't go and say anything rash, either. You know very well what I mean.'

'I do not,' Sibylla insisted angrily.

'You jolly well do.'

During the brief silence that followed, Laura was bewildered to feel all the tension go out of Sibylla's arm. The shivering ceased, too, and she appeared quite calm again. 'You're right,' she said. 'I have a *much* better idea!'

'Oh no!' Laura moaned, but it was too late; the fellow was almost upon them.

'Maurice!' Sibylla called out with every appearance of pleasure at seeing him again after so many years. 'I heard you were back but I hardly expected we'd meet so soon.'

Her familiar use of his name stopped him in mid-stride. 'Sibylla?' he said – his questioning tone being an oblique way of asking if he might respond in kind.

But she chose to interpret it the other way. 'Of course it's Sibylla,' she chided. 'Who did you think it was?'

He swallowed heavily and resumed his approach. 'Well, of course I knew it was you! I meant . . . never mind.' He smiled broadly and, coming right up to the fence, reached his arm over awkwardly to shake hands. 'How do you do?'

Sibylla offered him her cheek to kiss, which he was mesmerized into doing – darting Laura a puzzled glance as he did so.

She raised her eyes briefly to the skies and then, bitten by the same mischievous imp that had plainly got his teeth into Sibylla, offered her own cheek to him in turn.

Masking his delight in an exaggerated sort of gallantry, he turned to take up her invitation. But Sibylla's mood changed in a flash. 'Oh no you don't!' she exclaimed and pushed his face away, quite roughly.

'Ah ha!' He recovered himself swiftly and rounded on her in anger. 'Now we see it, don't we!'

'Do we?' Sibylla asked with equal belligerence.

'Your true colours. You haven't changed a bit.'

'And nor, I see, have you!'

'You don't even *look* a day older,' he sneered. 'Usually when one says of a woman that the years have treated her unkindly, that's what one means. But in your case, Sibylla, one means the very opposite. The years have *not* treated you kindly because they have left you exactly as you always were: disagreeable, malevolent, and evil-minded.'

They saw that he was trying to speak with a kind of magisterial aloofness, but they also saw the passion he was unable completely to hide – the way he jerked his head on words he emphasized . . . the fire that flashed in his eyes, borrowed, it is true, from the baleful red of the sunset behind them, but a fire nonetheless. In their different ways both women were taken aback, for the Maurice Petifer they had known would never have responded so surely and with such conviction. Sibylla was especially nonplussed. She wanted to hurl the insult back in his face, telling him he had not changed either, and giving him chapter and verse on it; but it was so patently untrue that not all her spleen nor all her contempt could bring her to do it.

So she did the opposite. 'But you *have* changed, Maurice,' she said coldly. 'You left us a hyaena, you return a jackal.' Nervously she wondered if they were not two names for the same creature – until she realized it would be an even finer insult if they were.

Maurice drew breath to say something further but then caught sight of Laura's expression and hesitated. She was grinning broadly. His sudden wariness made Sibylla glance her way, too. 'What's so amusing?' she asked coldly.

'Oh . . . don't mind me. I was just wondering if I shouldn't tiptoe away and leave you two together. You seem to be having such fun. I don't know! You haven't met in fourteen years and the minute you do, you're off again! Dog and cat!' She laughed.

The other two exchanged uncertain glances.

To give them a further nudge Laura went on, 'Are you going to fly at each other's throats every time you meet? You'll have people booking you like a duet when they fear the party might be a little dull. I'll be your agent, if you like.'

They had to laugh at that.

'Really, Laura!' Sibylla exclaimed crossly. 'You are outrageous.'

'And you're thirty-two,' her cousin replied sweetly, 'while *you*' – she turned to Maurice – 'are thirty-four!'

Sheepishly the quarrelsome pair faced each other again. 'Fourteen years is a long time,' Sibylla agreed ruefully.

He smiled wanly. 'Fourteen years and twenty days,' he said.

Jimmy Troy was delighted to welcome Giles that evening – until he heard mention of the Ratepayers' Association, coupled with phrases like 'spike their guns' and 'young Tory bucks.' Then he became restive. Finally, when the name of Jake Morvah arose, he suddenly remembered 'an urgent letter I've been putting off for the best part of two years,' and left the room.

'He'll come back when we're done,' Elizabeth promised Giles when she saw the disappointment in his eyes.

'The last thing I desired was to break up the happy domestic circle. It's really a very trivial request. I just want to ask you to insert a small, innocent-looking paragraph in the next *Vindicator*, if you'd be so kind?'

His hostess waited for the door to close before she said, in a near whisper, 'Actually, Jimmy takes the keenest interest in local affairs, but he refuses to show it. He knows your Cornish aversion to interfering "furriners," of which I am a good . . .'

'But he's not a furriner,' Giles protested. 'He's a Troy.'

'He's also a third-generation American – which they'd remember soon enough the moment he tried to dabble in local affairs.'

'But his grandfather was Cornish – James Troy.'

'Oh, I know all that. Jimmy is a third cousin to my first husband, Bill. So, although his branch of the family has been in America for the past half century, he'll still be considered a Cornishman. Whereas *I*, as I was about to say, will be an 'interfering furriner' until the day I die.'

'A title of honour in your case.'

She chuckled that he did not bother to deny it. 'Jimmy calls me his lightning conductor.'

Giles stared at the tapestry firescreen, letting his eyes trace the arabesques that substituted for flames in summer.

'You're an odd lot, you must admit,' Elizabeth prompted.

He nodded. 'And yet, Elizabeth, *you* have the last

laugh on us all, I think. If you hadn't married Bill Troy, the family fortune would have vanished by now.'

'Oh come!' Elizabeth was both delighted and embarrassed at the unexpected compliment.

'You know it would,' he insisted. 'Morwenna Troy had plunged the estate to the verge of bankruptcy – if not beyond. It was you who put it all together again.'

'And then I sold it all off!'

He waved his hand, dismissing her objection as too trivial to answer. 'There's no profit in tenant farmers any more. Selling it off was your best move of all.'

'Aha! Well now, I was hoping we'd get round, sooner or later, to the business of selling land – and buying it. So let's get your . . . what did you say – "trivial" request? – out of the way first, shall we?'

When he explained what he wanted, and why, she agreed readily enough to insert the little paragraph, which he had already drafted for her convenience. However, she did not at once return to the earlier topic – the buying of Culdrose. Instead she said, 'Perhaps you can enlighten me, Giles? I'm sure you know the full story. I've only heard snippets. What *is* the mystery concerning Jake Morvah? And why is he such an ambitious little firebrand?'

Giles shrugged. 'I was only five at the time,' he warned.

Elizabeth leaned forward with interest. 'At what time?'

'When he was born – or, rather, found.'

'Yes. I had heard he was a foundling – but he wasn't a workhouse child, was he?'

'Quite the contrary. In fact, he spent a large part of his childhood in this very mansion.' He pointed vaguely at the walls about them. 'Old Mr and Mrs Kitto were his grandparents – adoptive grandparents to be precise. It was their daughter, Roseanne Kitto, who adopted him. She later married Stephen Morvah and young Jake took his new stepfather's name by deed poll.'

'Ah, now it begins to fit together. Does anyone know who his true parents were?'

Giles cleared his throat. 'Do you have a particular reason for wishing to know, may I ask?'

She grinned. 'Or am I just playing Pandora! No, I do have a very particular reason, in fact. Since my divorce' – she uttered the word without shame or challenge – 'my lawyer has been Vosper Scawen. But he's over seventy now and is retiring next month. And it seems Jake Morvah will take over the whole practice. So I'd like to know all about him from someone I trust – having been the victim, myself, of a great deal of malicious gossip in my time.'

'Fair enough.' Giles nodded. 'Well then, for what it's worth, his real father was a blackguard called Percy Dumont. Came from a very good family over at Mawnan Smith. All dead or gone away now, though. But he turned out a dope fiend and a drunkard. Eventually he was reduced to living rough, sleeping in barns and under hedges . . . wherever he could. For a year or two he took up with a girl called . . .' He screwed up his eyes. 'Something Williams. Meg? Mary? Something like that – a Breage girl, another ne'er-do-well.'

'For a year or *two*?' Elizabeth echoed. 'Among people of that sort, two years would be an amazing show of fidelity.'

He shrugged, conceding her point. 'Be that as it may, it didn't stop him from murdering her.'

'Murder!'

'Very grisly. I'll spare you the details. Come to think of it, they must have been together *three* years, because Jake was about two when Roseanne Kitto found him wandering all by himself in the lane. Up Breage that was, the morning after the murder. Miss Kitto was born and reared there. Her father was only a humble stonemason at that time – but always very ambitious, you know. People would have laughed themselves hoarse then to think he ever aspired to owning a house like this.' Again he waved a hand about them.

'And she wasn't married to Stephen Morvah then, you say? But how could an unmarried girl be allowed to take in a child off the parish?'

'I don't know.' He shook his head. 'As I say, I was only five myself at the time. But the poor law guardians *did* allow her to do it – for whatever reason . . .'

'And her parents, too – I'm surprised they even countenanced it, no matter what the guardians said.'

'Again, I don't know. They must have had their reasons.'

Elizabeth peered at him intently. 'Don't you *want* to know? To me that's the most fascinating thing about Cornwall. There's the Atlantic on one side and the Channel on the other, no more than ten miles apart, and there's Land's End just over twenty miles away. So it's just a tiny little sliver of land. And all these secret lives are going on inside it all the time! Up in England it's all so shapeless. The fields and valleys and woods and hills just go on forever in all directions. You could never keep track of people and all the little details of their lives. But here one stands a chance – because everything *has* to happen inside that tiny sliver of land. Don't you see what I mean? Why did the Kittos allow their daughter to do such a bold thing?'

He laughed at her intensity. 'If you ever find out, let me know. Anyway, adopt him she did.'

'Did this Percy Dumont hang for the murder?'

'No. They say his parents smuggled him abroad. Anyway, he vanished for several years. Miss Kitto bought Wheal Fortune when the mine closed down and she turned it back into a farm again.'

'Still not married? What an independent-minded young woman she was, for those days!'

'I was there that night, actually – there was a big Midsummer Night bonfire at Wheal Fortune – the night Dumont came back and tried to kill them. He tried to throw them down a mineshaft.'

'Those Wheal Fortune levels are all joined up with my mines at Wheal Pallas,' Elizabeth put in.

'Of course!' He tapped his forehead. 'The original Troy mines. I'd forgotten you still owned them.'

A faint memory stirred in her mind. 'Was Percy Dumont nicknamed Scar Face or something of that sort?'

'Hatchet Face.'

'Ah, yes. It's coming back to me. Old Captain Body was my mine captain, God rest him! He told me thousands of tales about the local mines. I remember the one about Hatchet Face now – but I never realized Jake Morvah was one of the intended victims.' She closed her eyes and shivered. 'I cannot imagine a death worse than that – to drown deep in the very bowels of the earth. You know Cap'n Body was killed like that? When Deepwork mine flooded into Pallas Consols. Johnny Matthews and Arthur Cousins died in the same disaster. They hadn't a chance. Not a day goes by but I remember them – good men all.' She sighed and gave Giles a wan smile. 'So *that* was Jake Morvah's father. Are people quite sure? He's a very handsome young fellow – there's not a hint of a hatchet face about him, is there. Was Dumont really his father – beyond all doubt?'

'How can anyone be absolutely sure in such matters?' he asked – and was surprised to see her ears flush pink.

'Indeed,' she said, and dropped that particular topic rather swiftly. 'So, it was Miss Kitto who had the rearing of him. When did she actually marry Stephen Morvah?'

'Almost immediately, I think. As I say, I was only a child at the time. He helped save her, anyway. I watched it all happen.'

'Marry in haste . . .?' Elizabeth suggested.

'Oh, they'd been courting for some years – though I recall my mother saying once that Mark Bodilly was Roseanne Kitto's childhood sweetheart and everyone always thought she'd marry him one day.'

'Ha!' Elizabeth exclaimed at once. 'You've solved the mystery, man – why her parents agreed to let her foster the boy.'

'Have I?' He looked at her, mystified.

'Of course. It's as plain as a pikestaff, surely? It put the kybosh on any marriage to Mr Bodilly. He'd obviously have nothing to do with her while she had the brat at her heels – and her parents knew it. They already had their sights set on Stephen Morvah, the squire's son, a far better match, and an altogether more complaisant fellow – as he proved by marrying her. Voilà!'

Giles laughed at her earnestness – but could not avoid the thought that its intensity had something to do with drawing him away from that brief embarrassment she had been unable to suppress earlier. 'You said you wanted to talk about the buying and selling of land?' he prompted.

'Did I? Well, I knew one of us did. I thought it was you.'

'Culdrose,' he said.

'Yes. I suppose you've heard I was thinking of going to the auction . . . when is it? Two weeks today, I think.'

He nodded. 'A little dicky bird murmured something to that effect into the ear of my chief clerk one day this week.'

'Hm!' she responded drily. 'Vosper Scawen is retiring not before time. He runs a leaky ship. Now, of course' – she watched him keenly – 'there are some complications.'

He nodded curtly. 'You want to increase your arable acreage. I want to safeguard my flank – I mean, I don't want some builder to run up an estate of houses all down the side of my garden. And . . . well, as to other people's motives, we can only speculate. But it did occur to me that your wishes and mine are not incompatible – unless you actually want to *own* the land? Or would a long lease suit you just as well?'

'In which case it would be silly for us to compete at the auction.'

'Quite.'

She was silent a while.

'You see,' he added, 'I would be prepared to bid beyond what mere commercial wisdom would justify, *if* I were sure that you would be my tenant. Obviously, I'm not asking for some formal, legal agreement in advance. Just your assurance.'

'I'd not require the farmhouse itself,' she said at last. 'Just the outbuildings. What would you do with the house?'

He shrugged, suggesting it was of little consequence. 'You could put a manager in there? Or I could let it to a mutually agreed tenant. Or just board up the windows and lock the door. Mind you, your geese would sleep easier, coming up to Christmas, if the place were occupied.'

She smiled. 'It sounds very attractive, I must say. Having sold off a few thousand acres only seven years ago, it would seem a little odd to go back into the market for land now. Let me talk it over with my husband.'

'Of course. I'm only putting it forth as an idea. I didn't expect an immediate answer.' He saw a thoughtful glint in her eye and knew very well she was longing to probe his feelings about the prospect of having Maurice Petifer as a neighbour. The trouble was, he himself hardly knew what those feelings were; his mood could swing violently from fury to a sort of devil-may-care indifference. Then he realized it might help to discuss the business with her. 'I wish I knew what Petifer's intentions are,' he mused aloud. 'Have you seen him since the night of your ball?'

Her smile gave nothing away. 'The very next day, in fact. It is an addiction of mine to go and view houses that are up for sale. I have no intention of buying them, but I adore poking and prying into odd corners – especially the houses of people I know. So when Petifer told me he was thinking of buying Yeol Parc . . . and asked me if I'd give him the benefit of my *vast* experience – how could I refuse! My own partner's house!' She gave a little frown and cleared her throat. 'Partner in the *Vindicator*, I mean.'

Of course, Giles thought – what other way could she have meant it? 'What did he have to say about it?' he asked.

'Courtenay? Oh, he lost interest in the place long ago. And so, too, has Mr Petifer, I believe. I don't imagine I'm giving away any confidence in telling you.'

In other words, Giles thought, *the fellow asked you to let me know!* 'Well,' he said aloud, 'we shall just have to wait for the day of the auction, won't we.'

Jimmy Troy returned at that moment. 'Have we finished setting West Penwith to rights?' he asked cheerily; then, not waiting for an answer, added, 'Did I hear correctly – that Mrs Johnson returned on the afternoon train?' He stared at Giles's empty hands and tut-tutted. 'My wife is a wonderful hostess,' he remarked, 'if we have several hundred guests. But single figures confound her, I'm afraid. Scotch or bourbon?'

Giles grinned. 'I'll try some of your bourbon, thanks. And yes, your informant was correct: Mrs Johnson did return today. In fact, until they've finished working on her roof at Parc-an-Dour, she's staying under ours.' He added, 'She's Laura's cousin, you know.'

'Ah yes, of course.' Elizabeth took a sip of the port her husband had poured for her. 'I wonder if *she's* at all interested in Culdrose?'

'Why?' the two men asked in unison.

'Well, Parc-an-Dour's the northern neighbour, isn't it? She'd be every bit as keen as you not to have a rash of speculative houses going up there, I would have thought. Adam must have left her pretty well provided for – and the boatyard is doing a roaring trade, I hear. Land prices are at rock bottom. The only way they can go is up. And it's always a sensible thing – to buy land on the fringe of an obviously thriving and expanding town like Helston.' She looked at Giles and laughed. 'Sorry, am I just stoking up another nightmare for you?'

All the way home Elizabeth Troy's remark about stoking up *another* nightmare reechoed in Giles's mind. Did she really suppose it would annoy or distress him to have Sibylla as a neighbour? Or had she just been making a casual jest? In any case, it was, of course, the *original* nightmare she had really wanted to talk about – that Maurice Petifer might become his new neighbour . . . and all that might follow from it. Though they were hardly on terms of sufficient intimacy for such a conversation, perhaps she would have found some way of working around to it, especially if Jimmy had not rejoined them at just that moment. Now Giles felt a curious sense of disappointment – of wasted opportunity – and he realized he had, indeed, wanted to discuss his dilemma with Elizabeth Troy, precisely because there was that certain distance between them. But then again, his emotions that evening were so uncertain, so febrile, that his disappointment was immediately tinged with relief that he had held his tongue, instead! In short, he would merely have presented the spectacle of a man hopelessly torn between his head and his heart.

The primitive within him would gladly tip Maurice Petifer down the nearest mineshaft. The primitive would immure Laura in a doorless tower and ring it with bull mastiffs and boiling oil. The primitive would, this very night, haul the blacksmith from his bed and stand over the fellow while he fashioned the perfect chastity belt . . . at which point Giles's sense of humour got the upper hand and allowed him to shoulder the primitive aside.

Briefly he wondered what it must have been like in the days when no one would have laughed at such notions. He tried to imagine himself a crusader, setting off for the wars – how did such a man go about the business of actually placing such an instrument around his wife's person? Was it a mere item in some humdrum list: Lock up wine cellar; lock up silver room; lock up wife's parts . . .? Did the great man just stand there, holding that iron cage in his hands while she took off her clothes? And did she meekly step into it . . . forcing herself not to shudder as the cold steel was clamped about her? And there must have been several trial fittings for size; did she casually remark, 'It needs a little more curvature here, my dearest, and if you could file this edge a bit smoother . . .'? Did she connive at her own humiliation like that? Did she tell herself to be proud he loved her so jealously? And what words could a man say to his alleged soulmate while he performed an act of such monumental distrust? There were surely none in all the lexicon cavalier enough to bridge the shame of it. Yet how oppressive the silence must have been! What self-disgust must have plagued them as they flinched from comment on their own barbarity!

He tried to picture Laura as that woman, conniving at that particular notion of ownership . . . he tried to visualize himself in thrall to such an obsession. But it was beyond all imagining – laughably so. For that, at least, he was glad. And yet . . . and yet – that primitive was merely pushed aside, not dead. Buried deep within him, it relished such jealousies, and would nudge them into the light of his reason just as often as his reason rejected them.

There it was again! A picture flashed into his mind's eye, starkly drawn: Laura stands in the garden, playing croquet . . . and there, two hundred yards away, by the fence between Culdrose and Chynoweth, fronds of dogwood part an inch or two while a devouring eye gleams in the shadows behind them, turning a scene of charm and innocence into one of torment for him . . .

How many such visions, both real and imagined, lay in ambush over the months ahead, hid in jealousy's unsleeping calendar? He clenched his eyelids tight, shook his head violently, told himself that if he didn't get the better of these absurd fancies now, they'd reduce him to . . . something lower than an animal.

But how? It was easy enough to issue grand

commands: *Control yourself, man!* But should he curb his wandering fancy or give it such free rein it would trip over its own absurdity?

The trouble was he had not felt so *alive* in years. From the moment he heard that Petifer had returned to Cornwall his blood had run a little faster, a little hotter in his veins; like an old war horse who hears the distant tramp of legions, he could smell the blood that was yet to be spilled and he shivered in his stall. A new excitement had come into his life – and only half of him was ashamed of it.

At length, annoyed at what he was allowing to happen inside himself, he forced his mind onto other paths. Again he returned to his strange conversation with Elizabeth Troy. He remembered her momentary embarrassment when she had pressed him on the question of Jake Morval's paternity and he had hedged the bet by saying one could never be sure in such matters. But why should such a comparatively innocuous remark turn her ears bright pink?

Perhaps she herself was from the wrong side of the blanket? Now there was a thought to conjure with!

Then he recalled the gossip that had connected Elizabeth Troy with Courtenay Rodda – because of their commercial partnership in the *Helston Vindicator*, of course; people had to take a simple fact like that and give it the colour of scandal. It was hard to imagine a fine woman like Elizabeth Troy having an affaire with someone like Rodda. On the other hand . . . given the right circumstances . . .

One undeniable fact was that Oenone Beckerleg, Elizabeth's maid (and now David Troy's wife), had given birth to David's acknowledged daughter Davina on the very same day as Elizabeth had borne Trevanion. One didn't need much imagination to speculate on what might have happened nine months earlier.

Suppose, for instance, Elizabeth had returned home unexpectedly and caught David *in flagrante* with the maid! Perhaps she had flounced out again – straight into the arms of a Casanova – like Rodda, say, who'd been begging the Favour of her for months!

He laughed at the absurdity of it but also told himself that stranger things had happened. And it would surely require a shock of that magnitude to make a sensible and decent woman like Elizabeth fly off the rails with a man like Rodda. Laughter notwithstanding, he pursued the fancy a little further.

David Troy's hair, he recalled, was almost jet black; so was Zelah's – or used to be, though Laura had remarked only last week that it seemed to be getting lighter. Trevanion's was auburn, like his mother's. Could a man with such dark hair have been their father – what was the rule? 'Dark begets dark, even on light. Dark don't go pale, except in a fright'? Some such doggerel.

But no! Look at Sibylla's three. She herself was more dark than fair, though nowhere near what you might call black; and Adam had been almost snow-white; yet their three offspring had eyes and hair as black as jet. So there wasn't a rule after all.

Even so, that little blush of Elizabeth's had been . . . interesting. There must be something behind it.

The first person he met on coming indoors was Sibylla, who was standing in the hall, eating a strawberry. At first she held a second fruit behind her back, but then she offered it to him with a slightly shamefaced smile, saying, 'They are yours, after all.'

He declined the offer with a laugh. 'There you go again! Listen – as long as you stay in this house, they're yours as well. Don't think in those terms – even in the smallest matter. This is your home while you're here. I mean that.'

She popped it in her mouth and took him by the arm, propelling him toward the drawing room door. 'You're very good to us, Giles, which I truly appreciate, let me say.'

'Where's Laura?'

'Comforting Blanche. Apparently Maurice has been filling her head with nonsense about Madame Tussauds and the Chamber of Horrors.' She felt his arm stiffen at the name of Maurice and added, 'Yes, we shall have to start calling him *Young* Maurice, I suppose.'

'Because of Petifer? I'm damned if I will – pardon the French. Nothing will ever induce me to call *that* tripehound Maurice.'

'We met him this evening,' she said with an attempt at offhandedness. Though they had reached the drawing room she still held his arm – and was rewarded with another slight tic.

'Really?' he responded, using the excuse of pouring himself a brandy to ease her arm out of his. 'One for you?'

When she made no reply he turned to find her staring out through the now darkened window. His earlier image of a war horse sprang to mind and suddenly he knew that her intense dislike of the man – or hatred, not to make any bones about it – was like new blood in her veins, too.

He passed her the brandy she had not asked for and said, 'Success!'

'Success!'

The glasses touched; their eyes met and dwelled in each other's; Sibylla did not smile.

The hair bristled on Giles's neck. He had intended no more than a lighthearted gesture, a mask for his embarrassment at feelings he did not welcome but could not fully master; she had transformed it into a solemn compact between them. A sudden feeling of grandeur almost overwhelmed him – a fleeting certainty that together they could destroy Maurice Petifer and grind him finer than the dust.

The Culdrose auction was to be held at the farm itself, at half-past-two on the afternoon Elizabeth had mentioned: Friday, the eighteenth of July. Maurice Petifer had decided, after all, not to put in a bid – but that was no reason not to attend the auction, if only for the minor pleasure of watching Giles Curnow biting his nails to the quick. His plan, then, was to take an early luncheon at the Angel and walk the mile or so from there to the farm. He could do with the exercise, anyway; one of the holes in his belt seemed to have healed over since his return from the Cape.

At the bottom of Sithney Common Hill, however, he noticed a commotion up ahead, near the market. An urchin told him a horse had dropped dead between the shafts and that two farmers were about to come to blows over the loss. He decided to turn left and go in by way of Cross Street.

Then, as he happened to be passing Liston House, he thought he might as well call in and see if Elizabeth Troy was at home – and whether she had managed to have a word with Sibylla Johnson yet; if not, she owed him four pieces of chocolate!

Elizabeth, as it turned out, was not at home. 'She's putting that poor young Morvah fella through the grinder,' Jimmy told him. 'When she's reduced him to the consistency of good strawberry jam, she'll invite him home here for lunch. I'd kind-of like to tell her I've already eaten – and I'd like the added excuse that an honored guest unexpectedly called.' He smiled and held out his hand for Maurice's hat.

'We men are so squeamish,' he added as he led the way into the breakfast room, where the maid was just setting out a selection of cold meats and pies. There was a roguish glint in his eye as he concluded, 'I expect you'll want to eat at once? Get a good seat for the auction, eh?'

Maurice nodded. 'Actually, Jimmy, to tell you the truth, I've decided to make it a spectator's seat. That's what I came to tell Elizabeth. She said she might be in the bidding, too. So I wanted her to know she had a clear field as far as I'm concerned.'

Jimmy looked at him quizzically but all he said was, 'That tongue is excellent, but mind the peppercorns.'

'Is she in the bidding?' Maurice persisted.

The other shook his head. 'She's a law unto herself. But I'm sorry to hear you're dropping out. Beer? It's Rosewarne's Triple Export – I find it almost drinkable. I suppose you realize you'll be depriving the populace of a great show?'

Maurice laughed at his frankness. 'It can't be helped.'

They seated themselves; the maid fussed around them with napkins.

'I know that feeling,' Jimmy went on sympathetically. 'I, too, am not as young as I used to be.'

Maurice bridled, for, of course, his advancing age had nothing to do with it and he resented being bracketed with a dotard in his mid-forties. Jimmy noticed it and managed not to smile; if Elizabeth were in the room, she'd stop him right there. He stretched luxuriously and said, 'But the hush of advancing years brings its own peculiar comforts, too – as I expect you're already starting to discover. God, who would live through adolescence again!'

'Quite.' Maurice chafed under the constraints of courtesy. He breathed a couple of times, rather heavily, and then went on, 'Actually . . . well, it wasn't so much a matter of *anno domini* as straightforward common sense.'

Jimmy grinned at him jovially. 'Now you make me feel the difference in our ages. You're still young enough to believe there's a difference between the two – common sense and *anno domini*.'

'There's very good land at Gulval,' Maurice explained.

'And so it jolly well ought to be,' Jimmy agreed. 'They've been carrying the night soil of Penzance out there for the best part of five hundred years. A man would have to leap backward pretty nimbly after sowing seed there, I reckon.'

Maurice laughed at last. 'It's also much nearer home for me. I mean, most of my acquaintance is in Penzance.'

'Nowadays,' Jimmy replied. 'So who do you think Elizabeth will be bidding against – assuming she bids at all, that is? I heard Sampson has his eye on it – the builder. Or Mary Kitto, rather – she still runs that firm from her bed.'

Maurice thought rapidly. Jake Morvah was Mary Kitto's adopted grandson. Would that be how the Troys came to hear of the Kittos' interest? 'Is that speculation or pretty firm?' he asked. It occurred to him that, even if he wasn't interested in acquiring the farm for personal reasons, it might be worth the investment for straightforward profit – and he could make that blackguard Curnow sweat for a year or two into the bargain.

Jimmy chuckled. 'Getting interested again, eh?

Well, it would be for the best possible reason.'

The implication that any previous reason would have been ignoble was plain. Indeed, Maurice had never met a man who could make the unspoken bits of his thinking plainer. 'I wouldn't bid myself,' he said. 'But if Sampson's there, I could let him know I'd back him as high as two and a half thou'.'

Jimmy whistled.

'Fifty-two acres,' Maurice pointed out. 'As building land it'd be worth something between thirty and forty an acre. And the farmhouse and outbuildings must be worth a thou' on their own.'

'Not if you build over all the land,' Jimmy pointed out.

'No, of course.' Maurice laughed feebly, embarrassed that his enthusiasm should have led him to overlook such an elementary fact. 'Eighteen hundred, say. We'll see. It all depends whether Sampson's there or not. As I say, I wouldn't bid myself – so I fear I shall still be depriving the populace of its merriment.'

'That's a shame, Maurice. There's just not enough of it about these days. Did I ever tell you about my Uncle Stu?'

'No?' Maurice, glad the subject was closed at last, was eager to hear the tale.

Jimmy wiped his lips in his napkin, took a sip of beer, and leaned back in his chair. 'He wasn't a real uncle of mine at all, you understand, just a friend of my Daddy's that we learned to call Uncle Stu. He was one of a pair of twins that got separated when their mother died, when they were just a few weeks old. She was already a widow then. The other was a boy called Horace. Identical twins, they were, and I don't know what it is about those fellers but they always keep a kind-of hankering to be together again. Stu grew up on a farm in upstate Massachusetts, and Horace was sent to an uncle in Boston, a calico merchant and importer of wool. Well, the farmer and the merchant fell out soon after that – nothing to do with the two orphans, but it made no difference. They weren't more than a day's ride apart but they might as well have been on two different continents for all they saw of each other.'

He helped himself to another half tumbler and refreshed Maurice's over his none-too-strenuous protests. 'Anyway, like I said, there's something in one twin never gives up hankering for the other when they're apart like that. I can't tell you the coincidences they discovered when they finally did meet. For instance, on their twelfth birthday – the same day, of course – each of them, eighty . . . ninety miles apart, took a sudden notion to go visit the other. They both packed a pail of bread and cheese and an apple. And they both ran away from home. Neither made it, of course. They were picked up, sent home, and whipped. And that was the last of any attempt to meet up again until they were . . . oh, must have been twenty-five. Then that old hankering took a grip on them again – and this time they made it.'

Maurice surprised himself with a little laugh; it was almost like the storytimes of his childhood again. Jimmy eyed him somewhat sternly, as if to imply that his tale was not for mere entertainment – it had a moral. But he continued: 'Uncle Stu had to go down to Boston on business one week, so he wrote his brother and asked could he stay with him. Horace wrote back, delighted to say of course he could. Well, I guess you can imagine how it went. Come the end of the week, Stu just couldn't wait to hightail it out of there! And Horace was never more glad to see the back of any man before. They had *nothing* in common but their looks. They spoke different, thought different, liked different things – opposite things . . . there was just nowhere, nowhere and nothing, on which their minds could meet.'

'Were you there yourself?' Maurice put in. The telling was so vivid it seemed a natural thing to ask.

Jimmy smiled sadly. 'No sir! All that happened before I was born. Uncle Stu told me that tale when I was about ten. Two big boys from the rough end of town had stolen my favourite spinning top – a "canary," it was – made it and balanced it myself. Of course, there was nothing I could do about it. They were twice my weight and height – and there were two of them. But I told my Uncle Stu all the ways from there to Christmas that I was going to get my own back. And d'you know what he said? "Don't wait. Go do it now, son. Tomorrow's too late." His very words. Go do it now, son. Tomorrow's too late!'

Maurice saw the point of the story, of course, and smiled. Then, glancing at his watch, said he really ought to be going – or even today would be too late.

Shortly after he'd gone Elizabeth returned – with, as predicted, a rather pale Jake Morvah in tow. While the young fellow was washing his hands, Jimmy told her briefly about Maurice's visit.

'He's come to Helston for the auction, of course,' she said. 'That's why I took care to be out. I owe him four pieces of chocolate. I hope you dissuaded him from bidding today?'

'I did my best,' he assured her. 'I told him the time to get your own back is when it's taken from you. If you wait too long, what you thought was your own will have changed beyond recognition.'

Her eyes went wide with amazement. 'That was putting it pretty directly, Jimmy! I hope he wasn't offended – after all, it's hardly our business. Did he take offence?'

Jimmy smiled. 'I didn't put it in so many words, of

course. But I think he understood what I was driving at.' He paused and then added, 'I surely do hope he did.'

Maurice Petifer wandered up Meneage Street, picking his way around the potholes left by one or other of the public utilities and pausing frequently to stare in the shop windows. The displays were pretty meagre, he thought – not a patch on Penzance. Did he really want to come and live in this little backwater? Penzance was so much more cosmopolitan. On the other hand, give it its due – Helston had changed beyond recognition since the eighties, when he had last seen the place. Thanks to the railway, of course. The branch line had barely been opened a year when he left; now, what with overnight access to produce markets in all the big cities and an increasing flood of trippers in the summer, the town was noticeably more prosperous. If such progress continued, this might be a good time and place to catch it by the coat-tail.

He smiled ruefully at his reflection in Wearne's window. Did he really hope to deceive himself with such claptrap? If he were truly interested in buying land as an investment, Culdrose would be six or seven places down the list of favourable sites. Towns grow as inkstains spread, from the centre outward. It would be decades before the red-gray tide of brick and granite was lapping at the green boundaries of Culdrose. For a start, there were fifty empty acres between this very spot in Meneage Street, just before the workhouse, and Clodgey Lane, half a mile away up the hill. And then there was all that land between the church and the station. If Sampson was seriously thinking of buying

Culdrose, it would be as an investment for his grandson. So if he, Maurice Petifer, was going to buy the place, investment wasn't in view at all; let him be quite clear on that!

Uncertainty affected his stride. People began to overtake him. Many nudged each other and spoke in undertones after they had passed; some turned to stare at him with interest. He recalled Jimmy Troy's comment that he would deprive the district of 'a great show' if he pulled out of the bidding. He paused and took off his hat to wipe the lining with his handkerchief.

'Puffed are 'ee, boy?' called one he knew slightly.

'A trifle short of wind,' Maurice allowed.

'I got a horse home could let 'ee have a bit!'

They all laughed. Another cried, 'At least you won't meet no Dutch Boers up there!' The group around the fellow guffawed and they all hurried on.

The incident made Maurice realize what a figure of fun he had become among them. His anger rose. That settled it! He would most certainly not take part in the bidding. He would not even consider moving into a district so deprived of entertainment that a trivial little business like this could become the talk of the town.

It was the first time he had admitted to himself that his obsession of these past weeks was, indeed, 'trivial.' To do so he had to shrug aside the uncomfortable fact that it had been his obsession for a great deal longer – indeed, it had possessed him from the moment he arrived on the Rand and saw what fortunes were to be made there. With every diamond he found and every sovereign he banked, had come the satisfaction of knowing that one day he would return to West Penwith and flaunt it before those who had dismissed him as a nobody. Fantasies of revenge had sustained him through all those years of toil and self-denial. They hovered near the rim of his mind, but they were so juvenile he shrugged them uncomfortably aside and stepped out with a firmer pace for the farm.

And he would most definitely *not* be bidding.

Unfortunately, the mind only needs to determine it will not think about a particular topic for that topic to fill its every nook and corner. The most embarrassing fantasy of all came to mock him now. In it, Giles Curnow goes smash in some great commercial crisis. But Maurice Petifer, faithful unto death to his darling Laura, comes to the rescue. He buys up the business and gives it back to them gratis. 'It's just pocket money to me,' he murmurs loftily. 'Try not to get into trouble again.' Laura puts her arms about his neck and weeps into his manly shoulder – tears of gratitude and now-fruitless adoration. (Curiously enough, in none of his fantasies did he ever get her back; he merely left her pining in bittersweet regret for all that her meek submission to her parents' will had cost her.)

Other fantasies, equally picayune, frolicked in his mind, mocking his resolution. They made him want to curl up in embarrassment. At the fringe of his awareness lurked an intimation of a wasted life – a life driven by inanities like that. In some obscure way, too, it made him even more determined not to descend into the arena that afternoon.

Go back home now, he told himself – but immediately countered by asking what was there to be afraid of? If he ran from the challenge, he'd never be sure whether true backbone or mere empty bravado had kept him out of it. Besides, everyone would link it with the absurd sneer that he had 'run from the Boers.'

As he went in at the Culdrose gate, Elizabeth Troy drew level in her gig; Maurice was so immersed in his thoughts that she had to call out to catch his attention. Jake Morvah was at her side but Jimmy had obviously thought better of joining them.

'Oh!' He came back to reality with a jolt. 'I'm sorry I missed you at home. Thank you for a pleasant lunch all the same.'

'You should have curbed your impatience, you see. We managed to eat *and* get here in time.'

'I'm sorry I didn't now. Your servant, Mr Morvah.'

The lawyer nodded. 'Welcome back to Cornwall, Mr Petifer.'

Such intense, staring eyes he had! 'Are you still the Helston champion?' Maurice asked. When he had left the district, Jake Morvah had just won the all-comers challenge in Cornish wrestling at Wendron Ram Buck Fair.

He smiled gravely in reply. 'It's a young man's sport these days, I'm afraid, Mr Petifer. My mistake was to think agility and strength are superior to cunning – so I never paid enough attention to cunning. I never cultivated it.'

Unseen by him, Elizabeth pulled a face that said, 'believe that and you'll believe the moon is made of cheese!'

She halted the pony in the shade of a large elm, where Maurice tethered it to the fence. Several other horses were hitched near by and the buzzing of flies was intense. Elizabeth, who had brought a fan with her, beat them off more elegantly than the men. 'I know why you called at Liston House,' she said to Maurice. 'I'm sorry to disappoint you but the opportunity simply didn't present itself. My apologies. I suppose I owe you some chocolate.'

'Ah well . . .' He laughed and used a swatting gesture to wave away the topic as well. 'I must admit I've had second thoughts on the whole business myself.'

'Yes, so I gather. Jimmy gives me to understand

you're out of the bidding this afternoon?'

Maurice laughed in surprise. 'But he more-or-less told me *not* to give up now!'

She smiled wearily. 'That'll teach him to speak plainer in future. He's under the impression he advised the opposite. But never mind. You're your own man, I'm sure. What have *you* decided?'

He smiled at Morvah, who was listening avidly. 'To withhold my hand,' he replied.

'So you won't be bidding,' Elizabeth insisted. It was not a question – more like a demand that he confirm it in so many words.

Unseen by her, Morvah pulled a face that said, 'And you thought you already knew the meaning of the word *persistence!*'

'Not unless I see it going for a song. I mean, that would be the *only* reason for stepping in.'

She chuckled. 'In that case, I think your purse is safe enough today! Old Mrs Mullard will certainly not be selling Culdrose for a song, I feel.'

As they approached the corner of the haybarn, where the auction was to be conducted, young Billy Coad, the auctioneer's son, said – in the weary tones of an oft-repeated tale – 'On account of the heat, ladies and gentlemen, the auction has been transferred to the dutch barn behind the cowshouse. If you'll be so good as to hurry along, please – the bidding is about to commence.'

As they turned the corner into the dry passage between the courtyard of the bull pen and the haybarn Maurice almost bumped into Sibylla Johnson, who seemed to be waiting there for someone. For a moment they stared wildly at each other; his was the bigger shock for, somehow, he had not expected to see her here at all today. He raised his hat a fraction of an inch and said, 'Mrs Johnson.'

She nodded toward him, a barely perceptible tilt of her head, and replied, 'Mr Petifer.' Her face split in a too-radiant smile as she repeated her greeting to the other two.

'Such dark, satanic stares!' Elizabeth murmured to Maurice as they moved on toward the shelter of the barn. 'Do you have to practise or is it second nature by now?'

He chuckled, despite the fact that his heart was suddenly racing – with fury, of course. 'What is *she* doing here?' he asked bitterly.

'Well,' Elizabeth replied, 'since Parc-an-Dour practically borders on Culdrose – give or take a field – I'd say she has more right than most to attend.' On a mischievous whim she added, 'Why, she might even be intending to bid . . . er, if she sees the place going for a song!'

Somehow the notion that Sibylla Johnson might buy the place filled him with indignation – though he could not well have explained why. It was just that he had imagined himself the new owner so often lately that the thought of withdrawing, only to let *her* take it instead, was too galling to bear. 'What's she doing now?' he asked.

'Nothing,' she replied. 'See for yourself.'

He shook his head. 'I'd not give her even that satisfaction. Is she still just standing there? She's waiting for someone.'

'Nonsense!' Elizabeth sounded as if her patience was wearing thin. 'She's just passing the time of day with Harry Sampson, the builder.'

'Ah, so he has come after all!' Maurice darted a sharp glance at Jake Morvah. 'Are *you* in the bidding, then?'

'I?' Jake asked, spreading his fingers innocently over his chest.

'You know what I mean – you people . . . your family. Kitto's. Sampson wouldn't bid for a second-hand chimney pot without your grandmother's say-so.'

'Maurice!' Elizabeth chided, taking his arm and trying to steer him toward the dutch barn, which was already packed with people.

'What?' he asked belligerently.

'Firstly, it's hardly fair to ask him. And secondly, he's much too cunning to answer you.' She cajoled him with a nudge. 'And besides, what does it matter to you – now that you've placed yourself so far above this afternoon's little fray?'

He drew a deep breath and tried to calm his heart, which was bidding to leap out of his ribs altogether. 'It just never crossed my mind that she might be interested,' he murmured.

'Mrs Kitto d'you mean?'

He did not deign to reply.

The gavel banged as they entered the welcome shade of the great open-sided barn. Only then did it occur to him that he had not yet cast about to see if the Curnows were there. That showed how much the Johnson woman had unsettled him. He took a grip on himself and began a calm, methodical search of the assembly – or, rather, of the backs of a large number of heads. 'So many!' he murmured.

Elizabeth, who had developed a good eye for gauging a crowd during the days she had gone electioneering for David Troy, said, 'A hundred and fifty, I'd guess.'

The barn was large enough to hold them easily, without packing. They stood in loose groups – mostly, as is the way with crowds, toward the back of the area. 'And not more than a dozen of them seriously thinking of bidding!' she added as the gavel banged again and something like a silence descended.

Maurice could not see the Curnows among the crowd but he felt sure they were there somewhere.

'Good afternoon, ladies and gentlemen!' William Coad, the auctioneer, gazed around with that benevolent eye which, down the years, had lured many a bidder into believing he was still onto a bargain. 'As you know, today we're inviting your bids for the land and buildings. If all goes well, the live and dead stock will be offered immediately after. If both sales are concluded to the satisfaction of all, and if the buyer of the land and buildings does not arrange a private-treaty purchase of the contents of the house, they will be offered down in our salerooms this day week. I hope that's all clear now?'

Murmurs of assent and rustles of happy impatience answered him.

'Very well. The bidding is now open for Culdrose Farm, comprising fifty-six statute acres and two square perches – twenty in permanent pasture, the rest arable. Also a fine granite farmhouse of the Georgian period, recently reroofed by the finest builder in West Penwith.'

A chorus of laughter greeted this, for the builder in question had been his own cousin.

Then he pretended to notice Harry Sampson for the first time. 'Begging pardon, Mr Sampson!' he added. 'Present company excepted, of course.'

'Of course!' Sampson called back.

More laughter. Everyone was now at ease. Coad was a master of this sort of warm-up manipulation.

'Also two haybarns, a packing shed, ten pigsties, two mowies, a ten-stall cowshouse, a dairy, and . . .' He shook his head in perplexity. 'My dear soul – there's one more item but I'm blessed if I can remember 'n!'

'The duckpond!' someone called out.

'No,' he answered solemnly, 'that goes free to the highest bidder. Oh yes!' He looked at the roof above their heads – which once again filled with laughter. 'One fine, large dutch barn, capable of holding four hundred eager bidders – or two hundred tons of hay. Seriously, though – this is surely one of the finest agricultural properties to go under the hammer this *century*. Bid early and often, ladies and gentlemen – you won't get another chance like this for many a year. Do I hear two thousand bid?'

There was the traditional gasp at this piece of effrontery.

'You amaze me!'

'You come down here and bid two thousand, if you want,' called out a wit. 'I'll stand in for 'ee up there!'

'Eighteen hundred then! Fifteen surely? Who'll start me off then?'

'Nine hundred,' came a cry from the farther side.

'Nine hundred bid,' Coad echoed calmly – now completely businesslike. His sharp eyes quartered the room for signs of interest – a discreet nod here, the wag of a finger there.

'Who bid that?' Maurice asked Elizabeth.

'It sounded like Harry Tiddy, who used to be a tenant of mine,' she murmured. 'Just to oblige Coad, I expect. I doubt he's serious.'

'Can you see the Curnows anywhere?'

Elizabeth opened her fan and used its cover to mutter, 'Ask a little louder and they'll answer you themselves.' She nodded barely perceptibly to their right and fluttered the fan slightly.

'Nine-fifty!' Coad called out. To the crowd on his left he added, 'The bidder's to my right. Nine hundred and fifty pounds bid! Who'll make it a thousand?'

'Who bid that?' Maurice asked eagerly. He was craning his neck to catch a glimpse of Sampson, whose voice had come from the far side toward the back.

His eye met Laura's, then Giles's, then continued its search. Whatever their emotions, none showed the slightest change of expression.

So they were both here, he thought. That could only mean they were intending to bid. Curnow would never take an afternoon off from his business merely to satisfy his curiosity about who was to be his neighbour for the next few years; a messenger boy could do that.

'Do I hear a thousand anywhere?'

Maurice found Sampson then, at the very far corner of the assembly. He appeared to be taking no interest in the proceedings; instead he was deep in conversation with the man at his side. At that moment he nodded in vigorous agreement with some point the other fellow was making to him.

'A thousand!' Coad cried out happily. 'The bid is on my left. Will someone make it eleven hundred?'

'Who was that? Did you see?' Maurice asked Elizabeth. 'I missed it.'

'Oh dear!' She diverted his attention back to Coad, who was having a little trouble.

'Are you saying you also bid a thousand?' he was asking someone, also to his left. Then, to the crowd in general: 'Assist me, someone – I have two bids at a thousand. Give me eleven hundred, surely?'

Elizabeth chuckled and fanned herself again, absent-mindedly. Maurice, watching Sampson like a hawk, saw him nod again, but still in conversation with his neighbour.

'Eleven hundred I'm bid,' the auctioneer called out with relief. His eyes continued to dart hither and thither over the crowd.

Maurice almost laughed aloud in his triumph, for he realized he had discovered Sampson's code for bidding: He would pretend to be talking to his accomplice, but every time he nodded, he'd actually be making a bid! Then his blood raced as a further jewel of a discovery was added to this crown – for the accomplice moved a little and there, standing behind him, was Sibylla Johnson herself. Now he understood it all: Sampson was bidding for *her!* She'd give him some signal – touch the back of his calf with her parasol, for instance – and he'd nod away.

'Eleven hundred,' Coad repeated. 'The bid is to my right.'

In his excitement at his own cleverness, Maurice did not notice that this knocked his theory on the head, for Sampson was as far to the auctioneer's left as was possible.

'Twelve hundred!' Coad called out. 'This is getting better – I didn't even ask for that one. So who'll give me thirteen? I'm bid twelve on my left.' He scanned the faces to his right – but so impartially that Maurice had no idea where the bidders here on his own side might be. 'Do I hear thirteen, anyone?'

Then came a stroke of luck for Maurice. He was actually looking at Curnow when the man raised a finger and tapped his nose; Coad's immediate cry of, 'Thirteen I'm bid!' confirmed it. It would have been nice to see the satisfaction in Curnow's eye but just at that moment Elizabeth raised her fan again and obscured his view – not only of Curnow but of whoever it was who raised the bid to fourteen hundred – which was the sum Coad called out next, adding that the bid was still on his right.

So there were two bidders on this side, Maurice realized – Curnow and . . . who? Damnation take Elizabeth Troy! What did she need a fan for anyway? There was a good enough breeze in here, surely.

'It's still a mighty bargain, ladies and gentlemen – a grand farm like this for only fourteen hundred pounds? Someone will give me fifteen hundred, surely?'

Sampson laughed at some joke his accomplice was pretending to make, nodding heartily the while.

'There!' cried the auctioneer. 'Fifteen I'm bid. Now we're getting closer. At fifteen hundred pounds. The bid is on my left. Do I hear sixteen anywhere? The bid is on my . . . sixteen it is! A bid from my right.'

Maurice was just in time to see Curnow's hand fall to his side, but again he missed whoever it was immediately capped it with a bid of seventeen – and again because Elizabeth Troy would keep fidgeting with her confounded fan. He murmured in her ear that he wanted to get a better view and edged back a couple of paces. There he could stand facing inward and watch the Curnows out of one corner of his eye while keeping the other on Sampson and the Johnson woman on the far side of the gathering. During these manoeuvres he missed seeing Sampson nod his next bid of eighteen hundred, but Coad obligingly confirmed him as the bidder by saying he was to the left and turning once again to the right half of the crowd.

Almost at once he was able to cap it with a cry of, 'Nineteen, I'm bid. Nineteen hundred pounds. On my right. Who'll bid me two thousand? Come-us on – that's no great leap now!'

The auctioneer was still looking to the right. So, thought Maurice, there were, indeed, two bidders on this side of the crowd. Who was the other? It certainly hadn't been Curnow who had gone to nineteen hundred pounds, for Maurice had not taken his eyes off him. Nor did he do so now.

A moment later he was rewarded with the sight of Curnow rubbing his nose once again.

'Two thousand!' the auctioneer crowed. 'Thank

you, sir! At last there's someone who knows true value when he sees it. Two thousand pounds I'm bid, here on my right. Who'll put a hundred on that? Only a hundred now, surely?'

Sampson was still in animated conversation; but now it was the accomplice who nodded. It made no difference. 'And one hundred!' Coad called out. 'Two thousand one hundred, I'm bid. We're still far short of the true value, ladies and gentlemen, but we're on the road at last. Who'll make it two-and-two?'

'Two shillings and twopence!' called the wag who had sneered at Maurice about the 'Dutch Boers.'

'There's a man who knows his own worth!' Coad said without even looking at him. And the laughter he added, 'Where's the man who knows this farm's true worth though? Or woman, either?'

Maurice saw Elizabeth whisper something to Jake Morvah, again using her fan to hide the words. And again it distracted him from seeing who had bid the asked-for two thousand two hundred, which Coad immediately announced. 'The bid is against you on the left,' he added.

Expectantly Maurice turned to see if Sampson responded yet again. The Johnson woman inserted her head between the two men and said something; both of them nodded in agreement.

'And three hundred!' Coad called out at once. 'Two thousand three hundred pounds – the bid is from my left. Can I hear any advance on three hundred?'

Maurice felt all his anger returning at the sight of Sibylla Johnson's face between Harry Sampson and his crony – so smug she looked, so sure of her own cleverness! What did she want the farm for anyway?

'Any advance on two thousand three hundred?' Coad repeated.

Just to stop *me*, Maurice thought. She can't want it

for herself. She doesn't know the first thing about farming.

'I'll take bids in fifty-pound steps now,' the auctioneer added. Almost at once his watchful face creased in smiles. 'And two-three-fifty it is! From the right of the meeting, ladies and gentlemen, the bid stands at two thousand three hundred and fifty. Do I hear any advance?'

Sampson or his accomplice must have nodded, though it escaped Maurice's notice that time; however, the rise was instantly confirmed. 'Two-four! From the left now. The bid is against the right. I have two thousand four hundred from the left of the meeting. Any advance on two-four. Will no one make it two-four-five, surely?'

The smugness in the Johnson woman's eyes was unbearable. Maurice averted his gaze and stared out of the barn, across the fields. The thought that she might soon wander those acres, owning every inch of them, was intolerable. He would not – could not – stand for it.

The pain in the palms of his hands suddenly broke through his anger. He lifted them and stared at the deep ruts his nails had scored in the flesh; that they weren't bleeding was a miracle. He was still staring at them in amazement when he heard his own voice call out: 'Three thousand pounds!'

Sensation!

Every eye in the place turned upon him. The buzz of excitement rose to a mighty hubbub. The auctioneer just stared at him, unable to believe his ears – or his luck. But at last he found his voice and called out. 'Is that right, sir? I apologize for not recognizing you, but are you intending to bid three thousand pounds?'

Several people near the front of the crowd enlightened him as to Maurice's identity. Maurice himself, pale and shivering, shocked at what he'd done, stared miserably at Laura, who was staring back at him, her expression quite blank.

Tell me what to do! His silent voice roared in his mind, trying to project itself across that stunned space to her ear alone. *Help me get out of this!*

If she had only shaken her head . . . or closed her eyes . . . turned her back on him – anything except fix him with that baleful, empty stare . . . he would have taken his bid back, given any kind of apology, made any sort of a fool of himself.

But she did none of those things.

He nodded then, and turned to face Coad once more. So as not to appear quite so much of a fool, he now added, 'I'll make it four for the live and dead stock. And four and a half for the whole lot – house, contents, and all.'

These combined bids were actually not too far above the true value; at least people wouldn't be able to say he was that sort of fool who was soon parted from his money.

The auctioneer briefly consulted old Mrs Mullard, who gave him a delighted nod of acceptance. 'Going, then, for the first time, the farm at three thousand, the other lots withdrawn – I'll say again – the farm at three thousand, for the second time . . . are we all done at three thousand pounds? . . . Going . . . going . . . gone!' The gavel fell. 'All three lots sold to Mr Maurice Petifer – sorry I never recognized 'ee for a moment there, Mr Petifer – all three lots sold for four thousand five hundred pounds.'

Laura, her face the colour of ash on a winter morn, swept past Maurice; she held tight to Giles, but no one imagined it was for support.

Solemnly Coad raised the gavel and banged it again on his block – once, twice.

Maurice turned triumphantly to see how Sibylla was taking her defeat. But Sibylla had gone. Harry Sampson and his crony, however, were still deep in conversation, still nodding heartily.

Disappointed he turned to see what Elizabeth might have to say; over her shoulder he saw Coad threading his way among the crowd, making toward him. People were already beginning to drift away from the barn. To his surprise, several patted him on the back as they passed; there was no trace of irony in it, nor in their expressions, either. They truly believed he had pulled off some kind of coup.

Heartened, almost believing it himself now, he turned to Elizabeth again – only to flinch before the accusation in her eyes.

'Oh Maurice!' she murmured, folding her fan and tucking it away.

'I know,' he replied, morose again. 'But I told you, didn't I – it's beyond my control.'

The crowds had gone. The evening was well advanced. Peter Hosking and George Munroe, the two general labourers at Culdrose Farm, had spent an hour spiking up the litter and gathering the dung from the horses until no trace of the auction remained. 'You'd never know 'e'd changed hands at all,' Hosking said, surveying a scene that had been familiar to him for the past fifteen years now.

'Us'll know soon enough, I reckon.' Munroe spat a thumping quid of 'baccy at the dungpile.

'Reckon so?'

'Reckon so. Old Petifer weren't much of a feller when 'e left 'ere, back along. And 'e's been lording it over kaffirs out the Cape ever since. That's how 'e'll treat us, like kaffirs. Curses and blows – that's our fare from this day forth. You'll see, boy.'

Hosking cleared his throat meaningfully and inclined his head a fraction toward the gate at the top of the yard. 'Evening boss,' he called out. 'That's the last of it gone now.'

'Damme to hell!' Munroe swore under his breath. 'How'd he get there? Think 'e 'eard, do 'ee?'

'Shouldn't think so,' his mate assured him.

But they both studied their new master keenly for any sign that he had, indeed, overheard the unfavourable opinion of himself. If he had, he gave nothing away. 'Well done,' he said, his eye darting here and there, never resting. 'Is any stock under cover tonight? I see the herd down in the bottom field but I only counted fourteen. There were fifteen three weeks ago.'

'Mr Tresidder sold one down Helston last Monday,' Munroe explained. Tresidder was the stockman and general foreman at the farm.

'Hell, I never knew that when I bid!' Maurice laughed to show he was joking. Dutifully the other two laughed.

'You got three more pigs, though, boss,' Hosking added. 'That's where the profit went, see.'

Munroe decided to risk a joke of his own. 'As the feller said when he woke up with one short leg – there's compensations in it, for the other leg's longer.'

They both laughed and waited for the boss to join in.

But he was staring away across the fields. 'Yes,' he said absently. 'Compensations. The long and the short of it, eh.'

They realized he was hardly with them. Hosking cleared his throat. 'Is that all for the day, then, boss? Munroe and me, like, we'll be an hour late home now, see.'

'Of course you can go!' Maurice snapped out of his reverie and flashed them a broad smile. 'It was very good of you to stay on. I'll have a word with Mr Tresidder. You may leave an hour early tomorrow to make up for it.'

They were too flabbergasted to reply. Such a thing had never happened in all their working lives. Hosking had once had half an afternoon off when he'd been bitten by an adder – which he had thought considerate enough, even though his pay had been docked for it, too. 'What've 'ee got to say 'bout that, then?' he asked his mate when they felt safely out of earshot.

The other shook his head and sucked a tooth sourly. 'I don't like it,' he said. 'Not one bit.'

'How not?' Hosking asked in surprise.

'All sugar and spice. I can't abide a boss who's all sugar and spice. Curses and blows I could understand.'

'You aren't never satisfied with nothing, you aren't,' Hosking complained. 'What sort of boss *do* 'ee want, then?'

'One with a face as looks just like mine, boy!' Munroe laughed at long last, immoderately.

Maurice, who had been standing at the bottom rail of the yard, watching the sun set over Helston, wondered if they had ever been miners, or quarrymen – or in some trade that worked a lot with dynamite, anyway. Did they really imagine he couldn't overhear them when, to his mind, they were almost shouting their heads off! Or perhaps his hearing had become especially acute out on the Rand – where you strained your ears for the slightest snap of a twig, which could mean anything from rhino to porcupine. Still, he'd do nothing to disabuse them of their belief that he was as deaf as they; there was no knowing what they might let drop if they had no idea he was right behind them, picking up every word they uttered.

He knew why he was hanging on out here, of course. In a moment or two, when Hosking and Munroe had closed the gate behind them, he would have the place to himself. Old Mrs Mullard had gone to her daughter's for the night – well, for ever, now. Ma Harvey, the cook and housekeeper, had gone with her for a day or two, just to help settle her in. Molly Hendren, the dairymaid, had gone to a dance down in St John's, at the bottom of the town. Frank Tresidder was getting drunk on home-brewed ale at the Blue Anchor, as he always did on the third Friday of every month. And Mary Wells, the only maid the house had needed in Mrs Mullard's time, had gone for good – to marry Mrs Tamara Dawson's chauffeur.

The gate clanged to. He was alone. Nimbly he vaulted the rail and landed like a gymnast in an assault-at-arms; picking up his stride at once, he set off across the fields toward the boundary with Chynoweth Hall. A tiny voice inside him said he was being a fool . . . if he behaved like this on the very first night, it boded very black for the future . . . the steps he was talking were his first steps into madness. 'And you'll catch your death of cold,' it threw in as a last desperate caution.

Nothing he said had the slightest effect; his stride remained as purposeful as ever.

At last he reached the spot he had noted last time he had come this way – the evening he had found Laura and the Johnson woman, standing just the other side of the fence. He took out his binoculars . . .

'If you put those things to your eyes, I shall shoot you,' said a tree to one side of the gap.

A moment later the branches parted and Giles Curnow stood there. Over his arm was draped a double-barrelled shotgun, broken for safety – and also, perhaps, to show the two cartridges whose bright brass ends gleamed in the breech.

He had sounded more weary than angry; his appearance now confirmed the impression. He must have been waiting there an hour or more to be sure of making his point so effectively.

'Thought I saw a cirl bunting,' Maurice told him. 'Do you do much shooting with that thing? I hope not. You have a natural aviary over there, you know.'

'Glib as ever!' Giles sighed – and then put a fist angrily to his forehead and beat it a couple of times with a restrained irritation. 'No! These are not the first words I wished to have with you. Believe me, they are not.'

'I do believe you.' Maurice felt almost supernaturally calm. Ever since his unintentional – or, at least, unpremeditated – bid had made him the new owner of Culdrose, all strong emotion seemed to have deserted him. It was almost as if that one stupendous act had wound him up like a piece of clockwork, and whatever followed it now was part of some wholly mechanical sequence over which he had no control.

'Have you eaten?' Giles asked.

Maurice felt a strong emotion at last: astonishment! 'No,' he was surprised into admitting.

'Nor I.' Giles gave a dry laugh. 'No appetite, somehow. But now I do begin to feel peckish. Would you care to dine with me at the club? Or we could stroll down to the Angel and take pot luck?'

'Well, I'm damned!' Maurice was still unable to get beyond his surprise. 'Why not!'

Giles gave a thin-lipped smile, still more weary than anything. 'There are certainly a thousand reasons why not. I ought probably to shoot you now and have done with it. The wounds would . . .'

'You'd never get away with it.' Maurice thought it best to treat the suggestion as a huge joke.

'Oh, people would *know*, of course. I'd be the local hero till the day I died. And it would be wonderful for business, too. Would you dare add chalk to any flour you sold me, if you knew I'd done that! But knowing is one thing and legal proof is quite another. The wounds would be quite consistent with the "accident" I have prepared for us.'

'I say, Curnow!' Maurice gave a couple of awkward laughs and swallowed heavily.

'What?'

'There are limits, you know.'

'Quite!' Giles grinned, to show he really had been joking all along. 'Civilized limits, what? Civilized codes. And if people are prepared to be civilized, I believe we should stick to 'em, eh?'

'Absolutely, old man.'

Giles laughed. 'Well, young fellow,' he countered. 'Which is it to be – my club or the Angel?'

Maurice, on horseback, followed Giles, in his gig, to the Angel Hotel, keeping him in view but not attempting to catch up. To hold a sustained conversation between rider and driver is hard enough at the best of times; the narrow, echoey chasm of Meneage Street would have rendered it almost impossible. Besides, the arrangement was that they should meet, apparently spontaneously, at the stables behind the hotel – which they now did.

'Care to join me, young man?' Giles asked when the 'surprise' formalities were done.

At the last two words Maurice gave a little laugh of genuine surprise. 'Very good of you, old boy,' he replied, echoing their earlier exchange. As they picked their way in the gathering dusk across the cobbled yard to the rear entrance he added, 'Is that to be the style now – "young man, old boy"?'

'Why throw away any advantage?' Giles responded.

It did not seem to Maurice that Giles's extra six years were any longer an advantage. 'While you still have it, certainly,' he agreed.

Their entry, side by side, into the dining room caused something of a stir, which increased when they took their seats at the same table. The word in Helston was that Mrs Curnow had 'swoonded away' when the auctioneer's hammer fell and the buyer was revealed as her old flame, Maurice Petifer; even those who had been there found this version so much to their liking – not least for the attention it secured in the taprooms and street-corner parliaments of the town – that they concurred with a will and, for good measure, threw in all their powers of embroidery, too. The traffic past the door of the dining room was suddenly intensified and the number of people who seemed to think a friend might be in there eating his head off, but who were disappointed of finding him, was phenomenal.

However, the two men at the centre of all this persiflage were, to outward appearances at least, entirely unaware of it. They seated themselves, ordered sherry, and ran their eyes down the menu with amazing unconcern.

'Steak and kidney pie, I think,' Giles said.

'And I'll risk the lobster,' Maurice decided as he folded the menu and handed it back to the waiter. Then, to his host, 'Funny, I was never a great one for fish and suchlike before I went to Africa, yet the one thing I missed above all others when I was out there was . . . well, the harvest of our Cornish seas. I used to be able to close my eyes and see the quays at Newlyn, that gorgeous, yellowy granite and how it gleams when the sea washes over it. And I could see all the fishermen, in my mind's eye, landing their catches . . . the mackerel and cod . . . whiting, oh, and every kind of sole. The colour of it! The veldt is so parched and dry, you know. I used to long for the blues and greens and turquoises, and the cold of our sea. Especially the cold.'

Giles chuckled. 'And I'll bet there was many a day when the entire population of Cornwall would gladly have traded it all for just a week of the sort of weather you were having! We're an ungrateful race, when you think of it – always wanting what we haven't got.' He fixed Maurice briefly with his eye. 'Isn't there something you miss now – about the veldt, I mean? I have all the shipping timetables in my office.'

Maurice grinned. 'Actually, there is one thing I miss – biltong. I never thought I would, but I do. It's a sort of sun-cured meat. The way you make it is you shoot a kudu or a springbok – kudu is best – cut the meat into strips, roll them in saltpetre just to keep off the flies, and then simply hang them up to dry in the sun – which they do very quickly. Ten days and you could use the stuff for knocking in nails.'

'If it's that tough, how do you chew it?'

'You shave it. You take your penknife and cut a shaving, paper-thin, and pop it on your tongue. God, I'm drooling now at the mere thought!'

'And that's biltong.'

'Yes. Ask Elizabeth and Jimmy Troy if you think I'm exaggerating. They couldn't get enough of it when they were out there with me.'

All the while he spoke he listened to himself with amazement. He had driven over to Helston that morning determined not to buy Culdrose. If anyone had told him that by four o'clock he would have taken it over, lock, stock, and barrel, not causing so much as a hiccup in the day-to-day running of the place, he'd have sworn it was impossible; what, then, would he have said if that same prophet had gone on to predict that, before this extraordinary day was done, he would sit down to dine in public with Giles Curnow, of all people, and that they would talk of fish and biltong! Even now, in the thick of it, a giddying sense of unreality filled him.

'It makes one wonder why you bought Culdrose,' Giles went on mildly, continuing to speak over and between the arms of the two waiters, who brought their plates at that moment. 'We'll have a couple of pints of Rosewarne's Export,' he added to one of them. Then, back to Maurice: 'Why *did* you buy the place?'

Maurice shot him a rather desperate glance, implying it was hardly a fair question to ask in the present circumstances.

But Giles continued: 'I mean, will you keep it as a dairy farm? What are your plans for it?'

I have no plans, you oaf! I didn't even mean to buy the place.

That would make a fine confession! What about: *I'm going to let it all run wild . . . scatter acorns and beech mast . . . create fifty acres of wilderness for the birds and foxes.* That would give him something to think about!

'Keep it more or less as it is,' he replied. 'Slowly move out of cereals, I think. Keep the dairy side but go in more for flowers and vegetables. I think I'll try an extended four-course rotation.'

Giles chuckled. 'You've been talking with Elizabeth Troy.'

'I haven't as a matter of fact, old boy – not about farming, anyway. But people have told me how she pulled the home farm at Pallas out of the mire. She must have been one of the first people in the district to see what opportunities were opened up with the coming of the train.'

Giles took a mouthful of steak and chewed it thoughtfully, staring at Maurice all the while; his expression suggested that a certain amount of rethinking was going on. 'Summer would be the time to concentrate on,' he said at last. 'The railway hasn't just made it possible for our vegetables to appear on tables in London – or Liverpool – within twenty-four hours, it's also brought Londoners and Liverpuddlians here by the hundred. There are new hotels going up all over the place . . .'

'I know! I didn't even recognize the Esplanade in Penzance.'

'You should go and see what they're doing in Falmouth. You can't turn your back but another one springs up behind you. Anyway, the point I'm getting to is that some of the bigger ones deal with me direct, as wholesaler, and several of them asked me if I wouldn't consider going into fresh vegetables, too. Believe it or not, they mostly buy in London – to be sure of continuity of supply, you see. But it's absurd. One of them showed me – in that new hotel outside Mullion – he showed me a crate of cabbage he'd brought back from Helston station that morning. The head porter there showed him a mark he recognized. He'd put it on the crate himself two days earlier. Those cabbages were packed by Eric Polglaze – whose farm is no more than a quarter of a mile from the hotel! Did you ever hear anything more idiotic?'

The waiter brought their ale.

'Why didn't he just walk down the road and buy them, then?' Maurice sipped his glass and then took a good, deep draught, smacking his lips with relish at the taste.

'Another thing you missed in the veldt?' Giles suggested.

'In fact no. You could buy it in quite a few places. I don't suppose there's anywhere in the empire where you can't get Rosewarne's ales now. Why didn't your hotelier just . . .'

'Oh yes. Too many roads to walk down to ensure his supply. Too many unreliable small farmers. Too few hours in the day. It's so much easier to send a daily wire to Covent Garden and meet the milk train into Helston each morning.'

Maurice wondered why the man was telling him all this, or, rather, telling it in such detail. 'Are you going to do as they suggest?' he asked. 'Start wholesaling fresh vegetables?'

Giles eyed him carefully before he answered. 'If I'd bought Culdrose today, that's what I was going to do – guarantee a selected number of hotels continuity of supply in vegetables, roots, and salads for a trial period. Not as part of Curnow and Co, but as a separate concern . . . Culdrose Hotel Supplies . . . some fancy name like that. I don't know if you'd be interested?'

'Me?' The suggestion took Maurice completely aback.

'Why not? You'd make a better fist of it than I would. You certainly know more about farming. I'd have had to put in a manager. You could do fresh milk, too.'

Maurice was surprised at how swiftly his mind accommodated to the suggestion. 'Have you spoken to Elizabeth Troy about this?' he asked.

Giles shook his head. 'You're first.'

'She'd be a better one to start with. Pallas Home Farm is about twice the size of Culdrose, and it's more sheltered, and it's on better land.'

'You're first,' Giles repeated. 'Are you interested? I'm talking about next year now, of course, but even so there's no time to dither.'

Maurice laughed. 'You're not expecting an answer tonight, I hope, old boy?'

'How soon, then?' Giles did not smile.

'Do you mind if *I* talk it over with Elizabeth? If she's interested, then so am I.'

No emotion showed on Curnow's face – not pleasure, not relief. And yet Maurice had an almost overwhelming feeling that he had just said precisely what the man had wished him to say all along. His mind went back to Curnow's extraordinary behaviour an hour or so earlier . . . all that talk of shooting him, mingled up with expressions of goodwill and neighbourliness. And now this! For some obscure reason it put him in mind of the way they had played blind man's buff in the schoolyard as children; as soon as a fellow was blindfolded, all the others grabbed him and turned him this way and that, pushing him around until he was thoroughly confused. He had the feeling that Giles Curnow had just performed a vastly more subtle version of the same operation on him. He wasn't even the owner of Culdrose – not legally, anyway – and already he was tying himself down, selling the calf that wasn't even in the cow's belly as yet.

'Be honest, old boy,' he said. 'Is this what you really had in mind when you invited me to dine here tonight?'

Giles grinned. 'What else?'

The rest of the meal passed in the same amicable and thoroughly businesslike manner. They did not linger for coffee or liqueurs, but went straight back out to the stables. The moment they were gone, a group of men seated near by, who had been desperately pretending not to eavesdrop, burst out with expressions of amazement and stared at one another in disbelief: 'What's make of than then, boy? . . . Going into partnership together! . . . Butter wouldn't melt in their mouths! . . .' and so forth.

'I'll tell 'ee what I do make of that,' one said, leaning forward and laying a finger on his nostril. 'Money! That's what we heard talking there!' He fished a sovereign from his pocket and held it up, the way men hold rare wines to the light. 'There's what talks,' he told them. 'That'll open the door that never had a key. 'Twill buy a man's spirit and a lady's soul.'

A roar of laughter went up. 'You did say lady's *soul*, didn't 'ee, boy?' one asked.

'You heard what I said, plain enough. That's the glue will take two sworn enemies and yoke them in partnership, like it or not. That's the great persuader whose tongue we heard at that table there!'

'I think that passed off pretty well,' Giles said as they passed back up Meneage Street. 'Should stop the tongues from wagging?'

'Pretty well, indeed,' Maurice agreed; he was seated beside Giles, his mount tethered at the tail of the gig.

He had the feeling he was beginning to emerge from a kind of nightmare. He dared to think of Laura – and was relieved to find none of the usual emotions welling up within him, none of those adolescent yearnings, no falling away of the stomach, no hot-cold flushes of the blood. He felt perfectly calm again. He almost laughed out loud. It was over! It *had* been a nightmare – he could admit it now – and it was, thank God, behind him. Giles Curnow was a splendid fellow. They were going to build a wonderful business together. But it was not just his purse that would profit by their partnership; his whole life would be made so much richer by the fact that he could now treat Laura as an old friend and her husband as a new one! He only just managed to quell an impulse to throw his arms around the man and give him a ferocious hug.

'Yes,' Giles mused. 'People in business, you see, should have a certain dignity.'

'Of course.'

'I don't mean pomposity, mind.'

'No, no – God forbid!' Maurice wanted to laugh, wanted to tell him what a wonderful change had taken place.

'But we can't have people sniggering behind our backs.'

'Worst thing that could happen.'

'Well, not quite the worst – I'm coming to that. But pretty appalling, all the same. And I say behind *our* backs because you, too, are in business now, Petifer.'

'Indeed I am!' Maurice chortled. 'And I never felt happier.'

'Good.' Giles's voice remained quite even. 'And now to the worst thing that could happen, and that would be for you to show the slightest interest in my wife beyond what any neighbour might show. I'm sure you understand me, Petifer?'

'I do, Curnow. And I want to assure you . . .'

'But I'm not interested in your assurances, Petifer.'

'No, but just listen . . .'

'No, *you* listen. I'm not interested in your assurances. I wouldn't trust them an inch in any case – not after your behaviour today. But you can trust mine – in fact, for the sake of your health, you'd better. And I assure you that I intend to be a model neighbour to you, both in public and in private between ourselves. I'll put you up for the club and I'll deal fair and square with you in business, if you take up my offer – which I intended perfectly sincerely. In short, you play with a straight bat and I'll send you a fair ball. *But!* If you make the slightest move to re-establish the sort of relations you once enjoyed with Laura, I'll break every bone in your body. I'll flay every last inch of skin off your back. I'll smash you in tiny pieces. They won't carry you off in a stretcher – they'll need a sack. As long as that's understood?'

Maurice sat like stone at his side – feeling like stone, too. All his good intentions of a moment earlier had evaporated. The affection – yes, that was not too absurd a word for it – the *affection* he had begun to feel for the man he had once hated second only to Enoch Nisbet was gone.

'Understand?' Giles insisted.

Maurice turned to him with a broad smile and clapped him heartily on the back. 'Perfectly, old boy!' he replied. 'You have a wonderful gift for making things clear.'

'A hound it was, an enormous coal-black hound, but not such a hound as mortal eyes have ever seen. Fire burst from its open mouth, its eyes glowed with a smouldering glare, its muzzle and hackles and dewlap were outlined in flickering flame. Never in the delirious dream of a disordered brain could anything more savage, more appalling, more hellish be conceived than that dark form and savage face which broke upon us out of the wall of fog.'

Laura closed her eyes, clutched the magazine to her, and shivered. What manner of creature could it possibly be? Would it kill Sir Charles Baskerville, despite the best efforts of Holmes and Watson? Would the great Grimpen Mire claim yet another tragic victim? She glanced toward her bedside cabinet, where last

April's issue of *The Strand*, containing the final instalment of the serial lay temptingly within her grasp. Only an iron determination prevented her from reaching out for it.

There was a noise below, a familiar tread on the tiled floor, then on the stairs. Giles was home.

Seductive voices told her that if Sibylla hadn't taken all nine issues of *The Strand* away to London with her, she, Laura, would have finished the serial by now. She never read any of the Sherlock Holmes stories until the last instalment was printed, because she couldn't possibly wait a whole month for the next bit of the story to be revealed; but then, ashamed of her own impatience, she rationed herself to one issue per night, no matter how gripping the story nor how tense the situation in which she (or, more accurately, the victim in the tale) was left hanging. But, she now told herself, if those copies hadn't been whisked away to London, she'd know the solution to the mystery already. The agony would be over. She owed it to herself . . . it was only fair . . .

The seductive siren pleaded in vain, for Giles was by now lighting the lamp in his dressing room. 'You asleep?' he called out the moment he saw the strip of light under the door to the bedroom.

'And what if I were? You would just have woken me up.'

After a brief pause he said, in a particular tone, 'I think I'd have done that anyway. You're not feeling all done-in or headachey or anything, are you?'

She made no reply. Smiling to herself she cleared the counterpane of magazines and letters, stuffed them higgledy-piggledy into the cabinet, and turned down the lamp. *Down but not out*, she thought. The flame burned more orange when it was low, giving Giles's pale skin a healthy, bronzed tinge that pleased her more – because she knew it did the same kindly service for her.

'Eh?' he prompted.

She slipped her nightdress over her head, bundled it up, and hid it under her pillow. Then she lay on her side, with her back toward his dressing room door, and started snoring lightly. She did not close her eyes, however, for the looking glass in the middle door of the wardrobe would give her a full view of him as he entered; and in the gloom he would not notice her eyes open.

A moment later he was there, framed in the doorway. The lamp on his side of the bed was still fully turned up, so his tall, slim body was pale as marble against the dark behind him. He was naked, of course; he always came naked to bed from his dressing room, for he preferred to keep his nightshirt between the sheets, where, in winter at least, it could borrow the heat of the hot water jar. It had always amused Laura. After all, the idea of having separate dressing rooms for husbands must have arisen out of a desire for modesty; Giles's behaviour stood the whole thing on its head. However, he was not always in such an obvious state of arousal – in fact, it had happened decreasingly often lately; so much so that she, who had sometimes felt that his need for her was excessive in the early years of their marriage, had recently begun to look back on them with a sort of 'little-did-you-imagine' nostalgia.

For a moment he stood at the bedside, staring down at her provocatively slumbering body. Then he said, 'I see-ee!' – making the word rise and fall in a jokingly ominous tone. He lifted the sheet and counterpane and climbed in beside her. It was a warm night and they had no blankets; soon, no doubt, everything would be kicked off in the frenzy, anyway. A little thrill of anticipation ran through her.

Then came the part he didn't like her to see. Patiently she waited through the familiar sequence – the opening and shutting of his cabinet door, the furtive rustle of paper, the fiddling . . . the occasional 'damn and blast it!' and the starting again. Once or twice in years gone by the curses had come after it was over – and one such occasion had led to the birth of Phillippa. They didn't want *that* to happen again – or, rather, Giles didn't. He thought five children was a shamefully old fashioned number. Laura, being an only child, would gladly have had a dozen, for she loved the rough-and-tumble of a large brood almost as if it were a new lease on childhood for her, too. The children's infinite capacity for combining against authority was matched by her own for soliciting the help of one or more of them against the rest; children were such adorably *natural* traitors!

The fumbling was over; barring some lovely-ghastly accident, the family would not be enlarged by what was about to follow.

But what *was* about to follow? You never knew with Giles. He could be brusque one time and endlessly patient and tender the next. It often seemed to her that he used these occasions as an extra means of communicating things to her – things he would never put into words. He was, for example, a strong supporter of feminist ideas, much more so than Laura, who thought that being a Freethinker was bad enough for their business without rubbing salt in the wound. But he was always encouraging her to 'be more independent' – whatever that might mean. Sometimes it meant he wanted her to contradict him more, not just in trivial domestic things (where her word was law, anyway) but in *important* things like the Free Trade debate. That, in turn, meant she should read less trash (i.e., Sherlock Holmes) and more serious stuff (like *The Economist*). It meant she should develop interests and friends of which he might even mildly disapprove – because it was more comforting for him to be able to say, 'Laura is absolutely free to choose in things like that.'

But then, when she tried it out, his spirit would grow restive; his heart and intellect were suddenly at war. His mind would approve, his guts would churn away in resentment. Then he would turn their amorous moments in bed into a kind of wordless demonstration that he was master after all. In the ordinary colloquial meaning of the words, he was, indeed, a passed master of those conjugal arts. He knew her through and through, knew just where every secret pleasure lay hidden, knew what to do to tease them out, set them alight within her. Usually, it seemed, he used those skills quite unconsciously, making it appear as natural and as effortless as breathing. But when he was at war with himself like that, he turned into one of those virtuosi who simply cannot help showing off his prowess; he used his skills to astound her, to lay her prostrate and adoring at his feet.

In that, he both succeeded and failed, for it had the effect of divorcing her body from her mind; with the former he succeeded but with the latter he failed. At such moments she became almost a spectator of her own body, watching it succumb to wave after wave of ecstasy while she – the thinking part of her – remained in some inner fastness, unmoved and resentful. Above all she resented that he could take something which belonged so exquisitely to them both, which could not even exist without their perfect cooperation, and distort it for such a purpose. But because it was her intellect that remained aloof, and because the intellect does not exist in order to take sides but, rather, to see all sides of any question, she also found reasons in his favour. If he could not rid himself of his frustrations and conflicts in that way, she reasoned, they would build up into something far more threatening. In the end, her resentment transferred itself to her body, which begrudged its dependence on his.

At first, on this particular night, she thought he was once again playing the virtuoso with her. But then, as she felt her mind beginning its usual disengagement from her body's thraldom, it became calm enough to observe subtle differences between this and those earlier occasions. He was no longer crowing, in that wordless idiom of their bodies and limbs, 'Mine! All mine!' Its tone was still commanding, but it was more like a command to surrender, to melt, to obliterate her identity in his. More curious still – considering how detached her mind had learned to become when that mood was upon him – no sooner had the thought occurred to her than, rushing up out of nowhere, came an overwhelming urge to concede.

It was not simply that it would be so pleasant to lose herself in him, it was also a conviction the she *could* now merge with him; together they would acquire a new sense of selfhood, something so strong it would be absurd for either of them to indulge acts of individual will. Mists were evaporating before her eyes to reveal a new truth. Yet it was a truth that had always been there, just waiting for her to achieve this level of maturity, without which it would, even if visible, have remained quite beyond her grasp. *This*, it said, *is that elusive, yet perfect union which all the books and sermons and homilies on marriage prattle about but which so few married couples even glimpse, much less achieve! And yet it's so simple – there it is, so near! Take it now!*

It was a glittering prize, suddenly within her grasp.

What could she do but seize it? However, it was not like any of those partial and temporary surrenders she had conceded in the past. On those occasions her mind had, so to speak, simply taken a deep breath and held it for the duration of her body's immersion in that vast ocean of connubial joy. But this was like a road-to-Damascus conversion; it was total and it was for ever.

Giles, becoming aware that some profound change had overtaken her, responded, quite unconsciously, by ceasing to 'perform' in the virtuoso style. Indeed, for a moment he ceased to move at all. Usually when that happened – when, for instance, he was momentarily exhausted or out of breath – she would give a tiny sigh of complaint, jiggle herself a little, and set him going again; but now she just lay there beneath him, quite still, hardly even breathing. Then she began to shiver, imperceptibly at first and never violently, even at the height of the pleasure that now overwhelmed her. And he was so taken by surprise, so dazed by a sudden upwelling of love for her, that he was hardly aware of his own climax until it was almost over.

He emitted a small, shrill laugh that surprised them both. Normally an event like that would have set their common mood on a new course – they would have laughed a little, chatted in a contented, desultory way, and then fallen into a contented slumber. Now, however, the surprise of that strange, falsetto giggle – so unlike him – was itself defeated by the new solemnity that held them both. Later, when they had remade the bed and put on their night attire, she snuggled into his embrace and said, 'D'you think Sibylla and I chatter too much?'

'Yes,' he replied at once.

'No, seriously – is that why you dined out tonight?'

After a pause he said, 'No. As a matter of fact, I invited that . . . our new neighbour, I mean . . . I invited him to dine with me at The Angel.'

She struggled up onto one elbow and stared at him

in astonishment; he remained deliberately nonchalant. In a flash she knew why he had done such a thing – an act of which he alone, of all the men she knew, would be capable.

'Oh Giles!' She threw her arm about him again and buried her face in the crook of his neck. 'Dear, sweet . . . unbelievable Giles!'

It was his turn to be astonished. 'Why d'you say that?' he asked.

'Because I know exactly why you did it.'

It was part-and-parcel with his belief that everyone was a free spirit, she had just realized. He had always held that couples are not bound – because they are not capable of being bound – by the legal trappings and rigmarole of marriage. So, to make an enemy of Maurice Petifer, to deny him the usual courtesies that neighbours owe one another, would be, in Giles's eyes, a fatal curtailment of that freedom for her. He had done it for her sake!

She chuckled. 'I'll bet you told him he'd be welcome here at Chynoweth, both as an old friend and as a new neighbour. I'd *almost* bet you told him that if he wanted somewhere to stay while he had the old farmhouse done up, he was to consider himself our guest – except that you'd never do such a thing without asking me first. But I'll bet it's crossed your mind. Oh, Giles – you are such a *good* man – such a hard man to live up to. But I do love you, my darling. My dearest, sweetest darling. And tonight, for some reason, I love you more than ever.'

Her voice broke a little on the last words; she just went on clinging to him, trembling from the onslaught of her emotions.

And he hugged her tight in return, staring unhappily at the ceiling. He was beginning to wonder if he had not been, after all, just a little unwise in what he had said to the unspeakable Petifer, just before they had parted company.

It was the first Tuesday in October. The September equinox had been wonderfully free of gales that year but the present month was already threatening to make up for it. At noon south cones were hoisted all along the coast as far as Plymouth, sixty miles away. It was already blowing a half-gale by then and everyone said it was going to be a whopper. Laura and Sibylla took all eight children over to Falmouth to see the dozen or so tall ships – and many times that number of smaller ones – that had sought shelter in the protected waters of Carrick Roads.

The Roads were busy at any season, of course; ever since the coming of the telegraph Falmouth had been the most westerly port where oceangoing vessels could communicate with their owners. 'To Falmouth for orders' was a byword among merchantmen of every fleet. Even so, to see scores of vessels of every shape and size, all huddled together at anchor between the port and the rolling country of the Roseland peninsula, was a thrilling experience, especially to the children. They were almost blown off the ridge beside Pendennis Castle, which gave the best view of the Roads and the harbour.

'Remember that picnic at the Royal Cornwall Show this summer?' Henry asked.

'Yes!' It was a general chorus for they all knew what he meant. A sudden downpour had surprised everyone and the crowd ran for shelter under one giant oak tree, where they had jostled one another and stared out in dismay at the suddenly hostile elements. Now, overlooking the relatively calm waters inside the castle headland, they could easily imagine the vessels were doing the same.

On the way back home the two mothers almost regretted their foolhardiness in setting their noses out of doors on such a day, for the carriage was twice almost overturned – once at Laity Moor and again at Retanna, where the elevated country and the high stone hedges combined to make the gale especially powerful and treacherous.

'Thank God most of my roof is back on,' Sibylla exclaimed as they passed Parc-an-Dour at the end of Clodgey Lane. She rubbed at the steamed-up pane of glass with her sleeve and tried to make out the house in the gathering gloom.

'Most?' Laura asked, squeezing her head in beside her cousin's. 'I thought you said all.'

'Well,' she conceded, 'the main roof is on. It's just the bit over the kitchen, where it slopes down. It's behind the trees from here. I hope they've got it covered. I say! What on earth . . .?' She rubbed the pane again and peered even harder.

'Maurice Petifer!' Laura murmured. 'And Frank Tresidder . . . and all his workmen. What are they doing going into your place?'

The answer was, in fact, fairly obvious, since they were carrying a heavy tarpaulin and several hanks of rope.

'That's just what I intend to find out!' Sibylla replied grimly. 'The nerve of the man!'

She rapped on the carriage roof, twice; then, when it was clear that Hinks could not hear her above the wind and the clatter, she half-opened the door and leaned precariously out, calling to him to stop. When he at last brought the carriage to a halt they had travelled some way past the entrance to Parc-an-Dour, but, nothing daunted, Sibylla leaped down and stumped angrily back up the road, calling out to Hinks that he was not to wait.

Hinks leaped down, opened the door again, and asked, 'What do us do, missis?'

Laura stared after Sibylla, a gaunt, dark, angry figure under the wildly swaying trees, and said with some reluctance, 'We'd best get home as soon as we can. You may return here to collect Mrs Johnson after dropping us off.'

Up on the driveway to Parc-an-Dour, still a hundred yards short of the house, Tresidder nudged his master and jerked his head toward the gate behind them.

Maurice recognized the angry figure stalking along the driveway toward them. 'Stand by for a squall,' he said grimly. 'You go on and get started if you mind to.'

Alone he stood there, wondering what her first words would be and how he would respond. She was angry – one look was enough to tell him that. Should he turn it aside with a joke? Or be deadly serious? Better be serious, he decided – as serious, indeed, as the threat this storm now posed to her house.

'How dare you just come marching onto my property!' Sibylla called out when she was still some way off. 'Where's Dancey?'

Billy Dancey was her builder. The wind at her back carried her words to Maurice but made his reply inaudible to her: 'Looking after his other interests, I should think!'

Not that she was listening, anyway. She continued to shout as she drew nearer: 'You thought I was away, I suppose. Wouldn't see you! Well, you can just turn about and march straight out again – and take those men with you!'

She continued in that vein until she was face to face with him – quite literally, for she came on until only a matter of inches separated them. Spittle flecked her lips and her eyes burned with a wild, wintry fire. 'Well?' she yelled.

The gale snatched at her bonnet. In the subsequent tussle her long, dark hair fell free and streamed out toward him on the blast. Its fine tendrils lashed his cheeks, caressed his ears and neck, making a flimsy tube, dark within dark, in which he shouted back, 'Can't talk here. Come round the side.'

But in struggling to recapture her hair she caught him an uppercut with her forearm. He thought she was deliberately hitting him and grabbed both her wrists, much to her delight, for she had been screwing up her courage for an apology – which his roughness made unnecessary. For a long moment they stood thus, each caught off guard, though for different reasons – she because that shameful, cringe-making apology was still on the tip of her tongue; he because, for all his dislike of her, he would never have thought her the sort of woman who would go straight up to a man and strike him. It gave his perception of her an entirely new colouring, for, if she could shrug aside the restraints of ladylike behaviour so easily, could he not throw off the shackles society imposed on a gentleman with equal justification?

It passed in a moment. His more civilized self reclaimed him swiftly. He ducked out from under the straggle of her hair and, moving crosswind to her right, shouted, 'I'm trying to save your roof, you stupid, ignorant woman!'

All her fury returned at that. 'What business is it of yours, you arrogant, conceited man?'

'The business of any good neighbour!'

'Hah!' she almost screamed. 'Good neighbour?'

He waved a dismissive hand at her and turned on his heel. She, enraged still further by this impudence, flew at him and sent him staggering toward the house. He just managed to retain his balance, however, and ended up in the outer porch, whose door had blown inward. He came to rest with his back against the brick pillar beside the front door proper. She grabbed the outer door, whose upper half was glazed, and pulled it shut, holding it tight against his possible escape while she looked about wildly for a key or something to wedge it.

He watched her in disbelief. Deep within him something responded with a sort of maniac glee to the ferocity in her. It was for *him* and exclusively for him! He need only exist to stir that passion in her!

He raised both hands, fingers spread wide, and made a calm-down gesture at her through the glazing. Then he crooked his finger, inviting her inside.

Stubbornly she held fast to the handle with both hands and shook her head grimly.

You could say anything you liked to her now, he told himself. *The vilest obscenity . . . the most absurd nonsense . . . she'd never hear it over the wind!*

He decided to try it. He hadn't the courage of his thoughts, however, for he merely mimed the words, as if he were speaking slowly and clearly. But the words he mimed seemed to him the funniest of all, much subtler than nonsense or mere crudity. 'You are beau-ti-ful in your an-ger,' he mimed each syllable – and then laughed so much he ended in a fit of coughing.

He stopped when he felt the gale once more, whipping now among the dead leaves and dust in the porch. He straightened himself and turned to see her standing there in the open doorway, her face now calm and impassive.

'This is absurd,' she told him. 'Perhaps you imagine you are being a good neighbour. But I wish you'd understand that I do not want you for a neighbour at all. Good, bad, or indifferent – I want *nothing* to do with you, Mr Petifer. I wish you'd . . .'

'But why, Mrs Johnson? I wish you'd tell me. What have I ever done to make you . . .'

'I don't wish to discuss it, Mr Petifer. I merely express my . . .'

'But you must! I must know what I've done to bring about such hatred. Has it anything to do with that day at . . .'

'You are trying my patience, man. I just don't like you. Can't you get that inside your stupid, arrogant head? I never have liked you. I danced a week without stopping when you went out to the Cape. The day you returned was the blackest I . . .'

'You weren't even here!' he sneered.

She waved the objection away as too trivial to merit a reply. 'And I consider your behaviour since that day to be as despicable as it could possibly be. Though it is exactly what I might have . . .'

'My behaviour?' he echoed icily. 'With respect to Laura Curnow, you mean?'

'Respect!' she jeered.

'Isn't that rather more her business than yours?' he asked.

'How dare you!' she flared up again. 'She is not merely my cousin, she is also my dearest friend. Anyway, I don't propose to stand here and bandy words with . . .'

'I mean, if it doesn't distress her – my behaviour – if my behaviour doesn't distress her, why should it upset you so much?'

She just stared at him open-mouthed for a moment. 'Of all the . . .' she murmured at last. 'Have you really deluded yourself into imagining that your behaviour has *not* distressed her?'

'No.' He lowered his eyes and nodded a minor

concession. 'I know it has distressed her. But that's not the end of the story. It's nothing like as simple as that. You forget how well I know her.'

'*Knew* her.'

'*Know* her,' he insisted. 'She is distressed, but only part of her. The rest . . .' Suddenly he clamped tight his jaw and stared away, over her shoulder. 'You'd better ask her that yourself,' he concluded.

She stepped completely inside the lobby then, closing the door behind her. Swiftly crossing the two paces that separated them, she put her face once again close to his and said, 'If you truly believe that, then – by your own admission – your behaviour is even more despicable than I thought – and I didn't believe *that* was possible even. If you honestly imagine that some part of her is still under your malignant spell, then you, as a gentleman – I suppose you do fancy yourself to be a gentleman? – you ought to have packed your bags and gone straight back where you came from.' She narrowed her eyes and peered into his. 'Do you truly think she loves you still?' she asked in an incredulous voice.

He merely repeated his earlier words: 'You'd better ask her that.'

'You obviously do. So do you really consider it the act of a gentleman to come and live in the same town, even – much less to buy the neighbouring property and settle there?'

He gave a sad shake of the head. 'It's not a realistic question,' he told her, almost kindly, implying that her spirit was too dead to enable her to understand. 'You don't even begin to comprehend the power of these feelings you talk about so glibly. If you understood the first thing about love, you wouldn't ask any of these questions. But you don't. You don't know the tiniest thing about it. You're so eaten up with anger and bitterness against me – which I swear to you, I don't for the life of me understand, and I wish I did, I wish you'd have the mercy to . . . tell me . . . why.' His voice petered out and he just stood there, looking miserable.

And she just stood there, too, knowing that if she said anything more than the briefest of words, she'd burst into tears. She had no idea why. All she knew was that he had somehow engineered it. To humiliate her. She breathed in and out, rapidly, shallowly, several times, feeling her heartbeat go pitapat. 'God, you are such a . . . such a . . .' No word came. She began to panic. 'Such a swine!' she shrieked at last. She turned on her heels, pulled open the door, and ran outside.

The wind, which had risen several knots even while they had been in there, caught hold of the door once again and slammed it so furiously that the glass shattered; it fell in ringing shards to the tiled floor, where its clamour almost deafened them.

If Frank Tresidder hadn't come round the corner at that moment, there was no telling what might have happened next. 'We got 'er tied on now, boss,' he shouted above the wind. 'Come have a look-see, if you mind, afore we put the other ropes over 'n.'

Maurice, not trusting himself to look her in the face, walked a wide circle around her and so along the side of the house toward the kitchen. Sibylla recovered herself swiftly enough once he'd gone and set off in pursuit. 'Did Dancey ask you to do this?' she challenged. 'Where is the rascal, anyway?'

Maurice ignored her. His foreman, caught reluctantly between them, told her that the builder was at another site down in St John's.

'What's he doing down there?' she asked.

The man shrugged awkwardly and then turned with

some relief to show them the tarpaulin that he and the three others had managed to wrestle into place and finally to secure over the half-finished roof of the kitchen. If there had been any doubts as to the power of this gale, the fluttering roar of canvas against slate was enough to resolve them.

'It'll tear those eyes out inside half an hour,' Maurice said, pointing at the brass eyelets in the cover. 'Did you say there's more rope?'

Tresidder pointed to several hanks of it draped around the yard pump.

'Might as well use it all,' Maurice told him, and, taking one coil in his hand, went round to the windward side.

There he swung it around a couple of turns, like a discus thrower, before letting go. Up it sailed to the very ridge, buoyed on the wind, which carried it over and dropped it in the lee on the farther side. He turned to Peter Hosking and George Munroe. 'Hold fast to that, the pair of you,' he shouted. 'I'm going round to the ladder on the other side and I'll climb up there.' He pointed at the spot where the rope vanished over the ridge.

They exchanged dubious glances but neither man quite had the courage to argue with the master.

On his way back he passed Sibylla, who had stuck her nose into the teeth of the wind and then withdrawn herself to the partial shelter of the lee. 'I said I don't want your help,' she told him. 'I asked you most particularly to go away.'

He ignored her; but a voice inside asked him why he was being such a damn fool. Why was he risking life and limb – well, limb, certainly – for a woman he disliked and who couldn't stand the sight of him . . . a woman who was actually ordering him to go away?

Because she deserves it, he told himself.

Actually, it was because there was nothing she could do to stop him. And tomorrow, when the storm was over, and her half-finished roof was still intact, she'd have no choice but to be grateful to him. Yes, that was it! She'd *have* to be grateful to him! Oh, how that would rankle with her! How she'd grit her teeth and mumble and mutter when he returned to collect the canvas and rope after the storm had passed!

Gleeful again, and agile as a baboon, he shinned up the ladder to the eaves and then, with a half-twist of the loose rope around each hand, gave two jerks as a signal to the men on the far side; the moment they took up the slack, the strength of their pull enabled him almost to saunter up one of the rafters to the ridge.

Sibylla watched him, her heart in her mouth. She could not help admiring the speed and agility of the man, the way he anticipated the blast at the ridge and ducked beneath it so that, to cover the last couple of feet to it, he was practically sidling on his belly. At the ridge he sat upright and coiled the loose, downwind end of the rope around his waist a couple of times; sitting there astride the ridge, with confidence in every gesture and his hair flowing free, he made – she had to admit – a heroic sight against the darkening sky.

He shouted at Denis Williams to catch the loose end below and hold on tight; now he was held securely at both ends. From then on it went with hardly a word spoken, or needed. Tresidder threw up another loose rope, which his master then placed on the ridge exactly where it would have the greatest effect. Other ropes, tied at diagonals, he wove in and out of earlier ones like a fisherman making emergency repairs to a net, except that this had a mesh of gargantuan size. Last of all he wove his own safety rope into the network on his way down. The most dangerous moment of the entire operation came when he was on his way down the ladder, not noticing that one of the ropes was cutting diagonally across it, ready to trip him.

It was Sibylla's high-pitched warning rather than Tresidder's bass cry that saved him. For swank he descended the last half-dozen rungs like a circus artist – sliding swiftly down, hand over hand, with the soles of his feet bent inward against the uprights.

'Thanks for that!' he shouted at her, though she was only three feet or so away.

Then, with a satisfied grin he beckoned his men to follow him and left the scene without so much as a backward glance.

It was probably the grin that did it for Sibylla. So smug, so cocksure! She could just imagine him wearing it tomorrow when he turned up to collect his ropes and rick-cover. And the day after. And the week after. And God knows how many months after *that*. The very thought of being indebted to him in that way – indeed, in *any* way – was insupportable. She would rather see the roof of her kitchen go flying all the way to Truro than have to acknowledge the smallest debt of gratitude to that odious, smirking brute.

What could she do? She looked all about her but the evening had now grown quite dark.

No – the question was: What could she *un*do!

The ropes were tied to trees, gate hinges, the pump, a cellar grating . . . anything stout enough to withstand the force of the gale. One by one she tried them but the knots were self-tightening and the wind had already tugged them so hard that only a couple of men with long-handled pincers would get them undone.

'Aargh!' She raised her face to the storm-dark sky and gave out a cry of baffled rage.

As if in answer the heavens were split by a flash of lightning and a moment later the rain fell in stair rods – so obliquely that it felt more like a hosepipe trained upon her from the side than water falling from above.

She leaned into it, tricing herself up against its violence, and battled her way to the nearest shelter, which happened to be the woodshed.

Lightning flashed again, long enough to show her the hatchet the boy used for chopping the kindling. She picked it up and hefted it in her hand. A savage sort of calm descended on her as, heedless now of the downpour, she walked back out into the teeth of the storm. There, one by one, she hacked the ropes asunder.

Once that mighty wind got under the tarpaulin, nothing could withstand its force. Three of the eyelets had been tied directly to the bare rafters. The hurricane tore them out of the wall plate as if they were held with nothing stouter than panel pins. Then the entire roof came off as a single piece, which roared off downwind and took the tops off three fine Monterey pines, planted eighty years earlier to shelter the house on its north-west side.

But Sibylla hardly noticed. She was too busy nursing her arm, which was causing her the most excruciating pain she had ever known.

Doctor Thomas set Sibylla's broken arm, put it in plaster, and gave her a shot of morphine to dull the pain. It worked well enough until the small hours, when she awoke and began to cry again. Laura, her ears sharpened by the mothering of her own five – nanny or no nanny – went to her at once with some ordinary opium and managed to get her off to sleep again. After that she stayed with her, in case it wore off before dawn.

Sibylla had only a single bed, so Laura stoked up the fire, whose embers were in their last, dying glow. Then she brought a large eiderdown from their only remaining spare bedroom, which was next door, between Sibylla's room and her own boudoir. She wrapped it round her and, feeling very like the Caterpillar in *Alice*, sat beside the hearth and told herself it was going to be easy to get back to sleep. All she had to do was not try too hard. Just let her mind drift . . .

The wind poured around the house like a river in spate, roaring and soughing among the trees, shrieking through the telegraph wires that ran across the yard; she had lain awake through many a storm at Chynoweth but never before had she been so glad of its thirty-inch walls of granite and the massive slates upon its roof, not to mention the substantial new windows of teak and quarter-inch plate glass that Giles had put in two summers ago; the older Georgian sashes might have been more elegant but they'd have rattled like beggars' boxes on such a night as this. Even so, though the windows were all tightly closed, and never a rattle from one of them, the draught in the room was enough to lift the carpet at the threshold of the door, and stir the curtains around Sibylla's bed, and make the lamp wick gutter. Laura, sitting by the fireplace, could hear it roaring in the chimney, drawing the flames up at every gust.

She still couldn't imagine what had happened up at Parc-an-Dour. Obviously, Maurice Petifer had taken his men up there so as to secure something with that tarpaulin and rope. In a way, that was an even bigger mystery than what had happened to give Sibylla that broken arm. He couldn't stand the sight of her, nor she, him. So why had he gone out of his way to protect her property like that? It wasn't even as if Culdrose were downwind of Sibylla's place – in which case he might have had a justified fear of flying slates; but in fact, Culdrose was almost exactly upwind of Parc-an-Dour.

Anyway, whatever his motive, Maurice had certainly gone there to do *something* in the way of protecting Sibylla's property. And Sibylla had certainly gone after him 'loaded for bear,' as Jimmy Troy would say. And then what? Half an hour later, when Hinks went back with the coach and lantern to collect her, he found her lying unconscious and soaked to the skin beside a cellar light that had lost its iron grating. And then, when she was brought home and they fetched Dr Thomas to see her, he'd discovered her broken arm – 'fortunately a greenstick fracture,' as he said when resetting it.

Had there been a fight?

That was the most obvious construction Laura could put upon the bare facts – except that she could not imagine Maurice Petifer leaving Sibylla there in such a condition, no matter what she had said or done to provoke him. Her cousin, she knew, hadn't a good word to say for the man; she'd maintain he was capable of any villainy under the sun. Nothing was so vile that Maurice would refrain from doing it – according to Sibylla. Not for the first time she wondered what the poor man had done to deserve such hatred.

In their younger days the three of them had been almost inseparable. Sibylla had been the perfect chaperone . . .

No. She didn't want to think of those times now.

To get back to the point – no matter what Sibylla might say about Maurice, he would never have struck her. She could imagine that in the most extreme provocation (and no one could be more extreme in provocation than Sibylla!) he might possibly slap her face, just once. He would instantly regret it, of course, and be mortified, and profuse in his apologies. He wouldn't even notice that the triumph was Sibylla's, because she would have intended it from the outset. But anyway, that was the limit for Maurice – and there was no other lady in the world who could even provoke him that far.

Now there was an interesting observation . . .

No. She mustn't let her thoughts stray down there, either.

The fact was that Maurice could never have struck her a hard enough blow to fracture her arm. And even if it had happened by accident – suppose, for example, she flew at him, all teeth and nails, and he fended her off in such a way that she slipped and accidentally broke her arm – even so, he would never have cleared off and left her in that condition. Even if he'd gone to fetch help, he'd have got her in out of the rain and left a man at her side.

She must, therefore, have been alone when it happened – whatever 'it' was. She'd got rid of Maurice and his men – sent them off with a flea in their ears – and they'd taken their tarpaulin and ropes with them. Anyway, Hinks said he'd seen no sign of them, neither the men nor their equipment. And then, while she wandered around the place alone, some accident had befallen her. A falling chimneypot. A loose bit of scaffold or a ladder caught in the wind . . . even the branch of a tree . . .

Laura sighed. It was exasperating to have narrowed it down so much, only to have to wait Lord knows how many hours to learn precisely what it had been. Maybe Sibylla herself didn't know. It could have struck her out of the blue – or out of the black, rather. Giles would have to go up and investigate as soon as it was light. She made a note to tell him and then remembered he'd already decided to go; it was the last thing he'd said before dropping off to sleep.

That's what tiredness did for you.

But if she was so tired, why wasn't she sleepy?

She yawned – by way of encouragement.

Why did Sibylla hate poor Maurice so?

Laura had a vague memory of something that happened once when they had gone on a picnic to Land's End – about eight of them under the none-too-strict supervision of Mrs Williams, their teacher – and Maurice and Sibylla had gone off on a walk to Sennen Cove. She'd been a little cool to him after that, but merely cool – certainly she'd shown nothing like her present loathing for him. That didn't even begin until after he went out to the Cape. Quite a while after, in fact.

Another mystery.

Probably the incident at Sennen Cove had nothing to do with it. The trouble with knowing only a few facts was that you wanted to make them fit together no matter how tenuous the links between them. Laura realized that she herself only remembered the occasion because she had been so devoured by jealousy when the pair of them strolled off like that. It wasn't fair. Maurice was *her* beau, had always been her beau, everyone knew it and so . . .

And so . . .?

Nothing. Her mind was a blank, suddenly. She waited for something to come along and fill it. But nothing did.

She yawned and almost immediately fell asleep.

The fire was chill when Giles tiptoed into Sibylla's room at the dawn of the following morning. The two women he loved most dearly in all the world were fast asleep – his wife, coiled up in a cocoon of swansdown on the hearthrug, and her best friend, mercifully unconscious and pinned to the mattress by two or three pounds of plaster.

He smoothed her coverlet and then returned to his wife. There he stooped and, with a reverence close to being religious (for him, anyway), touched a pale blonde curl on her forehead.

'Maurice . . .' she murmured.

Shocked, hurt beyond degree, he straightened himself and, somehow, found his way back to the passageway without stumbling and wakening them. He had no idea where his feet were nor what obstructions might lie in their path.

It was not the name itself that had shocked him, he realized as he wandered, still in a daze, up the drive toward Parc-an-Dour. It was the smile on her lips when she said it. The Gioconda smile – which you can turn into anything your fancy, or your horror, dictates.

The wind was now a mere half-gale, soughing through the trees rather than roaring with the threat to topple them. Giles reached the main gate, still in something of a daze. At that early hour the Lizard road was deserted. He turned right toward the entrance to Clodgey Lane, which was less than a furlong away; Culdrose Farm lay an equal distance beyond it. The curtains there were all drawn back and several chimneys were gushing the dense smoke of freshly lighted fires. Wealth had not made a sluggard of Maurice Petifer, Giles thought. A moment later he saw the man himself, running as hard as his feet would carry him, not from the farm but down Clodgey Lane, from the direction of Parc-an-Dour.

Giles's first instinct, greatly to his surprise, was to turn and make for home; Petifer was the last person he wished to meet at that moment – indeed, at any moment. But contempt for his own cowardice combined with the more aggressive elements in his make-up and kept him on course for a confrontation.

For a few dozen paces he gave his fantasy free rein as he dealt with the problem of Petifer once and for all. He knocked the villain unconscious, dragged him down to the Loe (whose waters formed the southern boundary of both their properties), and held him beneath its surface until he struggled no more. But then his civilized, rather tolerant nature reasserted itself and asked him what sort of person he was allowing himself to become. What sort of a man was he letting Maurice Petifer make of him? Even as idle daydreams such fancies could be dangerous. By way of compensation – and just to show that primitive savage who seemed to want to take him over – he even prepared a thin smile of greeting for his enemy.

It was, however, wasted. Petifer was clearly in a panic of sorts – wild-eyed, hatless, his hair streaming behind him in the wind. 'Curnow!' he shouted. 'Thank God! Have you seen Mrs Johnson? Is she with you?' The words were forced out between huge and desperate gasps for breath. He stood beside the ditch, leaning across it with his hand against the stone hedge for support – the very picture of a man in the last stage of exhaustion.

'She's with us,' Giles assured him. 'Why?'

'Oh, thank God,' he repeated.

'But she has a broken arm. She has somehow acquired a broken arm.'

Maurice looked up sharply at the news. Then he frowned. 'A broken arm? Did she . . .?' The precise phrasing of the question eluded him; he glanced uncertainly toward Chynoweth, then Parc-an-Dour, and then at Giles again.

Giles pointed toward Parc-an-Dour. 'Up there. Something happened up there yesterday evening.'

A stony light filled the other's eyes. 'And I didn't dare believe it!' he said bitterly.

'Believe what?'

'It was the first thing I thought of – when I saw the place this morning – and then I said no, it couldn't possibly be . . .'

'Be what?'

'Even she wouldn't have been so . . . idiotic. Aargh!' He let out a sudden bellow of anger and hurt the fleshy side of his fist against the stone. 'The silly . . . stupid . . . vindictive woman!'

Giles advanced a pace toward him. 'What has happened, Petifer? Is something wrong at Parc-an-Dour?'

Maurice gave a hollow laugh. 'You may say that! Come and see for yourself. The place is a ruin.' Nursing his hand he turned about and started back the way he had come, taking the long strides of a man who has spent many years in the veldt.

Giles, though taller by several inches, had to break into a single trot every four or five paces to keep up. 'I was on my way there, anyway,' he said apropos nothing in particular. Or (it then struck him) apropos any faint suspicion that he was taking his marching orders from Petifer.

The other slowed down, saying, 'There's no hurry, actually. The damage is well and truly done now.' He glanced over his shoulder at the southern sky. 'If this turns to rain, the house *will* be a ruin.'

'You mean it isn't quite . . . look, what *has* happened up there?'

They turned into Clodgey Lane at that moment and Giles got his answer directly as the house came into view. Half a dozen men were crawling over its roof – the main roof, which had only just been reslated; they were struggling with a tarpaulin.

'Eh?' He turned to Petifer.

'Gone,' was the grim reply. 'Blew away in the night. Half the parish is buried under broken slate. You never saw such . . .'

'But how? It's only just been . . .'

'Listen, Curnow, I'm not going to say a word. People will only say I'm prejudiced. But . . .'

'People? What people?'

'You, for one. I'm not going to say a word as to what I think happened. You come and look at the place for yourself. Look at the evidence and form your own conclusions.'

They stepped out with renewed purpose toward the house. 'All I know about it,' Giles said, 'is that the ladies went over to Falmouth yesterday to look at the ships taking shelter, and on their way back they spied you and your men going in there with a tarpaulin.'

'Yes,' Maurice replied wearily. 'The good neighbour! I happened to notice that the roof over her kitchen is only half slated – *was* only half slated! It isn't even *there* now. Bill Dancey had left a tarpaulin over it, tied with baler twine or bootlaces or something. *He's* the real villain of this sorry affair, if you ask me. Anyway, I took my lads over there to do the job properly . . .'

'Why? Where was Dancey?'

'Where d'you think! The man's an utter blackguard. He's always juggling with three or four jobs at once. He was looking after one of his other sites down in St John's. I'll bet he thought to himself, *It's only a little kitchen annexe. Even if the roof does blow off again, it won't cost much to put it back.* That's his sort of cunning.'

'And the roof's now gone?'

Petifer darted him a glance, hinting there were a thousand things he might say. 'You'll see,' he replied grimly as they turned in at the gate to Parc-an-Dour.

They were now in the lee of an overgrown laurel hedge. The sudden lack of wind made Giles's skin feel warm, despite the rawness of the day. He glanced sidelong at his companion and tried to rekindle some of his earlier animosity – without success. For a moment it surprised him; then he told himself that anger or bitterness was, in a curious way, a compliment to the man. It gave him an importance he would not otherwise merit and would certainly never earn.

What did it mean that Laura whispered his name in her sleep? As St Augustine said, we are none of us responsible for our dreams. (He smiled self-mockingly at the thought that he had to turn to one of the fathers of the Church for this justification.) He wondered how he himself would respond if one of *his* old flames turned up like Petifer and intruded herself so insistently into their lives? His cousin Monica, for instance – he had almost thrown himself off St Agnes Head when she went and married . . . thingummyjig, that cavalry captain. Significant that even now he couldn't readily remember the man's name! Warburton, that was it. Or what about Gwendolen Walshe? He'd pined a whole year for her when she took the veil. If either of those ladies turned up, unattached and available once more, and bought the neighbouring property, they'd surely be on his mind. And could he honestly say they might not harry him into his dreams as well? Or nightmares, rather?

How could he be sure Laura wasn't having a nightmare of some kind?

He had a brief intimation of a further thought, something more disquieting than these easy and comforting excuses; but it vanished. His mind refused to pursue it.

When they drew close to the house, Petifer shouted a number of rapid instructions to his men on the roof. Giles could not help thinking that, in other circumstances, the fellow was exactly the sort of man he was always on the lookout to employ – a man you could trust, who'd know what to do, and whom you could leave unsupervised to carry it out properly. A man like that was as rare as hen's teeth.

'See!' Petifer stirred the toe of his boot among the broken glass in the lobby. 'That wasn't the wind did that.'

Giles made no reply.

Together they went round the back, where the full extent of the disaster was at once apparent. The kitchen roof had simply vanished – joists, rafters, battens, and all. The wall plate on the south side had been ripped from the stone and now hung down at a crazy angle into the wreckage of the kitchen below.

Petifer pointed silently at the three broken pines and the shards of roof that lay spilled among them before he led Giles to the outbuildings on the southern, upwind side of the house. There, still without a word, he pointed out several lengths of severed rope, each tied to a grating, a tree, a gatepost . . . a heavy anchorage of some kind. Each had been hacked through with some sharp implement. And that, of course, was the next item in Petifer's silent, guided tour around the evidence: the hatchet. It lay close to a hole beside the house, a hole from which a cellar grating had clearly been ripped.

'I've moved nothing,' he commented. 'This is exactly as I found it. When my men and I left here last night, those ropes were all tied fast to the tarpaulin we'd secured over the kitchen roof.'

The evidence was overwhelming, of course, and there was only one possible conclusion. Giles stepped back several paces to look once again at the damage to the main part of the house. 'When the roof blew off the kitchen,' he said, 'it must have taken out some of the bricks on that east wall. That's how it happened.'

'More than some,' Maurice agreed. 'The ridge pole ran about eight feet into the house. It's tied into the main lateral wall in there. Or it was, before I put my oar in. So it must have levered out a six-foot gash in the brickwork, at the very least. Which left most of that end wall just hanging. Then when *that* went, the gale got in under the main roof and . . . pfft! Blew it off like thistledown.'

Giles closed his eyes and shook his head.

Maurice laughed grimly. 'You now have a guest until Christmas,' he commented. 'Or next spring, more likely.'

Giles nodded forlornly and gave a single, bleak laugh. Again that fugitive thought crossed his mind and again it vanished before he could pin it down.

'Perhaps it *is* my fault,' Maurice went on. 'If I hadn't come up here and interfered last night, who knows? A few slates might have blown off the kitchen roof . . . Dancey's pathetic effort with *his* tarpaulin certainly wouldn't have held tight enough to pull off the rafters and all. It very likely *is* all my fault.'

Giles was about to protest at this nonsense when it struck him that that was probably what the man was fishing for. 'It *was* your fault, Petifer,' he replied, almost without thought. 'You surely know Mrs Johnson well enough by now to realize how she'd respond to any sort of help from you – no matter how good your intentions may have been. So when you shoulder her to one side and actually force it upon her . . . well!' He waved a hand toward the hatchet and the severed ends of rope.

'You agree that *was* her handiwork,' Maurice said quickly.

Giles just stared at him in a mixture of anger and contempt; but the other stared back, quite unabashed. 'Just between ourselves, of course,' he added. 'I'm man enough – and gentleman enough, I hope – to shoulder the entire responsibility for this, as far as the world at large is concerned, anyway.'

Giles was not deceived. 'You know you're safe enough in making that offer. You know it's the last thing in the world she'd let you do – shoulder responsibility for something she herself has done.'

'If *I* claim it,' Maurice agreed.

Giles frowned, not quite catching the man's drift.

'But what if you go back,' Maurice continued, 'and say I'm running round in a panic, telling the world it's not my fault, that I didn't mean it, that I was only trying to help? If *you* say that – and laugh at my pathetic efforts to shrug off the blame . . . she'd think it too good a joke to spoil.'

'Dear God, Petifer!' Giles put his fists to his temples and pressed hard. 'I don't know whether to . . . I don't know what to say.' He calmed down somewhat and peered intently at the man. 'Why are you willing to do this – take the blame on yourself? And anyway' – a further objection occurred to him – 'how do you explain the severed ends of the ropes?'

Maurice took out a large penknife, cut the first of them free and stuffed it in his overcoat pocket. 'What severed ends?' he asked as he went on to deal with the next. 'You must be imagining things, old boy.'

Giles continued to shake his head in bewilderment. 'In one way, I'm sure it's extremely noble of you, but can't you see how you're also blackening her character, man? You're saying she'd connive at a barefaced lie just to save her own embarrassment and to get you in hot water – that's a terrible thing to say about anyone, much less a lady.'

Maurice dealt with the last of the ropes before he replied. He gave Giles an oddly sympathetic look as he passed him on his way to pick up the discarded hatchet – which he held briefly in a manner that might *just* be construed as a joking threat. 'Lady?' he echoed. 'And gentleman? Well . . . we are, I suppose – yet what a thin veneer it is! Or don't you agree? I never knew how thin it was until these last few weeks.' He threw the hatchet into the dark maw of the woodshed and waved a hand about him. 'And now all this!'

'Are you referring to the threats I made that evening?'

Maurice shook his head; he seemed suddenly haggard and dejected, so that Giles had an intimation of the man's essential loneliness. 'No,' he replied and, tapping his forehead, went on, 'I'm referring to what's inside here. When I saw this place this morning, I was, of course, aghast. Yet I have to admit that some small part of me exulted at it. To my shame. I exulted that *that* woman could be so . . . so consumed by hatred for me.'

'You mean that she could give you such an important place in her life?' Giles suggested.

Maurice shrugged. 'I suppose so. I mean, that's one way of looking at it. Oddly enough, you know, I admire her! I don't mean I'm one of her admirers – God forbid! I mean there's something in me that almost exults to have been touched by a passion – even though it's the passion of hatred – but to be touched by something so strong and so compelling – it's . . . it's . . .' He shivered. 'Indescribable.'

Giles felt himself being seduced into this extraordinary way of looking at Sibylla's action; there was, indeed, a strange sort of magnificence in something so powerful and all-consuming as her hatred for this fellow. It made the ebb and flow of emotions between Culdrose and Chynoweth seem very feeble . . .

'Tell me,' he felt compelled to ask, 'why *did* you buy Culdrose?'

Maurice laughed, but with little humour.

When Giles realized that was the man's only reply he added, 'Apparently Elizabeth Troy told Laura that Jimmy advised against it. He was convinced you came to the auction as a spectator only.' He saw Maurice nod, perhaps unconsciously, and went on, 'Did something happen there to change your mind?'

This time the nod was quite conscious – and extremely reluctant. 'If it weren't for all this' – Maurice waved a hand at the wreckage of the house – 'I probably wouldn't admit it . . . maybe not even to myself. I mean, you know how you can hold certain facts in your mind and yet still shrink from seeing their implications? Well, it's like that. I truly came to that auction cured of my desire to buy Culdrose. But then, when I saw Harry Sampson bidding for it – at Sibylla Johnson's behest, of course – something in me just . . .'

'What d'you mean? At Mrs Johnson's behest?'

'No doubt about it. She was waiting for him when we arrived – Elizabeth Troy, Jake Morvah, and I – we almost bowled her over. She was on absolute tenterhooks. Then a moment later he arrived and she had a quick pow-wow with him – and then never moved from his side throughout the bidding. Oh, she was behind it all right.'

Giles was still bewildered, however. 'I don't see why that should have induced you to step back into the bidding,' he said.

Maurice gave a rather shamefaced grin. 'It's just that

I'd spent so many hours imagining myself the owner of Culdrose. And then, when – for the most altruistic reasons in all the world – I decided to pull out . . . only to see Sibylla Johnson step in . . . to imagine her walking over the very fields that I had just . . . Yes, well may you laugh! As I say, I'm not proud of it myself.'

Giles dabbed at the corners of his eyes. 'I'm not laughing at that,' he assured Maurice.

'What, then?'

Giles shook his head and sighed. 'It's no laughing matter, really. But are you honestly saying you only bought Culdrose because you thought Mrs Johnson was bidding against you?'

'Yes. Why?'

'Because I'm sure she wasn't.'

Maurice frowned. 'Are you quite sure?'

'Absolutely. She was only going to bid if you did. You're quite right in thinking she would bid through Sampson – or would *have* done, if there had been any need. But as you kept out of it – until your very dramatic intervention at the end . . .'

'But I *saw* them, Curnow! Every time Sampson nodded, the bid rose another hundred.'

Giles shrugged and apparently yielded the point. 'Oh well then, have it your own way.'

Doctor Thomas returned to Chynoweth that morning at about eleven, which, experience had taught him, was a good time for a small tipple of sherry and biscuits. The sharp pain in Sibylla's arm had by then receded to a dull ache.

'May I ask how it happened?' he inquired.

She ignored the question, saying, 'I'd almost prefer the pain, except I know I wouldn't really. But at least it occupied *all* one's attention. This ache is like a nagging little child, always whining away in the background but allowing one to *half* devote one's attention to other things.'

'Like grammar,' he said drily. 'When a patient can split an infinitive as robustly as that, my worries over split bones begin to recede. Do you recall how it happened?'

'Something to do with the wind,' she replied vaguely.

'I had already surmised *that*, dear lady.'

'You sound just like Sherlock Holmes, Doctor Thomas,' Laura said brightly as she entered the room with a vase of flowers, fresh cut from the winter garden. 'I expect you also noticed a slight smearing of paint – black paint – on our patient's arm last night? And not an inch from where it appeared to be broken! Highly significant, that. Also a small wooden splinter in her right hand – from a peculiar variety of pitch pine that grows only on the western slopes of a certain fiord in Norway – didn't you?'

'No?' he responded warily, being unused to the sort of humour the two cousins engaged in when together.

'No, nor did I,' Laura confessed and burst into laughter. 'We'd neither of us get very far in solving this mystery by Sherlockian principles, would we! May I offer you some sherry?'

After that he was reluctant to repeat his question a third time. When he had gone Laura went to help her cousin rise and get dressed. The first thing Sibylla did was thank her for stopping the man from asking all those unnecessary questions. Laura said, 'Unnecessary for *him* to ask, perhaps, my dear!'

Sibylla sighed.

'Actually,' Laura went on, 'there *was* a little smearing of black paint – not on your arm but on the sleeve of the coat you were wearing last night. And wasn't one of Dancey's men painting fresh bitumen on the cellar gratings last time you showed me over the place?'

Sibylla cleared her throat and sighed again. Then she looked at her hand. 'No sign of a splinter, anyway,' she remarked.

'But there may easily have been one – am I not right?' Laura insisted, staring intently into her cousin's eyes in the looking glass.

'I simply don't remember,' Sibylla insisted. 'I was going round, inspecting what . . . that man . . . whatsizname had done, and the next thing I remember was waking up here with a broken arm. Perhaps a tree fell on me? Did Doctor Thomas give me an injection of something? I still feel so drowsy. Did the children come and see me this morning? I seem to remember something of . . .'

'Of course they did. Martin is extremely envious of your plaster cast, I may say. And Agnes wants to paint flowers on it.'

'Oh, I remember that.' Sibylla closed her eyes and shook her head vigorously, as if to clear some blockage.

'These leg-o-mutton sleeves are just made for ladies with plaster casts!' Laura said with a laugh. 'Just see if it'll slip on if we leave the cuff undone. There!'

'Was it a tree?' Sibylla returned to their earlier topic.

Laura cleared her throat and drew a deep breath, but before she could speak there was a cry of 'yoo-hoo!' from below, followed by: 'All right if I come up?'

'Elizabeth Troy.' Laura's tone was not *over*joyed.

Sibylla looked at her in surprise. 'Have you fallen out?' she asked; then, raising her voice: 'Yes, dear, do come up!'

'There was something I hadn't yet told you,' Laura just managed to say before Elizabeth appeared at the doorway, her eyes large with prepared sympathy.

'My dear, I'm so sorry for all your troubles!' she effused as she crossed the room in one long swish of corduroy and silk and bent to kiss Sibylla on the cheek.

'It was far more painful last night,' Sibylla told her bravely.

Elizabeth looked down at the cast. 'Oh yes, that, too,' she said. 'Good morning, Laura, dear. How rude of me.' She kissed Laura, as well.

'Why, what did you mean?' Sibylla asked.

'Oh, I was referring to . . .'

'Actually,' Laura cut in. 'I was just about to tell her that. I'm afraid she hasn't heard . . . all the news yet.'

Sibylla turned pale. 'What? Has somebody . . . nobody's been . . . hurt? I mean, nobody else?'

'No.' Laura shook her head. 'It's Parc-an-Dour, I'm afraid. The roof was blown away in last night's storm.'

'It's not the only place to have suffered,' Elizabeth put in. 'There are slates missing all over the town. Joseph Faull, my neighbour, lost his barn.' She was talking mainly to allow Sibylla time to absorb the appalling news about Parc-an-Dour. The woman's response intrigued her, though. Far from being shocked she appeared, if anything, discomfited to hear it. And her next remark was more puzzling still: 'So, Maurice Petifer's so-called *assistance* was no assistance at all!' she said. Idly her free hand strayed over the dressing table, rearranging things to no purpose. Then, in a tolerantly dismissive tone she added, 'Well, they'd only done a couple of rows of slates – so I suppose it's not a great deal lost. It's annoying, though.'

Elizabeth and Laura exchanged glances.

'What's the matter?' Sibylla asked.

Laura swallowed heavily. 'I'm afraid it isn't just the kitchen roof, darling. You see – the way Giles explained it to me – the bit over the kitchen was blown away bodily, all of a piece. And it took part of the wall on that side with it. And that opened up a hole into the roof space, the loft, in the main house. And then the storm got in and . . .' She gave a helpless little shrug.

Sibylla closed her eyes and sank her head into the palm of her hand. 'Not the roof of the main house?' she begged.

Elizabeth laid a hand on her shoulder and squeezed.

Laura sat awkwardly beside her, on the few uncovered inches of the dressing table stool, and put her arms around her. 'I'm afraid so, darling. I'm so sorry.'

Sibylla began to sob.

The other two smiled wanly at each other and waited for her to grow calm again.

Her first words when she did so were, 'Well, we'll rent a house in the town. I can't possibly go on sponging off you and Giles any longer . . . Lord! How long is it going to take this time? We had that beautiful summer and all that dry weather . . . and now . . .' Again she fell to tears.

'It won't get wet at least,' Elizabeth assured her. 'I passed it on my way here. There's a rick cover secured right over the whole of the roof. The timbers are still there over the main house, you know – and quite a few slates, so the man told me.'

'Billy Dancey? I'm amazed he dare show his face there!' Sibylla was glad for a subject on which she could show a little spirit.

Elizabeth drew breath to say it hadn't, in fact, been Dancey but then saw Laura give a barely perceptible shake of the head and so she pursed her lips and said nothing.

'You'll certainly *not* move to any house in town,'

Laura insisted. 'What? And leave me defenceless here?'

Sibylla leaned her head briefly against Laura's shoulder and dabbed the tears from her cheeks. 'If only Petifer hadn't put that wretched cover on the kitchen roof,' she said experimentally.

'Mmm,' Laura replied.

'Is that what started it?' Elizabeth asked. 'No wonder he . . .' She faltered and looked guardedly at the other two.

'What?' Sibylla asked sharply.

Elizabeth glanced uncomfortably at Laura. 'Well, it was he who spread the rick cover over the main house this morning.'

'Yes,' Laura added. 'He was up there at the crack of dawn apparently. Giles went up first thing and found him there already.'

'Guilty conscience!' Elizabeth said.

'Giles?' Sibylla asked uncomfortably. 'Did he . . .?'

'Did he what?'

'Well.' She shrugged. 'I mean, the tarpaulin Petifer put on last night was tied to trees and bits of the outhouses and . . . things like that, you know. I just wondered if Giles happened to notice . . . you know – how the ropes came undone. If they *did* come undone, I mean. Or perhaps they uprooted the trees? I don't know.'

'Giles said nothing about trees being uprooted,' Laura replied.

'The ropes probably frayed,' Elizabeth told them. 'I've seen that happen with rick covers in a storm – when they flap, you know. If the rope is touching anything at all, it can fray to nothing in just a few minutes. Poor Maurice! And he was only doing it for the best.' She touched Sibylla's shoulder again and then went on. 'I suppose I was a little cavalier about your arm just now, dear. Did Doctor Thomas say it'd mend all right?'

Sibylla gave a rueful chuckle. 'He said I'm still young enough for it to mend completely. The nicest compliment I've had from a man in years! I expect I'll be breaking bones quite often in future, actually – just to hear him say it again.'

Laughing, they rose and went downstairs. A short while later Elizabeth said she'd only popped in to see how Sibylla was – and would she like to borrow some books – and she'd call again in a day or two, if that was all right?

When she'd gone, Laura asked her cousin if she'd like a bit of fresh air – a turn around the terrace, perhaps?

Artfully, Sibylla replied, 'The doctor didn't say I was to stay indoors all the time, did he?'

'Certainly not,' Laura assured her stoutly, thinking she was going to take up the suggestion for a brief turn around the terrace.

'Good! Then we might just as well walk up to Parc-an-Dour and take a look at the damage.'

Laura protested but Sibylla insisted, and when she insisted she usually won. So, with the sling tightened and a good woollen cape about her shoulders, they set off on a leisurely walk to Parc-an-Dour.

'I wonder what Elizabeth Troy really wanted?' Laura asked.

Sibylla bridled at the suggestion. 'I'm sure she just wanted to see how I was – and to commiserate over the roof. D'you think it'll be covered under the insurance? I wonder if Dancey's insured? I never thought to ask. That's where one misses having a man, you know. To do things like that. I'm sure Giles wouldn't forget it.'

'You manage wonderfully, darling,' Laura assured her. 'Everyone says so. It's just because you're in pain at the moment. I think we ought to turn back.'

Sibylla ignored the suggestion. 'Of course, you know, Elizabeth does have her *uses*. Apart from being a good friend.'

'Oh?' Laura encouraged her with a smile.

'Yes. She seems to get on quite well with the Petifer creature. She's also a pretty useful conductor of messages between us – especially the unspoken ones.'

'How can a message be unspoken?'

'Laura!' her cousin chided. 'You disappoint me. They're the most important ones of all. I'm sure she tells him . . . you know, the general lie of the land. She sounds out the ground for him. I don't mind. She's not at all underhand – I mean, she makes no bones of her friendship for both of us. Which is fair enough, I suppose.'

'You do gabble on!' Laura grumbled.

'I know.' She pulled a penitent face.

'Why?' Laura asked.

Sibylla gave an uncomfortable laugh. 'What d'you mean – why?'

'You know very well. You always gabble on like that when your conscience is troubled.'

Sibylla tossed her head. 'I'm not aware of it.'

Laura laughed. 'Oh yes you are. You remember that time – the first time Maurice Petifer took you to the theatre and you just happened to forget to tell me about it until Mary Beckerleg spilled the beans?'

'That!' Sibylla's voice was heavy with scorn. 'I like the way you say the *first* time. It was the *only* time.'

'You gabbled away for a whole hour before I took pity on you and told you I knew.'

'Yes – I haven't forgotten *that* little act of mercy, either!' Sibylla said darkly. 'Anyway, what, may I ask, am I supposed to have a guilty conscience about now?'

'Fun-nil-y e-nough,' Laura laid a delicate stress on

each syllable, 'the very same fellow. I'm putting you out of your misery early this time, you see. Giles told me what he found up there this morning. A hatchet lying just a yard or so from where Hinks says he discovered you unconscious last night. And three or four rope ends, all severed with that same hatchet – to judge by the blazes on the stone and wood nearby.'

Sibylla swallowed heavily and stared at the road ahead of them. 'I only hope he tidied them away,' she said at last.

'No.' Laura assured her.

She looked sharply at her cousin, who then added, 'Because Maurice Petifer did it.'

Sibylla frowned incredulously. 'He did what?'

Laura nodded. 'Yes – Maurice Petifer. He cut away the rope ends and he threw the hatchet back into the woodshed.'

'But why? I should have thought he'd be the last person to do a thing like that. Surely he'd want all the world to see what an idiot I am?'

Laura pounced. '*Do* you think you're an idiot, Sib?'

She hadn't called her by her adolescent nickname in years; somehow it restored an earlier intimacy, which marriage, parenthood, and respectability had caused to fade.

Sibylla nodded glumly. 'An utter blithering idiot – as your father used to say.'

'Why did you do it?'

'I don't know!' she replied angrily – most of it being directed inward. 'It's just the way he smiled when he bade me goodnight.'

She told her cousin all that had passed from the moment she descended from the carriage on the way back from Falmouth. 'So, you see,' she concluded, 'I told him I didn't want his help and he just brushed me aside and . . . went ahead and covered the roof over anyway. Actually, d'you know who he reminded me of? My father! D'you remember how he used to ignore all my objections . . . brush aside all my protests? Remember when he took some scissors and cut off all my lovely long hair? Not as a punishment but just because *he* said it made me look like a child.'

'He was right, though,' Laura dared to point out. 'You yourself admitted afterwards that men began to treat you differently once you stopped looking like a little Alice in Wonderland.'

'That's not the *point!*' Sibylla insisted, beginning to get agitated as she fought that long-ago battle all over again. 'The point is that he didn't reason with me or talk to me – I mean his whole attitude was *Daddy knows best, so just hold your tongue, little girl!* That's what made me so angry – the arrogance of him!'

'Plus the fact that in your heart of hearts you knew he was right.'

'Yes, yes, yes – very well!' Sibylla agreed angrily. 'And it was the same with the Petifer creature yesterday. I know he was right. It was just his *Daddy knows best* attitude that made me so angry. And then that odious smirk on his face when he left – and the thought that I was going to have to be *grateful* to him for ever after! Aargh!' She started to raise the wrong fist to the heavens and quickly changed it to, 'Ow!'

'That does it!' Laura said firmly. 'We're turning about and going back this minute.'

'Oh no we're not!' Sibylla spoke not argumentatively but with a low, savage growl.

Laura followed her gaze and saw Maurice Petifer coming down the drive of Parc-an-Dour at the head of a small gang of men.

A moment later they emerged at the gate and Petifer saw the two women holding their ground. He did not even break stride. He kept his eyes on Sibylla all the way; when he saw her draw breath to speak – though the wind was against him and they were still fifty yards apart – he called out, 'Mrs Johnson! I owe you my humblest apology!'

'Eh?' Her exclamation was so weak that even the wind would not have carried it to him; but her gaping mouth and furrowed brow said it all, anyway.

'Yes,' he continued as the gap between them closed, 'I believe that if I had not interfered last night and tied my tarpaulin to your roof, your house might still be intact.'

They were now quite close. Sibylla, too stunned to reply, just stared at him. He motioned his men to go on – which they did with a respectful tug at the forelock to the ladies. And while they were yet in earshot he added, 'If you will arrange for the builder's bills for the repairs to be forwarded to me, I'll gladly meet them.'

But the moment they were out of range he added, 'You blithering idiot! What on earth possessed you to do such a stupid thing?'

Laura burst out laughing – which just about kept the lid on the day.

'It's not funny!' Sibylla shouted – and then burst into laughter, too.

'I'm glad I've said something to amuse,' Maurice said stiffly; a brief memory of the hundreds of times these two women had made him feel small and excluded flashed through his mind.

'It's just because you're being so pompous, Maurice,' Laura told him. 'You know very well why she did it. You must have known it was a risk even before you began.'

'Ridiculous! I don't see that at all,' he protested; he was now more wounded than angry.

'Oh come on! You're not by any means an insensitive man. You know very well that anything you do is like a red rag to a bull where Sibylla's concerned, so . . .'

'Oh, am I still here?' Sibylla asked sarcastically. 'Yoo-hoo! Can anybody see me?'

Laura ignored her. 'Do I need to say more?' she persisted, fixing him with the keenest stare.

Discomfited, he shuffled a little and muttered that he was only trying to be neighbourly.

'No!' Laura insisted. 'Not *only* trying to be neighbourly. Granted that was one of your motives, but you can't look me square in the eye and say that was the *only* thing going on in your mind – now can you?'

'He can't look you square in the eye anyway,' Sibylla sneered.

Laura turned to her and, with solemn mockery, said, 'Leave this to Daddy, eh?'

Sibylla drew a deep breath. Her lips vanished in a thin line of whitened flesh, but she said no more.

'Can you?' Laura challenged Maurice.

He gave an uncomfortable shrug. 'I don't see what else. There was a gale blowing force nine or ten . . .'

'Maurice?' Her voice rose on a warning-questioning note.

'What else then?' he asked grumpily.

'And why are you pretending to take the blame for me now?' Sibylla put in.

Without even looking at her, Laura placed a symbolic hand over her cousin's mouth and continued to press Maurice. 'It didn't even cross your mind that the situation would be wonderfully piquant – to put the high-and-mighty Sibylla Johnson in your debt for a change?'

His eyes answered for him, but Sibylla didn't see it. She was too busy struggling free from her cousin's clasp. 'Whose side are you on anyway?' she asked.

'Ours,' Laura assured her. 'Listen – both of you.

This has simply got to stop. You realize that, don't you. If this sort of thing goes on, it can only get worse. It'll end in murder – and that's not just a figure of speech. One of you will do the other in. You're standing on the brink now. Why not take a quick peep down into the abyss and then draw back and agree to behave like sensible people from now on?'

Neither of them was looking at the other.

'What d'you say?' Laura persisted.

'I say you're an awful bully,' Sibylla muttered.

'And a spoilsport!' Maurice added.

Sibylla shot him a rapid glance and Laura realized that her cousin not only knew precisely what Maurice had meant but that she agreed. It had, indeed, been a kind of sport between them – to go at it like Kilkenny cats whenever their paths crossed. 'Shake hands on it then,' she was bold enough to suggest.

Sheepishly Maurice held forth a large paw, far from clean after the morning's labours at Parc-an-Dour. Sibylla looked at it askance. 'All got in a good cause,' he said. Shyly, then, she took his hand and shook it.

'Would you like me to show you the damage and what we've done in the way of emergency cover?' he asked.

They all went up to the house. Maurice repeated the explanation that Giles had already given to Laura, and she to Sibylla; neither woman interrupted him. As they passed the front porch he glanced at the shattered door and then at Sibylla. She gave him a wry smile and said, 'It certainly was a storm!'

Her imagination had combined with her guilty conscience to create a picture of a house that had been totally wrecked by her folly. When she saw it was, in fact, no worse than it had been back at the end of August, before they started putting the new slates on the roof, she cheered up considerably and said she was glad she'd come.

'Actually,' Maurice said, when they stood before the wreckage of the kitchen, 'I wasn't being *entirely* chivalrous when I said I was to blame. *Some* of the blame, at least, is mine, I must admit. If I had contented myself with simply anchoring the tarpaulin to the ground, it would have blown away without taking the whole roof with it. But I had to go and be clever – and tie it to the rafters as well. Mind you' – he cleared his throat meaningfully and stared at the low, scudding clouds – 'I never for one moment imagined that someone would go round with a hatchet behind me.'

'You can thank your stars I *wasn't* behind you with a hatchet last night,' Sibylla groused.

They managed a wan little smile at each other.

'There now, isn't that nice!' Laura cut in. 'What did you do with the rope ends?' she asked him.

He walked over to the hen run and stirred some cold ashes with the toe of his boot.

'Actually,' Sibylla said, out of the blue, 'you looked jolly dashing up there on the roof last night.'

They both stared at her in astonishment. 'What made you say that?' Laura asked.

'I don't know.' Her tone was half-embarrassed, half-aggressive. 'It just occurred to me.' She brightened and her jaw jutted pugnaciously. 'I've been trying to think of *something* pleasant to say for the last ten minutes, if you must know.'

PART TWO

Ins and Outs

[Marriage] is like a cage;
one sees the birds outside
desperate to get in,
and those inside
equally desperate
to get out

Montaigne

'Giles?' Laura reached across the bed and laid a finger on his arm. He looked down at her over the top of his book, *Reasons for the Existence of Deity*. It took a second or so for his eyes to refocus; if he had been a 'mere machine,' as he often claimed, she was sure she'd have heard gears and cogwheels grinding ponderously. 'In a moment, dear,' he promised abstractedly.

She laughed. 'I wasn't talking about *that!*' Then, more thoughtfully, 'Although . . . now you mention it . . .'

'What then?' he asked. 'The infuriating thing about these religious chaps is they all want to have their cake and eat it. They want to tell you that reason alone can never justify faith – indeed, that one has faith *precisely because* reason alone isn't enough – and yet they want to give you adequate reasons nonetheless. They've never been able to come to terms with it.'

'What would you call a child who can't remember to comb her hair or brush her teeth or change her knickers but who *can* remember that Oliver Cromwell died in sixteen fifty-eight?'

'I'd call her Blanche,' he replied at once. 'Ask me a difficult one.'

After a short silence she said, 'All right!' in a tone that implied she'd rather go on talking about Blanche, but, since he'd asked for it, she'd give it him. 'How do you feel about Sibylla having to stay on here for another couple of months – or however long it's going to be?'

He snapped the book shut as a gesture of some kind, and then was annoyed to see he'd forgotten to insert the bookmark first. 'Sanguine,' he said. 'Cheerful . . . jovial. I've already said as much.'

'She has a dreadful conscience about it all.'

He grinned. 'That's very understandable. I hope you're not about to say that *I* have in some way made it worse for her – rubbed her nose in it . . . that sort of thing? I've studiously avoided the slightest hint of condemnation.'

Laura shook her head unhappily. 'Perhaps that's the thing, you see. The fact that you *haven't* said a single word about it.'

'I have. I told her how very sorry I am – all of us are. And she's to feel *absolutely* that this place is her home for as long as she needs it.'

'Yes, but you haven't said a single word about what she *did*. Cutting those ropes and all that.'

He sighed deeply and raked the ceiling with his eyes. 'Like what? What should I have said? Have *you* said anything?'

'Indeed, I have. The day after it happened. I was quite severe with her – and Petifer. I told them to stop behaving like children.' She chuckled. 'I made them shake hands, just like you did with Henry and Agnes when they couldn't agree on putting up the curtain for their charades.'

'You didn't!' He chuckled, though her answer plainly surprised him.

'I did. They were so sheepish, but they obeyed.'

'Well, then' – he became serious again – 'one of us has done it. I can't see what I could add.'

'No, I know.' Her tone was more understanding now. 'It's difficult, I agree. But your silence on the subject must seem like the silence of reproof to her.'

He slid down the bed a little, allowing his nightshirt to ride up his body. He laid a hand gently on her shoulder and began to caress the line of her collarbone with the tip of one finger. 'What are you really trying to say?' he asked.

She shivered a little and then, closing her eyes, pulled him onto her. 'Don't hurry,' she said.

Twenty minutes later, when they were calm again, he repeated the question: 'About Sibylla and me – what d'you really want me to do?'

Laura pulled her nightdress down and smoothed it to her. Silk was such a gorgeous material. She snuggled herself into his arms and said, 'The other morning – in fact, it was the morning after the storm – she said such a strange thing. Would you judge her to be a self-pitying sort of person?'

'Absolutely not. She's the very last person on earth I'd accuse of that – after you, of course.'

'Well, she said something about Doctor Thomas telling her she was young enough for the fracture to knit together again perfectly. She said it was the nicest thing any man had said to her for ages and she was thinking of breaking a bone quite often in the future, just to hear him say it again.'

'Obviously she was joking.'

'Yes of course! But all the same Elizabeth Troy was there at the time, and I could see she thought it was something more than just . . . you know, a quip or something. And then later, when we were talking about insurance – this was after Elizabeth had gone – we were talking about whether Billy Dancey had insurance . . .'

'After the horse had bolted – as we now discover!' he put in.

'Well, that was her point. She said Adam would never have forgotten a thing like that when he was alive. She said that's where she missed having a man about the place.'

'I can go through all her insurances and annuities and things, if that's all she wants.'

Laura gave him a light punch and said, 'Giles!'

'What?'

'You know very well I don't mean *that*. I'm talking about her feelings, her loneliness.'

He swallowed heavily. 'I dread to think what you might suggest I *do* about it!'

'Oh, men!' Now it was her eyes that raked the ceiling. 'You could pay her little compliments. Say what a charming dress . . . how well her earrings match her eyes – that sort of thing. And when you bring me flowers, bring some for her, too.'

He cleared his throat significantly. 'I seem to remember doing precisely that when she first came to stay with us. The light in your eye would have stopped a rampaging elephant.'

'All right,' she conceded grumpily. 'I was wrong.'

After a silence he responded, 'You know what you're saying, really? You're suggesting I should flirt with her.'

'A little, yes.'

He drew in a sharp breath and shook his head dubiously. 'That's all very well when one meets a woman socially, at dances and things. I could flirt outrageously with Elizabeth Troy.'

'And don't we know it!'

'But . . . under the same roof.' He shook his head again. 'I don't know. Honestly I . . .'

'Well try,' she urged. 'It doesn't have to be much. Just the odd compliment – you know. Don't you think she's attractive?'

'Yes.' There was a kind of forced reluctance in the word.

'Well that sounded like a real vote of confidence!' Laura remarked.

'If you want to know the truth,' he blurted out, 'I have to spend quite a bit of my time trying to *ignore* how attractive she is. So there!'

'I'll help you,' she promised soothingly, reaching her lips to his and kissing them passionately.

'You' ll kill me one day,' he warned as he responded.

'Honey?' Elizabeth sank her head deeper into her pillow and watched Jimmy's face as he tried to decide if her tone sounded urgent enough for him to break off what he was reading and attend to her. Since what he was reading was half a ton of *New Alloying Techniques for Iron and Steel*, she wouldn't have thought it much of a contest – but apparently it was. 'Honey?' she repeated.

'M-hmh?' He snapped the book shut, to assure her he meant it, and was then annoyed to see he had forgotten to insert the folded slip of paper that served him for a bookmark.

It unfurled as he picked it up. She glanced at it and then snatched it from him. 'Bennetts' coal bill!' she exclaimed. 'I was hunting high and low for that.'

'Sorry!' He pulled a contrite face. 'What did you want?'

'This for a start!' She put the bill underneath the mineral water bottle she always kept at her bedside. 'And . . . I don't quite know. Advice? Your considered opinion, perhaps.'

He leaned away from her and put the book on the

floor. 'On any particular topic?' he asked.

'On a very particular topic – Sibylla Johnson.'

'Oh, well!' He sat up, grinning and rubbing his hands.

'Seriously,' she warned him. 'You know this latest disaster, the roof at Parc-an-Dour?'

'Yes.'

'And you know people are all saying it was really Maurice Petifer's fault for tying a rick cover on the roof and not making sure it was lashed down properly?'

'Yes. Maurice himself told me as much.'

'Well, I think he's lying.'

'Dear dear!'

'No, honestly. I think he *did* tie it down properly. But then there was a ferocious argument with Sibylla and she untied it, or cut it adrift, or something of that sort.'

'But that would be absurd,' he protested.

'I know,' she agreed unhappily. 'Nonetheless, that's what I think happened, I'm afraid.'

'But why would Petifer go around claiming it was his fault? Hardly to protect Sibylla Johnson! I should think he'd be only too delighted to crow over her if she was that stupid.'

Elizabeth shook her head. 'Would you? I don't think so. If you'd done something kindly to help a neighbour and then it turned out that she hated you so deeply she'd go and do a stupid thing like that . . . you wouldn't go about telling everyone, would you?'

He rubbed his chin thoughtfully. 'Guess not,' he conceded. 'Well, now – here's a how-de-do!'

'Isn't it though!'

He shook his head. 'It doesn't prove anything – not really. It's still only conjecture.'

She sniffed.

'No?' he asked.

'You know Joan Faull? Well she's cousin to Molly Hendren, the dairymaid at Culdrose. And Joan was telling her how they lost their barn and Molly said that Frank Tresidder came in to do the milking that morning and he'd told her someone had cut the ropes they'd tied over the rick cover at Parc-an-Dour. He was quite positive about it, and quite bitter, too. *And* he was in no doubt who did it, because, of course, they'd all seen the argument going on between Maurice and Sibylla the night before. But when the time came for the afternoon milking he'd changed his tune completely. He said he'd had another look at the ropes and it was clear they'd frayed. He said the boss was taking the blame for it on himself but personally he "didn't think as no one was to blame".'

Jimmy smiled. 'And what is the Elizabeth Troy explanation for that interesting turnabout?'

'Maurice obviously told him – told all of them that that was the story and they must stick to it.'

Jimmy shook his head in amazement. 'That man!' he murmured. 'What do you make of him now? He's not the man I remember meeting in the veldt.'

'I've been thinking about that. What was your expression for him out there? Carrying a torch? You said he was a man carrying a torch for a woman he'd left behind him. And how right you were!'

He stabbed a finger at her. 'And that's it. That's the change in him. I've been sort of half-aware of it without being able to pin it down. But that is it – he's no longer carrying that torch.'

Elizabeth frowned dubiously. 'Even though he went and bought Culdrose – of all the places on offer?'

He nodded unhappily for, naturally, it was a blow to his argument. 'I still don't understand that. When he left here – after I told him about Uncle Stu – I'd swear that buying Culdrose was the last thing on his mind.

Something happened up there at that auction to make him change like that. Anyway, leaving that aside – he may still have all his old feelings about Laura Curnow intact. Probably has. But he must realize by now that it's a hopeless cause. So if I say he's no longer carrying a torch, I don't mean he's indifferent to her, just that – well, there's no path for the torch to light any more. Anyway, he's found something just as thrilling – in an odd sort of way. He's found an abiding hatred for Sibylla Johnson. Yes!' He gave a triumphant chuckle. 'That, surely, is why he's nobly shouldering the blame for the disaster at Parc-an-Dour!'

'Why?'

'Don't you see? It fits perfectly. Put yourself in Sibylla's place for a moment. You loathe the man enough to go out of your mind for fifteen minutes and do a stupid thing like that – cutting those ropes. Next day you're full of guilt and remorse, but what does that odious Petifer go and do? Well, he shoulders all the blame, takes it all on himself. He *protects* you! Just think how she must be squirming at the very thought of it! That's why he's doing it. Because he must know how it riles her!'

Elizabeth's laugh suggested that, though there might be something in what he said, he was exaggerating his case too wildly; but suddenly a thoughtful light crept into her eyes.

He spotted it at once. 'What now?' he asked.

'I just remembered that when Maurice and I were looking at Yeol Parc together . . .'

'Are you going to buy that, by the way?'

'I still haven't made up my mind. And it's such fun to keep poor Courtenay on tenterhooks. How it must *rile* him, as you say!' She laughed. 'Anyway, when we'd finished looking at the house, we went out into the garden and he started talking about other properties on the market, including Culdrose. But he hardly talked about Laura Curnow at all. It was Sibylla Johnson, Sibylla Johnson all the way.' She turned to her husband. 'You're right, honey. He *is* obsessed with it – their mutual hatred.' She stared vaguely at the ceiling. 'Come to think of it, I have rather neglected him lately . . .'

Jimmy stared at the ceiling, too. 'The poor bastard!' he murmured. After a silence he dry-soaped his hands and became businesslike again. 'Try and find out what happened at that auction to make him change his mind.' Then another thought struck him. 'The really amazing thing about the whole affair,' he said, 'is that both of them are Cornish.'

Elizabeth frowned. 'What's that got to do with it?'

'How can they possibly imagine they can get away with trying to hide the truth like that! Frank Tresidder tells Molly Hendren tells Joan Faull tells you, and now you tell me. Where does it stop? The whole town must know by now.'

'Poor Sibylla,' Elizabeth murmured.

'Yes,' he sighed. 'There is that about it, of course. What about poor Sibylla, then?'

'She said a rather strange thing the other morning, after the storm.'

'After the storms,' he corrected.

'Yes. I asked her what Doctor Thomas had said – about her broken arm, you know. And she told us he'd said she was still young enough for it to . . .'

'*Still* young enough? I'm sure he'd never be so ungallant.'

'All right! She's young enough for it to mend without . . . I don't know. Whatever happens to *old* bones when they mend. Anyway, the point is she said it was the nicest thing any man had told her in ages.'

'It was a joke, surely.'

'Of course. She even said she was thinking of breaking her arm again next year, just to hear him say it once more. But even so, there's often a lot of seriousness behind jokes like that.'

'Many a true word . . .' he suggested.

'Exactly. Between you and me, I think there's more than a bit of quiet desperation going on there.'

'Well – she should marry again.' He studied her as he made the suggestion, to see if that was what she was driving at – because, to be sure, the next thing would be dinners, balls, outings . . . the whole Elizabeth Troy matchmaking machine running in top gear.

She remained impassive, her thoughts seemingly miles away.

'No?' he prompted. 'After all, it's almost two years now since Adam died. Martin's ten. He'll soon need a father more than he does her.'

Elizabeth shook her head vaguely. 'You're quite right, of course, but it's no good unless *she* feels it, too. And at the moment I can't imagine *what* she's feeling.'

He was wise enough – and knew her well enough – to venture nothing further. Soon she spoke again. 'You know how you can go through the day doing everything almost automatically? Well I can, anyway. Paying calls, marketing, reading the papers . . . you know. But every now and then something happens that just brings you up with a jolt? Like when Sibylla said that. Actually, it wasn't so much her words as the look in her eyes. You know she has those rather pale eyes? They looked so *haunted* at that moment. It was quite a . . .' She tapped her breastbone and abandoned her search for the right word. 'I haven't been able to forget it.'

He let a small silence grow before he asked, 'How do

we, er, *assist* her to see what she ought to do next?'

Elizabeth smiled. 'Well you could start by being nice to her.'

'I *am* nice to her,' he protested. 'When have I ever said so much as an unkind word?'

'It's more than that, dear. When did you last tell her what a pretty outfit she was wearing?'

He shrugged awkwardly. 'I'm sure I must have done. You know how one can go through the day doing everything almost automatically? Well I can, anyway.'

'Ha ha! When did you last tell her how lovely she's looking?'

'Elizabeth!' He exploded with laughter. 'I can't go about Helston saying things like that to every pretty woman I meet – even if it's the truth. Especially if it's the truth, come to think of it.'

'You can!' she insisted. 'You don't have to say it in words. You can convey it with a glance, a gesture. You can say it by your demeanour with her.'

'Flirt with her, you mean!'

'If you want to put it as crassly as that – yes. Flirt with her.'

He rubbed his hands jovially. 'With permission?'

'Of course.'

'You know where it might lead?' he teased.

'I know where it had better lead, Jimmy,' she warned in the same jocular tone. 'I don't care where you acquire your appetite – so long as you invariably dine at home!'

'Ah,' he said, as if he had suspected a catch in it from the start.

'Aah!' she said, as one commiserates with the loser of a contest.

He licked his lips and grinned at her. 'Hungry?'

'M-hmh.'

One of the first changes Maurice introduced at Culdrose was to go over to what was called the extended four-course rotation of the crops; that autumn they made a start by ploughing up nearly five acres of pasture and putting it in barley undersown with grass. That would release the other arable land for cash crops – Giles's scheme to supply local hotels. There was nothing more between them than a handshake, but both men fought shy of a formal contract.

The breaking up of the old pasture was the moment Maurice had been waiting for, not just because it would mark the first serious departure in the daily routine of the farm, but also because it was his chance to show the men that he was no mere dilettante who'd made a bit of money and now wanted to play at farming.

It so happened that in his boyhood his family had lived for a time at Rosudgeon, along the coast a few miles east from Marazion. That same year the old widow-woman who owned the next-door farm had rented her fields out to Johnny Tyack, a settled diddicoy who had a masterly way with horses. He planted the whole farm under oats that year. Oats were the favourite cereal in any stables since both the grain and the straw make good fodder. Johnny's son Henry, a lad of Maurice's age, had been sent over to do the ploughing.

Most Cornish farms are small enough to get by with a single draught horse, usually a percheron. On steeply sloping land, with a stony soil of variable texture, even that magnificent beast cannot pull a two-furrow plough all day, so there were not many farm labourers in the county who could manage a team of two with such an implement. The Tyacks, however, were an exception; the one thing they were not short of was horses – indeed, they rarely had fewer than fifty great shires in their stables at Carleen. They could move the heaviest engine or the largest calciner ever built by Harveys of Hayle up the steepest hill in the county. So to manage a couple of clydesdales while they pulled a two-furrow plough over the steeply dipping fields above the cliffs near Rosudgeon was – among the Tyack clan – hardly considered work for a grown man; which was why they sent a stripling like Henry to do it. And Henry had only charged Maurice sixpence (which, by sheer coincidence, was all his savings at the time) to teach him the craft. Though Maurice had smarted for years at the way the lad had hoodwinked him into parting with that coin, he now considered the instruction the best sixpenn'orth he ever bought in his life.

The things your muscles learn at that age they never forget. Riding a bicycle is the art everyone thinks of, but ploughing with a pair of horses is in the same league. Denis Williams, the regular ploughman at Culdrose, was a wizard with a single plough and old Punch, Culdrose's only draught horse. But he had hemmed and hawed and finally demurred when Maurice had bought Fervour, a second carthorse, at Harvest Fair. And he had stared with something close to horror at the implement that Watkins, the agricultural agent, delivered to the field just in time for the October ploughing: a smart, bright red two-furrow, reversible, walking plough. It was the reversible feature that had taken Maurice's fancy – and which caused Denis Williams the greatest consternation.

The traditional plough does not simply lift the soil, turn it over, and dump it back where it came from; in fact, it dumps it a foot or so to the right, creating a ridge. The ploughman turns at the end of the furrow and ploughs the ridge back where it came from. He turns the next furrow on top of the first and the return furrow on top of that again, creating a mighty ridge down the middle of the field with, of course, a small trench on each side.

From there on it's simple. Each succeeding furrow gets turned into the trench, filling it and leaving a new trench one furrow's-width farther away from the ridge. Eventually the ploughman reaches the boundary hedge and the field is ploughed – except that it is now disfigured by a ridge in midfield. The labourers have to come back with a horse and cart and shovel it by hand to fill the two final trenches, out along the boundaries of the field.

The reversible plough gets neatly round the problem. It comprises two ploughs, vertically back to back. The upper set is a mirror image of the lower; so, if the lower set turns the furrow to the south when you're walking east, the other set goes on turning it to the south when you face about and walk west. You start at the southern hedge, say, and work your way steadily toward the northern one – and you're turning sod every step of the way.

The moment Maurice saw this magnificent device, he knew he must have it – never mind that he had not so much as set his hand to one in his life. The rest of it – the traces and the three wooden swingletrees, which govern the depth of the furrow – were all familiar from the deep-breasted walking plough he had learned to use almost twenty years ago. So he bit the bullet, reached deep into his pocket, and paid over the outrageous sum of five pounds (wages for Molly Hendren, his dairymaid, for an entire quarter), and waited on tenterhooks for the thing to be delivered.

The night before the great day he lay awake a long hour, practising again and again in his mind the precise method of hitching in the horses. The dawn found him already up an hour, carrying in the oats, talking to Punch and Fervour, getting them used to the sound of his voice – or the voice of the hand that fed them. He curry-combed them and livened up their hides with a good stiff brush before giving them a treat of loaf sugar each. When he returned with their collars he was rewarded with that wonderful snicker and snuffle that horses reserve for those they truly love.

And they loved ploughing, too. The plough requires a different collar – deeper in the breast and with a lower hitch than the one used for ordinary draught work between the shafts. Punch and Fervour felt the difference at once, even before the hames and back-straps were fastened on in place of the deeply padded straddle they wore every day. Up went their heads, their nostrils flared, their eyes burned several degrees brighter as they realized they would be out in the fields all day, with the soft loam underfoot, and free of those cursed, unyielding wooden shafts on either side.

Denis Williams stood back and watched his master at work, first with an amused and patronizing eye, then with bewilderment when no disaster ensued, and finally with a grudging sort of admiration. And admiration was uppermost, too, when they moved out of the stables into the light of early dawn, for that was when Maurice claimed the place of privilege, sitting sideways on the broad, rippling back of Fervour with Punch on a lead behind him.

'You gwin make Fervour your land horse, are 'ee, boss?' Williams asked knowingly.

Maurice shook his head; no matter how many times he explained it, the man still hadn't got the hang of it. 'With a reversible plough there's no such thing as "land horse" and "furrow horse",' he said patiently and for the tenth time. 'Your land horse when you plough in one direction becomes your furrow horse when you turn around and flip over the plough for the opposite direction.'

But he could tell by the light in the ploughman's eye that the point escaped him still. He knew why the fellow was worried, of course – because when you turn an ordinary plough at the headland, the land horse is apt to turn more sharply than the furrow horse; you have to give his rein a delicate tweak and cry, 'Keep off!' to stop him treading the other's feet and bruising him or pulling off a shoe. Therefore you always try to make the one with the lighter tread and the swifter response your land horse; and you don't keep swapping them round.

'You'll see for yourself soon enough,' he promised the man.

The day could not have been better. There was not a cloud in the sky, or none was yet visible in that pale greeny light; and a gentle southerly breeze blew in off the bay, cool enough for them to welcome the sun that was clearly going to shine unhindered for most of the day. It was hard to believe this was the same countryside that, little over two weeks ago, had shuddered before the fiercest blast for many decades.

'We're lucky with the weather,' he commented.

Williams gave a dour shake of his head. 'There's still some big old swell rolling out there in the bay, boss. That's bad weather somewhere not too far off. Over to France, I reckon.'

'Well, if it holds off for today and tomorrow, it'll just about suit us.'

The only response to that was a sniff. The idea that they would finish almost five acres in only two days was clearly absurd to him. An acre and a quarter a day was more the mark.

Maurice smiled but said nothing. The spanning-in to the plough went pretty well according to the drill that had kept him awake so long the previous night. The main thing is to have no fear of the horses' feet –

or, if you can't help being afraid, not to show it. Farm horses, especially the great shires, are gentle by nature, neither vindictive nor stupid; but they respond badly to nervousness in anyone who works near them. With a quick, silent prayer Maurice dived in among their huge legs, pushing them this way and that, straightening the chains and finally hitching them to the swingletrees.

'We'll go as deep as I dare,' he told Williams, picking the last but one of the six holes that controlled the depth of the furrow. 'I don't know how stony this field is – do you?'

The man shook his head and stared out over the close-cropped grass. 'That weren't never broken in the twenty years I knowed 'n,' he remarked. 'I ploughed the one above the same year Pallas House burnt down. 'E weren't too bad, 'cept for a bit, like, that do run across the middle. All scratchy, that were.'

'Eight years ago,' Maurice said. 'Almost to the month.'

'You hear 'bout that out in Africa, did 'ee?'

Maurice nodded and went to the back of the plough, letting the ropes slip through his hands until he hitched them loosely round the handles. 'It took about four months, mind. But news always gets through in the end. News of home. There's hundreds of Cornishmen out there in the mines. Now!' He walked to the horses' heads. 'One quick check and we're off.'

Seagulls were already gathering a respectful distance away, which, for them, was no more than a few yards; their rivals the crows, shyer by nature, were congregating on the hedges and dotting the more distant corners of the field. The two shires were both champing at their bits, drooling an impatient ochre-coloured foam from the corners of their great, blubbery lips.

'All right, all right!' Maurice gave them a reassuring pat each on their mighty necks. 'We're off, my two fine lads. Pull together and best foot forward, eh?'

His eyes checked every chain and strap as he walked back to the rear end of the plough. 'All right with you?' he asked Williams, who kept pace with him on the farther side.

'So far as I can tell, boss,' was the guarded reply.

'Then away we go!'

He looped the ropes around his wrists and took a firm grip on the high-gloss varnish of the brand-new handles; they felt as if they were sticky but that, he realized, was his own sweat. He took a sighting on a wind-bent thorn on the far hedge, gauged the line to it against the line of the hedge to his left, wondering were they parallel. Then, satisfied he had it right, he clucked Punch and Favour into action at last.

'Steady now!' he had to call at once for they pulled with such a will they almost jerked the implement into a skid.

But then the soft-iron nose of the ploughshare took its first bite of turf and the blades sank as if the grass were pondweed. Soon the mould-boards were turning over two seamless ribbons of rich brown loam, running as neat and true to the hedge as a man could wish.

Not that Maurice relaxed. His knuckles were white on the handles and every muscle was tense as he watched for the slightest deviation of the line. And it was 'Hauly up!' and 'Hauly in!' all the way to the farther headland, where he cried, 'Hoo back!' for a well-earned rest – for himself, not the horses.

The sweat was running in rivers down his back and he was as breathless as if he'd run a mile; but he had the satisfaction of looking over his shoulder and seeing a furrow true enough to win the red rosette at the Royal Cornwall, any year. Already it was peppered and salted with crows and gulls, squabbling for the grubs, cutworms, wireworms, and earthworms whose dark world the plough had turned literally upside down.

'That's a good plough,' he said modestly to Denis Williams. 'The thing practically runs itself.'

The man laughed sarcastically, for Maurice was still breathless. 'Why, that's the first thing I noticed about 'n, boss. And the second thing was that 'tis made the wrong way. You should ought to have the land to your left, the furrows to your right. That's the wrong way round, that is.' He tapped the tail of the mould-board with the toe of his boot.

'We can soon cure that,' Maurice assured him as he clucked the horses back into action and, tweaking the left rein to keep Punch from treading Favour's feet, brought them round a full hundred and eighty degrees. His own body's memory amazed him. To save his own life he could not have described the twist of his hips that would jerk the plough out of the ground at the end of the furrow, yet his hips performed the trick without hesitation. The reversal of the blades was no ancient mystery to him, however, for he had practised the technique to perfection all last week – down at Watkins's yard rather than be seen making a fool of himself on home ground. Now he made it look like child's play. It was spoiled only by the fact that the horses had dragged it a couple of feet off line during their turn so he wasn't able to start the new furrow at the same point as the other had finished.

'Obviously a reversible plough needs a wider headland than the regular kind,' he commented.

Now, of course, he was turning the sod in the traditional direction, with the uncut turf to his left and the tilled land to his right. 'That suit you better, does it?' he asked the ploughman.

''Es, now you'm doing it right, boss,' the fellow replied. 'You keep *they* shares down now, all the darn time – don't 'ee turn 'n arsy-versy agin – and you'll do a proper job here.'

Maurice wanted to scream. He forced himself to say nothing while he counted out the next ten paces. He studied the rich soil of the ancient pasture, admired its texture, marvelled at the profusion of creeping, crawling life it apparently supported . . . anything rather than address his ploughman's obtuseness. Then he tried another approach.

'Surely this isn't the first reversible plough you've ever seen?' he asked the man. 'All the steam-ploughing machines use them. You must've seen them at the Royal Cornwall?'

Williams agreed that he had, indeed, seen them there. 'But they'm *natural* to steam, boss,' he objected. 'You can't hardly say as they'm natural to hosses, now can 'ee?'

'What's *natural* to horses?' Maurice asked, struggling to keep the despair out of his voice. 'Nothing is natural to horses. Not even horses are natural. These great beasts have been bred entirely by man – starting from tiny little Dartmoor ponies. So what d'you mean – "natural" to horses?'

'Why, what you'm doing now, boss – land to the left, furrows to the right. That's natural. You ask anyone. I been ploughing twenty year, boy and man – and that's the only way ever I seen. Stands to reason 'tis natural, then.'

The left blade hit a stone at that point. The two horses stopped on a sixpence and slackened off the traces enough for Maurice to pull the shares back. 'You may make yourself useful,' he told Williams.

The man took the shovel from its cradle and began digging. 'That's big enough for the hedge,' he said when he had unearthed it fully, and it was, indeed, the size of a football.

They carried it to the hedge where, after a bit of hacking with the blade of the shovel, they found a gap large enough to deserve it.

'Have you thought about it some more?' Maurice asked as they returned to the plough. 'Can't you see how this is going to save time? There's none of that walking along the headlands before you can start the return furrow. Apart from the actual turn at each end, every step you take you're breaking the sod. It's bound to take less time.'

Williams said nothing.

Maurice put his hand to the plough but gave no command to be off. 'You don't believe me when I say we'll finish this field by sundown – barring disasters – do you!'

The other stirred uncomfortably.

'Very well,' Maurice went on. 'I had intended doing no more than a couple of furrows each way and then handing over to you. But I'll tell you what. *I'll* do the whole of this field today – and challenge you to match me with the other one tomorrow. This field is two and a half acres. The other's two and a quarter, so it's a fair contest. How about that?'

The man grinned. 'With my old plough?'

'No! With *this* one, you oaf! Devil take your old plough! You may have your old plough. I'll make you a gift of it – as long as you never bring it near Culdrose again. All right? Meanwhile you may go back to the yard and fetch a hook and stick and start tidying up the hedge in here. That way you can keep an eye on me *and* make yourself useful.'

This mixture of good news and bad sent a mightily perplexed Denis Williams to do his master's bidding. In fact, it was more than merely good and bad news, it was both fabulous and appalling. A plough of his own! That was the fabulous part; it was more than he had ever dreamed of possessing. But, on the other hand, to be forced to work with this devilish new contraption, fit only for steam ploughs and suchlike nonsense . . . that was a bitter pill indeed.

By the time he returned with the hook and stick, Maurice, stripped to his waistcoat, had cut ten dark-brown furrows into the green of the sward – gilded now by the risen sun. Golden steam rose off the horses' flanks and the muscles of his forearms, already bronzed by a sun far hotter than this, rippled like molten copper. Yet how out of condition he was, he realized! Six months ago, the exertion he had made so far this day would hardly have tested him at all; now he was out of breath, could feel the itches that would turn into blisters before noon, and was already scanning across the fields for the first glimpse of Miss Sweet's buxom, welcome figure and the even more welcome sight of the covered basket with a flask of tea and great doorsteps of fuggan, the rich fruity cake Cornishmen eat with their 'croust.'

Miss Sweet was his new housekeeper. She'd originally applied as parlourmaid at Liston House and Elizabeth Troy, impressed by her qualities but having no place to offer, had – at Jimmy's suggestion – sent her on to Culdrose. Maurice had taken her on in place of Mary Wells, the housemaid who'd got married. Then Ma Harvey, who'd been housekeeper at Culdrose for donkey's years, had gone back to old Mrs Mullard as her companion. Maurice had asked around in a desultory fashion for someone to replace her and then, realizing how simple his needs were, had agreed to Miss Sweet's suggestion that she could manage the house on her own, with just Mrs Cowles of St John's to cook and Lizzie Waring of Wendron Street as a general – both of whom lived out. She had bargained heroically not just for Ma Harvey's old wage but half her own on top – which he had at last granted out of admiration for her nerve if for no other reason. She was a pretty woman, on the large side but very bonny. However, being in her mid-twenties, she was plainly not destined for marriage.

He had never for an instant regretted it. She ran the house to perfection, put up the most wonderful meals, kept immaculate accounts, and maintained his wardrobe better than he could have done it himself – and he was not a slovenly man. She was that rare item among servants (rare enough for even *Punch* to have stopped joking about it): a Treasure.

It was two long hours before she came out to the field that day, but by then he was broken to the task and well into his second wind. The sun was up, he was stripped to his shirt, the breeze fanned the light sweat on his brow, and he felt marvellous – master of the world, his world, anyway, and fit for any challenge.

'Oh this is the life!' he said as he threw himself down in the suntrap of the hedge near the gate. 'What fools they are that sit in their offices all day, pushing a pen! You're an angel, Miss Sweet,' he added as he lifted the white linen napkin that covered the basket and saw even more cake than he had dared to dream of. 'An angel of deliverance.'

'I shall be an angel of mercy beside your sickbed if you don't put this up, Mister,' she said severely, walking back from the plough handles and now carrying the waistcoat he had left draped over them. 'At least while you'm resting.'

Maurice pulled a face at Williams and muttered, 'Best not to argue on some matters.'

The man laughed and said he was right enough there.

Suddenly Maurice found himself wishing with all his heart he had not bought Culdrose, with its proximity to the Curnows and to Sibylla Johnson. The farm itself he loved, and would not part with it now, not for double what he paid; but the proximity of those two women, the one he loved dearest and the one he loathed most in all the world, was like a thorn in his flesh. If these identical acres were only somewhere else, over near Gweek, say – or, better still, over beyond Pallas Home Farm, where he'd have the Troys for neighbours part of the year – whenever they put up the dust sheets at Liston House. That would be absolutely splendid. Life would be absolutely splendid then.

'Penny for 'em, boss,' Williams dared to say.

'I was wondering,' he said. 'If we set a thick belt of these Lawson cypresses, the very quick-growing ones, you know, all down our northwestern and northeastern boundaries – except immediately between the house and the road, of course – we might do even better with this land. Trees like that give protection from the wind much farther than you'd think – and they wouldn't interfere with the sun if we set them just there.'

Neither of the listeners pointed out what immediately occurred to them both: that such a thick belt of evergreens would isolate Culdrose from both Chynoweth and Parc-an-Dour . . . except that Sibylla Johnson's place would still be visible from the farmhouse itself.

'Why not between the house and the road?' Miss Sweet asked calmly.

He stared at her long enough to force a tiny smile, for she knew the question had been bold. 'Yes, indeed, why not!' he agreed.

Maurice spent the best part of the following day buying hunting gear in Truro; he was now a member of the Cury Hunt, whose territory covered most of the Lizard peninsula and a few inland parishes around Helston. When he returned that afternoon, about an hour before sunset, he found a smiling Denis Williams already back in the stables, rubbing Punch and Fervour down with a handful of fresh wheat straw.

'You must enjoy mucking out, man,' he commented sarcastically, for it was understood that if the ploughman finished his work early, he was to help Peter Hosking and George Munroe muck out the heifers. They were already in their stalls for the winter, of course, and required mucking out several times a week. The bullocks, who were being fattened as stores, stayed out in the pen, which was covered at one end; they weren't mucked out until the spring, by which time the dung and straw beneath them would have risen close to the top of the walls.

'That's that new steam plough, boss,' he replied happily.

'Steam . . .?'

'The reimbursable.'

'Oh, I see. Where did you leave it? Not out in the field, I hope?'

'I changed the tips and put a bit o' grease on 'n and left 'n in the dutch barn.' He threw away the straw, gave Punch a final, affectionate pat, and made for the door. 'Best gone on with the mucking out, then,' he said with a virtuous sigh.

Maurice stayed for a while with the two horses, fascinated, as always, by their size and strength. 'See!' he murmured as he stroked and admired them. 'You *can* teach an old dog new tricks! I'll bet it was you two lads who *really* taught him, though. Wasn't it? Own up now, the pair of you. Amn't I right, now?'

He chatted with them a good while longer – telling them, among other things, that they'd soon have a nice little hunter filly to keep them company. Not that she'd bother two fine geldings like them, mind – lucky fellows! Then he set off to take a look at the two ploughed fields. As he passed the stores pen, Williams came out of the heifer house with a barrow of mucky straw. 'I'm glad you took to it – the new, *reimbursable* plough,' he called out.

'She's some beauty, boss.' He spat in the dung for emphasis. 'And that's a fact now.'

Maurice strode down the lane that formed the central spine of Culdrose. What a tyrant a farm could be! How it demanded every minute of his time and reflection! There were so many thoughts hovering at the rim of his awareness, waiting for his attention – thoughts about Sibylla Johnson . . . No! Thoughts about Laura Curnow first, of course. *Then* the Johnson woman. Thoughts about getting married again . . . they were all there, like hopeful debutantes in the anteroom of his mind. But the audience chamber itself was crammed to bursting with the needs of the farm. What barley to sow? How long would Lawsons take to send their catalogue of conifers? Should those two smaller fields be knocked into one? What about dropping cabbages next year and going in for daffodils instead? – now was the time to plant the bulbs.

Now was the time to look at plans for greenhouses.

Now was the time to get a bull of his own – old Mrs Mullard wouldn't have one.

Now was the time to . . . to mend that hedge, my goodness!

He stopped and pushed ineffectually at the wobbly stones with the toe of his riding boot, then gave up with a sigh. Now was the time to do everything on the farm. *Now* was a perpetual clamour, strong enough to drown out *soon*.

Therefore, he thought wryly, he was quite safe in promising himself that 'soon' he would address the problem of Laura Curnow.

And of Sibylla Johnson, to be sure.

It would be nice to have a variety of cypresses. Different greens – pale, dark . . . a bit of gold? Variegations, the nurserymen called it. He hoped the descriptions in Lawsons' catalogue would be comprehensive enough to make choices like that possible.

The first field he came to was the one he had ploughed. Already the sun and wind – and lack of rain – had turned its dark brown loam several shades paler. One more day and it would be perfect for harving – or harrowing, as they called it up in England. Disc harve tomorrow – Friday – again on Saturday, across the first cut. Sow on Monday, barley and grass . . . drag the chain harve over it . . . it could all be seeded, harved, and rolled by Tuesday evening.

He breathed deeply with satisfaction at the thought; the farm may be a tyrant but it could pat him on the head from time to time – and my, didn't it just feel good! Who needed women? They only complicated life.

Not for the first time he wondered why he had never mentioned that he'd been married out in the Cape. It wasn't that he'd deliberately tried to conceal the fact. But Sarie had already been dead two years when the Troys turned up. And neither of them had inquired if he'd ever been married and he just hadn't volunteered the information. And then, somehow, they'd progressed from that to assuming he'd always remained single. And where was the point in disabusing them? Sarie was dead . . . little Jannie had died . . . somehow he'd pulled his life together again.

The hair stiffened on his neck as he realized what was coming next – what memories were about to besiege him.

No! He shook his head and begged them to leave him alone.

But they would not, or could not oblige. Jannie would have been . . .

No! he begged himself even more piteously. And he closed his eyes, willing himself, as always, not to think of it. But the thought, as always, burst its way through: Jannie would have been five by now.

His dear little shoulder would have been just . . . *here*.

Maurice's fingers touched a bar of the gate, lightly enough to let him ignore the fact that it was merely wood, firmly enough to support his reluctant dream.

His tiny hand would have fitted . . . *so*.

Desperately, Maurice forced his hand into the widest possible spread, commanding it to take no part in this hurtful dream, recruiting the real pain of his muscles against that obscurer psychic pain within. But inexorably his hand closed upon that dream, and just for an instant the boy was there – more real than the setting sun, the wind, the farm . . . more real than the misery he knew he was now creating for himself. Inexorably his eyes closed upon a reality grown suddenly thin, while his inner eye opened upon a richer land, a serene and sunlit land where Sarie and Jannie stood smiling, eternally smiling, at him.

'I'm happy, Papa,' he said in that little piping treble which Maurice had cursed often enough during his life – and which he would now give his very soul to hear again. 'Aren't I, Mommie?'

And Sarie smiled, too. 'He's happy here,' she said in that beautiful, clipped accent of the Afrikander (at least, after meeting her, he thought it beautiful). 'We both are.'

A noise disturbed him. He clenched his eyes tight, fighting now to hold on to the vision that had ambushed him; the action forced a tear down either cheek. It was no good. They had gone. His inward eye sought desperately for those dear, dead shapes and found nothing – or a blackness worse than nothing. The blackness of the pit.

Sick at heart he opened his eyes on a world that – not five minutes earlier – he had thought rich enough to claim him body and soul, and send both to bed too exhausted to want much with dreams. He stared about him into the gathering twilight and at first saw no one, nothing that might have intruded on his vision like that.

But then he noticed her, a woman, standing still – or irresolute, perhaps – a hundred yards up the lane. 'Miss Hendren?' he called out in an uncertain tone.

The moment she moved he realized it was not, in fact, the dairymaid but Miss Sweet. 'Sorry,' he called out, hastily gathering the scattered shards of his everyday personality. 'It's Miss Sweet, isn't it – is anything the matter?'

She came toward him swiftly then, taking large strides. 'A handy woman in a fight!' He smiled as he remembered what Joel Harvey, a miner in the Rand, had said of another fellow's wife. Unlike that woman, however, Miss Sweet somehow retained every bit of her femininity – even though she would undoubtedly be 'a handy woman in a fight.'

'I'm sorry to bother 'ee, Mister,' she said as she drew near. ''Tis nothing, really. Only I caught they Curnow boys and the Johnson boys stealing apples in the orchard . . .'

'I thought we'd picked them all.'

'The crab apples.' She was right by him now; he could read the gleam of righteousness in her eyes.

'Oh well . . .' he said dismissively.

But she remained adamant. 'This year it's crabs, next year – Beauty of Bath, Peasgood Nonsuch . . . we shan't have one left.'

'Oh, very well. You're right, of course – as always.' He turned to watch the waters of the bay as they quenched the last arc of the setting sun. 'It moves so quickly at dusk and so slowly at noon.'

'I'm sorry if I disturbed 'ee just now, Mister,' she said in a softer voice. As he turned into the last of the sunlight she had noticed the tear streaks on his face.

'Oh, that's all right.' He was offhand. 'You say you caught them – all four of them? What did you do to them?'

'The two big ones got away – Henry and Martin, I believe. I got the two little ones barred up in the pigsty.'

Maurice gave an involuntary laugh and cut himself off abruptly. 'Meredith and young Maurice,' he said gravely. Then, to explain – if not excuse – his earlier levity, he asked, 'Didn't *you* ever go raiding other people's orchards when you were their age? We were terrors at it.'

'I suppose so,' she agreed reluctantly. 'I'll let they go scat-free, then?' She half-turned away, embarrassed still at having caught him in such a melancholy humour.

Suddenly he feared being alone. He wanted to see how Williams had got on with the ploughing but he also wanted Miss Sweet's company on the way back to the farmhouse. 'Come and see if your sharp eye can tell the difference between my ploughing and Denis Williams's,' he said. 'I'll give those two rapscallions the edge of my tongue before we let them go.'

She came and leaned on the gate beside him. 'That's my handiwork,' he said casually.

''Tis the talk of the parish,' she replied. 'Of all Helston by now, I shouldn't wonder. Is it true you learned ploughing off of Henry Tyack, backalong?'

He chuckled. 'Someone remembered that, did they? You see – you can't keep anything a secret for long in these parts. Yes. Henry Tyack *only* charged me sixpence to do a full day's work for him!' He waved his hand across the field before them. 'One of my wiser investments, I now believe. Let's go and see how much better Denis Williams has done.'

But when they saw the other field his heart sank like a stone. 'Oh no!' He lowered his forehead to the top bar of the gate and beat it there, several times.

'What?' she asked.

'Don't you see? He's ploughed it the traditional way. Hang on.'

He leaned forward, grabbed a lower bar, and vaulted himself over into the field, where a quick walk up the headlands told him all he needed to know.

'The utter, blithering idiot!' he shouted as he returned to the gate. 'He's used it the proper way – as a reversible plough. I mean, he made a sharp turn at the end of each furrow and flipped the plough over – just as I showed him . . .'

'Well, then?' she responded, still puzzled as to what irked him.

'Don't you see? He started in the *middle*! He's ploughed one half of the field toward the bottom hedge and the other half toward the top! He's left a great ridge down the middle, which we'll now have to scatter in the traditional way with six men using shovels and a horse and cart!'

'You do always start ploughing a field from the middle,' she said.

'Yes, I'm afraid that's what *he's* going to tell me, too.'

'Isn't it true?'

'Not with a reversible plough. I showed him. He *saw* me start at one hedge! Aargh!' He clenched his fists and shook them at the darkling sky.

She reached forward and touched his arm hesitantly – a gesture she turned rather smartly into an impersonal, housekeeperly brushing of his sleeve where it was marked with lichen picked up off the gate. 'I got a nice steak and kiddley pie in the oven,' she said.

On their way back, with the dusk now falling fast, they passed an old and rusty gate, just thrown against the hedge. He stopped, stared briefly at it, and chuckled. 'Actually, Miss Sweet,' he said, 'you couldn't have picked a better day, nor a better time of day, to come this way. See this old gate? I want you to help me carry it in to the yard. For the moment, however, we'll take it just to the end of the lane. Then, when it's come on dark and they've all gone home – well, as we go I'll tell you what we'll do with it.'

And so he did. While they carried it between them to the head of the lane, he described in detail the little trick he was going to play on Peter Hosking and George Munroe – and Denis Williams, come to that. 'A little time-bomb,' he called it.

And Miss Sweet, though the gate was heavy and she felt sure the rust was staining their clothes, was exultant to hear it. Perhaps Maurice Petifer had never – in his own mind – lumped her along with the other servants. Perhaps he had always set her apart a little. But his taking her into his confidence like this – well that was the first time ever he'd showed it.

He, for his part, enjoyed walking behind her – so as not to have to shout his explanation back over his shoulder. She was strong and supple, and the gate was clearly no burden to her at all; her stride was large and confident. Yet the overwhelming impression she conveyed was of grace and femininity.

'In the pigsty?' Laura was thunderstruck when a shamefaced Henry and Martin told her. In the pigsty! How dare she? The effrontery of the woman! What was she, anyway? A jumped-up chambermaid, that was all. Laura put on her bonnet and cloak and set off up the drive. She'd be a chambermaid still if Ma Harvey hadn't gone off to be old Mrs Mullard's companion. Miss *Sweet!* She'd give her Miss Sweet! Locking Maurice and Meredith up like that, as if they were common criminals. And all for a few crab apples. And in the *pigsty* of all places! Talk about adding insult to injury. She fumed all the way to the main gate.

Out on the Lizard road, however, the burden of her attack shifted. It was, she decided, more the fault of Maurice Petifer than of that jumped-up maid. True, he hadn't been there at the time – or, at least, Henry and Martin hadn't mentioned it – but he was the one who set the tone of the place. If the odious Miss Sweet felt at liberty to lock up two little boys like that – and not just any two boys but a Curnow and a Johnson – then she acted in a climate set by Petifer, a climate of what was permitted and what was not. Laura could not imagine a climate in which such offensive behaviour would be countenanced for a single moment. Yes, it was definitely more Petifer's fault than the mere servant's. By now she was near the farm-gate entrance to Culdrose.

''Night, Mrs Curnow!' the two labourers chorused as they passed her in the dark. She was so fuming she hadn't even heard them until they were almost level with her.

How did they know who she was, anyway? she wondered.

Then one of them chortled. 'Pig sty's down beyond the dutch barn, if that's what you'm looking for, missis!'

The pair of them collapsed in uncontrolled merriment at that.

She did not dignify their insolence with a reply.

However, their voices must have alerted Miss Sweet, for the front door of the farmhouse opened a moment later, framing the woman herself against the dingy brown wallpaper of the hallway. 'Mrs Curnow?' she called out. 'Mister's just gone down to set the little rascals free. Would you care to step inside and wait over a dish of tay? He won't be gone long, I shouldn't think.'

'I thank you,' Laura responded icily. 'But I shall deal with this in my own way.'

'I'll put the kettle on,' the woman replied brightly, as if Laura had suggested an amiable alternative.

'Little rascals,' indeed – the nerve of her! Laura seethed all over again. But the image of that awful wallpaper lingered enough to distract her. Maurice was obviously turning into a typical farmer. He'd do nothing with the house and garden unless someone nagged him half to death. That wallpaper had been ancient in Mrs Mullard's young days. She was half blind at the end, of course, and far too mean to spend money on a trivial thing like that. But Maurice had no such excuse.

She heard him ahead of her then, and started to walk more carefully, even going on tiptoe past the empty bull pen, down the little alley that led to the dutch barn. When she rounded the corner she saw him about thirty paces ahead of her, carrying a lantern – by whose borrowed light she was able to stay well back yet still avoid obstacles like the gleaming new plough, into which she would otherwise almost certainly have blundered.

She glanced at it curiously as she passed. She had heard the story, of course. It had gone all round town that day – how Maurice Petifer had done the handsomest bit of ploughing to be seen on Culdrose Farm in many a year, and who would have thought it of him! It was an impressive-looking implement, right enough. Unthinkingly she fondled one of its handles in passing, and then let go rather suddenly – and then wondered why.

She arrived at the farther end of the barn in time to see him clipping his lantern over the gate to the little forecourt in front of the sty, which he also opened. Nonetheless, in sheer exuberance, no doubt, he put one hand to the wall and leapt over it as nimbly as any acrobat. He was always lithe and athletic, she remembered. An image of him diving off the rocks at Land's End that day came to her; she dropped that one rather suddenly, too – but did not wonder why.

He tipped back his hat, bent his body forward, hands on knees, and, using a terrible stage voice, said to the door, 'Are you both in there?'

'Yes sir!'

The poor mites! They were nearly in tears.

'Do you know whose voice this is?'

'Yes sir!'

'And ain't you a-trembling and a-quaking in your boots to hear it?'

Laura frowned. The words were not at all like Maurice Petifer – and yet they were, somehow, rather familiar.

'Yes sir.' One more and they *would* be in tears. She

felt the pressure growing behind her own eyelids, too.

'Good!' He laughed and threw open the door to the sty. 'We'll say no more about it, then, eh? Sufficient unto the day is the trembling thereof, I always say.'

There was no sound from within.

'Eh?' he prompted, and gave another little laugh. 'I said that's an end to it. Enough's enough. Come up to the house with me and I'll give you each a *real* apple – much sweeter than those sour old crabs.'

Still there was no sound from inside the sty – or if there were, it was too faint to reach Laura's ears. She began to worry.

So, plainly, did he. He reached behind him and unhooked the lantern, bringing it forward to where it shed its light on the interior. At the same time he went down on his haunches. 'Oh!' he exclaimed. There was pity in his voice – and relief, too. He shook his head sadly. 'I'm not going to *eat* you, you know. I'm not going to flog you – no matter how richly you deserve it. D'you think I never stole apples when I was your age?' He stretched forth an inviting hand. 'Of course I did! D'you think I can't remember?'

After what seemed an age to Laura a diminutive hand stretched out through the dark of the doorway and slipped into his. A moment later Meredith's dark little bullet of a head peered hesitantly out – swiftly followed, in turn, by young Maurice – all of him. He took the lantern from his older namesake so that he could claim his other hand.

They turned their back on the sty and walked out in silence. Laura wondered why no one said anything – or, rather, she could understand perfectly well why neither of the youngsters spoke, but Petifer's silence was puzzling.

They headed her way. She shrank back behind one of the pillars of the barn, feeling sure they must discover her; but she need not have bothered. The two young boys were still in something of a daze at the lightness of their punishment, and Maurice was crying in perfect silence.

She was so shocked that, after they passed her by, each in his own peculiar form of sightlessness, she began to wonder whether or not her eyes had deceived her. But the image was burned too sharply into her memory for her to doubt it – Maurice drifting by with the tears coursing silently down his cheeks.

Why?

She thought back over what had gone before. His last act, before they left the sty, had been so jocular – assuring them that he, too, had raided neighbours' orchards as a child. Surely he wasn't so sentimental about those times that the mere memory of them would bring on tears? Not the Maurice she knew!

But then . . . *what* Maurice did she know?

And now it struck her that his last act had not been to give out that jocular reassurance; rather it had been when he stretched his hand forth into the sty to coax the two little boys out of it. That's when he had gone all silent – when Meredith's hand had reached out of the dark and found his.

But that was even more puzzling. What could such a gesture *mean* to him? Why would it bring him down in tears?

Their voices suddenly broke through her reverie – two piping little voices, gabbling away like a couple of fairground organs. Obviously they had overcome the horrors of their incarceration at last and were basking in Maurice's leniency. Fleetingly – until she saw the humour of it – she now felt slightly annoyed that he was *not* going to punish them, not even a little smack! The indignity of being barred in the sty would be no chastisement at all to them. Indeed, they were probably even now turning it into the greatest adventure. No, it was the parents who'd feel punished by that – a blow to their dignity and self-esteem.

Then the image of Maurice's face, haggard and streaming with tears, returned to her and drove out all other feelings. She knew she ought to follow them up to the house – make some excuse about having missed her way in the dark; she knew Miss Sweet would tell her master she'd followed him down to the sty and that if she didn't turn up in a moment Maurice would come looking for her. But her feet seemed rooted to the spot. She wanted to stay out here, near to the mystery – near to where she first became aware of it – until it was fathomed.

Glad, for once, of the dark, she reached out to where she had seen him pass – as if the very air might still cage something of that enigma. Her fingers moulded those cheeks she had so vividly seen, felt his tears – and she was suddenly close to tears again herself. Nor was *that* any less of a mystery than the unknown sorrow that had so moved him.

She withdrew a little, back into the deep dark of the barn, where she rested her forehead against the cold iron of the pillar and murmured, 'Oh, Maurice!'

'Are you there? Laura?' His voice came from the cobbled alleyway. The flame in his lantern flickered and guttered as he moved it this way and that, seeking her in every shadow.

'I'm over here!' She sniffed, straightened herself up, and gave a few needless pats to the few exposed curls that were not trapped by her bonnet. By then he was at her side, shielding his eyes as he held up the lantern to see her face.

'You've been crying,' he exclaimed in astonishment.

'I have not,' she protested.

He put a finger to her cheek and brought it away damp.

'Just the wind,' she said crossly. 'And the cold.'

'Ah, yes,' he said wanly.

She realized then how much he had wanted her tears to be genuine. A moment later she saw, too, that it might open the door on that mystery – a common starting point. 'Put the lantern down,' she said crossly.

'Aren't you coming up to the house?'

'In a moment. Just put it down. Don't keep blinding me with the lamp like that.'

'Sorry.' He did as she bade. He looked almost satanic – devilish, anyway – with the light shining up from his feet.

'You're right,' she said. 'I was crying just now.'

'Should I ask why?'

'Because of you,' she accused. 'Because you were crying when you led the boys past me here. I was standing just here as you passed, on this very spot. And you were just there, with the tears streaming down your cheeks. I saw it.'

'Well . . .' He inhaled deeply and added, 'All over now,' with a kind of enforced jocularity.

'But why?' she pleaded. 'Surely it wasn't just remembering apple scrumping in your childhood?'

'Not *my* childhood,' he said.

'What d'you mean? Whose, then?'

'Nobody's. I didn't mean that. I don't know what I meant. I don't even believe I was crying.'

He turned as if to go, leaving her to follow with the lantern. She reached out and touched his arm. 'Maurice?'

'What?' he asked irritably.

'I want to help if I can.'

After a long, brittle silence, he said, 'I don't need your help.'

Neither of them recognized his voice.

He did not cry again that night until he was safely in bed, safely in the dark, safely beneath his sheets. And then it was not for Sarie and Jannie, nor for the poignant memory of young Meredith's hand so warm and trusting – and so familiarly sticky – in his. It was for Laura, and the hardest decision he had ever had to take in his life. And the harshest words he had ever spoken, too.

At any social gathering, from the most select private dinner to a chance meeting of two or three interested parties at a street corner, a town councillor was considered fair game. 'Oh, Councillor Curnow,' they would begin, 'I'm so glad to find myself seated next to you . . .' This from someone who had gone on bended knees for the hostess to arrange it so. Or, more bluntly: 'Ah, Curnow – the very chap!' And what followed was almost invariably some special pleading on a topic close to the petitioner's heart – some nasty potholes in Meneage Street . . . late-night revellers from the Blue Anchor . . . disgraceful litter by the bowling green . . . or a suggestion to cover the river in Coinagehall Street and Wendron Street. This latter was a perennial complaint, for Helston was one of the few towns in the West that had a 'river' – actually a small brook – running in channels on each side of its main street. The channels were square-cut in granite, no more than fifteen inches wide and deep, but they were an ever-open trap for careless pedestrians and drivers. And so there was an eternal struggle between the 'practical people' who wanted them covered over and the 'sentimentalists' who wanted them preserved.

Therefore, when Jimmy Troy met Giles in Coinagehall Street, the week after Guy Fawkes night, and said, 'Ah, Curnow, the very man!' Giles prepared himself for the inevitable bout of ear-bending. 'You know what this town needs?' Jimmy went on.

'Let me guess. Fewer potholes in Cross Street? Repairs to the cracked paving stones in Church Street? Am I getting warm?'

'No sir! You're cold enough to chill ten gallons of fresh-drawn milk. However, if you want to discuss the town's needs at that petty level, your council could do worse than light a fire under The Amalgamated Union of Shovel Supporters, who seem to be holding their annual daily conference just round the corner, under the pretence of working for the Helston Gas Company Limited.'

Giles laughed. 'I wasn't aware that this town had *any* needs at a loftier level than that.'

'Oh, it has. Are you on your way home?'

'I'm just going up to the post office and then I thought I'd walk home. Who knows when we'll see sunshine like this again?'

'I'll walk part of the way with you.' He laughed at a sudden memory. 'When I left Philadelphia, you know, I was walking down to the train station for one last time, going to catch the train to New York and the boat to Southampton. And I met a friend who asked me was I going downtown to play pool, and I told him no, I was going to England. "Oh," he said – without a trace of a smile – "in that case, I'll walk part-way with you." I miss that sort of dry humour sometimes.'

'Whereas Cornish humor is wet, I suppose?' Giles suggested. 'Like our climate.'

'No. Cornish humor's all about people. I never heard a Cornishman tell a joke that wasn't about some named individual – and usually it's all about something stupid he's done. Occasionally she, but mostly he. Michael Vestey just told me a story about Maurice Petifer – a perfect example of the genre.'

Giles, who was desperately trying to think of an example to overturn Jimmy's theory – without much success – knew well that the man was dangling a bait before him. He resisted it manfully.

''Course, I don't suppose there's a grain of truth in it,' Jimmy mused.

'Oh, go on, then!' Giles capitulated.

They were passing the stand where all the horse buses waited just above the Angel. At that moment a motor car came noisily down the hill, firing raggedly as its driver – unrecognizable under all his swaddling and goggles – used the engine as a partial brake. The horses grew restless and their drivers had to run to calm them at the head. 'Can't 'ee hold that thing stiller?' they called to the man with the red flag.

'The law is the law,' the fellow replied with a knowing grin – for it was, of course, the horse trade in general that had lobbied parliament about putting a man with a red flag to walk in front of all motor cars. So now there was a general movement among motoring enthusiasts to make them regret it.

The car came to a racketty halt outside the Angel. The driver took a pair of wedges from under his seat and handed them to the flag man, who placed them under the two rear wheels. The driver took off his goggles and unwound his scarf.

'Doctor Thomas!' cried Giles and Jimmy in unison.

'Little beauty, isn't she?' he replied, staring at the little car with a would-be offhanded pride. 'The only Renault in Cornwall, I believe. Certainly the only coupé. You'd hardly credit it but there are three and a half horses under that little bonnet.'

'I guessed there was a *half* horse in there somewhere,' Jimmy told him. 'From all the racket, you know.'

Some of the bus drivers, for all their hostility, were drawn to inspect the vehicle at closer quarters. To oblige them the doctor raised the bonnet and soon vanished inside a thicket of the curious, the envious, and the admiring.

'Have you thought of buying one?' Jimmy asked Giles as they resumed their stroll.

'Not until they repeal the red-flag law.'

'Oh, that'll go – this year . . . next year. Even dear old England will have to recognize that *that*' – he jerked a thumb back over his shoulder – 'is the future. And, quite fortuitously, it's also what I wish to talk about with you – vis-à-vis Helston, don't you know. Will you dine with us tomorrow night? Informally. Don't bother to get all dressed up.'

'Well, we'd love to. Mrs Johnson, too, I take it?'

'Naturally.'

'Well, thank you very much.' He gave a backward nod. 'Are *you* thinking of getting one, then?'

Jimmy smiled as he parroted Giles's earlier reply: 'Not until they repeal the red-flag law. Well, I'll leave you here. I promised to get some cough mixture for Trevanion. Until tomorrow, then.'

Giles cleared his throat and hesitated.

'Oh yes!' Jimmy tapped his forehead as if he'd forgotten. 'Michael Vestey's scurrilous tale! It seems that when Petifer was but a young shaver – indeed, long before he even started shaving – his mother sent him to borrow a half-cup of pink distemper from a neighbour. And the young lad, having consulted with the cook, came back to his mother and said they didn't have such a thing as a half-cup in the house – would a whole cup half-full do instead? Vestey says that when young Maurice was at the village school in Marazion, he was nicknamed 'Whole-cup-half-full.' Now *that's* what I mean by Cornish humor.'

Laughing, he went into the pharmacy, opposite the post office.

Whole-cup-half-full . . . Giles wondered, not whether it was true, but whether it could possibly be revived. He liked it, anyway. Naturally, it would be beneath his dignity to repeat it, but he might tell young Henry, who might pass it around at school . . . and then the other boys would tell their fathers.

Or Sibylla? Yes! She wouldn't hesitate to spread it round. If it came to a choice between her dignity and the chance to poke Petifer in the eye . . . well, it was no sort of choice, at all.

As it turned out, Sibylla was the first person he encountered when he came home, apart from Mary Beckett, the maid who helped him out of his overcoat and galoshes, and then brought his slippers and the evening post. He told Sibylla the joke at once, and was pleased to see that Beckett hung around to hear it, too – pretending to pick flecks of mud out of his coat with her fingernail.

Sibylla clapped her hands with delight. 'Whole-cup-half-full!' she exclaimed. 'Well, Jimmy Troy may sneer at our scurrilous sense of humour but even he must admit we have a genius for hitting the nail on the head at times! Isn't that Petifer to a T! Whole-cup-half-full! Don't you think so, Mary?'

''Tis a good old tale, ma'am,' the maid agreed cautiously.

Laura appeared at the half-way landing at that moment. 'Mary,' she said sharply. 'If there's as much mud as all that on the master's coat, you'd best take it to the scullery and sponge it properly.'

The maid curtseyed and bore the coat away.

'A bit severe, what?' Giles commented as he kissed her on the cheek.

'You shouldn't tell such tales when the servants are around,' she replied. 'And you, Sibylla, shouldn't laugh at them.'

'Them?' Sibylla pretended not to follow. 'I was laughing at *him*. Whole-cup-half-full!' She tried to recruit a smile from her cousin. 'You have to admit it's apt.'

Laura smiled acidly. 'I don't, as a matter of fact. But if the revival of childhood nicknames is to become the vogue, why stop at just the one? I could, for instance, mention . . .'

'Don't you *dare!*' Sibylla leaped at her and clapped her hand over Laura's mouth. 'If you do, I swear I'll kill you. Promise you won't?'

'Mmh mmh hmm nhm,' Laura replied, her eyes sparkling merrily above her cousin's hand.

'Promise?' Sibylla tightened the clasp of her fingers to the very borders of pain.

Laura nodded vigorously, but when Sibylla released her, she raised both hands to show crossed fingers. 'I *will* kill you,' Sibylla warned.

Giles took Sibylla by the arm and gave her a warm, comforting squeeze. 'I shan't listen, even if she does break her word,' he promised her. 'Come on, let me shake you a cocktail. We're invited to dine *en famille* with the Troys tomorrow night, by the way.'

'Just you and me?' Sibylla grinned archly back over her shoulder at Laura, who was still on the bottom-most stair.

'No, alas,' he replied with a wink. 'I'm afraid they felt they couldn't exclude Mrs Curnow.'

Whole-cup-half-full! Laura thought angrily as soon as she was alone again. It simply wasn't true. And as for being apt!

Sibylla was very annoying at times.

She heard their laughter coming from the drawing room, whose door they had closed behind them.

Yes – very annoying, indeed.

Elizabeth raised a discreet eyebrow; Jimmy nodded. 'Well, ladies?' She smiled at Laura and Sibylla as she put her hands to the arms of her chair. Holden, the butler, hastened to draw it back for her. Giles and Jimmy, with Sibylla between them, both turned to assist her to rise – though the plaster cast on her arm was little hindrance to her. Laura, left to fend for herself, chuckled. Jimmy glanced somewhat sheepishly at Elizabeth. Giles shot an almost identical glance at Laura. Sibylla, noting these strange responses, left the room with a thoughtful glint in her eye; Elizabeth and Laura, immediately behind her, were talking of Dr Thomas's new car.

'Yes, indeed – the car,' Jimmy said as they seated themselves again. 'A rich man's toy. Doctor Thomas has a good private income, I believe.'

'He treats more of the poor than any other physician in the town,' Giles agreed. 'And without padding the bills of the better-off to pay for it. Fair dues to the man.'

'Hmm.' Jimmy passed the port to Giles and waved a hand in the direction of the cigars. 'Do you think it will always be a rich man's hobby – this motoring?'

Giles nodded. 'I can't see the price of a car falling below a hundred, can you? Even then – say they came down to eighty. That's still far more than a year's wages for the average working bloke. I'm sure it'll remain a rich man's hobby during *our* lifetime – how could it be otherwise?'

Jimmy poured his own port. 'One sees more and more of them on the roads every day.'

'Every *week*,' Giles allowed. 'Sometimes one goes two or three days without seeing a car at all.'

'Still, there *are* more and more of them – and despite the red-flag law. Why?' He asked the question as if it were the greatest mystery to him.

'Because they're such . . . *fun*, I suppose. Though perhaps you wouldn't find many who'd be willing to admit as much in this nonconformist county, where fun is another name for sin.'

'Fun,' Jimmy echoed. 'And just think what *fun* they'll be when the red flag goes, as go it must! D'you think we'll be able to keep such *fun* to ourselves and out of the hands of the toiling masses for long? I can remember when only ladies and gentlemen rode bicycles, can't you? Anyway – let us suppose, just for argument's sake, that at some time within the next ten years there will be several thousand cars in Cornwall, several hundred of which will be in the West Penwith area – almost all of which will drive into or through Helston when their owners go marketing or about their ordinary business.'

'Ah yes!' Giles lit his cigar and settled back. 'Of course. That's what you wanted to bend my ear about – something to do with the town.'

'Everything to do with the town, dear fellow. Can you imagine what the incursion of several *hundred* of those vehicles will *do* to the place? Not to mention the several *thousand* there'll be within two decades. I tell you, man, the towns and cities of this country are going to choke on those machines. And the villages and hamlets, too.'

'Oh, come!' Giles laughed at this plainly overheated

fancy. 'Anyway, what can we do about it *now?*'

Jimmy paused while he puffed his cigar to life. 'Something that's already overdue, in fact – even without the advent of the horseless carriage. Most days, I agree, the traffic in Helston isn't too bad, but have you ever tried to get *through* the place on market day?'

'Certainly not!' Giles replied. 'I shouldn't think any sensible person even tries.'

'Well, some folk *have* to.'

Giles suddenly realized what Jimmy most probably had in mind. To cut it short, he said, 'If this is working up to a plea for us to open up a byway around the town to relieve congestion – which is only experienced on one day a week, anyway – I can tell you now, Jimmy, it hasn't a chance. It's a non-starter, honestly. The traders would never stand for it – and they *are* the town council. Anyone who's desperate enough to want to get through Helston on market day can easily turn off at the top of Sithney Common Hill and go through Lowertown.'

'Aha!' Jimmy seized on the point. 'And maybe they will, dear fellow! Did you ever see an oxbow lake?'

Giles frowned.

Jimmy went on: 'It's an ancient portion of a meandering river that got left behind – literally a backwater – when the river decided to take a more direct course – or a different course, anyway. I guess something of that sort could happen to a town as well. One year it's a main highway, thriving and bustling. Next year – a stagnant little backwater, cut right off from the main artery. Just something the forward-looking traders of Helston ought to be thinking about!' He smiled benignly. 'I'm sure they all are wonderfully forward-looking, no?'

Giles blew out a thick, rich cloud of smoke and,

staring deep into his port, said, 'Well, it's not something to ignore for ever. I'll grant you that readily enough.'

Jimmy decided to let the matter rest for the moment. After a long and comfortably ruminative silence, Giles said, 'The way you leaped to assist Sibylla just now . . .'

Jimmy chuckled. 'You, too, I noticed. It was my fault, of course. I was nearer Laura than . . .'

'No, I wasn't thinking about that. I was wondering . . . the way you looked immediately at Elizabeth . . . has she . . . *said* anything to you?'

Jimmy's eyes narrowed. 'Like what?'

'Like "be especially pleasant to poor Sibylla"?'

Jimmy sniffed. 'Something of the sort. Why? Has Laura said the same to you?'

Giles nodded. 'Something of the sort.'

Jimmy made a vague gesture. 'Bit awkward for me, as a matter of fact. I know we're on first-name terms with Sibylla, but that's only through knowing you, and . . . present circumstances, you understand. Really, I don't know her all that well. I don't mean this as criticism in any sense. If I did, I wouldn't be so ungracious as to say it – to you of all people. But I don't find her a very *knowable* sort of woman. In a way, I mean it as a compliment. Despite all her good humour and . . . oh, you know what I mean. Her outgoingness – what's the word?'

'Gregariousness?'

'Well, sure, something like that. Despite all that, she is a very private person.' He licked his lips and eyed Giles cautiously. 'Is it fair to ask you how well she's recovered from her husband's death? Is it really as complete as she makes it seem?'

Giles pondered the question. 'Does Elizabeth think it may not be?' he asked at last. 'I know Laura suspects she hasn't. Is that why they asked us to . . . you know – butter her up a bit and so forth?'

'And did they both arrive at the conclusion simultaneously? Or separately? Or did one arrive at it and then inform the other? We shall probably never know. More to the point – and that's really why I'm asking you these questions, Curnow – do you actually agree with them? And if so, d'you think flirting with the lady – with or without our wives' consent – is such a terribly good idea?'

Again it was some time before Giles answered – and again his reply was far from direct. 'It's the damndest thing, you know, Troy – this business of civilization. Of being civilized and so forth. Would you call me a civilized man?'

Jimmy merely smiled. 'Go on.'

'You know why I ask?'

'Why yes, Curnow, I believe I do. In our dealings with the world we create a certain picture of ourselves – especially in business. We need everyone to believe we're solid, dependable types . . . the last sort of person to rush into a decision. *We* are the gilt-edged men . . . copper-fastened – all that sort of thing. But inside . . . oh, that's from a different blood-line! Am I right?'

Giles nodded sardonically. 'May I have the temerity to ask you a rather personal question?'

Jimmy pushed the port his way, saying, 'If a childhood sweetheart of Elizabeth's turned up out of the blue and bought Crowntown Farm – how would *I* feel? Is that it?'

Giles shook his head as he refilled his glass. 'No. Almost but not quite. I can imagine how you might feel. But how would you behave? It's the behaviour that matters.'

'In public? Or in private with Elizabeth?'

Giles looked up with interest. 'Ah – so there would be a difference!'

Jimmy thought about it and then, with a light laugh – as if the discovery surprised him slightly – replied, 'No. In fact, I don't think there would be.'

Giles tapped his own brow. 'The differences would all be bottled up inside here, wouldn't they?'

Jimmy nodded his agreement, a little uncomfortably, though.

'I don't think you ever met Laura's father,' Giles went on.

'No. But I've heard . . . things.'

'All of them true, probably. The man was an absolute tyrant. A monster of selfishness . . . oh, I couldn't begin to tell you the ways in which he held that household in thrall.'

'Laura was their only child?'

'I'm afraid so – though he'd have dominated them all no matter how many. He managed it, not through fear – he wasn't *that* sort of tyrant. Not a bully. He never raised his hand to a soul, and hardly ever his voice. He did it far more subtly – by sheer . . . I hate to use the word, but by sheer *charm*. He was the most seductively charming man I ever met.'

'Does Laura agree with you, may I ask?'

'We've never discussed it. But when I married her . . .' He broke off and, sinking his head in one hand, gave a single, bitter laugh. 'When I married *her!* What am I saying! *He* married her – to me! Her father. He simply made it impossible for her to do anything else. For the first two years of our marriage I think she loved me out of duty to him. No! Duty is too cold a word for it. She loved me because his will prevailed over hers – as it always did. Anyway, I was about to say that when I married her I made a solemn vow to myself – and a silent vow to her – that I would never, never,

never seek to bend her to my will in the way her father always did.'

'Ah! An important qualification there!' Jimmy smiled. 'In what way *would* you bend her to your will, then?'

'By reason – if at all. I mean, if you think of it, husbands possess quite a few powers over their wives – legally and by custom, anyway. I know it varies from marriage to marriage, depending on the relative strengths of the two personalities. I could – we both could – name dozens of marriages where the wives rule the roost. But if a man really wants to wield a big stick, he holds all the trumps.' He laughed at his mixture of metaphors. 'You know what I mean.'

Jimmy nodded but said nothing to impede the flow.

'Well, when I married Laura, I didn't want to wield the big stick and nor did I want her to rule the roost. I wanted it to be as near as possible a perfect union of equals – complementary, of course, but equals.'

Jimmy put on the grin of a devil's advocate. 'Let's just test this, Curnow, before we start pinning on the campaign medals. If she made a suggestion about your business . . .'

'*Our* business,' he corrected.

Jimmy lifted a finger. 'That's what we're testing. If she made a suggestion about it, would you go along with it?'

'If I agreed with it, yes.'

'Ha!'

But now it was Giles who lifted a finger. 'I know you think you've got me: I only accept *her* suggestions when they're really mine all the time. But it's not like that. I'll give you an example. Five years ago I was all set to open a new depot in Camborne. In here' – he tapped his skull – 'it was all cut-and-dried. I'd stopped even considering anywhere else. But Laura said no, we should open it in Redruth, instead.'

Jimmy pulled a dismissive face. 'Camborne and Redruth are practically one town. It was surely a small point to concede.'

Giles looked at him askance and then laughed. 'Oh, you businessmen with world-wide industries! Don't you see? Camborne is the more westerly of the two towns. The roads out of Camborne serve all the areas where our business already dominated the market.'

'Which was, of course, why you were so set on it.'

Giles nodded. 'Now you see it! Laura pointed out that we could thrive only by expanding – and that meant pushing out eastward, to Truro, and southward to all that country between there and Falmouth, where we already had a small depot. In other words – or one other word: Redruth! And I agreed with her. So that's what we did. *Now* do I pass your test?'

With jovial reluctance Jimmy conceded that he did.

'Anyway,' Giles went on impatiently, 'I'm not really talking about *practical* equality of that kind – important though it is. I mean, if a husband and wife don't even have *that* sort of equality, they haven't really started. But I'm talking about something that goes much deeper.'

'Tiger country.'

Giles nodded. 'The body and the soul. Tiger country indeed!' He gathered his thoughts again before continuing. 'This is the real nub of it, now. I always thought of myself as a civilized man – by which I mean . . . oh, the very opposite of Enoch Nisbet.'

'Laura's father?'

'The same. The very opposite of him in every way. You see, the thing about a man who enslaves his family in that fashion is that, in some curious way, he himself becomes enslaved to them. The pharaohs of Egypt, with ten thousand slaves to do their smallest bidding –

were they *free?* If you were offered "freedom" of that kind, would you even consider it for a second?'

'What you're saying is that it wasn't pure altruism on your part. The freedom you wanted to *grant* Laura you also wished to *claim* for yourself. Isn't that true?'

Giles stirred uncomfortably. 'Yes, damn you! Since Petifer bought Culdrose, *I've* been thinking about old flames, too!'

Unblinkingly Jimmy said, 'And also Sibylla Johnson? Was she, too, an old flame?'

Giles let out his breath as if Jimmy had winded him.

'You started it,' Jimmy pointed out.

'Very well then,' Giles agreed. 'And actually, if you want me to be completely candid – I began thinking about her in that way when she first moved down to Chynoweth, back in May, before we even knew Petifer was still in the land of the living – much less that he intended returning to Cornwall. And – worse and worse – she was never an old flame, either. So what does that make me!'

Jimmy chuckled. 'Quite an ordinary sort of *bloke*, I'd say. These thoughts would never lead to any sort of . . . activity, would they?'

'Of course not. And that's the thing, you see. Because I'm sure Laura has exactly the same sort of . . . what can one call them? "Daydreams" is too positive.'

'Idle fancies?'

'Perfect! You see how confused I am! I can't even think of obvious names for things. I was saying – I'm sure Laura has these idle fancies about Maurice Petifer, too. And I'm just as sure that she'd never let them lead to any sort of *activity*, as you so tactfully put it. *But that doesn't help!*'

Jimmy sat up, surprised at the man's vehemence. 'Why not?'

'Equality of body and soul . . . pfft! It's gone! It's nowhere! It's all shrivelled up in the furnace heat of my jealousy and rage. I discover I am not the man I thought I was, Troy! I understand Bluebeard. I understand Othello. I understand why Heloise's father, whatever his name was (God, I ought to know it – he's my brother across the centuries), I understand why he sent those men to castrate Abélard! I understand chastity belts.' He laughed, rather desperately. 'I'm trying to make a joke of it but really it's not even remotely funny. The one thing I don't understand is myself. I have discovered that I am not at all the noble creature I thought I was. I am a savage ape, baring my fangs and baying the moon – howling for blood to avenge a wrong that I nonetheless know will never be perpetrated.'

Without a moment's hesitation Jimmy Troy, now completely serious, said, 'It's a hard thing to tell a man in your condition, Curnow, but if you carry on like this, it seems to me you'll be doing your darndest to make sure it *is* perpetrated.'

'Oh God!' Giles whispered, burying his face in both hands. 'D'you think I don't know that!'

'The smell of the oil makes me feel sick,' Elizabeth said. 'There's something about hot oil – it's so cloying. Even in an open tourer you can't escape it. And the fumes!'

'Open tourer!' Laura exclaimed. 'Don't tell me about open tourers! The bonnets, the veils, the goggles, the scarves, the coats, the jerkins, the rugs, the swaddling . . . one feels like a chrysalis. Or what are those things in cocoons that you find behind wardrobes and chests?'

Sibylla laughed.

The others turned to see what amused her so.

'The way you go on!' she said. 'Anyone would think you'd rather spend the day on your knees scrubbing floors than go for a drive in a motor car. You know jolly well that if Doctor Thomas drew up beside you in Coinagehall Street tomorrow and offered you a seat for a little spin to Porthleven and back, you'd both absolutely leap at the chance – and never mind that it was *shrouded* in hot-oil fumes and you in nothing but a summer frock!'

'Ah, well . . . Doctor Thomas!' Laura replied archly, as if that would be reason enough to accept the invitation, despite all the awful drawbacks Sibylla had mentioned.

'Or Maurice Petifer,' Elizabeth said lightly.

Now it was the others who turned to her. 'Why?' Sibylla asked pugnaciously.

'Didn't you know? He's given in and bought a motor, too.'

'No!' Sibylla's face was a study in anger and frustration.

Laura was more watchful for she did not think Elizabeth's remark had been entirely casual. 'What sort?' she asked.

Elizabeth closed her eyes and hunted for the name. 'I know it's German. Or Austrian.'

'A Daimler?' Laura guessed.

'That's it. Daimler Mercury . . . or Mercy . . . something like that.'

'Daimler Mercedes,' Laura said.

'My!' Sibylla put in. 'You do know them, don't you!'

Laura smiled primly. 'If it's the latest one he's

bought, then it's a Mercedes Simplex with a four-cylinder, three-litre engine. It also happens to be the fastest motor car ever made. Mr Vanderbilt drove his at sixty-nine miles an hour last April. Which one has Maurice bought, d'you know? The tonneau, the phaeton, or the open tourer? I hope it's the tourer.'

'Why?' They leaned forward, smiles prepared.

'Because Cornwall will simply *drown* him!'

When their laughter subsided, Elizabeth said, 'You know a lot about it, my dear – especially for someone who was so scathing only a few minutes ago.'

'Oh, that was all directed at open tourers. I shall have the double-tonneau carriage work, of course.'

The other two women exchanged glances and aped her: 'Of course!'

'But how *do* you know so much?' Sibylla asked.

'Because I've made it my business to find out. I've seen Giles lingering over the motor advertisements in the papers, lately. And so, naturally, I want to have an opinion prepared when we come to make up our minds. At the moment it's a choice between the double-tonneau Mercedes Simplex (which I *pray* Maurice hasn't bought for himself) and . . . well, I think we ought to wait and see what sort of car Siddeley is going to produce – being patriotic and all that, you know.'

'Well, well, well!' Elizabeth was impressed. 'I must come and pick your brains quite soon. I, too, have seen Jimmy looking at the advertisements – so assiduously, indeed, that I felt sure they must have been for corsets. But no, they were for motors.'

Sibylla heaved a sigh. 'I still cannot decide which is best – simply to be able to make up one's own mind and go out and buy something, or to manipulate the man of the house into adopting one's own opinion and claiming it was his all along.'

Laura turned to Elizabeth, 'Why did you say

Maurice has given in and bought a motor, just now?'

'Oh.' She laughed, a little uncomfortably. 'I don't suppose it's telling tales out of school, but he mentioned to me, a couple of times, that his housekeeper, Miss Sweet, has been suggesting it for some time.'

'Miss Sweet!' Laura said contemptuously.

Elizabeth looked at her with surprise. 'Oh?'

'Don't talk to me about Miss Sweet! I had a run-in with that madam a couple of weeks ago.'

'You never said,' Sibylla told her accusingly.

'No. But I still don't see why you say Maurice has "given in"? She hasn't been his housekeeper for more than a couple of months. Did she start badgering him from the very first day? Mind you, I wouldn't put it past her – a thoroughly nasty piece of work, in my opinion.'

Elizabeth grinned. 'Between you and me, I don't believe Maurice required a great deal of persuading in the matter. I imagine she said something like, "Motor cars! Nasty, smelly, dusty things – I can't abide 'em!" Whereupon he replied, "Very well, Miss Sweet – I give in. Have it your own way! Pester me no more. I shall purchase one tomorrow." Something like that.' She winked.

But Laura was barely mollified to hear this version. 'All the same, I just bet we'll see *her* driving into Helston to do her marketing – and before any of *us* has even placed an order for a car. Oh, I *do* hope it is an open tourer!' She smiled viciously. 'And I shall be certain to order several gross of tintacks tomorrow!'

'My, you *do* have it in for her!' Sibylla said admiringly. 'What happened between you? Why didn't you tell me?' She found an ivory paper knife on the whatnot and used it to scratch absentmindedly inside her plaster-of-paris cast.

'Us,' Elizabeth corrected, watching Sibylla nervously, for the heirloom was irreplaceable.

'Oh, it was just so silly,' Laura said grumpily. 'She barred Meredith and young Maurice in the pigsty . . .'

'With the pigs?' Sibylla asked. 'When did this happen, anyway?'

'No. In an empty sty. But even so – to lock them in as if they were common little criminals!'

'When did this happen?' Sibylla repeated. 'Meredith said nothing to me about it.'

'No.' Laura sighed. 'Well, it all blew over and Maurice said we'd just . . . forget it. Pretend it never happened. Maurice Petifer, I mean. Henry and Martin were in it, too – only they ran away and never got caught.'

Then, seeing the bewilderment in them increase with each additional 'explanation' of hers, she told them what had happened, heaping all the blame on Miss Sweet. 'Maurice had spent most of the day in Truro,' she added. 'She took it upon herself in his absence.'

'Oh . . . that day,' Sibylla said, a little uneasily.

Elizabeth caught the hesitation in her tone and asked why she said it like that. Almost absentmindedly she relieved Sibylla's nerveless fingers of the precious paper knife.

'It was the day you went to Penzance,' Laura reminded her. 'It was all forgiven and forgotten by the time you returned.'

Sibylla pulled a guilty face. 'I only said I went to Penzance,' she confessed. 'Actually, I went to Truro, too. But I spotted Maurice Petifer there – thank God he didn't see me! – and so, rather than start a lot of stupid tittle-tattle, I said I'd been to Penzance.'

'But Giles met you off the Penzance bus,' Laura objected.

'I know.' She grinned. 'I took the train to Penzance

from Truro and then the bus home.' The grin broadened. 'Aren't I thorough when I decide to tell a little fib!'

'I wonder why Maurice never mentioned a word of all this to me,' Elizabeth mused. 'I seem to be the sounding board for all his woes lately.' She found a knitting needle stuck in a fold of the sofa and put it on the whatnot, within Sibylla's reach.

Sibylla turned the accusation onto Laura. 'And why didn't you tell me either?'

Laura made several vague, discomfited motions of her hand. 'It was all, as I say, forgiven and forgotten. And any mention of Maurice Petifer is like a red rag to a bull with you. And anyway, my quarrel was with Miss Sweet, not him, poor man.'

'I still think I should have been told. Stealing apples *is* theft, whatever way you look at it . . .'

'Oh, if you *must* know,' Laura said – to stop her from building up a head of righteous steam, 'I didn't tell you because of . . . well, something else that happened that night. To do with Maurice Petifer. Something so unexpected . . .' She relapsed into silence, annoyed at herself for having mentioned it at all.

'Well, you can't just leave it there!' Elizabeth said after a short silence.

'Very well.' Laura drew a deep breath and plunged into the tale of what she had seen when Maurice rescued the two little boys from the pigsty. 'The tears were simply streaming down his cheeks,' she said, feeling a lump begin to grow in her own throat at the memory. 'I never felt such *sorrow* in a man, nor felt such sympathy in me, either.'

'And then?' Sibylla asked. For once there was no scorn in her.

'Oh.' Laura became offhand. 'I waited a discreet minute or two and then followed them indoors, saying

I'd gone to the wrong sty and missed them. I still don't know why he was weeping like that.'

Elizabeth said nothing – which roused Sibylla's suspicions at once. 'But *you* know something, don't you,' she accused.

Elizabeth closed her eyes and shook her head. 'I'm not sure . . .' She opened them again and stared unhappily at Sibylla. 'I mean, yes, I do know something, but I don't know if he meant it to go any further.'

'What?' Laura laughed cajolingly. 'As somebody famous once said – you can't just leave it there!'

Elizabeth did not join in her laughter. 'You see, when he told me about it, I asked him at once why he'd never breathed a word of it when we met in the Cape. And he said it hadn't been deliberate. It just happened. I mean, he had nothing to hide, nothing to be ashamed of. He hadn't *wanted* to make it a secret, but the subject had simply never arisen. That was all.'

'Is it just *he* who's not ashamed of it?' Sibylla asked. 'I mean, is it something anyone else – any *decent* person – *would* be ashamed of?'

'Oh, Sibylla!' her cousin exclaimed crossly. 'Do give the man the occasional bit of credit. It's so monotonous, you know.'

'Very well, Laura, dear.' Sibylla gave a placatory smile. 'He's a first-class ploughman, or so I'm given to understand. Will that do?'

Laura turned wearily to their hostess. 'Anyway?' she prompted.

'Yes,' Sibylla added. 'From what he said to you, it sounds as if he almost regretted making it *appear* to be some deep, dark secret. I think he told you so that you could pass it on – in a cautious and circumspect manner, of course. To people of taste and discretion.'

'D'you really think so?' Elizabeth asked dubiously.

'It sounds like that to me, too,' Laura added hopefully.

Elizabeth drew a deep breath and squared herself to it. 'Well . . . it seems that some years ago – I'm not quite sure how many – four or five, maybe six – Maurice got married, out in the Cape.'

The other two women stared at her, open-mouthed, forgetting for a moment to breathe.

'She was a Boer girl by the name of Sara Viljoen. Sarie, he calls her.'

'How old was she?' Laura murmured.

'Nineteen. Her family weren't voertrekkers. They stayed in the Cape – down near Cape Town. Jimmy and I actually bought several dozen cases of wine from her uncle – though, of course, we didn't know of the connection at the time. That was the white wine we had with the fish course this evening. Viljoen of Stellenbosch – quite a well-known vineyard and quite a well-to-do family, too.'

'How interesting! Did he make his money in diamonds at all?' Sibylla asked pointedly.

'My God!' Laura flared up at her again. 'Do you never let it rest?' She turned back, all eyes and ears for Elizabeth.

Sibylla sank her head between her shoulders and sat in contrite silence. 'I don't really mean it,' she stage-whispered to their hostess. 'It's just that some moments are too good to let pass without a comment of some kind.'

Elizabeth shook her head. 'It's not a funny story, Sibylla,' she remarked. 'There was a dowry but he returned it to the family after her death. He asked them to endow a school for Hottentot children and to name it in her memory.'

'Oh.' Sibylla was truly contrite at that. 'So she died.'

'As if you couldn't have guessed!' Laura said acidly.

'*They* died,' Elizabeth corrected her. 'There was a little boy, too – no more than a couple of years old. John. Jannie, they called him. The Cape Dutch say their Js like a Y. They both died of tick bites – or of some fever you get from tick bites.'

Laura closed her eyes and willed herself not to yield to tears in front of the other two women; the lump in her throat, which had never been too far away, returned.

'I think it almost killed Maurice, too – not the fever, but the loss of his wife and little boy.' Elizabeth's voice began to break.

Laura, in her mind's eye, saw poor Maurice's hand reach out into the dark of the pigsty. She remembered the silence that had suddenly come over him as little Meredith's hand had sneaked cautiously out to clasp it. Now she could only guess at what thoughts must have preyed upon him at the touch of that little hand . . .

How vulnerable we are at the most unexpected moments. A tear she could not contain rolled slowly down her cheek.

'I know.' Elizabeth sniffed, too, and patted Laura's arm. 'I don't mind confessing I wept buckets when he told me.' She drew a deep breath and held it.

'God, just look at us!' Sibylla rose and paced aimlessly about the drawing room, angry that she, too, was moved – and even more angry that she could not conceal it from them. She snatched up the knitting needle and began to scratch furiously where her fingers could not reach.

Elizabeth took a firm grip on herself and almost babbled the conclusion to her tale. 'I think he contemplated suicide for a while. I'm a bit confused about what he told me after that, but there was something about going across the veldt – just walking and walking, intending . . . well, just to die of exposure or something. Not to come back, anyway. And that's when he found it – a diamond *pipe*. Isn't that what they call it? I think so. He was staggering along, close to the last extremity, when he literally stumbled over it.' She smiled wanly at the other two. 'That's the tale of it, anyway. I only hope I did right to tell you.' After a pause she asked, 'Did I?'

Laura recalled that long, silent moment, out there in the dark on that momentous evening – how ghostly he had appeared in the pale yellow light of the storm lantern – the anguish in his eyes when she had offered her help – the despair in his tone when he had replied, 'I don't want your help.'

Or had it been, 'I don't want *your* help'?

Had Elizabeth done right to tell them?

'Yes!' she said, with far more conviction than she felt.

Sibylla snapped the bone knitting needle under her cast. Her apologies were profuse but Elizabeth merely laughed and said vaguely that it could have been a lot worse.

The fastest motor car in the world! Molly Hendren told her friend Daisy Bucket that some famous old American millionaire called Venables had driven the car at over a hundred miles an hour, which was even faster than the Penzance Corridor Express. Soon everyone in the district knew all about it. They heard it not just from Molly Hendren and the other farm servants but from the actual horse's mouth – and the filly's, too. For even if Maurice Petifer had not breathed a word (and in fact he bellowed several hundred, or the same few words a hundred times over) the world would still have known it from Miss Sweet, who broadcast the news with equal abandon.

So the populace knew *everything* about the car. That it was blue, for instance. *And* that it was silver. And green. Also that it was a sobersided black. They could assure you it cost one hundred and ninety-nine pounds. That it cost *two* hundred and ninety-nine. That it cost three hundred and twenty pounds, sixteen shillings, and fourpence – anyway, that only a rich man could afford one. They knew it was on its way; plus the fact that it had been secretly delivered a week ago but had failed even to start; alternatively, it had been lost overboard in the German Ocean on November the twenty-eighth last and a replacement was on its way but would not now arrive until the new year. They were quite certain the motor would not be man enough to run on stalwart English petrol and that gallon tins of effete German 'benzine' would have to be sent all the way from its homeland – which would just teach Maurice Petifer to go buying unreliable foreign rubbish. In short, people knew everything that was to be known about the car (and a great deal more that was not) long before anyone even clapped eyes on it. The only thing they did not know was which among all these home-made varieties of fact would, when put together, comprise the truth. More especially, they had no real idea when the blessed thing would arrive and put an end to all the speculation.

But that difficulty, at least, was resolved before the great day itself; for in the early afternoon of the second Friday in December, young Victor Mead, one of the Post Office telegram boys, pulled his muffler tightly round his neck, tugged his little peaked cap down over his eyes, and cycled off into the teeth of a biting south-easterly wind to deliver a message of unequivocal exactness:

YOUR ESTEEMED ORDER OF FIFTH ULT DISPATCHED ON FLAT WAGON PADDINGTON THIS AFTERNOON PER PASSENGER TRAIN STOP ARRIVING HELSTON NINE SIXTEEN O'CLOCK TOMORROW SATURDAY MORNING STOP ADVISE OF UNARRIVAL STOP VEHICLE RUN PER YOUR INSTRUCTIONS STOP WILL START INSTANTER BUT MUST FILL PETROL TANK STOP GOLDSMITH DAIMLER CAR COMPANY LONDON.

By that Friday evening the news was all around Helston; by closing time it was known the length and breadth of West Penwith: The fastest motor car in all the world was coming to town tomorrow! The three Johnson children were in tears that evening as they set off for Falmouth on a long-arranged visit to their 'Uncle' Daniel Jago, their late father's partner in the Ponsharden Shipyards; but Sibylla, who was also celebrating the removal of her plaster cast, was adamant in honouring the arrangement, and so off they went. In any case, as she confided to Laura, not all the twenty-two wild horses crammed into the three-thousand cubic centimetres of the Mercedes Simplex's engine, would have kept her in Helston that Saturday. Laura replied that she herself had no intention of going near the station, either; she had far better things to do with her time, thank you very much.

At eight o'clock the following morning, the entire Curnow family was seated at the breakfast table. Saturday and Sunday were the two days of the week on which, as thoroughly modern parents, Giles and Laura took that first meal of the day with their children. It was approaching its end, amid a wreckage of kipper bones, bacon rinds, stringy bits of kidney, and butter remnants all liberally veined with charcoaly toast crumbs and marmalade smears, when Laura said, quite casually, 'I *do* want that new dress finished in time for Christmas.'

'The one made from that material you were talking about?' Giles asked. 'From Liberty?'

'Yes. I told them to send it down by train, because I was meaning to go directly on to see . . .'

'Ah, well, that's handy,' Giles cut in. 'I can call at the parcels office at the station and see if it's come. It so happens I'm going that way this morning . . . ah, on a little matter of business.' He pulled out his watch and added, 'Good heavens!'

'You?' Laura asked in surprise, for she could not think of any business at all up near the station – much less a business in which Curnow's might be interested. 'But what for? It's all just open fields up there,' she objected.

'Yes – it's to do with a field, as a matter of fact. It's something Jimmy Troy suggested to me. This particular field I have in mind would make a good site for a new slaughterhouse. It's practically inside the station boundary.' He pointed a finger around at the five children – or at the four who were old enough to understand. 'Not a word about it to anyone outside this house, you brats – or the price of the land will rocket.' He turned back to Laura. 'So you see – I can easily pop across the line and find out if your parcel's arrived. No trouble at all.'

Laura wiped the last crumbs from her lips and said, well, she'd come along anyway because, if it had arrived, she could go directly to Mrs Eaves, the dressmaker, who would then have absolutely no excuse for not having the dress ready by the twentieth.

'Can I come, too?' Henry asked casually.

'And me?' Gillian added.

'Me too, me too?' piped Maurice, Blanche, and – at last – even little Phillippa joined in.

'Why all this clamour to stand on a freezing cold station platform while old Chigwidden rummages among twelve months' stock of abandoned or lost parcels?' Giles asked.

'Because today's the day Mr Petifer's new car arrives there,' Henry said, with admirable honesty.

'So it is!' Laura exclaimed – as if she had quite forgotten last night's ructions with the Johnson children. 'Oh well, we can't miss that, can we! Come on, then. Hurry up, all of you!' And she rose, rubbing her hands as she shooed them about their post-prandial ablutions.

She studiously avoided her husband's eye, but as she left by the door he gave her elbow a squeeze and murmured, 'Heh heh! You didn't deceive me!'

'Nor you, me.' She grinned back at him.

He needn't have worried about the children having to stand on a draughty platform, however. The cleverest trick would have been to get into the station-approach road at all. So great was the renown of the new car, and so far and wide had the news of its arrival spread, that people had come from miles around just to be able to claim they 'seen 'n first.'

Giles took one look at the crush and told Hinks to drive on up the hill and stop by the next gate to the left.

'That's just a field,' Laura complained.

'But the grass is very short,' he told her.

'How can you be sure of that?' she asked. It sounded suspiciously like the sort of encouraging lie told by one spouse to keep the other quiet until it was too late to matter.

He smiled enigmatically. 'Because I was here only yesterday.'

She dug him in the ribs. 'You arranged all this! You knew there'd be a crowd.' She pulled him toward her and kissed him warmly on the cheek. 'Bless you.'

As soon as they were into the field the children scampered ahead, heels flashing up the slope, at whose crest stood the station and its numerous outbuildings; their wake was a trail of dark-green footprints in the velvety, frost-rimed grass. Looking about her, Laura realized that not even Giles, the most forethoughtful man in the world, could have arranged for sheep to be put into this field some weeks earlier – before they even knew that Maurice had ordered a car at all, much less one that would attract such crowds as this. 'There's more to this visit than mere gawking at a car,' she said.

He nodded. 'I told you.'

'So that story about buying the land wasn't just . . .' She frowned. 'Who owns this field, anyway?'

'If our meeting goes well,' he replied, 'you and I will own it.'

She gave him a foxy smile. 'Then the abattoir isn't just an invention, either! I felt sure you were pulling my leg.'

'In front of the children?' He pretended to be shocked. 'Actually, *abattoir* is a much better name for it than slaughterhouse. But won't this make the perfect site?' He stretched his hand toward the goods yard and engine workshop, which stood almost against the nearby hedge. 'Tell me if you disagree, of course. I won't proceed unless you also approve. Actually, I kick myself for not thinking of it before Jimmy. You see – we can chill the meat on the premises, run a siding right into the chill room, shunt refrigerated wagons in there, and load them directly. High-quality meat, properly hung at the correct temperature, properly chilled, and never warmed again until the cook puts it in the oven! How many other abattoirs in the country will be able to make such a boast? None in Cornwall, anyway – which is all that need concern us.'

They were almost at the station. A tall embankment, where trains marshalled and engines turned, had earlier masked their view of the road. Now they saw – or, rather, had it confirmed for them – that the entire approach on that side was as crowded as the main street of the town at Harvest Fair. 'We wouldn't have stood a chance of getting through there,' Giles commented.

'Who *does* own this land?' she asked.

'Vosper Scawen. He bought it as a little investment, I suppose – years before the railway arrived. He must have guessed this was the only place it could go.'

'But he'll surely know you don't want it for grazing the children's ponies,' Laura objected. 'Why did you warn them not to talk about it like that? Vosper Scawen's not going to let it go for a song, anyway.'

Giles chuckled. 'No, of course not. I just want them to develop the habit of caution, that's all. Oh look – there she is!'

He pointed toward the station in such excitement that Laura expected, at the very least, to see a tarpaulin being whisked off the gleaming monster. But he was pointing through the arch of the bridge to where, a short way down the cutting, the little saddle-tank engine could just be seen, dark-green and black against a cloud of its own steam. The crowd thronging the bridge, dangling their legs from the parapet, reminded Laura of pictures of Boat Race Day in London.

A cheer went up from the station platform, where the waiting party had seen it, too, and it soon communicated itself to the masses in the road, whose view was obscured by the station building itself. The bridge lay just to the west of the station; its abutments and the banks of the cutting beyond had the curious effect of absorbing the sound of the train's approach, especially when, like today, the wind was in the east. As a result the engine burst with a surprising roar of sound into the confines of the station precincts, taking by surprise even those who had their eyes glued to it.

The brakes went on with a screech, as if the driver, too, were astonished at the suddenness of their arrival; and the whole train shuddered to a halt just as it was in danger of overshooting the platform altogether. By now the Curnows had drawn level with the passenger building – though they were, of course, on the opposite side of the track from it. They therefore missed the fun of watching some three dozen startled passengers as they opened the doors and found themselves in the thick of such crowds as they had never before seen at the station; but, by way of compensation, they also got the first clear view of the flatbed wagon, covered with a green tarpaulin that formed itself into the unmistakable outlines of a large motor car.

'There's the great man himself.' Giles pointed out a group who had just detached themselves from the crowd; a moment later they climbed aboard the wagon and started fiddling with the ropes.

'No sign of Miss Sweet,' Laura said with gleeful relief.

Two gangers uncoupled the wagon and the guard's van behind it while a second saddle-tank engine came fussily up the relief line and halted just before the bridge. There it whistled impatiently, although the signalman must have known it was there since his signal box was entirely wreathed in its steam. He pulled a lever. There was the clank of switch-points, and the second engine chuffed down the link line to halt immediately behind the guard's van. As soon as it was coupled up, there was another toot and it shunted back up the link, this time pulling the van and the wagon, until all three were past the points. The car was still surrounded by Maurice Petifer and his impatient gang. Yet another toot (it seemed to be a competition as to whether the driver could get to his whistle before the signalman could pull whatever lever had to be pulled anyway) and the points clanged again. The engine chugged fussily down its final stretch of line, pushing the wagon to the ramp where horse-carriages were supposed to be loaded – though it was a facility hardly anyone bothered with these days. Certainly Maurice's was the first horse*less* carriage ever to use it.

The ramp was immediately to one side of the engine shed, right against the fence where – all going well – Giles planned to build the abattoir. Thus the Curnow family had the very best ringside seat for the unveiling of the new wonder. So, too, did the people on the station approach – at least, it was the nearest view they could possibly get from their vantage, or *dis*advantage, point outside the station itself. They pressed forward, threatening the integrity of the brick wall and railings in their efforts to improve their view. There were cries of 'Don't 'ee push so!' and 'Hats off!' from all over the place.

Maurice saw the Curnows at the very moment when he was about to pull the tarpaulin off the car. He paused and raised his hat instead. 'Good morning to you all! Going for a stroll?' He laughed. 'You passed by just in time. And good morning to you, too, Mr Scawen.'

Giles and Laura turned in surprise and then bade the old lawyer good morning, too. He apologized for creeping up on them. 'Didn't want to interrupt the excitement,' he explained. Then, raising his voice,

'You'll precipitate a riot, Mr Petifer, if you don't unveil that thing soon.'

Maurice put his hat back on his head and, without further ado, gave the signal to his men so that, between them, they whipped the tarpaulin off the car in one clean movement.

A gasp went up from the crowd; it was followed by a silence you could almost lean on.

'Magnificent!' Giles murmured, greatly against his will. But – one had to admit it – there was no other word for the splendid monster that now stood revealed.

'It *is* an open tourer!' Laura said at once – but even her glee at this cardinal error was tempered with the hush of admiration.

It was cream in colour, long and sleek, with deeply padded leather upholstery stained to a rich, dark tan – a high three-seater in the back and a slightly lower three-seater at the front. And there were no doors to fuss over and trap bits of clothing in.

'It's going to be *so* draughty!' Laura added happily. She was beginning to remember that she was not here to venerate the thing – though if ever a motor car deserved a little veneration, this was the one.

She glanced down at her children and was annoyed to see them utterly lost in wonder.

It was the design of the front end that impressed the most. Henry said later that it reminded him of a huge Cornish wrestler at that moment of greatest menace, just before a bout begins, when he leans forward and stretches out both arms to grapple his opponent. Those 'arms' were the two wicked-looking semi-elliptical springs, which jutted forward even beyond the wheels. Their upper and lower curves met, Gillian said, 'like crabs' pincers.' The bright copper radiator sat directly over the front axle, gleaming between the bastions of the two mighty front wheels; above them, like the peaks of a military helmet, projected the tips of the two front mudguards. And between them ('Like on the dog with eyes as big as dinner plates,' as Blanche said, not to be outdone in the quest for zoomorphic similes) sat two great lamps of burnished brass, jutting eagerly forward, ready, one would swear, to banish the night with beams as bright as the Eddystone lighthouse.

'Ah, but can it play in tune?' Vosper Scawen asked, almost inaudibly behind them.

Giles and Laura laughed heartily; the children turned back to the new idol, more impressed than ever with its hidden capabilities. A car that played *tunes!*

By now the ropes that had lashed it securely all the way from Paddington lay neatly coiled on the folded tarpaulin. The gangers put their shoulders to the wagon and rolled it the last few inches until its buffers were tight against the loading ramp; one of them wound the brake while the other put a baulk of oak across the gap between wagon and ramp. They were about to manhandle the vehicle down onto terra firma when Maurice put up his hand and cried, 'Stop!'

'What now?' Giles called up to him.

'Look at that crowd, man! I was intending to roll it off and tow it home by horse. But they're not going to be satisfied to see that, are they!' He sighed. 'I'll have to run her.'

Scawen added under his breath, 'And – *mirabile dictu!* – he just happens to have a tin of petrol with him!'

'A whole tin half full,' Laura murmured in reply; their eyes met and twinkled.

'It must break your heart, young fellow,' Giles called back. 'But you can't possibly disappoint your public, can you!'

'Well, old boy' – Maurice pretended to take the

question at face value – 'not that portion of it which appreciates a true thoroughbred among motor cars.'

'That's one to him,' Scawen allowed. 'We, I fear, lack the correct attitude of reverence for the wonders of the new century.'

Maurice sent Denis Williams across to the station forecourt, where his gig was parked. A moment later he returned with a tin of petrol. Then there was a hunt for a bit of metal to put between the lugs of the stopper, which was too tightly screwed down for even the horniest hand to undo. Eventually the brightest of them put the flange of the buffer between the lugs and screwed the can off the stopper that way.

Meanwhile, a small section of the crowd, growing restive, struck up with the revivalist hymn, *Saviour, Saviour, hear my humble cry!* The aptness of the closing words of the verse, 'Do not pass me by!' raised a laugh and soon most of the crowd was singing away with gusto.

'Look at Reverend Trebilcock's face over there,' Giles said. 'He can't decide whether to turn round and give them a helping of hot-tongue pie for their blasphemy, or take advantage of it and leap in with a sermon on the Devil and his toys!'

'It's their unending dilemma, isn't it,' Scawen commented. 'Do they go for sheer numbers, no matter how feebly each individual flame might flicker, or for sheer intensity – ending up with a religion of lone and scattered lighthouses along the dark foreshores of iniquity? They never can decide.'

The fellow spoke with such relish that Giles began to wonder. His own agnosticism (or Nothingerianism, as believing friends mockingly called it) was well known but he had never thought of the old lawyer as a fellow doubter. Was he therefore dropping these remarks to put him, Giles, in a favourable frame of mind for the hard bargaining that was soon to take place – not just *on* this very ground but *over* it, too?

'Ooh, what's that lovely smell?' Gillian asked.

'Petrol,' her two brothers told her contemptuously. 'Haven't you ever smelled it before?'

'It's as good as perfume,' she murmured, closing her eyes and sniffing deep draughts of the heady aroma.

'That might just be enough to get us home,' Maurice commented as he strapped the now empty tin in its proper place at the back of the running board. 'Let's see, now . . . fingers in ears, everybody!'

He raised the bonnet and made a number of adjustments before he unclipped the starting handle from its stowing place. All this drill he remembered from that wonderful day, six weeks ago, when he went to Plymouth, tried out the car, fell in love with it, and ordered it on the spot. In his fancy, to be sure, he had started it a thousand times since and there was hardly a lane in the whole of western Cornwall down which his imaginary Mercedes had not already driven. So he pushed the starting handle into its socket and engaged its two lugs with all the aplomb of a skilled professional. He even remembered the advice of the mechanic who had first introduced him to these mysteries, not to hold the handle in the obvious way, with thumb and fingers circling it – 'Because if she'd take it into her head to backfire on 'ee, she'd snap your wrist so quick as a green withy.' Instead, he took a careful grip, with his thumb on the same side as his fingers.

'Back to the apes,' Scawen commented.

One swing.

The motor made a hissing sound – *sss-sss-sss* – out-in-out.

Another swing.

Another *sss-sss-sss*.

And again.

Maurice hit his forehead at his own forgetfulness and went round to the petrol tank, where he pumped a little air pressure into it, to force the liquid forward to the motor. Then he opened the bonnet again and fiddled under it with a screwdriver. 'Have to bleed it,' he explained apologetically to his nearest audience, the Curnows and Vosper Scawen.

'Goodness gracious! Does the machine come complete with leeches?' the old lawyer asked.

A secular portion of the crowd was now singing, *Keep right on to the end of the road* . . . Reverend Trebilcock had lost his chance.

'Ah! Thar she blows!' Another flurry of the screwdriver, more fiddling with the bonnet catches, and once again Maurice took his deliberately non-prehensile grip on the starting handle.

One more swing . . . and this time the engine roared into life – at least, a roar was what everyone was expecting. But, as they gingerly peeled their fingers from their ears, all they heard was the deepest, silkiest, throatiest purr.

At that moment even the Reverend Trebilcock, the local expert in the business of sudden conversions, was himself suddenly converted to the worship of the new age. A roaring, clattering, banging, backfiring, sputtering motor – a little bang-bang like Doctor Thomas's, which was what everyone had expected – would have confirmed them in their worst prejudices. But that deep, velvety murmur, right at the lower threshold of human hearing, so quietly confident, so laden with *power*, spoke directly to ambitions and desires they had never suspected themselves of possessing. From birth their souls had been fortified against seductions from every conceivable quarter but this. It was a temptation that sailed in under neutral colours, past every sentry. And they yielded, every last man – and woman, too.

'Oh, Giles!' Laura whispered, moving to his side and taking his arm in hers.

He swallowed hard and drew in a long-delayed breath. 'I know,' he replied shakily.

Scawen shook his head and said nothing for once; but it did not stop him thinking, *I must be getting old*.

Maurice gave the starting handle an ironic kiss before he clipped it back into place. Then, pulling his huge gauntlets back on again, he grinned down at them and said, 'Anyone going my way?'

Laura just gaped at him, amazed that the very possibility had not even occurred to her until then.

The children, of course, clamoured to take up the offer, but she knew Giles would stay on to talk business with Scawen and she wondered how she could make it not seem like treachery to him.

She was on the point of saying no when it struck her that, if she did not ride in the car now, then the first woman to do so would be Miss Sweet.

'Thank you, Maurice!' she said brightly. 'We'd love to.'

One of the gangers put a stepladder over the stone hedge, making it easy for them to change sides with dignity. 'Shall we wait while you drive it down?' Laura asked.

'Certainly not!' he exclaimed. 'Get in and we'll all drive down. She's as safe as houses.'

Strong hands helped the children up onto the wagon, but their mother, with Phillippa in her arms, went the long way round and up the ramp. 'You boys go in front,' she told Henry and young Maurice. 'I'll sit in the back with the girls.'

As if in a trance the boys climbed into the front seat, gazing in wonder at the pedals and gear lever. 'Do not touch anything,' warned Maurice – the most unnecessary four words he had ever spoken, for the dashboard was a plain plank of wood, devoid of levers, switches, gauges, or controls of any kind.

The two older girls climbed into the back and bounced gaily on the deeply ribbed leather. 'It's all trembly and tingly, Mummy,' Gillian said as Laura joined them.

The crowds fell silent as Maurice himself climbed portentously into the driving seat; then they erupted in a great cheer. Laura and her children felt like royalty.

All this while she had not dared glance back at Giles; she knew well what disappointment and sense of betrayal she would read in his eyes. She knew she ought at least to wave at him, smile, laugh, say something . . . anything rather than this pretence at forgetfulness. She knew this was the worst way of all to behave. And yet she could not help it. For, no matter what she said, nor how much she tried to make light of it, if their eyes met, he would read the guilt in hers just as surely as she would see the accusation in his.

'Your material!' he called out just as Maurice was releasing the brake. 'For your dress!'

'Ah, yes!' she called back, giving him the briefest glance. 'I forgot. Actually, I remember now that I asked them to send it by post after all.'

Maurice pressed the clutch and there was a little grinding snicker as he engaged the bottom gear and the chain that drove the back wheels tightened. Then he tickled the accelerator and slowly let out the clutch.

But when it began to bite, he did what all novice drivers do and let it out too fast. The motor expired in a now familiar *sss-sss-sss*.

'Oh dear, what's wrong now!' Laura felt for his embarrassment as keenly as if it were her own.

There was a great, ironic cheer from the multitude.

He seemed quite sanguine about it, however. Henry was already fiddling with the catch that held the starting handle but Maurice put out a hand to stop him. 'We'll cure this with a little bit of swank,' he murmured; then, more loudly, 'Give her a push to the top of the ramp, you fellows.'

The gangers and his own labourers complied. At the top of the ramp he put her in gear again and, keeping the clutch depressed, said, 'One good hearty shove, now!'

'Wheee!' cried Blanche as they coasted down the slope.

Then 'Ah!' cried everybody as he took his foot off the clutch and the motor once again purred into life – this time driving the vehicle forward in earnest.

As soon as the rear wheels were off the ramp he turned sharp right, keeping the car on the wooden way by which carriages and handcarts crossed the lines. People near the gate that led out to the station concourse realized suddenly that he was now headed straight for them; they began scattering in some apprehension.

Still in bottom gear, letting the clutch in and out to control his snail's-pace progress, Maurice nosed the magnificent beast into the heart of the multitude before he finally eased her round to the left and down the slope that would lead, who could say how many hours hence, to Chynoweth and Culdrose.

'Bye bye!' Giles murmured as he stood behind the hedge and watched them vanish into the mêlée.

'Children!' Vosper Scawen commented drily. 'They're as faithless in their allegiances as . . .' His voice tailed off before he completed the comparison.

The word Vosper Scawen had failed to say rang on in Giles's mind and, once again – as had happened so often since Petifer had returned to Cornwall – he found one half of himself at war with the other. Common sense told him that what had just happened – and so publicly, too – was for the best. He knew that everyone in the district was talking about the 'piquant situation' that had arisen between Chynoweth and Culdrose. Not all the time, of course – he suffered no delusions of persecution on the subject; but he knew their minds turned that way whenever gossip and petty scandals were being aired.

Nor did he imagine that people were actually laughing at him behind his back. No one painted him with cuckold's horns. In an odd sort of way, he supposed, that showed the progress of civilization. In olden days, when cuckold's horns were all the rage, a wife need do no more than smile secretly to herself and at once the mockery would be pinned on her husband's brow. But in these modern times the subject would actually *lose* much of its interest if the cuckoldry were confirmed. Such a situation would not be nearly so interesting as one that was still all potential. 'Will-they-won't-they?' was the stuff of modern scandal; 'yes-as-a-matter-of-fact-they-do' was a mere bore.

Indeed, who so much as called it *cuckoldry* now? Even *adultery* sounded a bit old hat. The vogue was for *affaires*.

So the tongues of the district were kept in motion by the very lack of any confirmed affaire to gossip about. They fed on innocent moments like this, when the lady of Chynoweth (and her five children, to be sure) were to be seen parading through the town, bold as brass, with the gentleman of Culdrose.

'Side by side?'

'No. She was in the back, but even so, my pet . . .'

'And Curnow himself – did he know of it, d'you think?'

'Know of it! My dear life, he practically shoved her into the car and waved them goodbye!'

'What can he be thinking of!'

'Poor man, I say. What can *she* be thinking of!'

'Unless it's their way of showing the world there's absolutely nothing behind all this gossip.'

'Yes, well, there is that, of course. He always did pride himself on being such an *advanced* thinker.'

'It'll come to no good – mark my words. You can't pick and choose which of Society's rules you'll support and which you'll flout. It will end in tragedy . . .'

Giles only had to look into their eyes when he met them here and there about the town to know what was going on in that sordid mass of grey cells behind the smiles and the conventional greetings.

'I don't expect they're coming back,' Scawen said mildly.

'Eh?' Giles surfaced from his reverie, aware that the primitive man within him – the other half of the warring duo – had not had his airing. 'Oh . . . no. I'd forgotten them, as a matter of fact.' He waved at the field. 'All this . . .' he added vaguely.

'Oh!' The lawyer's tone was dismissive. 'That's soon dealt with. We're not going to fall out over a couple of acres.'

'An acre and a half.'

'One acre, two roods, and five square perches.'

'*Five* square perches?' Giles asked, as if it changed all his previous thinking on the subject.

'Don't mock the five square perches,' Scawen cautioned with an equally jocular severity. 'It's about the size of the building you're going to erect here, I should think.'

'Am I?'

'Well, I must admit I never supposed you wanted it for grazing your children's ponies!'

It was Laura's jest – indeed, it was practically her very words! For one absurd moment Giles caught himself wondering if there had been some collusion between the two of them. Then he remembered he hadn't even mentioned the matter to her until breakfast, a couple of hours ago. And *then* he realized that that was not in any case the reason he – or any good husband – ought to have for trusting his wife. A terrible gloom filled him. Once a man started down this road he laid himself open to every stray suspicion, no matter how absurd. At the end of this road, he warned himself, lay madness.

'What, then?' he challenged the lawyer. 'What's this building I'm going to erect on five square perches?'

'It's hardly my business,' was the bland reply. 'What it means is that, to me, as an isolated pocket of famland, the place is worth – what? Given its site on the edge of town . . . ten to fifteen pounds?'

Giles sucked in his breath sharply; ten pounds was the very most it was worth as farmland.

Scawen ignored the hint. 'But I can see houses here in the not-too-distant future. And I can imagine several small businesses that would flourish down here beside the railway . . .'

'I'm amazed you want to sell it at all!' Giles commented.

Memories were beginning to come back to him . . . something he had heard about Vosper Scawen years ago and had forgotten until this moment. It was triggered by that absurd thought about Laura's being in collusion with the man, of course. Scawen's wife Jane had been a considerable heiress; the lawyer had acted for her and later married her. That sort of thing always set tongues wagging, naturally, and what they had wagged about was . . . oh, the details had gone! It was something to do with Daniel Jago. No surprises there! Whenever the wagging tongues wanted a scape-goat – a father for a chance child, a cause for a broken heart – they fastened on Daniel Jago. Not so often these days, mind, for the man was now in his sixties; but fifteen years ago, when Giles had joined that adult world where such tittle-tattle was everyday fare, Jago's had been a name to raise a snigger in any company. But the details of this particular item of gossip now hovered, tantalizingly, just out of reach.

As he continued his haggling, part of Giles's mind detached itself and went in hunt of the elusive particulars. It was something to the effect that Jane . . . whatever her maiden name was. Hartley? Harding? No . . . it had gone. Laura would know – or Sibylla, even better. Sibylla collected every bit of gossip concerning Jago; they enjoyed a good laugh about it whenever they met. They were probably so engaged at that very moment, in fact.

He glanced at his watch.

'Yes!' Scawen took the hint. 'Me, too. Mrs Scawen warned me about standing around in the cold. Shall we call it a day and settle on sixty, then? Split the difference.'

It was outrageous, of course, but Giles bit the bullet and shook hands on the price. The lawyer had him over a barrel and was obviously not going to budge. 'Are you driving straight home?' he asked.

'No, I have one or two little errands in the town.'

'May I offer you a lift?'

'Ah yes!' Scawen smiled. 'You have room now, haven't you!' Then, more seriously, he added, 'Don't think me churlish, but I really ought to walk. In fact, I have been ordered to walk as often as I can. Join me, if you've time – I'd be delighted to have your company.'

He peered across at the station approach. 'And the insubstantial pageant has faded, it seems. How so many people can take time off on a working day baffles me.'

'It's the chance to see twenty-two horses packed inside a mere three thousand cubic centimetres, I think.'

Scawen frowned and then said, 'Ah yes – I see what you mean. And you're right, of course. I don't know what you're planning to do with this land, Curnow, but if I were you – and if I were still a young man, like you – I'd devote it to the motor car. I'd build motor cars here. Or sell them. Or repair them. Or something. It's obviously not one of those bubbles that bursts and vanishes.'

They passed the waiting carriage and Giles told Hinks he could go directly home. As the two men strolled down the hill into town, their conversation wandered wherever their stray thoughts led. Giles had a strong feeling that Scawen wished to broach some particular topic with him and yet was reluctant to do so. He himself was in the same boat, of course; he wanted to remember more about the Jago story. At last he grasped the bull by the horns.

They were talking about land and the things one could do with it. Scawen described the once-bare fields over near the Helford River, which his wife had, over the past three or four decades, turned into the most magnificent gardens.

'D'you know, Curnow, she even took a course in rock-blasting so that she could make the cliff terraces. She was the first person to use dynamite in Cornwall – only a year after it was invented.'

'Didn't her family once own property over this way?' Giles asked.

'Her father did. Her mother was Cornish but she

died before they moved back here to Cornwall. Her father, old Wilfred Harvey, bought Montpelier House – the Dawsons' place now. Your man Hinks could tell you about it. His father was the Harveys' butler.'

Harvey! That was the name! How curious that one little detail like that – not even a relevant detail – could unlock the rest of his memories! The whole story came crowding back suddenly.

And now, too, he could see how the confusion in his mind had arisen, for it was not merely *Daniel* Jago who enjoyed that 'certain reputation.' His father, Kinghorn Jago, had enjoyed it before him – indeed, the joke was that he'd passed it ou to Daniel in his will. The gossip was that one of Daniel's many conquests had been Jane Harvey – before she married Scawen, of course. It was said she'd even started to run away with Daniel and had only drawn back from that abyss when Kinghorn confessed he had run away with Jane's mother many years earlier, and that he was probably her father – which made her Daniel's half-sister, of course. The things people got up to in those times! No wonder the gossips remembered them. And how tame they were compared with today's meagre fare: 'I saw Mrs Curnow and her five children in Maurice Petifer's new car today!' Yes – it hardly compared!

But the point of the gossip about Scawen's wife and Daniel Jago had changed subtly over the years. In the beginning, to be sure, it had all been about the elopement; but when it turned into the elopement-that-never-was, the focus shifted onto Scawen himself – how clever he was . . . how patient he'd been . . . how, against all the odds (for he was just a little country lawyer with no money or family connections to boast of), he'd fought off a dozen rivals to win the hand of the richest heiress to settle in Cornwall in living memory.

To Giles's surprise an enormous sense of relief now filled him. It was not just the pleasure of turning a dim memory into one that is bright; it was something to do with Scawen's triumph itself – the way he had won through, the patience that had paid off at last – it meant something to him, Giles, in the depths of his present perplexity.

'D'you know the Dawsons at all?' Scawen asked.

'My wife knows them better than I. And her cousin Sibylla better still. She's a great friend of Tamara Dawson.'

'Ah yes – Mrs Johnson. I confess I was surprised not to see *her* here this morning.'

'Were you?' Giles asked. 'Well *that* surprises me. Or are you joking? You know she and Petifer are at daggers drawn.'

Scawen chuckled. 'That's what I meant. I'm sure nine out of ten people in that crowd came because they fully expected his car to explode, or fail to start, or fall to bits, or something. That's what I thought would have drawn her.'

'Only if you could have guaranteed it,' Giles said. 'As a matter of fact, she'd arranged some weeks ago to spend this Fri-to-Mon over in Falmouth with Mr Jago.'

'Ah!'

Did his pace falter? Giles could not be sure. As a lawyer of course, he'd had a lifetime's training at suppressing his surprise. 'She and her children, of course,' he added.

Now Scawen did reveal his surprise. 'Of course,' he said, looking somewhat askance at Giles for thinking the qualification might be necessary.

'Well . . . Jago has a certain reputation,' Giles pointed out in his own defence. Inwardly he was rubbing his hands with glee. By no stretch of the imagination could he have hoped to broach this subject directly.

Scawen thought the matter over before he said, '*Had* a certain reputation, surely. The man's now in his dotage – like me!' Then, apropos nothing in particular, he added, 'Adam Johnson was his partner in the Ponsharden Boatyard, of course. My wife still has a little money in that venture, you know.'

Even at the time it struck Giles as such an astonishing thing for a cautious man like Scawen to let slip that it could not possibly be accidental. The old lawyer wanted to tell him something – and this was his idea of a suitable opening. 'I didn't know that,' he responded. 'I look over the books for Mrs Johnson, as it happens – ever since her husband died. As you probably know. But, of course, the source of the capital doesn't show in them.'

'Partnerships are the strangest institutions,' Scawen mused aloud. 'They depend so much on *absolute* trust. One has no way of saying, "Here is the limit of my personal commitment." One is either in it to the hilt.' He tapped his forehead. 'Here as much as anywhere. Or one gets right out of it.'

'Ah!' The obvious inference of the man's words was a warning that Sibylla ought to take care over her inherited partnership with Daniel Jago. Giles didn't for one moment believe that was Scawen's intention, but he had to pretend he did – or show that he knew the lawyer was hinting at something much more personal. 'I've wondered from time to time, you know – whether to advise Sibylla to offer to let Jago buy her out. It's not that I believe he'd cheat her out of anything in the regular way, but boatbuilding's an up-and-down sort of trade . . .'

'Don't I know it!' Scawen put in.

'And with his back to the wall . . . well, it'd be only

human for him to put his own interests first. Especially as Mrs Johnson is well provided for in other ways.'

They paused to let a nursemaid with a pram out of a shop. Scawen did not immediately start to walk again; instead he fixed his gaze on Giles and said, 'Believe me, Curnow, in my opinion Daniel Jago would sell his house, his boats, his very *soul*, rather than see Mrs Johnson go short of a reel of button thread!'

It was such an exaggerated reassurance that Giles could only stare. Then Scawen smiled and added, 'She and her children, of course!'

Giles, hearing the deliberate echo of his earlier words, laughed and repaid the compliment: 'Of course!' parodying Scawen's earlier surprise at the same afterthought.

The lawyer pointed at the tobacconist's shop across the street. 'And here is the first of my errands,' he said. 'What do the French say? "*Tout casse . . . tout lasse . . . tout passe!*" My wife's favourite motto.'

Giles offered a paraphrase: 'In the end nothing matters, eh?'

'No no!' Scawen looked shocked. 'It means patience conquers all!'

'I thought that was supposed to be love. *Amor vincit omnia*. No?'

Scawen shrugged and turned to go. 'Same thing, perhaps,' he said.

Sibylla (*and* – as both Giles and Vosper Scawen had solemnly pointed out to each other – her children) returned from their visit to Uncle Daniel's just in time for lunch on the Monday before Christmas, which was a week later than had originally been planned. As

Sibylla explained: 'Daniel's such good fun, and the children are so fond of him – and he dotes on them, of course – and they love messing about in the boat-yard . . .' The list would have meandered on for some time if both Giles and Laura had not assured her that, although she and the children had been sorely missed by all at Chynoweth, not the slightest offence had been taken at her extended absence and they were delighted it had all gone so well.

Reassured by this, Sibylla passed immediately to her next anxiety – her need to visit Billy Dancey at Parc-an-Dour. She looked out of the window and said, 'Oh dear, it gets dark so early these days . . .'

'Winter solstice today,' Giles put in. 'If we had the courage of our agnosticism, my dear, *this* is the day we'd celebrate.'

Laura pulled out her watch and said there were masses of things she still hadn't bought for the holiday – and also she wanted a word with Elizabeth Troy before she left.

Sibylla looked up sharply. 'Where is she going?'

'They. Jimmy's going, too. Apparently, they always take the train to London on Christmas Day. They have the entire carriage practically to themselves and the food in the restaurant car is superb, she says. Why? D'you want to see her, too?'

'How long will they be away?'

'Until early January. She says you can haggle the prices in the shops right down, after Christmas.'

'How millionaires hang on to their money!' Giles commented. 'It's a wonder our friend next door doesn't go with them.'

Sibylla ignored him. 'We could go and join them – after Christmas,' she suggested with some excitement.

'You've only just come back from London,' Laura objected.

'That was in *June!*' her cousin protested. 'Years ago!'

Laura smiled and glanced shyly at Giles. 'It's a thought, isn't it. It really is years since I've been to London. And if it's true about everything being much cheaper in January . . ."

Giles shrugged. 'You don't need my leave to go, my dear.'

'Why don't you come too?' she suggested. 'It's just as many years since you took any proper time off. We can go to the Opera. And look at *all* the motor-car showrooms.'

'Aha!' he pounced. 'Now we come to the nub of it!'

'Well!' She pouted. 'Are we never going to buy a motor now – simply because Whole-cup-half-full has bought one?' She giggled suddenly and turned to Sibylla. 'You should have seen them last Wednesday, when we had that snow! Did you get snow in Falmouth?'

'No. Sleet.'

'Pity. That would've been even better. They set off to do the marketing in Helston . . .'

'Who?'

'Who d'you think! Whole-cup-half-full and Miss Sweet of course – proud as peacocks. Him at the wheel, her in the back, dipping her head right and left like gentry. Bright sunshine when they set out. Snowing half a blizzard by the time they came back. And that *pathetic* hood that's supposed to stretch over the back seat is worse than useless – especially in snow . . .'

Giles noted how Laura's eyes shone as she recounted every little detail of their neighbours' discomfiture – which, in truth, had not been nearly so bad as she was making it seem – and he wondered when he had last seen them shine with such a sparkle over anything to do with him or their children. Had she already forgotten she'd asked him to accompany them to London? Had she also forgotten that he had to say no two or three times, just as a matter of form, before he'd yield and say yes?

'Anyway . . .?' He cut in to remind her.

She halted in mid-story and stared at him blankly.

'London,' he said testily. 'One needs to know the arrangements.'

'Oh well!' She waved her hands about with a vague air of discontent. 'If you refuse to come with us, I suppose Sib and I will just have to make do with each other's company.'

He poked the cruet until it was at the dead centre of the table and absolutely four-square with its edges. 'So be it,' he said.

Laura turned back to her cousin. 'So are you coming to see Elizabeth before they leave?'

Sibylla looked awkwardly at Giles, she being more sensitive to his unhappiness, for once, than Laura. 'I'd love to,' she said, 'but . . . well, I really ought to go and see how Dancey's getting on with the reroofing.' She grinned, trying to cajole Giles out of his ill-humour. 'Didn't I say something very like that before the storm in October? Am I beginning to repeat myself?'

He laughed then and said, 'I've been going up there almost every day, as a matter of fact. He has all the slates back on, but now, of course, he has to plaster the backs of them – and I won't let him do that with these frosts. So I've got him replastering the ceilings in the two main bedrooms. He can light fires there to keep off the chill.'

'Bless you, Giles!' She rose and squeezed his arm on her way to the door. Then, turning to Laura, she said, 'Give Elizabeth Troy my love and say we *may* see her in

London in January. But I really ought to go and look over Parc-an-Dour this afternoon. I can't leave all the donkey work to this good man.'

Giles rose, too. 'I'll go with you. Dancey will only try and talk you into things you shouldn't permit.'

She saw the double entendre that he had missed and turned to stare at her cousin with wide open eyes and a shocked smile. Laura laughed. 'Actually,' she admitted, 'I only married him for that lovely innocence. Don't do anything to spoil it, will you!'

Five minutes later, as Giles and Sibylla trudged up the frost-rimed drive, he said, 'That was an uncalled-for little exchange between the two of you.'

'But it was a *joke!*' She leaned forward to look into his eyes. 'Or are *you* joking now?'

'Gotchar!' He chuckled 'All the same – it's not the sort of joke Laura would have made before . . . I mean since . . .' He tried to think of a time that would not reflect upon Sibylla.

'You mean since I moved under your roof!' she said heavily. 'You see – I *am* a thoroughly bad influence.'

'Heigh-ho!' he said.

After a pause she went on, quite serious now: 'Things are all right between you and Laura, aren't they, Giles? You probably think we talk about *everything* – no secrets between cousins and all that sort of thing. But we don't, you know. She'd *never* talk to me about anything that may happen between you two.'

'Ah – so you think *I* would!' He laughed at the trap she'd unintentionally sprung for herself.

'Yes,' she said unabashed. 'Because I'm really the only person you've got, aren't I.'

'Not at all,' he protested.

'I am. Men don't talk to each other about things that really worry them, do they! Do you?'

'And nor – as you've pointed out – do women. At

least, not you and Laura, it would seem.'

She waited for him to ask what there might be to talk about in any case – which was all the cue she needed; but he was too canny to oblige. She tried again: 'I'll bet you've tried to talk about it to Jimmy Troy – and couldn't say a word . . .'

Giles took an enormous, and for him uncharacteristic, gamble – something he would not have done if his mind hadn't meanwhile been turning over several of the things Vosper Scawen had said to him on their walk from the station that day. 'I've no idea what you're referring to,' he assured her, 'but if you suppose I never talk with anyone on matters of intimate concern, you're wrong. For example, I had a most interesting talk with old Vosper Scawen the other day. The same day Petifer's motor car arrived. The day I bought the field up there. Did you know his wife once almost eloped with Daniel Jago?'

'Stuff and nonsense!' she thundered. 'I'm surprised at you of all people, Giles, for even listening to such bunkum, such utter drivel!'

Her vehemence took him aback – and so, too, did the form of her reply. He had fully expected her to say, 'Did Vosper Scawen tell you that?' – which would have been the response of ninety-nine out of every hundred other people.

But not Sibylla!

Now why? That was surely very interesting.

Similar thoughts must have been going through her mind, too – for she now tried hastily to retrieve the situation. She dug him in the ribs and laughed. 'You're still joking, aren't you! And I fell for it! As if Vosper Scawen would ever admit such a thing to you, even if it were true – which, as I say, it's not. Daniel Jago's had more guiltless babies fostered on him, and more broken hearts laid at his door, than he's had days and nights in which to . . . you know what I mean – father the babies and break the hearts in question.'

'I wonder why?' Giles mused, trying now to probe her responses more delicately.

'Because of his father's reputation. Now he really *was* that sort of man. And if you want to know some *real* scandal about the Scawens, I can tell you that Kinghorn Jago *was* Jane Scawen's real father. The story that he and her mother were stopped from eloping isn't true. They actually did elope. Got almost to Bristol, in fact. They were prevented from marrying but baby Jane was already on the way by then. That's Kinghorn Jago for you. But *Daniel* is a gentleman. He'd never behave in that fashion.'

'Not now he's in his dotage,' Giles agreed.

'He's not in . . .' Sibylla began to say quite heatedly. But then she broke off – making Giles turn and look at her sharply – and said in a much fonder tone, 'Yes, you're right. In his dotage. Yes . . .' A strange, almost indulgent smile parted her lips.

'I suppose,' Giles went on casually, 'it was just his misfortune to have been born to a father with a reputation like that, *and* to be so devilish handsome himself.'

'Oh, really?' Sibylla was as offhand as could be. 'Would you say he's a handsome man, then?'

'*Was* handsome, then – and a bachelor, into the bargain. Devilish bad luck, that!'

'I suppose he was handsome,' Sibylla said, as if the notion had never crossed her mind before. 'I've only ever known him as Adam's partner – and more lately, of course, as a very dear friend.'

They arrived at the gate and looked up and down the empty road. 'No sensible person is out in this weather,' he said. Then, turning to her with a rueful smile, added, 'Now we've got *that* out of the way, I'll say yes,

I admit it – you are one of the very few people I *could* talk to about . . . things that burden me. And yes, there are one or two matters I would very much welcome your opinion on.'

She turned pale. 'To do with you and Laura?'

'Yes. Let's walk on, shall we? About me and Laura. But the thing is, d'you see – would you feel a traitress if you just happened never to mention to her any conversation we might have? It's asking a lot, I know, but if I thought you might be passing on things that I say . . .'

'I'd never do that unless you asked it.'

He shook his head. 'That's not my point. If I thought you were, then the temptation to use you as a mere message carrier between me and her would become irresistible. And really, you know, I'd value your help far more for what *you* are.'

'And what am I?' she asked with a dismissive laugh.

'Quite an impressive person, in my view,' he replied quietly. 'You've weathered a most grievous loss with wonderful dignity, and you've emerged from it greater in stature . . . greater in every way. You know Laura better than anyone, perhaps – certainly better than I do. You love her, too, which is not always the case within families. And I flatter myself you're also quite fond of me . . .'

'Giles! Stop, for heaven's sake!' Laughing with embarrassment she took his arm and butted her forehead against his shoulder. 'You know I'm more than fond of you.' Then, after a pause, she added, 'Did you honestly mean all that?'

'Every word of it, Sibylla. I promise I won't embarrass you by repeating it, but I wanted you to understand that it's no frivolous request I'm making. It's not a whim.'

She held on to his arm, afraid to let go in case it seemed like a rejection. And anyway, it was comforting in the December chill. 'I'll listen, if you like,' she offered. 'I'm quite good at that, though I say so myself. But I don't know about giving advice.'

He was silent awhile, and then uttered a small, self-deprecating laugh. 'Now I don't know where to begin!'

'Try the day Culdrose Farm was sold. You see why I may be reluctant to give advice!'

Giles began hesitantly. 'You're right in one way, of course. My present doubts and tribulations do, indeed, date back to the moment that man returned to Cornwall. But they don't concern him, not really. Nor Laura, either – if that's what you're thinking. They concern *me* – the sort of man I've discovered myself to be.'

'Ah!' She sighed. 'I ought to have known it wouldn't be straightforward – not with you.'

They turned off the Lizard road, up the lane that led to Parc-an-Dour. 'What d'you mean?' he asked.

'Well, Giles – there's no point in having a conversation of this kind unless we're both going to be completely frank. Agreed?'

'Of course.'

'Then I have to tell you that I don't think you understand yourself at all. I don't believe you ever have. And, if Maurice Petifer hadn't come back from the dead, I don't think you ever would have.'

'Oh,' he said bleakly.

She laughed and squeezed his arm. 'But that's your strength, man – not your weakness! It's what has enabled you to take a couple of grocery shops and build them into the biggest wholesaling business in Cornwall. I often used to compare you and Adam when I saw you together. You were such opposites – which is why you got on so well together. Adam was a lovely man, a wonderful man . . .'

'Absolutely. I couldn't agree more. He . . .'

'No, let me finish. He was a splendid man, but he needed someone like Daniel to help him make a success of the boatyard.'

'Just as Daniel needed him.'

'Indeed! As he has discovered these last two years! Still – I hope that's all settled now. And that, by the way, was my reason for staying on the extra week.'

'Ah – I thought there was more to it than indulging the children.'

'Yes – we've found a new manager who can supply all those qualities Adam had in such abundance. But I'm straying from the point – which is that Adam *knew* himself . . . was always aware of what he was doing and why . . . never surprised himself.' She poked her head forward and challenged him. 'I'll bet you've surprised yourself more than once since Petifer returned!'

Giles fanned his face ironically. 'You may say so, indeed! I always thought myself such a *civilized* man!'

'Ye-e-es?' She drew the word out on a questioning sort of laugh.

He stared at her in amazement. 'You mean you don't think I am?'

'Not remotely!' Her laughter rose in a crescendo.

'Oh!' His surprise winded him.

They turned in at the main gate of Parc-an-Dour. 'You're a pirate, Giles. A privateer. A freebooter. Did you play rugby at school?'

'Of course.'

'I'll bet you played on the wing. You took the ball and ran eh? No shoulders-down and push with the common pack for you!'

He stared uncomfortably at the house. 'And if I did? That doesn't prove anything.'

'Ah! So I'm right, then!'

'Anyway,' he grumbled, 'you can't be a pirate in this day and age. You'd end up in prison.'

'Not all pirates – only those who don't realize times have changed. But don't seize on that one word as if it said everything about you.'

'What, then?'

'No – this is going all wrong. *I'm* not meant to be telling you about you. You're supposed to be telling me. So go on – what have you learned about yourself since Petifer came on the scene?'

'D'you know, that's three times you've called him by his proper name – without a sneer – in the last five minutes. What happened to Whole-cup-half-full?'

'This is too serious for little games, Giles.'

'Ah! So you admit it usually is a matter of "little games"?'

'Get on with it! You're using any excuse not to answer me. What surprises have you discovered?'

He swallowed hard and replied, 'That I am a . . . pirate – to accept your description. A man of intense violence, anyway. If I thought I could "get away with murder," as the saying has it – I jolly well would! I'm not joking, now. I meet Petifer about the place – as one is bound to do from time to time, of course – and we chat away like two neighbours ought . . . I mean, I know people's eyes are on us. Everyone's just hoping for some sign of ill will between us. You should have seen us up at the station on the day his Mercedes arrived! He offered Laura and the children a lift . . .'

'I heard all about it, my dear. Mrs Laity – who comes in and cleans for Daniel – she couldn't wait to tell me!'

'And there I was, smiling and waving as they drove away – but in my imagination I was pulling out his fingernails, boiling him in oil . . . stretching him on the rack . . . things I'm so ashamed of!'

Sibylla began to laugh. He asked why. 'Oh!' She waved him away. 'I do *much* worse things to him than that!'

'What?'

She lowered her head and shook it vigorously. 'I couldn't possibly tell you a thing like that!'

They arrived at the house at that most inconvenient – or, perhaps, most convenient – point in their discussion; and for the next half-hour or so they were, perforce, engaged in the tedious business of inspecting the builder's progress and refusing him permission, yet again, to plaster the slates to their battens while there was the slightest chance of a frost.

Dancey then packed up his tools in disgust, saying that in that case there was nothing more he could do there. He took his two assistants with him, 'to work for them as appreciate me.'

'Like the landlord of the Blue Anchor,' Giles murmured immediately after the man had gone.

They stood at the window over the entrance and watched the three of them trot down the drive. Giles added, 'Nothing but a cheery taproom fire and the prospect of a foaming tankard would make those three run like that!'

'Talking of a cheery fire . . .' Sibylla said brightly. And she set about gathering bits of scrap wood, old lath, battens, and paper and soon got the embers of Dancey's fire into a fine old blaze. 'There may be some bread and jam down in the larder,' she added. 'I know – let's make some toast, eh?'

Ten minutes later he licked each of his fingers free of the jam and wiped them in his handkerchief and said, 'The bread was not the freshest – as you admitted yourself. And the jam was decidedly granular. Why, then, does it taste ten times better than fresh bread, perfectly toasted, at some stuffy At Home?'

She took his handkerchief from him, wrapped it round her finger, and offered it to him with the words, 'Lick for Mama!'

He obeyed.

She wiped some jam out of the cleft between his lip and chin, saying, 'Because stolen fruits are always sweeter, my dear.'

He frowned. 'Stolen?' The firelight played on her cheeks and sparkled in her eyes.

She laughed. 'Yes. We stole them from Dancey.' She passed him back his handkerchief.

'Ha ha!' He took it and wrapped a clean portion around his finger. 'Lick for Papa,' he said.

But he did not wet it on her tongue. Instead, he brushed her cheek with his knuckles. 'Firelight becomes you, Sibylla,' he murmured.

'Go on, then,' she said, closing her eyes and raising her lips toward him. She held her breath.

He leaned across the few inches that separated them and kissed her – a gentle brushing of their lips.

He had not kissed any other woman since marrying Laura. It was the oddest sensation, at once familiar and yet . . . excitingly novel.

It was a very gentle kiss. If she had responded to it, he would have kissed her again, with more passion. He could feel it building up inside him, like a head of steam. But she did not respond – except insofar as she did not withdraw her lips. Instead she opened her eyes and stared into his – such cool, intelligent, knowing eyes she had!

Eventually it was he who broke that delicious contact between them.

'Yes, well . . .' she said, giving him a dispirited little smile. 'Now we know *that's* no answer – not for either of us – don't we!'

She saw the sadness in his eyes and mistook it for a

painful acknowledgement of the truth in what she had just said. She gave him a warmer smile then, and a quick, effusive kiss on the cheek. 'I'm not *playing* with you, Giles, my dear. Honestly. But that's been building up between us for a long time. If you're honest, you'll agree. And so we had to get it out of the way before anything else. We had to prove it's no kind of answer at all. We had to put it behind us. And now I really do want to help – in any *real* way I can.'

The firelight still played on her cheek and danced in her eyes. He reached forward and tucked a curl behind her ear. It was going to be a long campaign. 'Good!' he said.

It looked as if someone had exploded a small bomb in Elizabeth Troy's bedroom. There were dresses she might wear, dresses she certainly would wear (unless she changed her mind during the next three days), dresses she certainly would not wear (unless . . . et cetera), and dresses she would *never* wear again but wouldn't pass on because one never knew, did one. Laura surveyed the carnage and said, 'It's hopeless! You can't possibly reduce this to any semblance of order in only three days, Elizabeth.'

'Oh, believe me, I can! I'm always like this. Jimmy used to threaten to take two hotel rooms and two cabins on the ships we sailed in – one for us to actually use and one for me to make my chaos in. But you come back the day after tomorrow and you'll be amazed. Whoever thought of the luggage-in-advance service was one of the great benefactors of mankind. It concentrates the mind wonderfully to have to get it all ready a whole week before you travel.'

She hurled yet another dress toward the chaos and said, 'Oh, let's leave it for now. My head's in a whirl. I'll come back to it later, all refreshed. There was a time, you know, when I used to dread the very thought of going to London.'

'At the time of the Pallas Disaster Appeal?'

Elizabeth looked at her sharply. 'No. During all that nasty litigation. What made you think of the disaster appeal?'

Laura smiled. 'I thought it would surprise you. I was there the night you spoke, you know – at the Central Hall, Westminster. You were wonderful, I thought. I was so envious!'

'Good heavens, why?'

'Oh, I could never stand up in front of hundreds of people like that and speak.'

Elizabeth smiled fondly at the memory. 'I never thought I could, either. Courtenay Rodda arranged it all, of course. He said not a word to me until just before the meeting – sprang it on me. I could've killed him at the time but it was for the best.'

'He spirited you away quickly enough afterward, too!'

Laura could not swear to it but she was almost sure Elizabeth blushed. Her reply, however, was smooth enough: 'Yes, well, if you'd been up and about early enough the following morning, you'd have seen me walking down Grand Junction Road, Paddington, and into Hyde Park with David Troy. And make what you like of *that*, too!' She paused a moment and then gave a reminiscent little laugh.

'What?' Laura prompted.

'Oh, catching David out there so early in the morning. I thought he was being so romantic – hanging around under my balcony all night like Romeo, you know. And actually he had the same dirty mind as other people had about me and Courtenay – I name no names, mind.' She smiled innocently at the ceiling. 'In one of our arguments, after we got married, he accused me of deliberately *taking* him on that walk so as to leave the coast clear for Courtenay to make good his escape!' The humour went out of her then and she concluded, rather sadly, 'I hate it when people take something like that – something that, to you, is very romantic – and twist it for some ugly purpose, don't you?'

'Yes,' Laura agreed, slightly bemused. It sounded like a veiled rebuke yet she could think of nothing she had done to merit it.

'It's cold up here.' Elizabeth rubbed her hands vigorously. 'Let's go down. It's almost time for tea.' As she led the way out onto the landing she added, 'I'm slightly surprised not to see your cousin with you this afternoon. Is she still not back from Falmouth?'

'No, she came back just before lunchtime. She said the *children* adore it so much over there and their Uncle Daniel spoils *them* dreadfully.'

Elizabeth looked at her with an amused eye. 'You sound skeptical.'

'I think she's the one who enjoys it most.'

'I'm *sure* she does!' Elizabeth said with heavy emphasis and then, putting a hand to her brow and beating it in self-accusation, added, 'See! I'm doing it now. I expect it's nothing more than – oh, something quite light and romantic.'

'What is?' Laura asked, genuinely puzzled.

'Nothing, dear. It's quite wrong to start such hares, even if one is obviously joking.'

Laura's bewilderment increased. 'You must think me terribly obtuse, dear, but . . . are you hinting at something between . . . surely not . . . Daniel Jago and . . .?'

Elizabeth stared at her, as if she thought Laura might be pulling her leg. 'You mean it never crossed your mind?' she asked.

'Crossed my mind? Daniel Jago and Sibylla?' Laura felt winded. 'But Adam and Daniel were partners!'

'Hah!' Elizabeth's laugh carried a trace of bitterness. 'So were David Troy and I!'

'I mean business partners, not partners in marriage.'

Elizabeth seemed annoyed at herself for having spoken at all. 'As I say – I'm now doing the very thing I said I hated only a moment ago. Anyway, why isn't she here? Didn't you tell her Jimmy and I are going away for Christmas?'

'Oh, I'm coming to that.' They arrived at the drawing room door and Elizabeth ushered her in with a flourish. 'Ah, what a lovely fire!' Laura continued as they advanced toward the crackling blaze, hands already outstretched before her.

'Well?' Elizabeth prompted when they arrived at the hearth.

'Before I tell you that,' Laura replied, 'let's just clear up the previous matter – what you were joking about – Daniel Jago and Sibylla.'

'It was only a joke, dear,' Elizabeth replied testily. 'And not in very good taste, as I admitted.'

'But is it just something that crossed *your* mind or have you heard other people joke about it, too?'

'You mean is my mind uniquely dirty! Well, of course I'm not the only one to remark on it. Are you honestly saying it never crossed your mind, either? She goes off to Falmouth half a dozen times a year – if not more? And always stays with . . .'

'But Daniel Jago must be getting on for seventy!

Sibylla's less than half his age. It's absurd! Anyway, they're partners in the boatyard, so of course she stays with him. I think *I'd* be more suspicious if she didn't – if she made a deliberate point of *not* staying with him.'

'Yes,' Elizabeth said soothingly. 'I quite agree with you – it is absurd. The very idea!'

'But people obviously have passed comment on it.'

'People! They have nothing better to do. What were you going to tell me, anyway – something to do with Sibylla?'

'And with me.'

The maid came in with the tea.

'Cucumber sandwiches,' Elizabeth said offhandedly. 'You don't mind, I hope?'

'In December?'

'Yes. Jimmy's so proud of his heated glasshouse. We have cucumbers coming out of our ears! He's gone for a drive with Maurice Petifer, by the way. They should be back at any minute.' She glanced at the clock on the mantelpiece.

'Anyway,' Laura said, determined not to be balked a third time, 'Sibylla and I are arranging to travel up to London together after Christmas. We'll stay with our Uncle Drogo in Fitzroy Square, of course. But won't it be fun! We can go round all the shops together – and dining out and the theatre.'

'Ah!' Elizabeth said awkwardly.

'What's the matter? You haven't changed your mind? I mean, all that packing going on upstairs – it *is* for London still?'

'Oh, yes.' Elizabeth took in a deep breath. 'It's just that Maurice Petifer happens to be joining us, too. Er . . . I don't know whether that makes any difference to you?'

Despite Elizabeth's disparaging comments on the over-supply of cucumber at Liston House, the two women devoured the sandwiches with gusto. The last morsel had gone by the time they heard Maurice Petifer's car turn in at the gate. Guiltily Elizabeth handed the empty salver to the maid, telling her to cut fresh replacements as fast as she could. The car's motor expired with a splendid backfire, crowned by the delighted laughter of the two men.

'Boys!' Elizabeth said with a jaded, tolerant smile.

'Giles would be just the same,' Laura assured her. 'All one needs do is mention the words *motor car* and he loses twenty years – the wrong twenty, unfortunately.'

'Yes, I'm surprised he's not coming to London with you and Sibylla. The chance to inspect just about every motor car ever made is not to be sneezed at, surely? Wouldn't he change his mind?'

'He says he can't spare the time – which is true, I suppose.'

Elizabeth grinned. 'Perhaps he'll think again when he hears Maurice will be there.'

'I'd hate *that!*' Laura said vehemently. 'If that's the only reason he'd change his mind, think how dishonoured I'd feel!'

'You mean you won't tell him?'

Laura looked uncomfortably away. 'No, I don't suppose I will. I say, those men are rather a long time coming indoors.'

'I expect they're grovelling under the bonnet. D'you think the smell of engine oil is like opium? What about Sibylla? Will you tell her? It might be fun if you didn't! I won't give you away – I mean, I'll say I forgot to mention it to you, if you like.'

'Why should it be fun not to tell her?'

'Well, she does dramatize it all rather grossly, don't you think? She *vaunts* it – if there is such a word . . .

her much-vaunted aversion to poor old Maurice.'

'I'm sure she feels it quite genuinely.'

'Oh she *feels* it, right enough,' Elizabeth agreed. 'But then, just think how unreliable *feelings* can be!'

The remark puzzled Laura; after all, what could anyone do with an aversion *except* feel it? However, their conversation was interrupted at that moment by the sound of the car starting up again outside. Elizabeth hastened to the window and was just in time to see it setting off down the drive once more; and this time it was travelling at speed, dispensing with the red flag and the man to wave it. Instead, Jimmy was standing up in the well between the front and back seats, holding a handbell, and ringing it continuously with all the vigour he could muster.

'What new game is this?' Laura asked in the same jaded tone Elizabeth had used earlier.

But Elizabeth made no reply. Laura saw she'd gone white as a sheet. 'What is it?' she asked

Elizabeth turned and hastened toward the door. 'I've just had the most dreadful premonition.'

She was still two or three paces from the door when it opened. Hinks, who had driven Laura down to Liston House, stood irresolute in the doorway, staring from one lady to the other. The anguish in his eyes was enough to let them know something dreadful had happened.

'What is it?' Laura asked him.

'If you please, ma'am, it's the little boy . . .'

'Trevanion!' Elizabeth went to him and grasped his arm. 'Say it, man! What's happened to him?'

'I don't believe 'tis too serious, ma'am,' he replied unhappily. 'But he've lost his senses.'

'What d'you mean – lost his senses?'

'What has happened? Just tell us what *happened!*'

'He got kicked by a horse, out in the stable, ma'am.'

'Oh, my little boy!' Elizabeth ran past him, distraught, forgetting her hat, her cape, her outdoor shoes.

Laura did not immediately follow 'Was it the noise of the motor car?' she asked him under her breath. 'That loud bang?'

He nodded unhappily.

'Well listen – don't say a word about that to Mrs Troy, d'you understand?' Laura recalled how Jimmy (and Maurice, to be sure – but Jimmy above all) had laughed. He'd never forgive himself for that laugh if Trevanion were left with some permanent injury.

'I believe I do understand you, ma'am,' Hinks replied.

'Is our carriage ready?'

'Yes, that's the other thing I came to say, ma'am.'

'Good. Go back outside and tell Mrs Troy I'm on my way with her hat and cape. You drive round and I'll meet you at the front. I suppose they've taken him up to Doctor Thomas?'

'I heard them say the cottage hospital, ma'am.'

'Right. We'll go there. And remember – not a *word* to Mrs Troy about the bang from Mr Petifer's car being the cause of it.'

She snatched up capes, bonnets, and outdoor shoes at random, knowing they both took much the same size in clothes; she was standing on the drive, waiting for the coach, well before it came lumbering out of the stable yard.

'Let's stay calm!' Elizabeth said as soon as Laura was safely inside. 'There's nothing to be gained by going to pieces,'

'Of course not. And you heard Hinks say he didn't think it was as bad as it looked. He's seen a lot of mishaps with horses in his time, I'm sure.'

'Trevanion's so frail, though.'

'Nonsense!' Laura sounded quite cross. 'He may have the build and bones of an elf but he has the constitution of an ox. What about that time when he nearly drowned in Australia – you remember you told us? Didn't the doctor there say he'd never seen a quicker recovery? And what about when he and young Maurice were four and they fell in that patch of stinging nettles? Maurice had a rash for a week but you couldn't see a mark on Trevanion next day. No, my dear – frail is not the word to use about that young fellow!'

And so it went all the way up Meneage Street to the cottage hospital – Elizabeth putting up Aunt-Sally worries for Laura to knock down with her compassionate scorn. When they arrived at their destination – which, as its name implied, had no more than a dozen beds – the day nurse came out of the casualty surgery and gave Elizabeth a well-practised smile; it simultaneously conveyed the gravity of the situation and the hopeful prognosis she and the doctor had already formed. She led her at once into the surgery.

'I'll wait out here,' Laura told her. Elizabeth gave no sign of hearing the promise.

Laura turned and gave a little start, for there at the window, staring out into the last of the twilight, stood Maurice Petifer. 'I didn't see you there,' she said.

He, too, gave no sign of hearing her.

She looked about and saw they were alone together. She crossed the room to join him. Her boots seemed to make the most enormous noise on the hard linoleum, no matter how delicately she set them down. An air of unreality pervaded everything around her.

'It wasn't your fault, Maurice,' she assured him. 'Horses have been kicking people ever since they were invented.'

'I just had to show off!' he murmured bitterly.

'You didn't see the nurse's face just now. She obviously doesn't think it's as bad as it looks. And Hinks, too . . .'

'Let's give the ladies a fright, I said!'

'And Jimmy agreed, I'll bet? If I know him, he was the one who suggested it first.'

Maurice gave an uncomfortable shrug.

She pounced. 'There you are! If you're to blame, then so is he – but actually neither of you are – I mean, is!'

'I can't bear it in here,' he said. There was an edge of desperation in his voice.

She looked around indecisively. 'I can't leave . . . I promised Elizabeth I'd wait.'

'We can just walk in the garden outside,' he suggested. 'Just round and round the lawn or something. I'm suffocating in here. Carbolic . . . and . . .' He shivered.

They stepped out by the front door and onto the close-cut lawn, already crisp with frost. After the light of the waiting room it now seemed almost pitch black outside. 'They say we may have a white Christmas,' he remarked.

It was such a clumsy attempt at conversation that it hung like lead between them, making it impossible *not* to talk about the only fear that possessed them both.

And it was a measure of Laura's terror that her next comment was: 'It is one's greatest nightmare, of course: to lose one's child. Children are so vulnerable.'

Maurice stopped dead and stared at her, though the lighted windows behind her made her expression unreadable; she, however, could see the anguish in his. And then, of course, she would have given all she owned just to be allowed to take those words back. She was about to apologize, to explain that she had been so preoccupied with Trevanion's fate that it had driven everything else from her mind, when he murmured, 'So – Elizabeth didn't tell you!'

Cowardice, or at least an unwillingness to admit she had spoken those words despite what she knew, made her say, 'Tell me what?'

He sighed. 'In my spineless way, I rather hoped she would.' He turned from her and took a step into the darkness beyond the small carpet of light cast from the window.

She, more hesitantly, followed, now committed to the fiction that she knew nothing of his tragedy. 'What?' she prompted.

'I wanted you to know – and Sibylla, I suppose, to be honest – but I didn't want to be the one to tell you.' He turned suddenly to face her, though now his face was little more than a grey blur in the gloom. A thin, crescent moon was setting behind him, over the dark whaleback of Sithney Common Hill. 'If I tell you now, I want you to understand that it's not to gain your sympathy.'

He took several more steps into the dark, leaving her to follow the sound of his voice and his crisp tread in the frosted grass. 'The thing is, you see, I got married when I was out in the Cape – an Afrikander girl called Sarie . . .'

'Maurice!' she interrupted, thinking she could not sustain the deception much longer.

'We had a baby boy – Jannie. He died. Sarie, too. They both . . . died. Four years ago.'

'Oh . . . Maurice!' she whispered, afraid to speak aloud in case her voice gave her away. The tears were already flowing.

He drew a deep breath and said, 'I'm over it now. But that's why I can't bear places like *that!*'

He raised his hand to point to the hospital but, misjudging her distance from the softness of her whisper, struck her more than a glancing blow on the elbow. 'Oh, I'm sorry!' he exclaimed, diverting all his agony into an incident too trivial to sustain it. 'I can't even do the simplest thing right!' He began to rub her elbow clumsily.

She put her arms around him then and hugged him tight. 'It didn't hurt,' she said. 'It wasn't *that* which hurt.'

He just stood there, tense and motionless, letting her hug him but making no response.

He hardly felt like Maurice, she realized bitterly; indeed, he hardly felt like a person at all – just an unreachable monolith, wrapped up inside heaven only knew how many layers of motoring clothes.

'I've told you before,' he said. 'I don't want your sympathy.' But his voice was thin, close to capitulating to grief.

Still she clung to him, not knowing why – or knowing full well why, but not wanting to admit it.

He began to shiver. If he grew any more tense, she thought, he would surely snap in two. 'Maurice?' she whispered, turning her face toward him and pressing her lips to his neck.

'Laura? Don't!' he pleaded, also in a whisper. His hands grappled hesitantly with her arms, trying – not even half-heartedly – to pull them off him. Soon they gave up the struggle and began to caress her there instead . . . then up to her shoulders, to her shoulder blades, pulling her tightly to him now.

She did not realize she had been holding her breath until she heard it escaping in one long sigh. Then, afraid to break contact with him, she nuzzled and grazed her lips upward, over the line of his jaw, hard enough to feel the bone and flesh through his beard, and so onward across his cheek to within an inch of his lips. But she left him to make that final move . . .

begging him with a little moan to make it soon.

And he, as much a prisoner of his body as she was of hers, had no choice but to bend and press his lips in a kiss for which both he and she had hungered fourteen long years.

Familiarity with Giles and the warm but perfunctory kisses of a comfortable marriage had dulled her perception. She had forgotten the sweetness, the strength, the very taste of a stranger's lips on hers – and that baffling mixture of opposites it provoked in her: a desire to repel the invader at the same time as yield to him. Fight or flee? Her stomach hollowed at the impossibility of that choice. Nerves that had slumbered fourteen years came awake as if they had merely nodded off five minutes earlier. She thought of Sleeping Beauty. Her joy at what she was doing – and her terror at doing it – were so overwhelming she almost swooned in his arms.

'No!' he exclaimed suddenly, straightening up and pushing her from him. 'No!' He blundered into a young hazel tree, showering them both in ice crystals. Her eyes, growing accustomed to the night, could now make out the dark reticule of its branches against the starry sky. 'That's why I said I don't want your help.' He made it sound like an accusation. 'I don't want your sympathy, either.'

'Sympathy?' she echoed in a voice close to despair. 'D'you think that's what this is? Sympathy!' She put all the scorn at her command into the word.

For a while he said nothing; then she heard him murmur, 'Oh God!' He breathed in deeply, in several fits of shivers, and then let it out in one explosive rush.

'Maurice?' she said cajolingly, trying to inject some note of lightness into their situation.

'No!' he replied, making the word sound almost like a plea. Then, more fiercely: 'No, no, no . . .'

The branches above her shivered. She realized he

was banging his forehead against the trunk. His motion helped define him, for when he stood still he melted into the dark of the shrubbery around. She went to his side and gripped his arm fiercely. 'Stop it!' she hissed.

Panting, he rested his forehead against the tree and said, 'What have we done?'

But she did not want to speak – not of what they had done, nor of what they had *not* done, nor of what they might yet do. She did not want mere words to weasel their way between him and her at this particular moment. She peeled off her glove and raised her bare fingers to his cheek. 'Maurice!' she whispered as she stroked him there, from the ridge of his cheekbone to the angle of his jaw.

Nerves that had died in her fingers came back to life, too; there were new sensations in every part of her body. Or forgotten sensations. The forgotten sensations of Maurice . . . the feelings that he and he alone could awaken in her.

Then she realized it was not her feelings that had forgotten him but she herself; her feelings had merely slumbered, awaiting their moment – awaiting *this* moment. And now it had come they were not about to let it slip from their grasp once more.

'No,' he repeated, but there was no strength left in the word. Once again it was the feeblest plea.

'Kiss me?' she whispered, drawing even closer to him. Now her eyes were so accustomed to the starlight she could see him clench his eyes.

'If I do . . .' he began. His inability to complete the thought made it seem like a threat.

'I know,' she assured him as she slipped her body between him and the tree.

Again their lips met and again she yielded to that baffling contest between repulsion and surrender. But now the balance was tipped the other way: The urge to repel the invader was already dwindling fast.

When Giles and Sibylla arrived back at Chynoweth they were surprised to find that Laura was still out. Then a maid told them what the postman had told her when he made the second afternoon delivery – as a result of which they both hastened out again at once, making for the cottage hospital. Sibylla headed for the drive but Giles said they could cut across the children's paddock, the uppermost corner of which shared a boundary with the hospital garden.

She followed him with some reluctance, complaining that the word 'boundary' was a trifle vague, and adding that she wasn't going to go climbing through any old hedges in the dark at her time of life. He assured her there was a gate – crossing his fingers that it wouldn't be rusted solid at the hinges. Before the children were old enough to have ponies the Curnows had rented the field to the hospital janitor, who kept two cows there for the milk. The gate hadn't been used since then.

'You're not just *saying* that I hope,' Sibylla warned. There was an odd, nervous sort of skittishness in her since what had happened between them – or, perhaps, what had *not* happened between them – up at Chynoweth. It was as if she were trying out variations of her old personality in hope of finding a better fit to the new circumstances.

He made no reply.

'Are you?' she pressed.

'I'm just amazed you could even ask such a question,' he told her then. 'First, when have you ever known me tell a lie about a thing like that? Second, what sort of company have you kept that would trot out falsehoods, just to keep you quiet?'

'Sorry!' She took his arm and giggled. 'You'd be surprised how many people do when it's only women and children they're dealing with.'

'Well, not me,' he assured her.

'No, that's true.' She gave his arm a further reassuring squeeze. 'You're a very dependable man, Giles. Very solid. Very reliable . . .'

'Very dull!' he added.

'Oh no!'

'I sometimes think Laura is of that opinion. Tell me honestly – and since you say you and she never discuss such matters, I suppose I can honourably ask you. I mean, it wouldn't be like asking you to pass on things she's actually said . . .'

'Honourably?' she echoed, interrupting him quite suddenly.

'Yes?' He made a half-question of the word, being surprised at the inquiry in her tone.

'Oh, very well,' she went on, implying it was the last word she'd have chosen.

'Why does that seem to surprise you?' he pressed.

'I'd have thought the gloves came off some time ago. However – what did you want to ask?'

He dropped the topic then but meant to return to it later. 'Can you see your way?' he asked.

'Well enough to avoid . . . that!' And she giggled again as she neatly stepped around a pile of horse droppings. 'Ask away!'

'Well, do you think this is all a bit of a storm in a teacup, really? I mean, Laura and I have had a very smooth marriage – very uneventful. And that's another thing!' He forgot his question and started on a different tack. 'When two people have been married almost fifteen years they develop ways of conveying their wishes and feelings that are peculiar to themselves. Laura knows very well that if she suggests something and I say no, that's never my final word on the subject.'

'Why say it, then?' Sibylla asked sharply.

'I don't know. It was just a sort of habit that started from . . . no, I don't even know that. We've always done it. She suggests something. I say no – or look dubious. She starts giving me good reasons for whatever it is. I say well . . . perhaps. She gives me more reasons. I give in and say yes, jolly good, you've convinced me. Really, I suppose, it's just more *interesting* to do it like that. What could be more boring than for her to say let's do so-and-so and for me to say yes. The end! It's a ritual, that's all I'm saying.'

'And you think Laura has broken this ritual?'

'Yes. About coming to London. *You* noticed it – when she just accepted my no like that.'

'There, there!' Sibylla laughed and made a pantomime of stroking his back. 'What if I were to ask you to come to London with us?'

'No.'

But she could hear the smile in his voice and said seductively, 'We could go round all the motor-car showrooms.'

He sighed. 'I'm not sure I could spare the time.'

She could hear him trying not to laugh.

'I said *we* could go round the showrooms, Giles. I fully intend to buy a motor car, with or without your help. I'm damned if I'm going to let Whole-cup-half-full flaunt his Mercedes all over the place, with no competition from decent people.'

'Well . . .' he chuckled.

'But I would *so* welcome the opinion and advice of a leading expert on absolutely everything from the plastering of roofs to the correct choice of lubrication oil!'

'Heigh-ho!' he exclaimed, giving way to his laughter finally. 'London it is, then!'

Now she turned herself into a cat and snuggled briefly beside him. 'Did I do it properly?'

'I couldn't tell it from the real thing,' he assured her.

She became serious again. 'And now what was your question? You were saying, I think – perhaps even complaining – that your marriage is as calm as a millpond?'

'Yes. I was going to ask if you thought all this Maurice Petifer business was just a storm in a teacup? On a millpond, after all, the smallest ripples could *seem* like mighty waves.'

Like the memory of Sibylla's lips on his, he thought. What was it really? A tiny, momentary lapse – a ripple, if ever there was one. But it sent mighty waves through him that were going to rock the vessel of his soul for some time to come. Laura might not be the only one who found their 'dependable, solid, reliable' marriage a teeny bit dull.

He became aware that she had not responded to his question. 'Mmh?' he prompted.

She sighed. 'D'you really want me to tell you the truth, Giles? Or at least, the truth as I see it?'

'Of course. Why?' He gave a small, apprehensive laugh. 'Is it so desperately grim?'

'That depends. I remember when Adam started playing golf – or after he got quite good at the game – good enough to hit the ball more or less in the direction he wanted. He came home one day and he described a little incident where he'd been just about to hit the ball up onto the green and one of the other fellows warned him about two hikers walking across the links. It annoyed Adam because the hikers were miles away — and miles off his line, too. "But blow me!" he said. 'I went and hit the ball almost straight at 'em!' And you know how he always liked to find a moral in little everyday things like that – and he said this only showed how often we'd avoid mishap if we didn't go looking for it here, there, and everywhere!'

Giles trudged on in silence at her side.

'Does that make sense?' she asked.

'Only too clearly. But the trouble with all those *sensible* things is that one knows jolly well how sensible they are but one still goes and does the opposite. The drunkard knows, as he raises the next glass to his lips – he knows it won't do him any good. Yet still he knocks it back. The embezzler knows he'll be caught one day with his finger in the till. But he goes on stealing, nonetheless.' He drew a deep breath before he added, 'And I know that benign neglect would be far and away my wisest course . . .' He left the corollary unspoken this time.

Sibylla supplied it in a wan little voice that hardly seemed to belong to her: 'But it is so . . . *thrilling* to hate!' Her articulation gained strength on that word. 'Yes! It is the most seductive sport of all – more addictive than drink, more compelling than the zest of successful embezzlement. More . . . than anything . . .' She abandoned words and turned to him, her eyes flashing with light borrowed from the windows at the rear of the hospital, which now were close. 'You know what I mean, don't you! I can tell you do.'

He could not deny it yet he was unwilling to agree aloud.

'Stop!' she said suddenly, gripping his arm and making him stand still and face her.

'What?' he asked after a moment of bewildering silence. It was so frosty they could hear cows chewing the cud two fields away.

'Sometimes everything comes together at once,' she

replied. 'Was there ever a moment like this in your life? Sharp frost like this . . . no moon . . . brilliant stars above . . . crystal-clear sounds. Hear that dog barking? He could be a mile away. I remember a night like this once. I don't know where it was or who I was with or where we were going. But all these things have come together once before in my life.'

'And?' he prompted, not seeing the point.

She hugged herself tight to his arm and shivered, not with the cold. 'Oh, Giles! One day we'll be dead! D'you ever think of that? Moments like these will cease to come together for us – ever again. It's horrible . . . horrible'

Nonplussed, he simply stood there, trying not to trespass upon an emotion that was too fragile for him to grasp. Death had not intruded much into his thoughts as yet; he had only just turned forty.

Then he heard a sound that brought all his senses to the alert at once. It was Petifer's voice, saying the one word, 'No!'

Sibylla drew breath to speak but he put a finger to his lips and then, disentangling his arm from hers, ran tiptoe over the grass toward the front of the hospital, from where the sound had come. The nearer he drew to its source, the more stealthy his movements became, until at last he was stalking like a cat – seeming to grow each leg forward rather than move it.

He saw them at last, silhouetted against one of the lighted windows on the front façade. And after that it was etched in his mind's eye for ever: Laura raised her hand to Maurice Petifer's face; she held a handkerchief between her fingers and with it she wiped his cheeks, first the right, then the left. 'Kiss me again,' Giles heard her say.

Then *blasted* Sibylla found the gate and tore the fabric of the night with the shrieking protests of a pair of long-unused hinges. 'Yoo-hoo, Laura!' she cried. 'Is that you?'

PART THREE

A Natural State

Sir, it is so far from being a natural state
for a man and a woman
to live in a state of marriage,
that we find all the motives that they have
for remaining in that connection,
and all the restraints which civilized society
imposes to prevent separation,
are hardly sufficient to keep them together

Dr Johnson

The Troys, for once, spent Christmas in Helston. It turned out that Trevanion, though badly bruised on his thigh by the kick, and severely concussed in the subsequent fall, had broken nothing and suffered no obvious damage of a permanent kind. He was, however, poorly enough to oblige Elizabeth and Jimmy to postpone their visit to London for a week; so it was not until the following Thursday, the first day of 1903, that they and Maurice Petifer travelled up on the Paddington Corridor Express. The three from Chynoweth took the same train on the following day.

Though the Curnows had met the Troys during that Christmas – in fact, at the meet of the Cury Hunt on Boxing Day – and they had talked briefly of things they planned to do during their visit to London, somehow the fact that Maurice would also be of the party simply hadn't cropped up.

Maurice stayed at the same hotel as the Troys – Earl's, in St James's; Sibylla and the Curnows had booked into Whittaker's, just around the corner in Jermyn Street. Indeed, the two establishments were so close that, when the Curnows were dressing for dinner on the evening of their arrival, Sibylla gave an excited knock on the door that connected her room to Giles and Laura's, calling out, 'Guess what I can see! Is it all right if I come in?'

Laura glanced hastily at Giles, who, though he was decently into his shirt and trousers, was still struggling with his starched front. She was about to tell her cousin to wait a couple of minutes when Giles called out, 'Enter if you dare!'

Sibylla came bubbling in at once, fully dressed, right down to her diamonds; she wore a magnificent silken sheath of aquamarine blue trimmed with bits of pearly grey ostrich feather. 'Does your window look out on . . . yes, it does!' And, careless of the fact that Laura was still in partial deshabille, she drew back the curtain and said, 'Quick, or you'll miss her.'

'Sibylla!' Laura protested.

'What?' Sibylla looked at her for the first time. 'Oh, put this round you! Don't fuss!' And she threw her Giles's dressing gown. 'Look! Look!' she chortled, turning at once back to the window.

Giles, with only three studs fastened, went to join her.

'Giles! Someone'll see you!' Laura exclaimed crossly.

'See what?' he asked without turning round.

Laura rose and went rather grumpily to join them. 'What is this eighth wonder of the world, anyway?' she asked.

Sibylla made a megaphone of her hands and, though the window was shut tight, pretended to shout: 'No, no! The green chiffon's much prettier! Yes – that's right!'

Giles laughed. Laura saw what they were watching, then. A hundred yards away, on a level with their window, they could see into the rooms at the back of Earl's Hotel – specifically into Elizabeth Troy's dressing room, where she was standing, fully clothed, before her looking glass, unable to decide on which of several boas to wear.

'Fancy leaving her window open like that!' Laura said disparagingly.

'She's only *just* opened it,' Sibylla said in her defence. 'She waited until she was decently dressed. She's a terrible fresh-air fiend, that's all. Nurses are.'

But Laura was no longer listening. Her heart missed a beat when she saw another set of curtains open, another window thrown wide, and another fresh-air fiend standing at the threshold of the night, breathing in the soot and smoke of London. Maurice Petifer!

Sibylla spotted him, too. She turned sharply to her cousin and saw in her face the consternation she was just a fraction too slow to conceal. Sibylla turned to Giles and, seeing his gaze still upon Elizabeth, let the curtain drop. 'That's quite enough excitement for one evening,' she said. 'We'll know her final choice when we meet for dinner.'

'Giles, dear,' Laura said tartly. 'That's hardly the way to appear before Sibylla.'

Sibylla turned and looked him up and down. 'Yes,' she said sharply, as if agreeing with her cousin, 'you're a disgrace, you wretched boy! Go and do it again!' And she gave his shirt a mischievous tweak at the front, pulling it almost entirely out. She let go at once and stared in horrified fascination at what she had done. All the men's shirts she'd ever seen were buttoned round the thigh and through the fork to stop them from riding up. A slow grin spread over her face. 'Is that one of these tunic shirts?' she asked. Then, before he could confirm it, she grabbed a handful of the cloth at the small of his back and tugged hard, emitting a hoot of laughter as it came right out. 'How wonderful!' she cried.

'Sibylla!' Laura was furious by now. This new recklessness in her cousin's behaviour – which she had noticed building up over the past week or so – was really going too far.

'Oh come on, coz!' Sibylla chided. 'This is a holiday!

Pretend we're on the sands at Torquay.' As fast as Giles tucked away the liberated linen, she tweaked it out again.

'If we were on the sands in Tonga-Tonga,' Laura replied, 'I shouldn't behave like that! Giles, do show just a *little* decorum, please.'

'Laura's right,' Giles said, catching hold of Sibylla's wrists and pinning them to her sides by sheer superior muscle.

'Oh, such a big, strong, handsome man!' Sibylla growled as her eyes dwelled in his, issuing an obscure but merry challenge. 'If ever you want to get rid of this fellow, Laura, just say the word!'

'If you ask me, I'm beginning to regret I came to London at all,' Laura muttered.

Sibylla looked swiftly at her once again – and just for a moment Laura caught sight of the anger that was fuelling all this horseplay. 'For some reason, Laura dear, I find that very hard to believe,' she said coldly.

Laura had completed her dressing in the meantime. She was wearing a slightly fuller-skirted dress than her cousin, in dark-blue silk shot with crimson and just a hint of a bustle; it was covered by frills at the back, which could have been the last dying vestige of the train her mother might once have worn. She gave her hair a businesslike pat and handed her cape to Giles for him to place round her shoulders. 'We'll wait for you in the lounge,' she said. 'I shall have a cocktail!'

'Eh?'

'You'll probably dress quicker if you don't have an audience of ladies to show off to.'

'Precisely!' Sibylla added with a giggle as she flounced theatrically from the room in the wake of her cousin.

But the moment they were in the corridor her manner changed completely. She fell in at Laura's side, took her by the elbow, and gave her rather a hard nip there. 'You knew!' she accused.

'Knew what?'

'Don't think you can deceive me. I could read it all over your face. That was Maurice Petifer at the window below Elizabeth's. And the sight of him standing there didn't surprise you one tiny bit.'

Laura, who had been thinking hard since she realized her face had given her away, had already decided that her best defence was to attack. 'Sibylla, dear,' she said coolly, 'I think I ought to tell you that your attitude to Maurice has become rather tedious to your friends. You overdo it so much. You make such a parade of it.'

An elderly couple, dressed for the theatre, came out of a room just ahead of them. They bowed gravely to one another and Sibylla was prevented for a moment from making any reply. 'You take the lift, please,' Laura said to them with a smile. 'My friend and I are in no hurry at all.'

When the wrought-iron cage had plummeted out of sight Sibylla said, 'Did Petifer himself put you up to this?'

It was such an extraordinary question for her to ask – when one considered all the responses she might have made and the fact that she'd had plenty of time to ponder them all – that Laura was thrown out of her stride. 'How could he have?' she asked.

'Ha!' Sibylla pointed at her as if she now stood accused out of her own mouth.

This brief exclamation left Laura completely nonplussed. 'What's that supposed to mean – *ha!* Anyone can say *ha!* in that tone and pretend it's full of deep, dark significance.' She went ahead of her cousin down the first flight of stairs.

'It means that I note you are not at all interested as to

why Petifer might put you up to making such an absurd suggestion to me. All you're interested in is establishing that he could not possibly have done so. You wish me to understand that you and he have not met – and so the opportunity did not arise. But we both know that's a lie – don't we!'

'Do we?' Laura felt her mouth go dry.

But Sibylla – apparently – didn't even consider the point worth pursuing. She said, 'I'll never forgive you for this, Laura. I don't know what you think you're doing – whether this is a solo game or whether you and Petifer both are playing – but I'll never forgive you.'

They had reached the foot of the flight. A gentleman and a lady, puffed from climbing the stairs below, stood aside to let them pass. Laura asked if they happened to have noticed where the lounge was and they told her it was on the ground floor. The two cousins thanked them and descended in silence to the halfway landing. Then Laura turned to Sibylla and said, in a placating tone, 'Let's try and discuss this whole thing in a calm, sensible fashion, eh? I assure you you have completely the wrong end of the stick – in fact, even the stick is a pure figment of your imagination. The whole situation is fraught with difficulties as it is. But I can't even begin to discuss it with you if you're going to go all operatic on me.' She smiled with an even greater appeal than her words had already delivered.

Sibylla, who had been enjoying her anger enormously and wanted to air it a little longer – though she fully intended doing the unthinkable and forgiving her cousin entirely before the evening was out – looked away in annoyance.

Laura darted her head to follow her. 'Mnh?' she prompted. 'You know it's not really possible for us to fall out, darling. We can snap each other's heads off.

We can even quarrel. And no one in all the world can wound me as deeply as you – if you really set your mind to it. But the one thing we can never do is fall right out with each other, can we! Besides, I really do need your help and advice. I'm in such a state over all this . . . confusion.'

Sibylla blinked rapidly and then squashed a little tear on her knuckle. 'Damn you!' she said with a sniff.

'Damn me!' Laura repeated bleakly, and then gave a weak laugh as she pointed to a huge sign showing the way to the lounge. '*And* what's more, I'm going blind!'

'I'll bet Giles will miss it, too,' Sibylla said, taking her arm as a provisional gesture of forgiveness.

'He didn't see Maurice, did he?' Laura's tone implied it was a simple statement of fact but her attitude turned it into a worried question.

'Why should I be able to read Giles's moods better than you?' Sibylla asked defensively.

'There you are – going all prickly again!' Laura chided. 'I ask a simple question and you immediately assume I'm accusing you of something.' She grinned mischievously. 'I wonder *why*? Is there something to be guilty about?'

'Laura!'

Laura's smile broadened 'You're blushing!'

'I am not.'

'Go and look in that mirror, then.'

The waiter came up and she ordered 'two cocktails.' He told her that narrowed the choice to about forty different drinks. She told him to bring two of whatever the barman considered to be his speciality. The waiter pursed his lips, nodded, and withdrew.

Laura grinned. 'He thought he'd enjoy my discomfiture,' she said. 'The ignorant provincial lady! I don't like Londoners.'

'I don't think that fellow was even English,' Sibylla objected. 'One of your Russo-Prusso-Belgo-Gallo tribe!'

They settled in some well-padded chairs upholstered in bottle-green plush, which set off their dresses nicely. 'I do like this hotel!' Sibylla said. Then she remembered their earlier conversation and changed her smile for a frown. 'Though I still haven't forgiven you for saying nothing about Petifer being in town, too.'

Laura traced the outline of a complex knot in the rosewood veneer on the little whatnot at her side. 'Because I thought you already knew, if you must know. I thought *you* were keeping it back from *me*. I was wondering how long you'd sustain the deception.'

Sibylla stared at her in amazement. 'How could you possibly have thought that?'

'Because it was you who invited Giles to join us for this visit – after he'd said he couldn't spare the time. I thought you must have discovered about Maurice for yourself somehow, and then told him – and, naturally, he'd change his mind at once.'

This explanation merely increased Sibylla's incredulity. 'Dear girl!' she exclaimed. 'I mean . . . the implications of what you're saying simply amaze me. How long is it since I asked Giles to come, too? The night you took Elizabeth up to the hospital. What's that? A fortnight ago yesterday. For the last fifteen days you've been under the impression Giles knew about Maurice coming to London, too – and yet you haven't breathed a word to *him* about it? Is that true?'

Laura nodded unhappily. 'I was waiting for him to speak about it. And when he didn't, I thought he must also have his own reasons for keeping silent.' She returned to the attack. 'But you see how wrong *you* were – jumping to conclusions like that – thinking I deliberately kept it back from you as some kind of trick!' Then, feeling she was hitting out too hard, she smiled and softened her words. 'And you see how important it is for us not to leap to conclusions about each other's behaviour and motives, darling? We must talk more frankly with each other, and trust each other, too.'

Sibylla shook her head slowly, still nonplussed at Laura's blindness. 'And it doesn't cross your mind that what's sauce for us two geese is also sauce for the gander who's probably still struggling with his studs upstairs? I can promise you that, to the best of my knowledge, Giles is going to get the most dreadful shock when he finds Petifer is here as well. So what price all those mistrustful things *you've* been thinking about him for the past fifteen days?'

The waiter brought them each a cocktail of rye whiskey and vermouth with a dash of bitters, which he called a 'Manhattan.' They each took a sip and gasped with pleasure at the bitter-sweet afterburn.

'He's been pretty mistrustful of me, too,' Laura pointed out.

'And can you blame him!'

'Why?' Laura looked at her in surprise.

'Think, girl! Think back to that evening. He came up to the hospital with me. What d'you suppose he saw to send him quietly back home without saying a word? Good heavens, do you find yourself in Petifer's arms, dabbing the tears off his cheeks with your handkerchief so often that one occasion more or less escapes you?'

'He saw me?' Laura pretended to be shocked though she knew Sibylla was trying to play some cruel trick on her – no doubt thinking it the greatest jape.

'He saw both of you.'

'But you never even said he was there. I thought you came across the paddock by yourself. Was he there behind you all the time?' She continued to pretend to take this persiflage seriously – though the more she thought about Giles's behaviour since that evening, which was utterly normal, the more convinced she became that Sibylla was fibbing and that he had seen nothing.

Sibylla shrugged uncomfortably. 'My loyalties were absolutely evenly divided, so to speak.'

Oh yes, Laura thought. *Very likely!* She said, 'Well, if he'd been close enough to hear, he'd have known there was nothing to worry about. Can't you imagine what Maurice was telling me out there?'

'No thank you!' was the sarcastic reply.

'Oh yes you can! You just don't want to. What memory would make it impossible for him to remain inside a hospital? What story would he tell me that could still make him weep after all this time?'

'But you already knew about it,' Sibylla said accusingly.

Laura stared scornfully back, knowing she was not really as obtuse as she was pretending to be; when it looked as if Sibylla might still try to brazen it out, she said gently, 'When it comes to your turn for him to tell you – he asked me not to tell you, by the way – when it comes to your turn (and it will!), I want to be there. I want to hear you tell him, "Oh, Maurice, that's old hat! Don't be a bore! I've known about it for donkey's years!" I don't think even you, loving him as deeply as you do, could treat him like that.'

'Just as *you*,' Sibylla sneered 'loving him as *you* do couldn't either.'

To her surprise, Laura merely nodded in agreement and stared down into her empty cocktail glass.

After that, there seemed to be nothing further to say.

When Giles finally appeared, immaculate in his evening dress, Laura slipped away on the pretext of powdering her nose. He objected that they were late already, but she replied that it was by no more than fashion required. Watching her departing back he let out a sigh of vexation and said, 'Now that's the thing that annoys me about your sex, Sibylla. She's had fifteen minutes to powder her nose – so when does she choose to do it?'

Sibylla, too, gave a sigh of vexation, and said, 'She's left us alone together, Giles, dear, so that I can tell you some rather frightful news.'

'Oh?' He turned sharply to her.

'Whole-cup-half-full is here, too.'

Giles started looking about the lounge, peering into the darkest corners.

'No. Here in London. He's staying at Earl's, too.'

'*With* the Troys?'

She nodded.

'But why didn't they say anything? Good heavens – surely they realize what . . .'

'They did. They told Laura. Elizabeth told Laura.'

His eyes narrowed. 'When?'

'Weeks ago.'

He sat down then and, weaving his fingers together, sank his jaw onto the bridge they formed. 'And she said nothing! Or not to me, anyway.' He glanced at her and raised his eyebrows, turning it into a question.

'Nor me. I spotted him just now, when we were watching Elizabeth across the way. He was in the window below. I looked at Laura and saw at once it was no surprise to her.'

He frowned into the emptiness ahead of him. 'But *why* did she say nothing?' Then, with a bitterness that surprised even her: 'I can guess!'

'She thought you already knew. Or, rather, she

thought Elizabeth had told me and that I had told you. She thought we had our reasons for keeping it from her.'

Giles stirred uncomfortably; his eyes flickered toward her and then down to the carpet. It was the moment she had been waiting for. 'You have got to start talking to her again, Giles,' she said quietly.

He picked up Laura's empty cocktail glass and sniffed at it. 'What was that muck?'

'Giles?'

'Aye!' He nodded glumly. 'You're right, of course. But it's bloody difficult, if you'll pardon the French. In the old days, talking wasn't necessary at all.'

'Perhaps that was the trouble. Anyway, lack of communication certainly *is* your trouble now! One of you has to begin.'

He nodded, with little enthusiasm.

'When?' she asked relentlessly.

Cornered, he said, 'Tonight.'

'Good!' She put the seal of her approval on his word, making it a promise. 'And meanwhile, what do *we* do, you and I, about the odious Maurice Petifer?'

He relaxed, for this was easier ground to him. 'I don't have the same difficulty as you in being civil to the fellow. If the Troys thought they'd bring him and me together and see the sparks fly for their amusement, they'll be gravely disappointed. What do you intend to do?'

Now it was she who raised an empty cocktail glass and sniffed at it.

The chance was too good to miss. Grinning broadly, he said, 'Sibylla!' in the same sharp tone as she had used on him.

She saw the humour of it and smiled sourly at him. 'I'll just have to take a leaf out of your book, I suppose. I certainly don't wish to be sport for the Troys.'

He rose, having spotted Laura threading her way toward them across the lounge. 'Do you think they *have* been hoping to extract a bit of amusement out of this situation?' he asked.

'Not maliciously,' Sibylla conceded. 'But they like to think of themselves as a pretty worldly-wise couple. Aloof from our provincial little embroilments, don't you know.'

'Yes,' he said, 'I do know. I know exactly what you mean. We must put our thinking caps on. Wouldn't it be wonderful if there were some way of turning the tables on them!'

The greetings were frosty enough. They would have been even frostier if Giles had not seen the smile on Elizabeth Troy's face when Maurice Petifer joined them; for her it was no more than a smile of welcome but to Giles it seemed like a smirk. Then, pitting every ounce of his willpower against his natural aversion, he forced himself to smile, too, shake the usurper by the hand, murmur that it was good to see him again, wish him a prosperous new year, and receive his felicitations in turn.

Sibylla, taking her cue from Giles, also managed to shake his hand without a trace of a squirm, though all she could manage to say was, 'The same goes for me, Mr Petifer.'

Everyone was over-sensitive that evening. In the normal course of events Sibylla's precise identification of her feelings with Giles's would not have irked Laura at all; in fact, she wouldn't even have noticed it. But now, coming on top of their recent conversation – and especially the way Sibylla blushed when Laura had jokingly asked whether her cousin and her husband had any reason to feel guilty – it seemed almost as shocking as if Sibylla had put her arms around Giles and given him a hug. By contrast, she thought that Maurice behaved impeccably, in kissing her hand he kept a good two inches of air between his lips and her knuckles, making a very formal demonstration of it – for the benefit of all.

Jimmy Troy, who had been going to suggest a relaxing drink before they set off, sensed that 'relaxing' would be out of the question; so he glanced at his watch and said they ought perhaps to postpone their cocktails until they arrived at the Café Royal.

'Oh, is that where we're going?' Laura asked, making a rather brittle effort at gaiety.

'The food is good . . .' Jimmy began.

'Don't say food, say *cookery*,' Elizabeth scolded.

'Or even *cuisine*,' Laura suggested.

'The vittles is scrumptious,' he insisted, putting on his backwoods-Yankee voice. 'And I'll take my dyin' there's more fame per square yard than you'd catch in a week at Madame Tussaud's.'

It was the first crack in the ice.

'Talking of fame, the Café Royal was Oscar Wilde's favourite haunt,' Giles remarked as they meandered back through the hotel foyer toward the street.

Strangers turned and stared in shock. Jimmy caught up with Giles as they approached the door. 'It isn't only the *love* that dares not speak its name!' he murmured, taking his arm. 'You'll have gathered it extends to the lovers, too!'

'How absolutely absurd!' Giles replied. 'I'm sorry if I embarrassed you and the ladies, though.'

'Not at all. In my view such matters should be right out there in the full light of day. They turn pale and sickly in the dark and become even more corrupting.'

They drew close to the others, out on the foot pavement, as he made this final comment. 'My my – did you hear that!' Sibylla said. 'Corrupting, eh? What delectations can you have in store for us this evening, Jimmy?'

'Nothing that the late great Oscar would have disapproved of, my dear,' he assured her – but, Giles noticed, he glanced quickly around before he spoke the dreaded name.

'Cab, sir?' asked the portly commissionaire, rubbing his gloved hands together for warmth.

Jimmy turned to the others. 'What's the vote? It's half a mile – a gentle stroll along Piccadilly. Shall we walk up an appetite? Are the ladies shod for such an ordeal?'

They decided to stroll – 'As long as we can take a cab back,' the ladies cautioned.

The commissionaire plucked at Jimmy's sleeve and murmured that Piccadilly was not a suitable street for ladies after dark and they would be better advised to go along Jermyn Street and then up Regent Street. But the fellow hemmed and hawed and generally took so long about it that the others were almost into Piccadilly by the time Jimmy caught up with them and passed on the man's reservations.

'What?' Elizabeth asked scornfully. 'Does he think we're too delicate to be exposed to the sight of a few ladies of the night?'

Sibylla, who had been all set to fall in with Jimmy's suggestion, rallied to Elizabeth's camp: 'Does he think we don't have such creatures in Cornwall?' she asked stoutly.

'In Helston even!' Laura added, not to be seen lagging.

'Really?' The other two women turned to her in fascinated surprise.

'Well, I presume so,' she said awkwardly.

The men just strolled along at their sides, listening with astonishment, but hardly daring to join in.

'Did you say a *few*, darling?' Jimmy asked when they reached the corner of Piccadilly.

Elizabeth's heart sank as she glanced up and down the street. The scene reminded her of a time when they had removed some old wooden panelling in the burned-out shell of Pallas House, several years after the fire. A colony of bats had made their home there. The soft, velvety way those creatures had slithered and crawled . . . and the way they had squealed – an odd little chattering squeal that sounded like depraved laughter – it was all somehow reminiscent of the dimly lighted vista that now stretched before her despondent gaze.

'Fortunately, there seem to be very few of them on this side of the street,' Sibylla pointed out.

'And we don't have to *look* at them, after all,' Laura added.

And so they set off along the south side of the street, heads front, eyes left. After no more than a few dozen paces, however, the pretence became impossible. They were drawing near the better-lighted area around the Burlington Arcade and Elizabeth saw that her analogy with the bats had been wide of the mark. The laughter was not depraved; it seemed quite warm and heartfelt; and the ladies were more like charming and delicate butterflies – if any zoological comparison were needed. She gave a little laugh and turned to Laura. 'D'you remember recently you mentioned that night I spoke at the Central Hall?'

'The speech Courtenay Rodda arranged in secret and sprang on you at the last minute.'

'Yes. Poor Courtenay! I embarrassed him dreadfully, I remember – here in Piccadilly. We drove this way in a cab afterward and I looked out of the window and remarked – in all innocence, I do assure you – that the fashionable young ladies of London seemed to be going in for shorter skirts!'

Their laughter vied with the merriment across the street and several heads turned their way.

'Did Courtenay explain?' Giles asked. 'I'd love to have heard that.'

'He did it very creditably,' Elizabeth said in a tone that was half jocular, half reprimanding. 'He drew my attention to the fact that this is the area of gentlemen's clubs and the apartments of the bachelor swells – including the Albany, just the other end of the Burlington Arcade . . . and left me to draw the obvious conclusion. I thought it was most tactfully done. I say! We're more than half-way there – do let's cross and walk on that side! I want to see them at close quarters, don't you?' It was the two ladies she canvassed. 'Are they really as pretty as they appear? And what are they saying to the men?'

The two cousins were silent, though the very fact that they made no protest spoke for them.

'I don't know,' Giles said dubiously, looking to see whether Jimmy had any opinion.

'It's not as if we're just out of the nursery,' Sibylla pointed out hopefully.

Jimmy smiled at her. 'Well, my dear, *you* at least have no guardian of your purity here to say yea or nay.'

His wife bridled at that. '*I* am the guardian of my purity, thank you very much.'

'And so am I!' Laura added her voice to the protest.

Elizabeth took her arm. 'Then what are we waiting for?' A dart of her head included Sibylla, who linked with Laura's other arm; together they wove in and out of the traffic, which at that hour was light and fast.

Jimmy gave the other two men a resigned smile.

'Personally,' he said, 'I blame the motor car.'

Five minutes later they arrived, without insult or mishap, at the Circus, where they paused briefly to admire the Shaftesbury Memorial – a statue of the boy Eros standing on one leg and firing his arrows into the ground, roughly at the point where Piccadilly and its Circus meet.

'Why is he not aiming up into the air?' Sibylla asked.

'It's a pun,' Maurice told her – or, rather, remarked to the world in general. 'He's *burying* the *shaft* of the arrow in the ground – the *Shaftesbury* Memorial, see?'

After a brief silence Giles said, 'Is that really so?'

Maurice laughed. 'I have it on the authority of the flower lady who sits in his shadow all day. Probably the one who's there now. Hang on!'

He nipped across the roadway and returned a short while later with three hothouse carnations and three little posies of violets. 'Different lady,' he said, 'but she confirmed the tale, all right. The violets are from Cornwall, needless to say.'

United for the first time by genuine laughter, they crossed Regent Street and entered the opulent world of red plush and gilded plaster that is the Café Royal.

Jimmy advanced on the head waiter with outstretched hand, which took the man by surprise, though, being a true cosmopolitan, he masked it swiftly enough and shook Jimmy's hand as if they were old acquaintances. Jimmy said, 'I hope you've kept us a good table, Charles. Jimmy Troy and party.'

The man summed them up in one quick sweep of his eye and led them to the best in the house, where six waiters drew back six chairs like a movement in a ballet. Laura gallantly placed herself to Maurice's right, between him and Jimmy; Elizabeth, likewise, took the seat between him and Giles; thus they spared Sibylla the painful possibility of an accidental brush of elbow upon elbow or, worse still, knee upon knee – though now she had to look at the man for the next two or three hours. They smiled at her – smiles of sisterly commiseration which suggested that nothing could be perfect in this vale of tears.

Jimmy proposed Manhattans all round, saying that if they'd never tasted them before, this was the place. The two cousins caught each other's eye and said how nice that would be.

'Do you always shake waiters by the hand?' Maurice asked as he spread his napkin.

'Head waiters, always. They never forget you – except in Italy, where everyone does it.'

'And how did you know his name is Charles?' Giles asked. 'I suppose you've dined here before?'

'No. I asked the head waiter at Earl's. They all know each other.' Then, speaking to Elizabeth, he asked, 'And what did your descent into that slough of wickedness outside tell you, my dear?'

She lowered her head and gave him a grim smile of challenge. 'You expect me either to mutter something embarrassed or to pass it off with a few frivolous words, don't you!'

Jimmy hung his head in shame. 'Oh Lord,' he asked the gleaming array of cutlery before him, 'what have I started?'

'*Did* you learn anything?' Laura asked her.

'I think I did. I mean what I expected to hear was a lot of smutty banter or, at best, some suggestive innuendo.'

'Oh!' Giles exclaimed with mock sympathy. 'And you were disappointed. How dreadful!'

'Giles!' Laura chided. 'This is serious.'

She turned back to Elizabeth, who, to lighten the atmosphere after Laura's rebuke, said, 'Not *terribly* serious, actually. But it did strike me quite forcibly that some of those men were holding very easy and relaxed conversations with some of those ladies – and not in the least bit smutty, either. There was one group talking about the new comedy at the Alhambra. And there was another little threesome – two girls and a man – discussing whether Brighton was better than Margate for an outing . . .'

'What's peculiar about that?' Sibylla asked. 'You could hear conversations like those at any dance or dinner table.'

'You could hear those *topics* discussed but . . . I don't know – it's very subtle. They were talking with such ease and freedom.'

'So do we,' Laura objected.

'Yes, but we're old friends, getting long in the tooth and all that. Those were young people. Don't you remember how ghastly it was for us to try and sustain ordinary conversations at their age?' She grinned at Jimmy. 'Of course, I never knew *you* as a young man.'

He put a doddery hand to his ear and, assuming a reedy, quavering voice, replied, 'You'll have to shpeak up, m'dear. Losht me confounded ear trumpet again.'

Elizabeth ploughed on through their laughter. 'I mean I never knew you when you were *really* young – in your late teens and early twenties.' Then, to the others, she added, 'But *you* know what I mean, don't you? You four knew one another when you were that sort of age. You must remember those awful sticky moments when one ran out of conversation at dances and garden parties – and one's mind was stuffed with dozens of things that one really wanted to talk about. But they weren't on the Approved List of Suitable Topics for Young Ladies and Young Gentlemen – so on we muttered and on we mumbled . . . endless platitudes about the weather, the Season, the last ball . . . the next ball . . . *eurgh!*' She shivered theatrically.

Laura, who had thought Elizabeth's earlier remarks rather fanciful, now saw quite clearly what she was driving at. 'Yes,' she put in eagerly. 'Of course, one is so relieved to have all those dreadful days behind one that one gladly forgets how dreadful they were.' She raised her brow at Sibylla, canvassing her agreement, too.

Sibylla, aware that Giles had resented Laura's earlier reprimand, tried to bring him back on what she now felt was a general wave of agreement with Elizabeth's ideas. 'What about you, Giles?' she asked. 'Of course, you did the sensible thing, didn't you!'

'What was that?' he asked, slightly taken aback at a compliment that might yet prove two-edged. One never knew with Sibylla.

The sommelier brought their cocktails. Two waiters and their *commis* brought the hors d'oeuvres for their selection. Charles took their orders. The two Cornishmen asked for steak and kidney pie with boiled cabbage and carrots – the nearest thing on the menu to a Cornish pasty. The other four chose dishes with French names.

Giles was quite ready to drop the subject and let his question to Sibylla go unanswered; not so Laura. 'What was the sensible thing Giles did, darling?' she asked her cousin. 'Apart from marry me, of course!'

'Oh, it was the *way* he married you,' Sibylla replied, helping herself to hors d'oeuvres. 'I mean, Elizabeth's quite right. Those awful, awful dances and picnics of our coming-out days . . . they make one cringe just to remember them. But Giles never went through any of that.' She turned to him. 'Did you?'

He pulled at the lobe of his ear and gave a diffident laugh. 'I was too busy learning the difference between arabica and robusta coffees and how to candle eggs and . . . things like that.'

'You see!' Sibylla looked about at the others, as if Giles had just confirmed her assertion.

'No!' the two women said in unison. Elizabeth added, 'Why was that the *sensible* thing?'

Sibylla tossed down the rest of her cocktail and fanned her cheek with a jovial flutter of her hand. 'Because he knew that all those sticky, embarrassing rituals of courtship . . .' She turned to Elizabeth. 'That's really what you're talking about, isn't it: courtship. All those awkward, stumbling conversations – which were just elaborate ways in which young men and young women tried to convey to each other . . . well' – she cleared her throat awkwardly – 'we all know what we were really trying to convey!'

'I don't.' Jimmy blinked his eyes owlishly at her.

Giles, sensing a little sport – and seeing a way of steering the conversation off his particular brand of cleverness, whatever it might be – agreed. 'What did I *miss?*' he asked.

Sibylla looked at them coolly. 'Oh, now you imagine you're going to embarrass me, don't you!' She licked her lips. 'So let's just see who embarrasses first, shall we!'

Laura shot an alarmed glance at Elizabeth and then said to her cousin, 'Don't let them provoke you, darling. They know jolly well what you're talking about. And so do we. That's what being civilized means – except that *some* people' – she glared pointedly at the two men in question – 'are apt to forget it from time to time.' She smiled at Maurice to show he was not being included.

But he took it as an invitation to have his say. 'I was hoping,' he told her lightly, 'to hear how and why your husband was so clever.'

Sibylla was now torn – furiously torn – between gratitude to him for reopening the door her cousin had so pointedly closed and indignation that she would now be going through it at his behest. 'Well,' she said coldly, 'there are some men who are *not* always so civilized – they simply manage to conceal it better than the rest. However,' she went on before he could rise to that, 'Giles was astute enough to know that all our endless twittering at those balls and parties was neither here nor there. The sugar-coating round the pill might be romance, but the heart of it was commerce. It was a commercial bargain that lay at the end of the romantic little path – you give me this, I'll give you that. And Giles was making sure he could deliver his side of that bargain – weren't you, dear.' She flashed him a brief, dismissive smile and, turning to Jimmy, added, 'That is a very good Manhattan.'

Two little movements of Jimmy's finger brought a replacement, almost instantaneously, and one for himself as well. Meanwhile, beaming at Giles, he said, 'And I guess he has, too, delivered, eh?' Then, to fill the rather thoughtful silence that had descended, he turned to his wife and added, 'But we seem to have strayed rather wide of your original point, my dear – which, if I'm to believe my ear trumpet, was that the bucks and bawds of London town find it quite easy to discuss seaside resorts and theatrical presentations. It was not, you'll agree, an especially profound observation – but perhaps you were about to develop it into one that is?'

'Ho ho, Jimmy Troy!' she exclaimed. 'Just for that, my boy! The point I was about to make was that, *whatever* they were discussing – those bees and bees of London town – a particular transaction lay at the end of it all. A "commercial bargain," I think you called it, Sibylla? Similarly we, in our courtship years, whatever *we* were discussing, be it the weather, the Season, et cetera, we, too, knew that a commercial bargain also lay at the end of it all. More complicated, I grant you, than the rather brief and simple one between the busy bees, but . . . how shall I put it?'

'Delicately!' Maurice suggested.

'The two bargains,' she concluded, 'are not, in their essentials, a million miles apart. Delicate enough, Maurice?'

He raised both hands, yielding the point to her. Then, turning to Jimmy, he said, 'You were wrong, Troy. Mrs Johnson didn't lead us away from the point at all.'

'No!' Sibylla said, again angry at having to concur with a lead from the odious Petifer. 'Anyway, why are we talking about this, at all? What's your hotel like?' she asked Elizabeth. 'Whittaker's seems quite select, I'm glad to say.'

'Good view from the windows?' Maurice asked.

Jimmy, seeing that Sibylla was about to have an apoplexy, leaped in with: 'Just "that little patch of blue which prisoners call the sky." He beamed around at the others and whispered, 'Oscar!' adding in his normal voice: 'I think we owe that little bit of homage to this restaurant's most illustrious former patron, don't you?' More deft fingerwork produced replacement cocktails for the other four. The waiter lifted an eyebrow at Jimmy, who replied with an almost imperceptible shake of the head.

But it was not quite imperceptible enough to slip beneath Laura's gaze. She laughed. Elizabeth asked what the joke was. Laura said, 'This husband of yours, who can speak whole volumes with just a lift of a finger or one shake of the head.'

'For example?' Elizabeth pressed her.

'Just now that waiter said to him, "D'you want to

get these people really blotto, sir?" and Jimmy replied, "No, thank you, I believe they're quite tipsy enough already." And it was all done with one raised eyebrow and one teeny-weeny nod.'

'*I'm* not tipsy,' Sibylla protested.

No one quite knew how to respond.

'Go on, Giles!' Laura urged at last. 'You back her up this time – don't leave it all to Maurice.'

Husband and cousin glowered at her.

'At the risk of being a bore,' Elizabeth cut in hastily, 'I should like to be permitted to develop my thesis to its ultimate point – trivial though it may prove to be.'

'And that is?' Jimmy asked.

'The easy familiarity we witnessed out there in Piccadilly – between people of an age who would, in other circumstances, be rather awkward with one another – how do we explain it?'

Jimmy smiled. 'Pretty obvious, I'd have thought! The ultimate question, which, if we're honest, lies behind almost all dealings between the sexes – "Shall we or shan't we?" – is already answered, one way or the other, for both parties.'

She shook her head. 'I don't think it's that . . .'

'But it must be,' several others insisted.

'All right, but not in the simple way Jimmy implies. The fact that the Ultimate Question – as he so charmingly calls it – is already answered puts them all on an absolutely equal footing. *That's* what explains their effortless ease and openness with one another. Those young women are the *equals* of those men.' She grinned mischievously around at the circle of faces – thoughtful, perturbed, intrigued, dismayed – and added, particularly to the other two ladies: 'We've had a little glimpse of the future tonight, my dears . . . how easy and relaxed it'll be when we're *all* allowed to descend from our pedestals!'

Giles cleared his throat and ran a finger round inside his collar. 'Did you say *trivial?*' he asked. 'It's over my head, I'm afraid.' He turned to Laura. 'Do you feel you're on a pedestal, my dear? Does it make you giddy up there?'

Laura racked her brains desperately. For some reason she did not want to agree with Giles in anything tonight – and Elizabeth's words (though Laura realized she intended them mainly to amuse) made her even more eager to strike out on her own. But the fact remained that there was no part of her life with Giles where he did not treat her as an equal. He hardly consulted her over the trivia of the business, of course, but no important decision was ever taken without consulting her. 'We've come a long way since my father's time,' she admitted.

'Hah!' Maurice snorted. 'A fuzzy-wuzzy caveman with bones through his nose and a vocabulary of five words would have come a long way in comparison to *that* man!'

The other five stared at him in astonishment.

'It's the truth!' he protested. 'And isn't that what we're all supposed to be doing this evening – telling the truth?'

'If that's so' – Sibylla leaned across the table and stared at him ferociously – 'here's one for you: You don't even know the meaning of the word!'

Their eyes locked; his jaw muscles rippled busily. Clearly there were a dozen replies on the tip of his tongue. Nobody breathed. Then he gave the most casual grin and said, 'Perhaps we'd better not, then.'

Sibylla preened herself for her victory – until she saw her cousin's face and realized she had, in fact, lost that round. Then she turned to Giles and said, 'Actually, it wasn't fair of you to put that question to Laura. All the world knows what a model husband you are.'

'Then where's the unfairness in that?' he protested.

'Not in you – but it's still in society at large. A man who wants to make a prisoner of his wife has dozens of laws ready to hand. He doesn't even need to use them. The threat is enough: "I'll cast you out without a penny and take the children from you!" And he could, too. Just let her make one little transgression! But he can transgress as often as he likes and that same law will do nothing to stop him. D'you think all those men out there in Piccadilly are bachelors?'

Giles shrugged. 'What can *I* do about it? Anyway, I still don't see why it was unfair to ask Laura a perfectly straightforward question.' He turned to his wife again. 'Do you?'

In the most diplomatic tone possible she said, 'I think Sibylla's point is that we shouldn't see this issue in such personal terms, dear. The question is not whether my husband is the salt of the earth (which he is) or' – she turned with a smile to Maurice – 'whether my father was an antediluvian monster (which he was).'

'I stand corrected,' Maurice conceded.

But Giles was less easily soothed. 'What is the question, then?' he asked heavily.

Jimmy rubbed his hands at the approach of the heated trolley bearing their various dinners. 'The question is whether our tempers will improve as our hunger is appeased, old fellow.'

Everyone laughed – far more than the observation justified. And each of them knew why. There was a feeling abroad that they had all, somehow, enjoyed a miraculous escape – though from precisely what peril none of them could have said. Yet it was so strong that Maurice caught Sibylla's eye and actually smiled. And, what is more, before she could stop herself, she smiled back.

They were in a convivial, even high-spirited mood as they straggled out onto the foot pavement in front of the restaurant; they were certainly relaxed enough not to stand on ceremony – which goes to explain what happened next. The commissionaire blew his whistle and a growler came forward to pick them up. 'Ah, good,' Jimmy said. 'Now we can all go back together.'

Normally, of course, the three ladies would have mounted first, but – in their not-standing-on-ceremony humour – Jimmy hustled them aboard so that, as it happened, each husband followed his wife; they were all chattering and laughing at the tops of their voices. Laura and Giles went in first, then Elizabeth; but no sooner had Jimmy followed her than the driver, who was holding open the door, closed it firmly and whistled up a waiting hansom. To Sibylla and Maurice he said, 'Beg your pardon, sir, madam, but I 'it a pothole in Carnaby Street not a hower since and it's done that damage to me horfside front as I doubt she'll carry the weight o' six no more. There'll be a stiff 'un in the 'Ackney Horfice tomorra', but for tonight, four's the best I kin manage.' He turned to the driver of the hansom, who was just drawing up. 'Oi, Nobby! Two for ya, mate!' Then, addressing once more the rapidly sobering pair of revellers, he concluded as he leaped back into the driving seat: 'This gentleman of the trade'll carry you right royal.'

Elizabeth, who had been struggling with the door of the growler, managed to open it at last. 'Here, Sibylla! Change with me,' she called out. But by then it had already drawn away from the kerb and was picking up speed toward Piccadilly Circus.

In the hush that followed, Maurice looked at Sibylla and said solemnly, 'Well, I won't kill you if you promise not to kill me.'

After a brief pause she heaved a sigh and said, 'It seems my life is one long round of sacrifices.'

'Where to, Guv?' the driver asked.

Maurice opened his mouth but Sibylla spoke first. 'Just drive around, please, cabby.'

'But whatever you do, stay out of Carnaby Street,' Maurice added as he climbed aboard.

'D'you agree?' Sibylla asked him as they set off, also toward the Circus. 'You and I are long overdue a serious conversation – and this is a heaven-sent chance to have it.'

'Jimmy-sent, more like it,' he told her.

'And I absolutely insist on paying my half of the . . . what d'you mean – Jimmy-sent?'

'While you ladies were away he had a little private word with the commissionaire at the end of which a small coin changed hands and the man slipped outside. Didn't it strike you as funny that the growler came forward, even though this hansom was first in the line? And then Jimmy himself ushering us in with delicate little touches on the elbow while he distracted us with his flim-flammery? I don't believe that growler had a defective wheel at all. And in fact, just between you and me, Mrs Johnson, I don't believe there are pot-holes in Carnaby Street, either!'

Sibylla digested this a moment and then burst out, 'D'you mean this is Jimmy Troy's idea of a joke – to wangle you and me together?'

'Both Jimmy and Elizabeth, I think. The pair of them are highly amused by the situation that has developed around Chynoweth and Parc-an-Dour and . . . the neighbouring property.'

'Agh!' Sibylla raised both her gloved fists and shook them at Eros, beneath whose outstretched wings they were at that moment passing. 'How dare they!'

He cleared his throat. 'Don't you think we're mostly

to blame?' he asked. 'Me above all, I admit. In fact, I rather hoped that was what you wished to discuss with me.'

'What?' she asked, still nursing her anger.

'A *modus vivendi?* How we can arrange our lives so that we cease to provide such sauce for the jaded tongues of West Penwith to relish? All four of us, not just you and I.'

They passed out of the Circus and into Coventry Street, making for Leicester Fields. A lamp on the far side of the street showed her jaw muscles working hard.

'You and I are the key to it, though,' he said.

'You are!' She flared up at last. 'If you just sold up and went away again, that would solve everything.'

'Would it?' he asked calmly.

'You know bloody well it would!'

The shocking word forced a wedge of silence between them. At length he said, 'Why do you hate me so much, Mrs Johnson?'

'You know very well why.'

'I know bloody well why! Because of what happened at Land's End that day.'

'That was only the last straw. The tip of the iceberg.'

'I was very young at the time. I didn't know how to deal with . . . situations like that.'

'Now you do, I suppose!'

'You'll have to take my word for that.'

'Well, I certainly don't propose to put it to the test – if that's what you were hoping for!'

Maurice suppressed a smile and held his peace. The cab entered Leicester Fields at a smart clip. 'Surely it was a very *little* incident,' he offered at length.

'No doubt to you it was,' she sneered. 'No doubt your life is positively crowded with "little incidents" of that degraded nature.'

'Alas, no,' he sighed. 'Would that it were! However, we stray . . .'

'I don't wish to talk about it any more,' she asserted.

'On which point of *absolute* agreement, may we turn our attention to the present situation – forgetting whatever origins it may have had in the distant past? The question is, what do we do *now?*'

'I've told you. Sell up and go! That would solve everything.'

'And I asked: Would it?'

'You know it would.'

'It might have done,' he replied in a conciliatory tone, 'until a few weeks ago.'

'Nothing has changed in the past few weeks.'

'I think you know it has,' he said quietly.

To his surprise, she blushed. At least, he thought he saw a tinge of red in her cheeks and ears, but in the dim light he could not be sure. Her flustered behaviour, however, would certainly support the suspicion. It amazed him – and started whole new trains of thought in his mind. When he had accused her of understanding very well that things had changed recently, he was referring to Laura's behaviour with him. It had not crossed his mind – until now – that changes in the behaviour of the *other* two parties might simultaneously have taken place.

'It has not,' she insisted, rather too tardily to carry much conviction. 'Anyway, what are you referring to? If this conversation is to be all hints and innuendoes, I'd rather go straight back to my hotel.'

'I'm referring to . . . I'm sorry, I have to put this rather vaguely in case I'm maligning the lady, but . . .'

'Which wouldn't surprise me!'

'Oh!' He almost doubled up in bogus pain, adding in a foppish voice, 'Your barbs can be so crew-ell, Mrs Johnson!' Then, returning to his normal tone, 'Can I just finish what I was going to say? In the backend of last fall I told Elizabeth Troy . . . certain things about myself – about my life in the Cape. I don't know why I didn't tell the Troys when I met them out there. But the subject didn't come up then . . . and that led them to make certain assumptions about me. And those assumptions followed me back here and so put me in the position of living a sort of lie – quite unintentionally, but there it was. So I told Elizabeth the truth. If you have no idea what I'm talking about, all this must sound like the ramblings of an idiot.'

Sibylla said quietly, 'I know what you're talking about, Mr Petifer. And – contrary to what you may suppose – I am not so consumed with my aversion to you that I do not sympathize. However, I must add that I think you could have found some way of letting us know earlier. You were, as you rightly say, living a lie. And it was not the bravest thing – leaving it to Elizabeth Troy to tell us.'

'Us?' he asked. 'Who is *us?*'

Sibylla had been so eager to accuse him of this petty cowardice that she had overlooked (which is not *quite* the same thing as forgotten) her recent conversation with Laura. Now it was too late. She pressed on robustly, hoping to find some way of extracting her cousin later: 'Laura and me. You did *intend* Elizabeth to tell us, didn't you? She was in no doubt about it.'

This revelation left Maurice wondering why Laura had forced him to go through the whole confession again, as if she knew nothing of Sarie and Jannie. The conclusions he drew from it were naught for his comfort. 'Yes,' he replied. 'And now I wish with all my heart I had said not a word to anyone.'

Sibylla, who had found her anger easy to sustain as long as Petifer met her fire with fire of his own, now realized that she was beginning to sound shrewish, even to herself – when every quarrelsome word of hers was met with submission from him or, at most, his quietly reasoned objection. So she deliberately suppressed all sign of hostility as she said, 'And believe me, I wish with all my heart, Mr Petifer, that you had never bought Culdrose.'

'So do I, Mrs Johnson. Indeed, so do I.' He gave a single, ironic laugh.

'And yet you obviously see some humour in the situation!'

'The humour is that I came to Helston that day, intending not to bid. I had luncheon with Jimmy Troy, who talked me into it.'

'Did he?' she asked with sudden interest.

'In his own obscure way. However, walking between Liston House and the auction, I thought better of it once again and reverted to my earlier decision. I went into the auction, fully determined to stay out of the bidding. The reason I laughed just now was that it was *you* who changed my mind.'

'Me?' she asked in astonishment. 'But I didn't say a word to you, apart from a how-d'ee-do.'

'No, but when I saw you bidding . . .'

She gave a little half-laugh, half-gasp. 'Then your eyes deceived you, Mr Petifer. I didn't bid a single brass farthing.'

'No?' He leaned forward and grinned at her. 'You didn't tip the wink to Harry Sampson? And he didn't pretend to be deep in conversation with . . . I've forgotten. The fellow who was with him.'

'One of the Meagor boys – they all work for Kitto's. I was talking with them, yes, but there was no pretence about it. We were, in fact . . .'

'But Harry Sampson gave a definite nod every time the bid went up on the left. You three were over there on that side. I saw it all.'

'Then you saw what your own anger told you to see, Mr Petifer. I do assure you – I was talking to Sampson about getting Kitto's to rebuild the stables at Parc-an-Dour after Dancey had finished with the roof. Even then I was far from satisfied with Dancey, you see.'

Maurice closed his eyes and slumped back in his seat. 'So Curnow was right,' he murmured. 'He also assured me you didn't bid. Oh, folly upon folly!'

She stared at him incredulously. 'D'you mean the only reason you changed you mind and bought Culdrose was to stop me getting it?'

He nodded unhappily but then said, 'No! It wasn't as simple as that. I thought you were bidding just to stop me from becoming the Curnows' neighbour. But since I'd *already* decided not to, anyway, your action seemed high-handed, officious . . . oh, what's the word? It was as if you were rubbing my nose in my own decision. Or as if you were telling me I needn't have bothered to behave so nobly because *you* wouldn't have let me buy the place anyway. Oh, Sibylla! I don't know what the reason . . . I'm sorry – that just slipped out. Mrs Johnson! I don't *know* what the reason was. I just wasn't going to let *you*, of all people, rub my nose in anything!'

And now it was Sibylla's turn to laugh – and in that same ironic vein too. 'D'you want to know the real joke?' she asked.

'Probably not,' he answered glumly.

'I don't know who was bidding on our side of the ring, but the person bidding against you on *your* side was none other than Elizabeth Troy. She bids with her fan. She does it like this.' She gave a brief demonstration with her left hand and then apologized for digging her elbow in his chest.

They were now driving into Trafalgar Square, between the National Gallery and St Martin's-in-the-

Fields. 'The fellow must have heard the West Country in our voices,' Maurice commented. 'We're obviously going to be shown the sights.'

Sibylla stared up at Nelson on his column, a dark, brooding shape against the night-glow of the sky. 'He must be cold up there,' she said.

Both of them knew they ought to turn their minds to the topic they had agreed to discuss, but neither could now think of an easy way back to it. Maurice seized on Nelson instead. 'Extraordinary, when you think of it,' he commented. 'He was an open and flagrant adulterer for Lord knows how many years. He equally openly disobeyed orders from the Admiralty – a crime for which he would have flogged any subordinate of his. And what does this nation of hypocrites do? It raises the largest monument in the kingdom to his memory!'

'Ah!' Sibylla said fondly, glad at last to find some topic on which she did not have to be angry or scornful. 'But it was such a romantic story, wasn't it! The love that held him and Emma together across continents and oceans . . . that survived so many snubs and gibes!' There was an odd, faraway look in her eye, almost as if she had been alive in those times and were speaking of it from her own knowledge.

'But,' Maurice pointed out, 'she was married to Sir William Hamilton all that time.' He was intrigued to see how animated Sibylla had become on this particular topic.

'*He* didn't mind,' she assured him. 'He was a great crony of Sir William Troy, you know – the two foremost collectors of their time. You should ask Hamill Oliver to show you their correspondence one day. He's catalogued it all. There's one letter in which he admits he's very glad that such a distinguished man as Nelson has taken Emma under his protection and is keeping her contented. Old Hamill showed it to Adam once.'

'Tactfully put!'

'What d'you mean?' She bristled again.

'Taking her under his protection. That's a tactful way of putting it.'

'Oh, I see.' She began to talk rapidly. 'It's not a situation people discuss a lot, of course, but I'm sure it's far more common than the *lack* of discussion would lead one to suppose. I don't think there was any coolness at all between Emma and Sir William. I think from a purely domestic point of view she was probably far happier with him than she ever was with Nelson. I think she was the sort of woman who had both domestic needs and romantic needs, and she . . .'

'Ah,' he remarked, 'the *rare* kind!'

'Oh!' Sibylla said crossly. 'Don't be obtuse! You know what I mean. She was the rare kind – if you want to put it that way – in whom the domestic passion was as overwhelming as the romantic one. Nelson was useless when it came to satisfying her domestic desires – every bit as useless as Sir William was in satisfying her romantic ones. All power to her, I say, that she found a way out of her difficulty! Her tragedy was that the world found out, too.'

'Not that they took much care to conceal it!'

'No,' she agreed primly. 'That was their mistake. But I think Society then must have been full of such *understandings*, don't you? Considering how many arranged marriages there were and how naïve most girls were before their weddings.'

They were now leaving the square, trotting past the decrepit facade of the old Admiralty building. Maurice wondered briefly how often Nelson had walked in through those doors to fight battles that were every bit as perilous to him as any he directed from his own quarterdeck. Then, returning to Sibylla's comments, he was about to point out that unmarried girls had probably been less naïve in Regency days than they were now – when it struck him she was probably not talking about Regency girls at all. 'Society probably still is like that,' he commented.

'Oh . . . yes,' she said off-handedly. 'For all I know.'

He persisted. 'I mean, girls are still kept pretty naïve. *And*, at the risk of reopening an old sore, so were boys, too, in my young day – with what lamentable consequences you and I both know only too well!'

'*Tskoh!*' Now she was cross again. 'Why are we talking about this, anyway? It's got nothing to do with what we ought to be discussing. The *modus vivendi* you mentioned.'

After a pause he said, 'I suppose it hasn't.'

After a further pause she said, 'My idea, as I said, is quite simple. You should just sell up and buy some other farm – which should be easy enough for your wounded dignity now you know I'm not seeking to rub your nose in anything. But every time I suggest it, you imply it's too late. I hope you don't mean what most people would assume you mean by that alarming phrase?'

He made no reply to that.

'Well?' she prompted impatiently.

'I find it very hard to discuss this with you, Mrs Johnson. Laura is your cousin, after all, and you and Giles have always been good friends. And even if that weren't true, you are presently a guest under their *roof* (if you'll pardon the word).'

'Oh!' she sneered. 'You just can't avoid every little unpleasant dig, can you!'

Impulsively he squeezed her arm. 'I'm sorry. I meant it as a little pleasantry – something to soften the atmosphere. That's another thing which makes serious discussion almost impossible – this thunder and lightning that keeps following us around.'

She laughed against her will – and, he noticed, she quietly eased her arm out of his grasp instead of snatching it ostentatiously away. 'You're a snake in the grass, Maurice,' she said. Then she added, 'I'm sorry. It does just slip out, doesn't it!'

'All the same, I think we'd better stick to Mrs Johnson and Mr Petifer. We behave badly enough in public as it is – even from behind *those* formal barriers.'

To his surprise she giggled. 'We do, don't we!'

'But,' he suggested, 'we could stop sparring when there's no audience about . . . except' – he waved a hand vaguely at Buckingham Palace, which they were now passing – 'Her Majesty.' Only three windows – high up on the left – showed the slightest glimmer of light. 'They can't have much of a gas bill,' he remarked.

She did not laugh. Reluctantly she said, 'Very well, Mr Petifer. I realize that any useful discussion of this present situation may involve my cousin and her husband. If I now hesitate, it is because I have no wish to give you ammunition to use against me at some future time.'

'Ammunition?' he echoed in surprise.

'To discuss them at all, is a kind of treachery – when they're not here. But . . .'

'All right,' he interrupted, allowing his anger to show. 'Let's all four meet. I don't suppose it'll do any good. I mean, I don't think there's the slightest chance any of us will tell the truth at such a meeting. But if it will make it easier for your tender conscience to contemplate telling the truth at a further meeting . . .'

She dug him sharply in the side with her elbow. 'Don't be so prickly, boy!' she said. 'I was about to add that if you will describe the situation to me from your point of view – omitting nothing – I will then decide whether it is worth the risk of being called a traitor by you at some future occasion. And that is the *only* condition on which I am willing . . .' She stopped and bit her lip. 'No,' she said firmly. 'Let's neither of us climb back on our high horses. That's not a condition; it's only my *suggestion*. No more than that. If you have a better one, I'm willing to listen.'

'You ask for the truth,' he said, 'from one who doesn't know the meaning of the word.'

'Get on with it!' she scolded.

He collected his thoughts then and began. 'When I came back to Cornwall . . .' He shook his head and tried again. 'It started before that. When my wife and child died like that – one week bonny and healthy, next week gone . . .' He was suddenly at a loss for words.

'You needn't tell me about the effect of a sudden death like that,' she said quietly as they passed into the narrow, dark little lane known rather grandly as Constitution Hill.

'It all came back to me just before Christmas – when I thought my stupidity in making the motor backfire like that . . . when it looked as if Trevanion was in danger of his life . . . I'd forgotten how *angry* I was. At the whole wide world. I wanted to take my revenge on the whole wide world. Did it have the same effect on you?'

'Yes.' She wanted to hold his arm, to comfort him – but then she suspected that might be the very trick he was hoping to play on her.

'I thought I was over it by the time I came back to Cornwall. The truth is I was like a boxer, a badly mauled boxer, still on his feet but not really in touch with the world at all. They don't feel the pain, you know, when they're groggy like that – not until after.

Anyway, I thought I was over Sarie's death, and Jannie's – and I *certainly* thought I was over my disappointment about Laura.'

'Did you know . . .' she began – and then changed her mind. 'No. I won't interrupt. Go on.'

'Really I was like that boxer. One push and I'd have fallen over. You remember that ball at Liston House – oh, no, you were still in London – then, of course. Anyway, did either Laura or Elizabeth ever tell you about that night?'

'No. Nothing out of the way, at least.'

'If she'd been correct and distant and charming and all the things she ought to have been – as I say – I was in such a weak state at that time, she could have pushed me into any corner she chose, or out the door.'

'I'm sure Laura was all those things,' Sibylla could not help saying.

'On the surface, yes,' he agreed. 'But underneath – oh, she was like a frightened gazelle.' He fell silent.

'What?' she asked.

'Frightened gazelle! I remember shooting a frightened gazelle once, in the Cape. I shot hundreds, of course, but this one I'll never forget. As beautiful a Tommy's Gazelle as ever you saw – and there was no *need* to shoot her!' His voice rose in anguish on the word. 'Every other animal I ever shot, it was either for the pot or to save my own life. Or someone's life. She was the only creature I ever shot for . . .'

When his silence grew unbearable, Sibylla suggested, 'The only one you shot for the fun of it?'

'No.' He was trembling. 'Not fun. Something much . . . darker . . . deeper. Something I don't even want to think about. I shot her *because* she was so frightened . . . *because* her eyes were pleading with me to let her go free. My God! I just *had* to show my power, you see. I just . . .' His voice broke and he could not continue.

She looked away from him, hoping the dampness in her eyes would not swell into actual tears.

He saved himself with an ironic laugh. 'I am not, you will gather, a great admirer of Maurice Petifer. There now – we have something in common at last!'

A tear rolled down her cheek. She brushed it angrily away and snapped, 'Get on with it!'

'Yes!' He drew in a deep breath and squared his shoulders. 'Quite right! What I was going to say was that Laura had the same frightened gazelle look in her eye that night at Liston House. And, once again, I couldn't help it. I had to show my power. I met Elizabeth Troy the following day. She showed me over Yeol Parc, which I was also thinking of buying.'

'Pity you didn't!'

'Pity I didn't! But anyway, what I'm driving at is I know just how it must look from the outside. It must look as if I came back with this one, single-minded idea – to win Laura's heart and take her away from Giles. But up in here' – he tapped his brow – 'I've wavered about like a reed in the storm. As I say, *anything* can knock me off course. I told you – I had no intention of buying Culdrose. And then I saw you (or, as you now say, I deluded myself into seeing you) enter the bidding, and – *biff!* A red mist rises before my eyes, and I'm back on my feet, punch-drunk as hell, jabbing away at every shadow in sight!'

There was another pause. The cab swung round the site of the old reservoir and turned toward the Wellington Memorial and Hyde Park Corner. 'Any pertickler way ye'd care to go now, sir?' the cabby asked.

St James's was less than half a mile away now but Maurice opened the light in the roof and told him to go on up Park Lane.

'You don't object?' he asked Sibylla as they set off again.

'No,' she said, as if it slightly surprised her. 'Anyway – for whatever reason – you *did* buy Culdrose didn't you.'

'And regretted it at once. And I mean that very first evening. It was a fit of insanity buying that place but I recovered from it at once. That same night I resolved – just like a child making a new year's resolution, you know – I resolved to be a model neighbour and not give the Curnows any cause for distress. And then – damnit! – Giles has to invite me out to dinner and threaten he'd kill me if I so much as laid a finger on Laura!'

'No!' Sibylla exclaimed. 'He didn't!'

'He did. And then down came that red mist again . . .'

'It rose *up* last time,' Sibylla could not stop herself from pointing out.

'Tricky stuff – red mist,' he assured her. 'Anyway, my response to *that*, of course, was to promise myself that somehow, by hook or by crook, I'd snatch her away from him. Ho ho – nobody talks to Maurice Petifer like that! But fortunately I recovered from that bout of insanity before I actually *did* anything to further it. And then came the storm and all those excitements, and then . . . I don't really know what happened next . . .'

'Miss Sweet happened next!'

'Oh yes! Why does Laura dislike her so intensely?'

Sibylla cleared her throat. 'I'm not going to vouchsafe anything, remember – until I've heard *all* you have to say. But it does occur to me to ask why you employed a woman like that as your housekeeper?'

'A woman like what? What's wrong with her?'

'Everything's wrong with her! She's pretty. And young. Or young*ish*. And single. And she has blatantly set her cap at you!'

He gave out a roar of laughter. 'Is that what you think of her?'

'It's what the whole world thinks of her.'

'Well let me tell you – and the whole world, too, if you have its ear – Miss Sweet and I enjoy the most correct and proper relationship.'

'I believe you Mr Petifer, sincerely. But I believe I'm in a minority – and one that does not include my cousin.'

He stared at her, appalled. 'She thinks that . . . Miss Sweet and I . . . no!'

'I believe she does – and that is why she cannot bear the woman.'

'But . . . good God!' He made a gesture of tearing out his hair. 'I only took her on as my housekeeper because I knew how the tongues would wag about my becoming Laura Curnow's neighbour! I thought what else can I give them to wag about? I meant to deceive the world but not Laura Curnow. A housekeeper who was young and pretty and single – as you say – seemed heaven-sent for the task.' He broke off and stared at her in dismay.

'What?' she asked.

'Jimmy-sent, actually. Back we come again, full circle! He was the one who recommended her to me. No no!' He laughed. 'We mustn't start seeing his shadow behind every tree. It amuses him to manoeuvre you and me into this hansom . . . by harry! I hope he's frozen half to death, waiting out there on the pavement in St James's, so as not to miss the sight of our faces when we return! But he's not so machiavellian as all that. Anyway, what I was saying was that I only took Miss Sweet on in order to divert the gossiping tongues away from poor Laura. And now she's gone and taken it as some personal slight!'

'What a web!' Sibylla murmured.

'And it all ties in,' he went on glumly. 'This is the bit where you may lose your temper with me again, but Laura's attitude to me has changed greatly over the last few weeks – ever since Elizabeth told you and her about Sarie and Jannie, I think. I don't know if that's a coincidence?'

'It isn't,' Sibylla assured him, in a tone as glum as his own.

He allowed the silence to grow a while before he said, 'You can't go on refusing to talk about it now. I don't want to take Laura away from Giles. I admit I did once – or imagined I did. But no longer. Now the boot is on the other foot.'

Speaking with the utmost reluctance, Sibylla said, 'You remember the night Miss Sweet barred the two young ones in the pigsty? That was another thing that didn't exactly endear her to Laura, by the way! But you remember she came over to Culdrose that night?'

'Yes?'

'And after you let the boys out and brought them indoors you went out again to find Laura?'

'Yes?' He was growing distinctly uneasy now.

'And she told you she'd lost her way in the dark? Well, she hadn't. She saw you letting the boys go free. She was just about to step forward and give you the verbal hiding of your life when she saw you open the door and take one of the children by the hand.'

'Meredith!' He almost breathed the name. 'He was the image – just for a minute – he was the image of Jannie.'

Sibylla frowned. 'But . . . Meredith is six!'

'So is Jannie,' he said. 'Or would be. In one way, you see, he has never died for me.– neither of them.

Not a day goes by but I imagine what he'd be doing . . . what he'd look like . . . the things he'd say. I have to keep them alive because they're all I've got left now.'

To him it was a statement of fact, a rather prosaic admission, something he lived with every day and had long since ceased to find remarkable. But to Sibylla it was something so unexpected that it slipped under every guard, every fence, every tripwire she had ever rigged between her soul and this detestable man. She burst into tears.

Maurice just sat there astounded, wanting to comfort her and not daring to try. 'It's all right,' was all he could think of to say. 'Honestly! I'm hardly even sad about it now. It's what I live with. I'm used to it.' Then, when that had no effect, he added, 'And that's really why I no longer want Laura back in my life. She'd take their place. She'd blot out their memory. The trouble is, it's woken up all the wrong instincts in her. I can't understand it.'

'Can't you, Maurice?' Sibylla asked huskily, sniffing back her tears and talking a grip on herself once more. 'Can you really not understand it? Then you're an even bigger monster than I thought.'

Elizabeth, in the growler, gave up her attempt to change places with Sibylla, on the pavement, and reseated herself with a sigh of exasperation. The view through the window was suddenly clear. Giles gazed out and thought he had never seen anyone looking quite so forlorn as Sibylla appeared at that moment. It had been two weeks since that kiss – two weeks, four days, and eight hours – and still it haunted him. Why had she done it? Not, as she pretended, to demonstrate to him that an affaire was out of the question. He now felt sure she had started to kiss him out of desire, need, attraction . . . call it what you will – she had kissed him because she wanted to. And then, half-way through, when she felt the strength of her own response to him she had become frightened. And so, realizing she must either commit herself body and soul to him – no, not to him but to *them*, to that mysterious togetherness in which lonesome man and lonely woman can lose their separate beings – or draw back from the abyss, she had panicked and tried to pass it off as a lesson, a smart little pedagogical trick.

She claimed it was impossible for there to be anything of a romantic nature between them, but her eyes had never, then or since, endorsed the declaration. And his spirit refused to accept it, too. Over and over again in his mind's eye he saw her face in the firelight, her darling face, drawing closer to his, her dark, mysterious eyes gazing into his, her lips parting gently, moving closer and ever closer to his, the appealing curve of her cheek . . . He tormented himself with every small detail, delaying that most poignant and heartbreaking moment of all, when their lips finally met and he felt their amazing softness, their strangeness, their ineffable sweetness.

He clung to his memory of that moment, making it stand for all those ideas his conscience was still strong enough to prevent him from thinking 'aloud,' as it were – in the echoing emptiness of his mind. Not once did he admit to himself that he had fallen in love with Sibylla; but while he could cherish that kiss and recall its every sensation with such powerful clarity, the admission was superfluous; the words would have forced him to choose.

For the oddest thing of all was that he still loved

Laura. Admittedly they were going through 'a bad patch' now, but it was not the first and no doubt it would not be the last. He could even acknowledge that his love for his wife was in every way bigger than these new and unexpected feelings for Sibylla. But by that very token they were also more diffuse – scattered over so many workaday aspects of their lives. He could look at her totting up the accounts, or listen to her near-snoring beside him at night, and even so feel himself brimming over with a love for her too large to contain. Even in moments when he seethed with anger at her – for her refusal to snub Petifer at every occasion, for instance (and, yes, he knew very well how irrational that was of him) – even then he could be beside himself with his love for her. Indeed, by an odd sort of contradiction, he could afford to be so angry with her precisely because his love felt large enough and strong enough to contain those most destructive and corrosive emotions. Their acid would bite its hardest, exhaust its strength, weaken, and die – and their love would emerge intact, harder-shelled than ever. He knew, too, that he could indulge his new feelings for Sibylla because of that very strength; they would never threaten his love for Laura or their life together.

He was aware, too, that turning forty last September – though he had insisted on making no fuss about it at the time – had been a shattering moment for him. He had suddenly realized that all the positive choices of his life had powerful negative effects, too. He had always known that, in deciding to take on his father's business, he was, in effect, automatically deciding *not* to be a tinker, a tailor, a soldier, or a sailor – or to follow any of a thousand other trades and professions. A man would be a fool not to know such a thing. And yet those other possibilities had always been there, out of sight yet not utterly out of mind. They remained as potential alternatives, buds that had failed to develop but which had not shrivelled and fallen away, either. He could still wonder what he was *really* going to be when he grew up.

But in those dark days around his fortieth birthday he had felt the buds dying at last, leaving him with the knowledge that the life he had chosen was now the *only* one he could pursue. Sibylla was, perhaps, the one alternative bud that refused to die.

Again and again he treasured the memory of that moment of overwhelming tenderness between them . . . the sweet, soft touch of her lips . . . the compelling nearness of her, which no mere words, no clever thoughts could banish.

So there it was, then, he thought glumly. It was something *physical*, after all. Oh, unlovely word! He could hear it as it fell from the lips of preachers, moralists, and those awesome dames of his youth who set themselves up as arbiters of right and wrong for all the world: *physical!* What a temple of shame they had erected around the sneer. And now, how impossible it was to relate that shame, that stain of uncleanliness, to the pure, lifegiving warmth of their kiss.

These ideas, which he had wrestled with for the past fortnight – or two weeks, four days, and eight hours – passed through his mind in a sort of flash-review as they drew away from the Café Royal. Even the most complicated ideas can pass in the twinkling of an eye if one has become sufficiently obsessed by them. His last sight of Sibylla was, unaccountably, of her lifting her face to Maurice Petifer, turning from darkness into light, and smiling broadly at some remark of his.

'I can't feel anything wrong with any of the wheels of this cab,' Elizabeth said.

Jimmy, deep in the dark of his corner, chuckled.

She turned on him sharply. 'Did you arrange for that to happen?'

The chuckle broadened into a laugh. 'I didn't think I'd pull it off, though. I knew Petifer would hang back to last because he always does. It was getting the three of you in before Sibylla.'

'But how? You didn't talk to the driver . . .'

'The commissionaire,' Giles said angrily. 'He had a word with the man before you ladies rejoined us. That was it.'

'Why, Giles, you sound as if you disapprove!' Jimmy chortled.

'Of course I do. I see nothing amusing whatever in inflicting on Sibylla the company of a man whom she heartily detests. Fortunately, it's a very short journey.'

'Yes,' Jimmy agreed, as if he were taking up Giles's point and developing it further. 'We shan't have long to wait. I want to see their faces as they get out. I guess he'll drop Sibylla off at Whittaker's first.'

'Let's see.' Elizabeth, completely reconciled to Jimmy's little jape, knelt on the seat and peered out of the tiny rear window. 'Oh no!' she exclaimed a moment later.

'What?' the others chorussed.

They had been delayed in the Circus by a black maria and an ambulance, so they were only just entering Piccadilly itself. 'Their cab had a skewbald horse, didn't it?'

Jimmy agreed, the others weren't sure.

'Well, if I'm right, they've just turned off along Coventry Street.'

'What?' Giles and Laura started upright and snapped the word in unison. Then they glanced at each other and muttered face-saving things like, 'Are you sure, dear?' and 'Surely it must have been someone else.'

'It was them, all right,' she replied. 'There's no hansom drawn by a skewbald anywhere else in sight. You're going to have a long, long wait, Jimmy Troy.'

Laura and Giles, shaken by the vehemence of their response to Elizabeth's words, were now doubly shaken by the implications of the detour Maurice and Sibylla were taking. It could only be at their own request since both knew London well enough not to be deceived by a cabman seeking to pad the fare. To Giles and Laura it felt like treachery – though not for the same reasons.

'I do hope they're not settling their differences and trying to reach a *modus vivendi*,' Jimmy said.

'It would make life a lot easier if they did,' Giles countered.

'Sure,' Jimmy agreed at once. 'But less interesting. They're such fun, our two hate-birds! I never thought I'd sit at a dinner table where one person told another to his face that he was an outright liar – and for the whole show to go on as if she'd done nothing worse than tell him he had a smear of butter on his chin. They make it sound so natural.'

'Yes, but Maurice *knows* Sibylla,' Elizabeth pointed out. 'He'd go home a very disappointed man if she didn't come out with at least one of her remarks during the evening.'

'Quite!' Jimmy said. 'They just *love* arguing. How their eyes glow! They practically applaud each other. I keep wanting to cheer, too, don't you?' He included the Curnows in the question. 'I guess that's why the rest of us feel no real embarrassment to speak of.'

'I feel a little embarrassed at discussing them behind their backs,' Giles said. He waited for Laura to back him up but she kept silent.

They took the corner into St James's. Jimmy turned to his wife. 'Are you going to wait with me?' he asked. 'See their faces?'

'I am not!' she asserted roundly. 'One of the glories of staying at a swell hotel is that one can have a hot bath at midnight. And actually, Jimmy, I don't know if you realize it, but the bathtubs at Earl's are big enough for two!'

Jimmy laughed but it was clear he intended staying to see the faces of the two 'hate-birds' as they ended their enforced ride together.

'Elizabeth Troy does love to shock,' Giles commented as he and Laura made their way upstairs.

To his surprise Laura answered, 'We've never taken a bath together.'

In fact, he was so taken aback that all he could think of by way of response was, 'We've never had a bath big enough.' He turned the key in their door and pushed it open for her.

The moment they were both inside she threw her arms around him and said, 'We have now!'

'Here?' he asked, conventionally perturbed but secretly intrigued by the thought.

'Where else?'

'People might see us going in or coming out.'

She laughed. 'Which would be worse?'

He heard a tinge of despair behind her humour and, taking a grip on himself, managed to recover something of his usual aplomb. 'Either could be disastrous for me. People who go around accidentally dropping the name of Oscar Wilde can't be too careful. I'm probably the talk of everyone in the hotel by now.'

'But you said his name at Earl's, not here.'

'As Jimmy said – they all know each other in these places.'

She threw her arms around him and clung to him tight. 'Please?' she begged. She was shivering.

'What is it?' he asked, gently caressing her back. 'Tell me.'

'I hated this evening. Jimmy may laugh but I hated to see Maurice and Sibylla at each other's throats like that. I feel as if someone's thrown me down the bottom of a very deep well, or a mineshaft. Hold me! I feel like I'm drowning.'

'Oh darling!' He held her as tight as he dared, feeling for her a love he had almost forgotten – a physical love whose intensity had been crowded out by all those other forms of love that grow over the years. He suddenly wanted her with a passion that would not be denied.

She felt the change in him at once. 'Giles!' she murmured with an accusing, skittish grin.

'It's something I often dreamed about,' he told her softly.

'Truly?'

'What about you?'

She slipped from his embrace with a laugh. 'I don't have to answer that.' She began undressing hastily, careless of where each garment fell. 'Let's not bother about a bath.'

'No,' he told her primly, taking more care with his own, much easier disrobing. '*You* put the suggestion on the agenda. You tricked me into revealing that it had always been my dream. So *you* jolly well don't back out of it now.'

But when they were actually in the bath together her skittishness deserted her and she became languorous and rather demure. 'Has it really always been one of your dreams?' she asked lying back against him and letting him pretend to soap her breasts.

'What about you?' he challenged again.

'I suppose I have thought of it,' she confessed.

'But you never said a word.'

'Nor did you.'

He sighed, unable to deny it.

'Why not?' she pressed.

'Don't know,' he replied awkwardly. 'Because you're my wife, perhaps . . . I suppose.'

'What does *that* mean?' she asked with more spirit.

'Well . . .' He was even more awkward. 'It would be a bit like . . . I don't know – *using* you. As if you were one of those women we passed on our way to the Café tonight.'

'Is that what they're for?' she asked dreamily, relaxing against him once more. 'To stop husbands from . . . to take away the dreadful necessity to *use* their wives?'

He swallowed heavily; she felt his adam's apple bob up and down. She leaned her cheek against his and whispered, '*Use* me, Giles. Forget I'm your *wife*. Forget I'm a *person*. Just use me! Make me feel useful.'

'But . . .' He began to protest.

'Don't argue. Don't stop to think. Please, my darling – do something to break these awful chains that hold us prisoner now. Be a rocket and lift me out of this suffocating mineshaft. *Now!*'

Elizabeth came round to Whittaker's while Giles and Laura were still at their breakfast; she joined them for coffee. 'No Sibylla?' she asked as she settled herself in what was obviously Sibylla's place. The waiter came to lay another setting.

'We don't actually inhabit the same room,' Giles told her.

'Giles!' Laura chided. 'Jimmy is allowed to say outrageous things like that but don't you start.' She turned to Elizabeth. 'May I ask – will he be joining us shortly?'

'We don't actually inhabit the same room,' she said, mimicking Giles's intonation. Then she laughed. 'Actually, last night I wish we hadn't. He sniffed and snuffled until the small hours and now the poor boy seems to be going down with a cold. I wonder why!'

Laura could not help laughing. 'When did he get in?'

Elizabeth raked the ceiling with her eyes. 'I don't know. It was over an hour. When did Sibylla get in?'

Her question included Giles, who grinned and answered, 'I don't know. We were otherwise . . .'

'We didn't hear,' Laura said. 'We were asleep.'

'So! That must have been quite a detour they took. And she has slumbered on this morning!'

'Has Maurice?'

'Oh no. He's finished his breakfast and has gone for a walk in Green Park. He's made a list of all the motor-car showrooms within striking distance and he's bought a map on which to spot them. He was going to take Jimmy and me around, but now, I suppose, it'll be only me – so I was rather wondering if Giles would like to come, too, in Jimmy's place.' She smiled and added, 'To chaperon me, of course!' She turned her smile on Laura. 'Or perhaps Sibylla has a chill, too?'

Laura, seeing no connection, frowned.

'Didn't you say last night that the pair of you ought to call on that uncle of yours today? Drogo Nisbet?'

'Ah.' Laura understood then. 'Well, yes, I did say we *ought* to. So perhaps we shall. Did Maurice say anything to you about . . . last night? Was he at all embarrassed that anyone had noticed their absence?'

'Well, I didn't exactly challenge him outright, Laura!'

'No, but *you* know. One can tell these things if one is at all interested.'

Elizabeth conceded the point with a little shrug. 'We

did talk about it briefly. He appeared, if anything, a little puzzled when he tried to summarize the event for me. But I wouldn't say he was embarrassed, exactly. He admitted that he did at last understand why Sibylla dislikes him so intensely.'

Laura took an inspired leap. 'Did he mention Land's End? Did he say it was something in connection with Land's End?'

Elizabeth shook her head. 'He didn't say anything. He just said he understood better. But he still looks puzzled.'

'Why the funny look in your eye at the mention of Land's End, then?'

Elizabeth smiled and stared off into the distance. 'I've not been back there in ten years,' she said. 'Ten years ago, in the August of 'ninety-two, David Troy, George Ivey, Lilian Rodda, and I went there for a picnic. Lilian accidentally kicked George while they were horsing around in the water. He very nearly drowned – and he knew it. He told us after that when he thought he was going to die, he was filled with a great rage at his own stupidity – that he'd wasted thirty-odd years of his life as a lawyer when all he really wanted was to be a painter. That day changed his life.' She fell silent.

'But . . .' Laura began, not seeing any connection between that and what Maurice may or may not have said; but Giles's finger on her wrist silenced her, too.

Elizabeth drew a deep breath and went on, 'He proposed to Lilian that very same afternoon. She'd been dithering a long time and I suppose the realization that she'd almost lost him for ever made up her mind, too. And also . . . David Troy proposed to me, straight after that. And I accepted him – though I had no such excuse.' She smiled at Laura then. 'It's a place fraught with significance for all of us, you see!

Have you any inkling why it should have some meaning for . . .'

Giles cleared his throat significantly and rose to his feet. 'Sibylla!' he exclaimed. 'Good morning! You're looking absolutely radiant.'

Sibylla eyed him with the deepest suspicion. 'Has he been hitting the bottle already?' she murmured to Laura as she took her seat. 'Good morning Elizabeth. You actually *are* looking radiant.'

'Thank you,' Elizabeth responded, somewhat surprised. 'Jimmy has a slight chill but Maurice Petifer is determined to drag me around all the motor-car showrooms between Paddington and Streatham, so I came over to find if Giles would like to share the torture.'

'I had a nice long talk with Maurice Petifer last night,' Sibylla said, adding to the waiter, 'I'll have two kippers please. And lime marmalade if you have such a thing? Don't bring the toast until I've finished with the kippers.' To the others she explained, as the man departed, 'They always do, you know.'

'Did I hear you say a *nice* long talk?' Laura asked incredulously.

Giles looked at the two cousins and wondered how he could ever have fallen for Sibylla, even momentarily, even in the most superficial way. He wished he had told Laura she was looking radiant for, of the three ladies at that table, it was most true of her, and he had seen the disappointment flicker in her eyes when he had complimented Sibylla.

'Yes. We have decided to bury the hatchet – and not, as Jimmy would no doubt say, in each other's skulls. I'm sorry he's not well, by the way. I hope he didn't catch his chill waiting on the pavement for our return. We were gone almost an hour – just driving around. It was very kind of him, to go to all that trouble and expense in arranging it, but he needn't have waited.'

Laura realized she was giving all these frank details about her and Maurice so that no one would later suspect her of trying to hide anything; but the question prompted by that was why anyone who knew the pair of them would have the slightest suspicion that there was something to hide in the first place?

So perhaps there was!

'We've decided,' Sibylla went on, 'that it must be very tedious for the rest of you to have the pair of us going for each other like Kilkenny cats all the time . . .'

'Oh, well, I don't know,' Elizabeth said, a judicious lilt in her voice.

' . . . those of you, I was about to add, who are not positively amused by it. So, rather than be either a bore or a spectacle, we have agreed to behave like two civilized beings. In public, anyway.'

'Ah!' Elizabeth pounced on that final qualification. 'And in private?'

Sibylla flashed her a lips-only smile.

'Haven't we heard all this somewhere before?' Laura asked.

'Ah . . . yes, but we mean it this time,' Sibylla assured her.

Giles turned to Elizabeth. 'I think I will take up your kind invitation, my dear, and chaperone you with the dreaded Petifer.'

'Oh, you lovely man!' She laughed. 'I know it'll be the most dreadful bore for you, but there you are – into each life a little rain must fall.'

Laura looked at her cousin. 'And I suppose it's Fitzroy Square and the dreaded Uncle Drogo for us.'

Sibylla nodded glumly. 'Into each life . . .' she echoed.

Just for the adventure, the two cousins took an omnibus up Tottenham Court Road, alighting at its junction with the Euston Road. 'Oh, look!' Laura exclaimed the moment they turned into Warren Street. Sibylla followed her pointing finger across the narrow street and saw a small, dingy workshop bearing the sign: ELECTRICAL INSTALETIONS. 'Well,' she said, 'as long as he can spell positive and negative I don't suppose it matters.'

'No – next door,' Laura told her.

And there, Sibylla saw, stood a motor-car showroom, proudly displaying an aristocratic Panhard and a sporting-looking Renault like Dr Thomas's. They burst into laughter. 'And we thought we were escaping it all!' Sibylla said. 'I wonder if it's on Maurice Petifer's list.'

'The Renault has a propeller shaft, just like a ship,' Laura informed her. 'Maurice's Simplex has a chain, like a bicycle.'

'How can it have a propeller shaft, like a ship, when it hasn't got a propeller?' Sibylla asked.

'I don't know. That's what it said in Giles's book. Actually, it was Blanche who pointed it out to me.'

'Oh well, I'll ask her when we get back!'

'Don't!' Laura advised. 'She'll surely tell you!'

They stared at the Renault awhile without becoming any the wiser. 'Wouldn't it be funny if we bumped into Maurice and the others here,' Sibylla remarked.

Laura said, 'I wonder how he and Giles are getting on.'

Sibylla wondered why she did not put Giles first but passed no remark on it.

'I notice you're calling him Maurice now,' her cousin continued.

'Not to his face!'

'Oh? Interesting. Have you and he honestly buried the hatchet?'

'Yes. We decided we were setting you and Giles a bad example.'

'Àh,' Laura replied with a grin. 'You've noticed, have you!'

'Yes, I'm like that. I notice even the subtlest things. Last week, for instance, a man punched me in the face in the street in Helston. And though I'd never met the fellow in my life, he only had to punch me twice more before I was saying to myself, "This chap doesn't like me very much." I'm quick, see!'

'Sibylla!' Laura cajoled, taking her arm and giving her a push. 'You are in a funny mood.'

'Well, honestly, Laura! "You've noticed, have you"! I'd have had to be blind, deaf, and dead for a month not to have noticed.'

'Poor you!' Laura felt suddenly contrite. 'It must be awful sharing a house with two people who can't hide their feelings better than Giles and me. Still – I think everything's on the mend now. Last night he and I went from being just about as hostile to one another as we've *ever* been to . . . well, the very opposite. We haven't felt so close in years.' She giggled. 'Now tell me the same thing happened with you and Maurice – I don't think!'

'That's right, dear,' Sibylla replied acidly. '*Don't* think – if you can't come up with something more likely than that. I'd sooner bale out Loe Pool with a whelk shell than actually have to be nice to that man. But we can at least be coolly correct in public. And, before you repeat Elizabeth's feeble joke – there won't be an "in private" to concern yourself about. Oh!' She turned and rested her head briefly but fiercely on her cousin's shoulder. 'Please don't let's be all brittle like this. I'm delighted for you. Really I am. All I've ever wanted to do is help in any way I can. I've told Giles all along what a fool he was being.'

There was a pregnant pause before Laura said, 'What d'you mean?'

'I mean the way he's been behaving . . .'

'No. What d'you mean, you've told him *all along?* All along what?'

'Well . . .' Sibylla was nonplussed for a moment. 'Ever since he started behaving like a bear with a sore head about you and Maurice. I told him – the very worst way to gain your cooperation is to be surly, resentful, and uncommunicative – to imply a criticism without ever stating it – to create an aura of righteous indignation without ever saying what's made him indignant.'

'Yes, all right, don't go on and on.'

'I'm only answering your question. Don't we turn left here?' She pointed down Fitzroy Street.

'We can go down this or the next. I don't want to go down this one.'

'Why not?'

'Because it has one of those dubious houses in it.'

Sibylla grinned. 'Has it? How d'you know?'

'One of Uncle Drogo's maids told me.'

'None of them ever breathed a word of it to *me*.' Sibylla's tone suggested that that made the entire thesis very unlikely.

'Perhaps it was someone else, then.'

'Perhaps it wasn't anyone at all,' Sibylla told a bollard – which was actually an old cannon from the Battle of Waterloo, filled with concrete and stood on its muzzle.

'All right, then, I'll tell you who it was. It was Maurice Petifer, when I mentioned where Uncle Drogo lives.'

'How would Maurice know about a place like that?' Sibylla sneered.

'I don't know. I'm hardly likely to ask him, either!' Mischievously, she added, '*You* could, though – now you're such pals! I suppose bachelors have to know these things. What else can they do?'

She added that final thought to make herself sound worldly-wise and tolerant, but Sibylla seemed to take it as another barb against her. 'Oh,' she said airily, 'there's *lots* of other things they can do. They can engage pretty young housekeepers, for instance.'

They had just crossed Fitzroy Street. Laura, having declined to go down it, now turned abruptly away from her cousin and set off with some determination to run the moral gauntlet of the dubious house – whichever one, among thirty almost identical dwellings, it might be.

Sibylla followed in her wake, making no effort to catch up. She inspected each house carefully, on either side of the street, as she passed it, looking for one that might bear out Laura's assertion. They all looked eminently respectable – but then they would, of course. They'd hardly put up a brass trade plate! But perhaps there'd be a discreet little card in the window. What could it possibly say? She had never even thought about such things before.

That she could do so now was thanks to Elizabeth Troy, of course. She'd made such curiosity seem almost respectable. And the men only aided and abetted her. Sibylla had expected either Jimmy or Giles – certainly Giles – to protest last night in Piccadilly; but, instead, they'd been terribly, terribly suave and had given the whole subject quite a different aura.

A gray-haired woman in her forties, dressed in widow's weeds, stood at a ground floor window, watching Sibylla with an impassive gaze. Ring the doorbell and ask her which house it was! Why not? If she spent many hours of the day at that post, she must surely know the answer. Sibylla chuckled to herself at the very idea. What would the woman think! She'd assume Sibylla was seeking work at the establishment in question. She flushed at the very thought.

And there was another puzzle: How *did* a woman get work in such houses? If they looked as respectable as any other house from the outside, how would you even find where to begin? It was something to have reached the age of thirty-two – in fact, thirty-three *tomorrow!* Heavens, she'd almost forgotten her own birthday! It was something to be knocking on the door of thirty-three, to be the mother of three (and never mind all the convolutions by which *they* were begotten!), and to realize there was that whole secret world going on around you, a world of which you were completely unaware.

The woman in black made a slight movement as Sibylla drew level with her window. She was now holding a card against the pane. *Female required within*, it said. *Good horizontal position.* The woman was staring up at the rooftops of the houses opposite, as if she had no idea what her hands were doing. What an odd way of putting it! This was a district for quaintly worded signs, all right. *Good horizontal position!* Why not say, *Scullery maid wanted within – not required to climb stairs*, or something more specific like that? Sibylla walked several paces before she realized why the card was, in fact, already quite specific enough.

So that was the house! Laura had been right after all – or Maurice had. She turned and looked at it again. The card had vanished but the woman was staring at her with an inviting and hopeful smile on her face. Sibylla was aghast to realize that *she* was actually being canvassed as a suitable candidate for that 'horizontal position'! Her heart skipped a beat and then thumped like some wild creature set at liberty inside her ribs. Flustered, she turned and ran a step or two before she realized what a spectacle she was making. Then she forced herself to stop and walk at the same sedate pace as before. At the end of the street, where it opened out into Fitzroy Square, she turned for one final glimpse of the house. Though she could see the window, its angle was now such that it revealed nothing but a reflection of the houses opposite.

Two ladies – in their thirties, Sibylla guessed – were walking down the street, the way she herself had just come. With a smile she waited to see if they got the same treatment. They were dressed so quietly and respectably, and were engaged in such earnest conversation, that, Sibylla decided, if she were the woman in black, she wouldn't even bother to show them the card.

The woman in black obviously decided otherwise.

Sibylla almost laughed aloud to see the shock with which they responded. Like her, they hastened their pace, though they did not quite run. Like her, too, they quickly slowed down again. But then, unlike her, they stopped and began an animated conversation. The shorter of the two looked back at the window, pointed to herself, then to her friend. And then, after a further brief consultation, they turned about and went back to the house – where they were admitted even as the taller one was raising her hand to the doorbell.

So that was it – as simple as that!

A gentleman took her by surprise, striding swiftly past her and on up the street. He gave her an amused, over-the-shoulder glance but did not break stride. As she knew he would, he paused before the House (as she now thought of it), straightened his tie, and pulled at the bell. A moment later he, too was admitted.

And that was it again – as simple as that! Had she not been shown that card she'd never have guessed it. Indeed, she might well have passed such a scene every day of her life and never once been the wiser.

'What's keeping you?' Laura asked, having cooled her temper and returned from half-way across the square.

Sibylla heaved an ironic sigh. 'I've just missed my chance!' she replied. But when Laura pressed her she said it was too trivial to explain.

'They seem to be preparing for some unusually large festivity at the Honor Club,' Laura went on.

The Honor Club, which was next door to Uncle Drogo's, was for respectable working ladies of the West End. It provided a lending library, a gymnasium, nightly table d'hôte, and copious hot baths; on different evenings each week there was a medical clinic, a dramatic reading, an improving lecture, and a dance.

'Ah,' Sibylla said vaguely.

'Probably their new year play,' Laura suggested. 'Last year, Aureole wrote, the racket went on past midnight.'

'Mnh,' Sibylla replied. She was still stunned at what she had just witnessed. It was quite possible that at that very moment the gentleman and one of those women were upstairs, taking off each other's clothes! Perhaps even both women! It seemed so incredible that it was hard to believe it hadn't all been a dream.

A further thought struck her: Those two women hadn't known about the House in advance – and they certainly hadn't come there looking for it. Their surprise at seeing the card was proof of that. So they could have had no idea as they entered the far end of Fitzroy Street, making toward the Square, that they would not reach it – indeed, that by the time they might have expected to reach the Square, they would, in fact, be upstairs in one of the houses, getting undressed with a man they'd never met before! If the façade of the Honor Club had developed a human face at that moment and given her the most enormous wink, she would hardly have been more flabbergasted.

'A bit of luck!' That's probably how those women would describe it to their friends: 'I had a bit of luck today, my dears!' Sibylla tried in vain to imagine the sort of life in which such an unthinkable train of events could be dismissed quite casually as 'a bit of luck.' She gave a little involuntary shiver.

'Well, no wonder you're cold!' Laura scolded. 'Just standing there like that. Uncle Drogo's seen us, so there's no turning back now.'

Sibylla drew a deep breath and put the incident from her mind – for the moment, anyway. She gave their uncle a wave. 'He's at his window early today,' she commented. 'Perhaps moneylenders' debts fall due at the beginning of January? He won't come and talk to us. I just know it. Why do we keep coming?'

'Not to see him, anyway. I want to meet Aureole.'

Two young nuns, making house-to-house calls, came out of the Honor Club at that moment; they smiled to see a pair of well-dressed ladies and held out a collection box in the most confident way. Laura made sure that the money was for a good secular purpose – days in the country for slum children – before parting with her two florins, saying firmly, 'One from me and one from my friend here.'

Sibylla tried to read the expression in their eyes, and tried to imagine what sort of a life they really led – the best or the worst? But the eyes were inscrutable – though the smiles were limpid and their gait sprightly as they went on to their next conquest. The pickings around Fitzroy Square were obviously rich.

Laura forgot them at once and returned to their earlier topic: 'Is Uncle Drogo really a moneylender?' she asked.

Sibylla shrugged. 'Aureole won't tell me. All she'll say is that he deals in *things*, and when I ask what things, she says, "This and that – whatever comes to hand." Which isn't very informative.'

'It's more than anyone's ever told me,' Laura remarked. 'Though that maid I mentioned did once let slip that he could buy up every house in the Square.'

Sibylla grinned suggestively as she rang the bell. 'Well, there's one house that might repay the investment rather quickly.'

Laura gave a puzzled frown.

'Well, not *in* the Square, perhaps, but not too far out of it. We've just walked straight past it.'

'Oh, that!' Laura replied scornfully. 'I think Maurice was just bragging – showing how worldly wise he is. I don't believe there is such a place. I looked at every single one and they're all obviously quite respectable. I don't suppose you even glanced at them – you're in a strange sort of faraway mood today.' She gave the bell another pull.

'There was one house back there I had my suspicions about,' Sibylla confessed. 'The one where a lady in black was standing by the window. Did you see her?'

'Yes?' Laura turned to her. 'You don't mean *that* house, surely?'

'Did she greet you in any way? I mean, nod to you, smile at you . . .?'

'No. She just stared at me rather vacantly and then gazed at the houses opposite – also rather vacantly. Why?'

'She didn't attempt any kind of communication with you?'

'I've already said no,' Laura responded crossly. 'Why d'you ask, anyway? Are you going to tell me she rushed out of doors to ask for your autograph or something?'

'No!' Sibylla laughed and turned away to hide her smile of triumph. *She* had been chosen; Laura, on the other hand, had not been considered attractive enough! But the smile lost some of its lustre when she recalled what she had been considered attractive enough *for!*

'Where is the dratted girl!' Laura asked in the same cross tone – and found herself asking it right in the face of the dratted girl herself. 'Oh there you are, Biddy. What kept you?'

The woman curtseyed as they passed. 'If you please, m'm, the mistress sent me to answer double knocks so I waited till you rang twice, only it's usually Maggie's job.'

'Lord save us!' Laura flung off her cape and dumped it in the woman's arms, then her muff, then her coat; her gloves went with the coat automatically, being held on one long cord from sleeve to sleeve. 'Double knocks just means *quality*, as you say in Ireland. Single knocks are other callers, or members of the quality who simply want to leave cards. It doesn't mean you have to wait for two actual knocks – it's just a way of speaking. Is the master at home?'

'Sure he's in his dressing gown, sitting at his window, m'm.'

'No, no!' Laura cried in despair. 'When I say "at home," I don't mean is he in the building. I know he's in the building. I saw him at his window. I mean, is he at *home?* Is he receiving . . . Oh, never mind.'

'The mistress says would you kindly go up to her, m'm.' Biddy took Sibylla's neatly folded outdoor clothing and laid it out, with Laura's, on an ancient carved chest in the hall.

'The mysterious mistress!' Sibylla echoed under her breath as she and Laura mounted the stairs. Then she halted, for it suddenly struck her that sheer chance had, that morning, furnished examples of the four womanly rôles: nun, wife, mistress, and . . . the two women seen in the distance down Fitzroy Street. How odd! she thought. Then, a moment later, she realized it was even odder that she had never once considered herself to be a mistress. Well, it was odd if you just looked at the facts of the case – from the outside; but from her point of view, seen from inside her own skin, it didn't feel odd at all. She raised her eyes and looked at Aureole, waiting for them at the stairhead and wearing her broadest smile and the skimpiest of silk negligées.

She felt no kinship with the woman at all.

Both Laura and Sibylla (when she had an establishment of her own) served sherry and biscuits to visitors around mid-morning, although neither of them took such refreshment when they were alone. Nor, however, did they regard sherry as falling wholeheartedly into the category of 'alcohol,' by which they meant gin, brandy, whisky, and other spirituous liquors. So when Aureole de Verity, now slightly more decently clad in a dressing gown, took a firm grip on the gin bottle, they protested with a clean conscience that neither of them touched *alcohol* before six of an evening. It was a golden rule of life. Half a minute later, so overpowering was Aureole's magnetism, both were happily proving that *aqua regia* (a mixture of nitric and hydrochloric acids) was not the only solvent of gold; *aqua Aureole* (three parts gin, one part French, and a dash of angostura) was just as effective when the gold was alloyed to a rule of life.

'I've never done this in all my days!' Sibylla assured her, feeling rather glad she had lined her stomach with a good breakfast that morning. She could swig away without harm.

'I did, once,' Laura confessed. 'Only once – the morning I married Giles – I drank a large tumbler of gin and Indian tonic water.'

Aureole chuckled. 'Did you think you needed it, then?'

'My maid seemed to be of that opinion.' She turned to Sibylla. 'Tamsin Chandler – I don't know if you remember her? Afterwards, when I came back from the honeymoon, she confessed that all she'd really done was dip the rim of the tumbler in a saucer of gin and then fill it up with tonic water. Yet I got as tipsy as anything on it. The power of suggestion, eh?'

Sibylla took another gulp, smacked her lips with relish, and said, 'Another thing I've never done in my life . . .' And then she thought better of it.

'What?' the others pressed.

'Taken *two* gulps of gin,' she said lamely, as if that had been her meaning from the beginning.

'Anyway . . .' Aureole rubbed her hands. 'Do tell me all the Helston news. There's nothing about it in the London papers, which are shamefully out of touch with the real world. The last I heard was that Maurice Petifer had returned from the dead. What has happened since then?'

'Who told you that?' Laura asked.

Aureole pointed at Sibylla. 'She got a letter from Elizabeth Troy just before she returned to you. Poor Mrs Troy sounded rather miffed – mainly, I suppose, because returning from the dead is a hard act to follow, as we old troupers say.' She leaned forward and smiled at Laura. 'Has he kissed you yet? You're getting a bit long in the tooth, you know. So are you making hay during the brief summer that is left to you?'

'Aureole!' Laura flushed pink and covered her confusion with another swig. 'Really!'

'He's bought Culdrose,' Sibylla threw in. 'The farm that marches with Chynoweth.'

'And with Parc-an-Dour,' Laura pointed out.

'Poor man!' Aureole tutted. 'Farming between Scylla and Charybdis. Is he up all hours, wasting his strength at the plough or whatever farmers do? I'll bet the matriarchs of Helston are simply *hurling* their daughters at his head.'

'He doesn't go about at all,' Laura replied. 'We hardly see him. I'm sure he gets scores of invitations but he doesn't go about. He's in both hunts but he didn't go to either ball last month.'

'He hardly needs to,' Sibylla said mischievously, not taking her eyes off her cousin. 'He has a pretty young housekeeper to help keep the winter's blasts at bay.'

'Pretty young or pretty *and* young?' Aureole asked at once – also, following Sibylla's hint, watching Laura closely.

'Both,' Sibylla told her.

'She's built like a leviathan and she's thirty if she's a day,' Laura put in scornfully.

'Oh!' Aureole waved the information aside. 'Middle-aged indiscretions are of no interest whatsoever – unless' – she fixed a beady eye on Laura again – 'one knows at least one of the parties very well. Tell me something more about him.'

'He got married out in the Cape,' Laura replied evenly, challenging her to try and be witty about it.

'But his wife and his little son both died – of the same fever, whatever it was.'

Aureole put down her glass and took Laura's free left hand between her own, as if she was trying to guess its weight. 'In short,' she said, gazing intently into Laura's eyes, 'he's a hard man to dismiss from one's thoughts. Do you try? I expect you do – almost every day.'

Laura felt an odd sort of lassitude come over her. It was nothing to do with the gin, she felt sure – or very little – but it had everything to do with this odd, intense woman, not the least of whose oddities was her ability to live in intimacy with Uncle Drogo. Laura had never met her before today, though she had seen her on previous visits, flitting about the house like some huge, silent moth. And yet, she felt, Aureole knew her almost as intimately as did Sibylla; her eyes seemed to reach into one's soul and divine all its secrets. The questioning tone she adopted in speculating about Maurice, and Laura's responses to him, was mere politeness; in fact, she was saying to Laura, 'I understand.'

And she did!

'I should like to meet him sometime,' she concluded. 'Could it be arranged, d'you suppose?'

'Very easily – today or tomorrow!' Laura laughed at her surprise. 'I don't know if Sibylla told you in her note – we're up here with the Troys. They're staying at Earl's and the three of us are at Whittaker's. Maurice Petifer is staying at Earl's with the Troys, too.'

'Tomorrow or the day after, then,' Aureole said with an air of finality. 'Send a message to let me know which. I can hardly wait.'

'Sibylla will bring him,' Laura said. 'She's *just* starting to learn how to behave in a civilized manner when circumstances force them together. Now all she needs is practice.'

'I'll do no such thing!' Sibylla asserted loudly.

Laura wagged a monitory finger at her and said primly, 'Now, Sibylla, dear – you know how stale you become if you neglect your exercises.'

'Well, I'd rather . . . I'd rather . . .' She sought desperately for some image that would convey the very depths of awfulness. 'I'd rather enter the house with the dark mauve door in Fitzroy Street and stay there a whole year than spend one single hour with Maurice Petifer on the slopes of Parnassus.'

'What do you know about the house in Fitzroy Street with the dark mauve door?' Aureole asked.

Laura merely frowned in bewilderment – which was only increased when Sibylla replied, rather blasé, 'If you must know, I was almost recruited there as I passed it by on our way here. Laura and I had a teeny contretemps and were walking slightly apart at that moment – so I can't answer for her.'

'What are you babbling about?' Laura asked crossly.

Aureole was miming with her hands, as if they held a card up for display, and quizzing Sibylla with her eyebrows.

Sibylla nodded. 'A good horizontal position!' she quoted with a knowing laugh.

'Go back, child!' Aureole urged. 'You may not be too late.'

'I would, I fear.' Sibylla hung her head, as if in deep sorrow, and then went on to describe the incident with the two ladies.

Laura meanwhile had leaped to all the right conclusions. 'And is that the house the gentleman entered?' she asked. 'The one you were watching when I came back to you?'

'Yes.' Sibylla became quite serious all of a sudden. 'I

can't get over it. I mean I can't get it out of my mind. I mean, one knows such things go on, of course – and in a vague sort of way . . . I mean, in an *abstract* sort of way, one understands what takes place. But when one sees it like that – when one is almost caught up in it, accidentally, like that, it's . . . it's . . .' She sought vainly for words to express the ineffable and ended lamely: 'It's different, somehow.'

Aureole turned to Laura. 'What are you thinking? Did she try to recruit you, too? Hold up her card like this?'

Laura shrugged. 'I don't know. She had such a sad expression on her face – or not so much sad as *drawn*, you know? I didn't like to look at her again. I was gazing across the other side of the street as I went by.' She grinned, suddenly. 'Why, Aureole? Has she tried to inveigle you, too? You seem to know a lot about it.'

But Aureole gave her a withering smile. 'The house where *Les Girls* are my age, dear, is down in Charlotte Street!'

Laura stopped her ears with her fingers and shook her head. 'I've heard quite enough!'

'But I know all about the house with the dark mauve door,' Aureole went on, speaking to Sibylla, 'because the maids come home complaining about that woman and her recruiting card. Some of them, anyway. Some of them hand in their notice with a rather smug little smile – for which one can't blame them, since they can earn as much in a week under that roof as they'd get in a year under this one.'

Laura, slowly unplugging her ears, only half heard this but Sibylla's eyes opened and her jaw dropped.

'Yes, indeed!' Aureole laughed. 'That's why I advised you to go back at once, dear!'

'Isn't it funny,' Laura remarked. 'I've never discussed this topic with anyone, ever, in my life, before this. And now we're talking about it for the second time in twenty-four hours. I wanted to hit Elizabeth last night – talking the way she did.'

Aureole looked in amazement at her – and then at Sibylla, much as to say, 'What wild creature is this you've brought me?'

'Why on earth?' Sibylla asked in equal astonishment.

'All that nonsense about bargains.'

'You seemed to agree with her at the time.'

Laura grinned guiltily at Aureole. 'That was just because I wanted to annoy Giles – *at the time*. But actually I thought she was talking poppycock. She said the bargain between those women and the men who . . . who . . .' She wanted to say 'use them,' but she and Giles had now sanctified those words and made them unavailable for the purpose.

Sibylla misunderstood her difficulty and was amused. 'Go on, dear,' she said. 'We know the word. Just pretend you said it.'

'The men who *hire* them,' she said with relief. 'Elizabeth Troy said *that* bargain is essentially the same as the bargain between husbands and wives. Well, it may be for her, but it certainly isn't for me. And I wish I hadn't been so out-of-sorts with Giles last night because I'd have told her so to her face!'

No woman in all the world was quicker than Aureole to catch particular nuances in others' conversations, even if they hung by a thread to the merest fraction of a syllable. The way Laura said, 'Well, it may be for her' . . . the slight menace with which she dragged out the word 'her' . . . quickened Aureole's interest at once. 'Does this Mrs Troy sail under flags of convenience?' she asked. 'Perhaps I should ask you to add *her* to my collection, too! If Sibylla brings Maurice Petifer, perhaps you'd bring Elizabeth

Troy, dear?' she asked Laura.

'Well,' Laura replied defiantly – choosing to answer the first question rather than the second – 'neither Trevanion nor Zelah is by David Troy, although he was her husband at the time. Her "flag of convenience" as they say!'

'How d'you know that?' Sibylla asked, almost angrily – certainly with a great deal of scorn in her tone.

'Because they've got Courtenay Rodda written all over them. Not just their colouring but the way they walk, the way they speak, even the way they laugh.'

'I thought you liked Courtenay Rodda,' Sibylla said accusingly.

'I do. That's got nothing to do with it.'

'It sounds as if Elizabeth Troy liked him rather *too* much,' Aureole said, putting herself in the line of fire.

'And rather too often,' Laura added. 'She was quite reckless. They were seen at it down on the rocks at Trequean Zawn, and in the old Pallas quarries, when they were derelict, *and* at Yeol Parc . . .'

'My goodness!' Aureole put her hands to her head, as if her scalp were about to fly off. 'What are all these revelations? And how d'you find time to plough the fields, and catch pilchards, and dig for tin, and all those other terribly Cornish things?'

But Laura now had the bit well between her teeth. 'Old Pallas quarries could tell a tale or two, if only rocks could speak. That was where Bill Troy – Elizabeth's first husband – took Oenone Beckerleg's virginity and almost got her into trouble.'

'I must pack my bags at once!' Aureole murmured.

But Laura was far from done. 'And now Oenone's married to *David* Troy, Member of Parliament for West Penwith! I tell you – there's a deep vein of corruption runs through that whole family. Anyway, the thing I really wanted to say – the bargain between man and wife is *not* like . . . that other one.'

Sibylla placed her glass down with supreme skill, exactly on the intersection of two bits of cross-banding on the occasional table at her elbow. True, she took rather long about it, but the result was perfect. Well worth the agonizing wait. 'Just because Elizabeth Troy may have had her babies by someone else – a dear family friend like Courtenay Rodda – it doesn't mean she never loved her husband.'

Laura frowned. 'That's not in question, dear.'

Aureole looked at Sibylla in puzzlement.

Sibylla smiled at her. 'I can understand your bewilderment, Aureole,' she said. 'You don't know the background to this. But that's what my dear, darling cousin is really trying to say: She didn't love her husband. That's what she's *really* hinting at.'

'I am not!' Laura protested.

Sibylla ignored her. 'Bargains?' she explained. 'Forget all that. It's not about bargains. It's about faithfulness. You see?' She smiled.

'No, dear – I don't,' Aureole told her.

'I don't think you ought to drink any more of that, cousin dear,' Laura said severely.

Sibylla laughed. 'It's about faithfulness,' she repeated. 'And my cousin is an expert on faithfulness! But never mind that. My point is, you see – what I'm *trying* to say . . .' She sighed and, for a moment, completely lost the fox. Then suddenly she brightened. 'Yes! That was it! What *I* say is that a woman can have a dozen children, all by different men – no, not by different men. I mean by one man. One good family friend like . . .' She frowned and turned great, frightened eyes on Laura. 'What was his name?' Her hand, seemingly liberated from her will, trawled the air aimlessly around her, as if it might pluck back the name so recently uttered.

The blood drained from Laura's face and the slight intoxication to which she would have admitted deserted her at once. Sober, shaken, she sat bolt upright and said, barely above a whisper, 'A good family friend like Daniel Jago!'

'Yes!' Sibylla laughed and hit her palm to her forehead. 'How could I forget! Just because a good family friend . . .' Her butterfly-hand gestured the words she had spoken and forgotten. 'It doesn't mean . . .' She frowned. The echoes of the name of Daniel Jago were just beginning to penetrate her consciousness. 'It doesn't mean . . .' She stared at Laura in horror – aware at last of what she had admitted. Then her face creased in agony and she fell in a rumpled heap upon herself, curling up in the ample chair. 'Oh, Adam!' she moaned. 'It didn't mean I didn't love you!'

Sibylla's eyelids flickered a little before they opened. She obviously remembered where she was and what had happened, because her face screwed up in a pain that was not the pain of unaccustomed daylight on the eyes. And indeed, the illumination in Aureole's apartment was barely enough to read by. 'Oh God!' she moaned and turned over on the sofa, facing into the dark where seat and backrest met.

Laura caressed the side of her neck with gentle knuckles and tidied away a few stray hairs. 'There's a cup of tea going begging,' she said. 'Fresh made.'

Sibylla groaned again.

'I'll pour you one anyway.' She half rose to go but

her cousin darted out a hand and grasped at anything in reach – a flounce of Laura's dress, as it happened. 'Stay,' she pleaded.

'It's only over there. Look, I can almost reach it without getting up.'

Sibylla maintained her grip with silent determination.

Laura gave her a comforting squeeze and sidled along the sofa to where she could reach the handle of the teapot. 'There!' she said a moment later. 'All done with one hand and nothing spilled. Sit up and drink it like a good girl. You'll feel so much better.'

The 'good girl' lifted her face slightly away from the chintz upholstery, so that her voice no longer sounded muffled. 'You must despise me now.'

'Sibylla!' Laura chided gently.

'Or are you going to try and say *you* have no standards, either?'

'Sit up and drink your tea before it gets cold.'

'Bloody tea!' It was a quiet, almost monotone explosion. 'Bloody chintz! Bloody nineteen hundred and three. And four. And five. And . . . fifteen. It's never going to get any better!'

It made Laura laugh, despite herself.

'Oh yes, that's the other possibility,' Sibylla said sarcastically. 'I could be just a figure of fun – not even *worth* despising!'

'You're more fun to be with than anyone else in all the world – if that's what you mean.'

Sibylla began to cry, not bitterly, but with large, almost restful sobs. Laura caressed her arm and waited for it to pass.

A thought popped unbidden, and unwelcome, into her head. How often, she wondered, had a scene like this been enacted – but with Daniel Jago playing the comforter? How often had his strong, soothing hands caressed her while she wept those tears of remorse?

She did not want to think about it and yet her mind would not let it go. What would induce an upright woman like Sibylla to commit adultery with her husband's partner – a husband she had undoubtedly adored, moreover? There had never been the slightest doubt that she had loved Adam. Sibylla was not one to hide her emotions, good or bad . . . although, come to think of it, she had hidden her feelings for Daniel Jago pretty cleverly all these years!

Or had she? Jimmy Troy had once remarked that the best place to hide a nail is in a bag of nails. Sibylla had always shown the greatest affection for Daniel and often spoke of him in the warmest tones.

Laura realized that in pursuing this line of thought she was avoiding the question of her cousin's true feelings for Adam when he was alive. She remembered something Giles once said, when they were trying to breed a pony for the children with a white blaze on its nose by selecting a dam and sire with the appropriate markings. Giles had wondered if it would work. 'When you look at Adam and Sibylla – and then at their three offspring, he said, 'it's enough to make a professional livestock breeder despair!' How had they never suspected, even fleetingly, that there was an obvious alternative explanation? Perhaps Giles had! He would never have spoken of it to her, though. He would have considered it 'not quite nice' to mention – what with the two women being cousins and so on.

Sibylla's tears dried up. 'Now I'll look awful,' she grumbled. 'Even worse than this chintz. Is Aureole there?'

'She went to talk to Uncle Drogo. Perhaps he will see us after all.'

'Curiosity alone should ensure that now!'

Laura ceased caressing and gave her a robust pat on

the shoulder. 'I don't for one moment think she'll tell him.'

Sibylla stopped breathing.

After a moment Laura gave her a shake. 'What now?' she asked.

'It's just beginning to sink in. The whole of my life is changed. I've just changed . . . everything. Nothing will ever be as it was before.' She sat up, almost knocking Laura off the sofa, for she was perched on the very edge only. Then, throwing her arms around her cousin she said, 'Promise me you'll never breathe a word of it?'

'Of course!'

'Never never never never *ever!* Not even to Giles?'

'Especially not to Giles!'

To Laura's surprise she felt her cousin stiffen; a moment later Sibylla sat upright and stared at her in a manner slightly puzzled and slightly accusing. 'Why d'you say it in that tone?'

'What tone?' Laura wondered why she was being put so suddenly on the defensive.

'*Especially* not to Giles!' Sibylla echoed.

'I didn't say it like that. I said, *especially* not to Giles.'

'What's the difference?'

'All right!' Laura conceded testily. 'They sound very similar. I can't remember *how* I said it now. Anyway, what's it matter? I know what I meant. I meant that we're going to live cheek-by-jowl for the rest of our lives probably, and it would be intolerable for you if you ever suspected for one moment that Giles knew your secret. I also meant I love you very dearly, as a friend and never mind being cousins, and that I will never never never never *ever* tell a soul. Not *even* Giles! Is that better?'

Sibylla's eyes puckered and if she had had a tear left

to shed, it would have fallen then.

'And you're right,' Laura added solemnly. 'You do look awful. Drink your tea and we'll go and dab some cold water on your face.'

Five minutes later, greatly more composed in both features and spirit, they returned to the sofa and rang for a maid to bring fresh tea.

'The cup that cheers but not inebriates,' Sibylla quoted. 'I shall never touch alcohol again.'

'Or, on the other hand, you could learn to hold it!' Aureole said cheerily as she entered the room. She was fully – and rather magnificently – dressed now in a long, sleek gown of moiré silk in the deepest bottle-green. Nervously she rearranged a necklace of pale-green emeralds, saying, 'I know – jewellery before noon! Shocking. But then I never was *quite* a lady, was I! And nor' – she turned amused eyes upon Sibylla – 'it now appears, are you! Welcome to the sorority, my dear – though *majority* would be a better name, perhaps!'

'I don't think it's a laughing matter, Aureole,' Sibylla said. 'You shan't jolly me along until I say I'm proud of it.'

'But you are, of course,' Aureole replied in a confidential, comforting tone. 'At least, you ought to be.'

The cousins stared at her in bewilderment. 'D'you really think it's the majority, Aureole?' Laura asked incautiously.

'We all have something to hide, don't we,' was the almost prim rejoinder. 'I'm sure you do. Look me in the eye and tell me you're as blameless as a newborn babe!'

Laura flushed.

Aureole gave a triumphant smile and returned to Sibylla, eyeing her up and down with a critical scrutiny. 'Well,' she conceded at last, 'you *look* composed enough once more – your countenance as smooth as marble, your dress straight from the press. But what about up here, eh?' She tapped her own brow. 'I suspect that all the mess has gone and hidden up there.'

Sibylla glanced at Laura, imploring her for some lifeline. Laura said, 'Would it help if you told us more about it? Not to satisfy my curiosity – though you must know that's like a fever by now – but because . . . well, *I* often don't know what to think about something until I hear myself giving an opinion on it to someone else.' She glanced at Aureole, hoping for her support.

The older woman smiled wanly. 'The main purpose of speech is to deceive, as you well know, my dears. That's why one should always listen most carefully of all to oneself. One learns precisely what kind of wool one is currently seeking to pull over one's own eyes.'

'Thank you, Aureole,' Laura said drily. 'I hope I may never need you in a *real* emergency.'

Sibylla, feeling the attention slipping away from her (as Aureole had intended her to feel), said, 'Adam knew all about it, as a matter of fact. It was like Nelson and Emma.'

That rivetted two pairs of eyes right back where they belonged!

'He knew?' Laura echoed in amazement.

'Not at first. Oh dear!' She stared glumly into her empty hands. 'Where to begin?'

'At the beginning?' Aureole suggested.

Sibylla nodded absently, now staring off into the distance through the window. 'Is it morning or afternoon?'

'Morning. You only slept about thirty minutes.'

'Slept! That's a kind word for it.' After a pause she murmured, 'What was the beginning?' Then she looked around sharply and fixed her eyes on Laura. 'Did you honestly *want* children when you married Giles?'

'Of course!' Laura gave a puzzled, slightly embarrassed laugh.

'No, I don't mean that "of course" kind of wanting – or wanting them as a matter of course – because they come along anyway and there's not much you can do about it unless you're like Tamara Dawson and are *determined* never to have them. I mean *want*. You know? So you can hardly think of anything else. So that you look at other women's babies in bassinets and have to restrain yourself from lifting them out and making off with them. So that you wait for your husband to doze off every night and then you can cry yourself to sleep, because once again you haven't been quickened. Did you ever *want* to have a baby as deeply as *that*?'

Laura touched her arm. 'Darling!' she said softly.

'Well that's how it was for me. Can you imagine how hard we tried? And how it felt when month after month the cardinal . . . paid his remorseless visit? Poor Adam! The doctor told us to try doing it twice every day for three months. I don't think he could even bear the sight of me by the time we abandoned that. And I was at the end of my tether, too. I went over to Flushing on the ferry – this was when Adam and Daniel were first talking about setting up their partnership in Ponsharden. I took that little ferry over to Flushing and said I was just going for a walk. Actually, I was determined to drown myself. I felt so guilty! I was convinced it was all my fault – because of something that happened at . . . well, I just *was*, that's all.'

'Sibylla!' Laura squeezed her arm; tears were starting now.

But Sibylla smiled at her and said, 'Peace, child! It

gets brighter now. That was the lowest ebb-point of my life. I never felt more worthless. I'll tell you how worthless, in fact. I sat there, on Trefusis Point, and I couldn't even find the will – the grit – to walk down into the water. I thought, I'll only bungle that, too . . . the sea won't accept me . . . I don't know.' She laughed without humour. 'Anyway, when I didn't return, Daniel and Adam came looking for me. By chance – except, are these things *ever* by pure chance? – Adam took the road inland and Daniel came along the foreshore to Trefusis Point . . . found me in tears . . . listened to my tale of woe and . . . well, very kindly suggested a rather obvious answer to the problem.'

Laura caught Aureole's eye. Both knew there was something richly comical at the heart of this laconic gloss on what had happened, yet neither felt in the least bit like laughing.

To put some emotion in its place Laura said, 'I think that is . . . rather beautiful, Sib.'

'The following year, Martin was born. Of course, everyone knows you can't go by the colouring of a newborn baby – hair and eyes. But within a year I think Adam began to have his doubts.'

'Did he say anything?' Laura asked. 'Of course, by then Agnes was born, wasn't she.'

Sibylla nodded. 'I lived in dread that Adam would find out. I don't mean to imply that Daniel and I were at it like rabbits – so Adam wouldn't have found out by catching us together. There was only that one time at Trefusis.'

Laura cleared her throat.

'Yes, I know!' Sibylla responded wearily. 'There were two or three other times, a few months after Martin was born. I was so afraid Adam would twig what had happened and lock me up in a tower for ever.

So I made sure of at least one more.' She stared out of the window again and smiled to herself. 'Daniel and I made sure,' she added dreamily.

'And Meredith?' Laura prompted after a short interval.

Sibylla looked at her and laughed. 'You do want your money's worth, don't you! Yes, Meredith was different. I think Adam had not only twigged by then but he'd actually grown used to the idea. He accepted it. Fact of life. Pity – but there it was – couldn't be helped.'

Laura smiled. 'I can just hear him saying it.'

'Yes, well, he never actually *did* say it, of course. Not in so many words. But there was that sort of feeling between us. He realized I wasn't slipping into Daniel's bed at every opportunity. In fact, he knew I wasn't slipping into Daniel's bed at all – only when, how can I put it? Only when absolutely necessary. Besides, he and Daniel were such good friends by then. He told me once they were more like brothers than partners – for all that Daniel was twenty-five years older.'

'D'you suppose they ever talked about it?' Laura asked.

The question appeared to shock Sibylla; obviously it was not one she had ever asked herself. 'No!' she asserted at once. Then, 'I wonder . . .?' Then, 'I must ask Daniel that. God! I'll kill him if he says yes.' She laughed at her own inconsistency and turned to Aureole. 'You're right – as always, damn you!' she said with a jocular sort of crossness. 'One *must* listen to oneself to see what quality of wool one is trying to pull over one's own eyes.'

'And the pattern,' Aureole said coolly. 'I was just getting interested in the pattern. We had reached Meredith.'

Sibylla buried her face in her hands, parodying shame. 'I think Adam wanted another child by then, just as badly as I did. Anyway, without being too blatant about it, he left Daniel and me in a situation where . . . well, where Meredith could become something more than just a gleam in the eye.' She saw Laura's disappointment at the blandness of this précis and added, 'I'm not going to give you chapter and verse, dear!'

The maid came with the tea at last, saying she was 'sorry it had tooken so long, only they had to send round the corner for the pertickler blend.'

Sibylla, dry of mouth, finished her cup with unladylike speed and relish; she poured herself a second even as Laura was being passed her first. 'There's my sordid tale, then,' she said blandly. 'And now you see what a shameless viper you've nurtured in the bosom of your family all these months!'

'Actually,' Laura again canvassed Aureole's agreement as she spoke, 'I think it's the most heartwarming . . . story I ever heard. I was going to say "confession" but it wasn't any such thing. I don't think you have the slightest cause for shame.'

'Laura!' Sibylla was alarmed.

'What?'

'Giles would have an absolute *fit* if he could hear you now. *You* may see nothing wrong . . .'

'I don't! I think any woman would have done the same as you – feeling as you did. And you said it yourself – you and Daniel didn't, ah, go at it like rabbits.' She borrowed her cousin's phrase with reluctance.

Sibylla bit her lip like a naughty girl and said, 'Not while Adam was alive, anyway!'

'Oh!' Laura coloured to the roots of her hair. 'Well now!' She sipped her tea in some agitation.

Aureole chuckled. 'I think the point Sibylla wanted to make, dear, was that although you may respond to this beautiful and moving tale as between one woman and another, a man might see it in an altogether harsher light. Your compassionate indulgence of your cousin's actions might cause him unnecessary alarm – if you ever tried to convey them to him.'

'Not Giles!' Laura laughed confidently.

Aureole shook her head. 'It's not so long ago they *were* locking us up in towers, as Sibylla put it. And clamping chastity girdles around our loins. You ask Giles if he hasn't thought of chastity girdles from time to time since Maurice Petifer came home from the Cape!'

Laura burst into shocked but delighted laughter. 'I'll do no such thing! Honestly, Giles just isn't like that! He'd have a heart attack if he even suspected I'd thought about such things.'

'Oh, so you *have* thought about them!' Sibylla commented.

'No!' Laura blushed once more. 'Only as a . . . I mean, not seriously.'

Sibylla was relentless. 'Before Maurice came back or since?'

'Since,' Laura replied wearily. 'Obviously!'

The other two women exchanged knowing glances. 'Obviously!' Aureole echoed.

The Fiat Corsa was too sporting; the touring version of Maurice's Mercedes too bombastic; the Thorneycroft too aristocratic; the Cadillac, the Ford, and the Winton too ugly – with their great, black, rectangular radiators on the front; the Scout was too small; and the de Dion-Bouton looked splendid but hadn't enough seating. These were Giles's judgements. For him the choice narrowed down to the Opel tonneau, the Clement Talbot, and a very practical Lanchester, whose rear seating could be transformed into a goods platform. The salesmen at each showroom thought he was making a joke when he said he'd bring his wife to look at them before he decided.

But it was love at first sight between Elizabeth and the Thorneycroft. Giles might think it too aristocratic for the Curnows but it seemed just about right for the Troys – or for one of them, anyway; Jimmy could go and buy his own if he disagreed. However, being old enough to distrust love at first sight she waited until they had seen all the other cars on Maurice's list and then went back to the Thorneycroft showrooms in Shepherd's Bush. There she took the vehicle out into the field behind the garage and put it through a series of tests that left the salesman's nerves in shreds. The car, however, survived and she paid cash, so the man's belated new year resolution to go into something quiet, such as testing new explosives, evaporated. He even threw in two free tins of petrol and gave them a list of stations that would exchange empty tins for full and charge only for the petrol.

She insisted on dismissing their cab and driving Giles and Maurice back to the West End. Giles muttered something about the man with the red flag. 'Oh, we shan't bother with all that rigmarole,' she replied. 'Especially in the dark. Everyone's ignoring that rule.'

'It's not just a rule,' Giles pointed out. 'It's the law.'

'More honoured in the breach than in the observance. Don't be such a stick-in-the-mud, Giles. Maurice has no qualms, have you!'

Maurice cleared his throat and said, diplomatically – if not quite to the point – 'The electrical lighting seems quite powerful, especially that headlight.'

'There!' Elizabeth said. 'Come on, or we'll be late for the opera.'

And so, with their boyish enthusiasm overcoming their mature sense of responsibility, they climbed aboard and set off up Holland Park Avenue. The two driving lamps, mounted in front of the radiator, were low enough to pick out every ridge and hole in the carriageway surface; but the lamp beside the windscreen on the passenger side – which visually balanced the splendid brass hooter on the driver's side – made them look like penny candles as it cut a swathe through the darkness almost as bright as day. Maurice, who had a similar 'headlight' on his Mercedes, loosened the wingnut sufficiently to let him spray the light around, like a powerful jet of water from a garden hose. All the way up to Notting Hill he froze one pavement vignette after another in its mighty jet: startled maidservants off to post a letter; cheerful urchins, leaping and waving; early drunkards, hiding their faces – thinking it some new form of police bull-lantern; vagrants, chilled past all curiosity, hoping to pick up a few pence before the workhouse opened its doors and removed them from the capital's conscience for the night. And at Notting Hill Gate itself he managed to pick out a London bobby, waiting to ambush them from behind a lamp standard.

Thanks to this early warning, Elizabeth was able to cross the road and, by partly mounting the foot pavement on the farther side, avoid the constable's lunge when (too late) it came; the poor fellow was left standing in the middle of the road, blowing his whistle. Giles huddled down between the two criminals on either side of him and prayed the man had been too blinded by the headlight to make a note of their faces.

Elizabeth let out a whoop of triumph. 'That'll teach

him! Have a quick peep, one of you. What's he doing now?'

Maurice turned round. 'Scratching his head . . . taking out his notebook. We're safe – thanks to some pretty nifty driving!'

'Not to mention some fairly deft work with our searchlight,' she said, returning the compliment. Then her tone turned suddenly angry. 'Who *do* they think they are!' she asked.'They're supposed to be catching *criminals* and keeping public order.'

Giles sat up straight again and asked what her definition of a criminal might be.

'A person who breaks a *serious* law,' she told him. 'Oh, damnation!' She stared in dismay at the road ahead and took her foot off the accelerator. An official-looking man in a peaked cap was standing firmly in the middle of the road, flagging them down. 'Well,' she went on, 'I suppose it was too good to be true! Listen – this is our story: None of us even noticed a policeman at Notting Hill, all right? We're utterly astonished to hear of his existence.'

She stood on the brake and slewed to a halt just inches from the toe cap of his highly polished boot.

But he was not a policeman. Quite the reverse, in fact. He saluted smartly and said to Elizabeth, 'Begging your pardon for flagging you down, madam, but I'm here to warn all automobilists that the police have set up a speed ambush ahead, just before the Victoria Gate, if you're at all familiar with London.'

'I'm familiar with the Victoria Gate,' Elizabeth assured him. 'My *second* husband almost proposed to me there once.'

The man made a good job of hiding his surprise, though he eyed the two men with new interest, wondering what number she was at by now.

'And who are you?' Elizabeth asked.

'Patrol-man Saunders, madam, of the Automobile Association. I . . . er, see you aren't actually a member yourself.'

'Have a heart! I only bought the car fifteen minutes ago.'

'Ah, well then, perhaps you'll permit me to explain the advantages of joining? We are, of course, making the most energetic representations for changes in the law and for the raising of the speed limit to thirty miles an hour outside towns . . .'

'And inside them?' Giles asked.

'Twenty, sir. Also we're fighting the proposals in the new bill before parliament to force drivers to buy licences.'

'What?' Elizabeth was scandalized. 'Are we going to have to be *licensed* to go about on our own highways now?'

He nodded gravely. 'If parliament has its way, madam. Five shillings, it'll cost. And *each automobile* will have to be licensed, too – quite apart from its owner. Each vehicle will be compelled to bear a distinguishing number – fore and aft.'

Elizabeth exchanged glances with her two passengers; they were all thinking of that bobby reaching for his notebook – and what he might have written down if this pernicious bill were ever to become law. 'But that is quite outrageous!' she said.

'Indeed, madam. And we are fighting it most strenuously, as I said, on behalf of all members. But for the benefit of the individual member I should also point out that we maintain regular bicycle patrols along all roads where the police are known to set up speed ambushes, like what I'm a-doing here, this evening. And in the most notorious cases we form our members into convoys and escort them safely through enemy territory . . .'

Elizabeth had heard quite enough to satisfy her that the Automobile Association was articled in heaven; she took out her five shillings and joined on the spot.

'The ruinous expense of motoring!' she sighed as they set off again. 'Where will it end? I think that, as none of us is carrying guns, we'll make a discreet little detour via Lancaster Gate and avoid the police ambush altogether.'

After a moment's thought Giles said, 'It's not the ruinous expense that worries me so much as the way decent, respectable people like you and me are being turned into criminals.'

'Oh, you should talk to Jimmy about that,' she said. 'It's one of his hobby horses – how the automobile will spell the end of civilization as we know it."

'He told me it's going to strangle Helston.'

'Oh yes, that's a favourite.' She swung left out of Bayswater into Leinster Gardens, narrowly missing a telegram boy on a bicycle. 'It's going to kill every town in the land. He's a real Cassandra – or do I mean Jeremiah?'

'D'you mind my asking, Elizabeth,' Maurice interrupted. 'But have you, in fact, driven a car before?'

'You saw me!' she replied, swinging right and cutting the corner into Lancaster Gate.

'Where?' he asked in surprise.

'Back there in Shepherd's Bush. In the field behind the garage.'

'Ah! No, I didn't necessarily mean just this car. Obviously I knew you hadn't driven this one before. I mean any car.'

She laughed. 'Same thing in my case.'

'Oh!' His hand tightened on the bracket that held the headlight. 'So, ahem, this is your first time behind the wheel – of *any* car?'

'I've watched lots of people,' she explained defensively. 'You. Dr Thomas. Courtenay Rodda. It's not difficult. You put your foot on this pedal to go faster . . .'

'Yes, yes!' the two men shouted. 'We know.'

'And this one if you want to stop.'

Giles and Maurice were almost catapulted through the windscreen. Elizabeth laughed and apologized; by way of compensation she offered Giles the chance to drive.

'I've never been behind the wheel in my life, either,' he said. 'Let Petifer try.'

'But it's easy,' she assured him. 'The main thing is not to crash the gears when you change.'

'Yes,' Maurice put in, half-admiring, half-distrustful. 'If you've never driven before, how d'you manage not to crash the gears. It took me a whole day – *and* I practically wrecked the gear box.'

'Oh, but it's easy. You let the whine of the motor get up to about F or F-sharp below middle-C, then clutch in, foot off the accelerator, let it drop an octave, and she'll just slip into the next-highest gear. And it's the opposite if you're changing down, of course. With your Mercedes it's a bit lower, I've noticed – around C-sharp or D below middle-C.'

Maurice gave Giles a wan little smile and said, 'Perfect pitch! They just don't think like you and me, do they!'

Giles shrugged and waved a hand toward Elizabeth, offering her as an exhibit. 'It works, though. Plainly.'

'Do you want to try her out or don't you?' she asked him. 'I'm dying to play with that headlight.'

She had wonderful fun all the way home, the culmination of it being in Berkeley Square, where she caught a lady and a gentleman in a compromising position near a darkened upstairs window. She left a trail of cursing, blinded cabmen in Piccadilly and St

James's, and the normal good humour of the commissionaire outside Earl's was distinctly threadbare as he asked them if they would 'kindly leave the ve-hiccle rahnd the corner in Jermyn Street.'

'Well, what a wonderful, wonderful day it's been!' Elizabeth exclaimed as they left the Thorneycroft pinging and hissing at the kerb. 'Thank you so much, Maurice, for all your sterling work as a scout.'

'Hear hear!' Giles concurred. 'Especially as you're not really in the market yourself, young man. Very good of you.'

'We mustn't crow or gloat too much, though,' Elizabeth warned. 'Poor Sibylla and Laura must have had a dreadfully dull time compared to the three of us.'

On the following Monday afternoon, Giles made his second round of the showrooms to give further scrutiny to his shortlist of cars, though he was fairly certain already that the Lanchester was the one he wanted. This time he took Laura and Sibylla with him. When he told them he thought the grand-touring version of the Mercedes was too bombastic, Laura saw clearly enough what he meant; all the same, it was a magnificent monster and part of her wanted to buy it regardless. It annoyed her that the Troys had bought the Thorneycroft, for she, too, had fallen in love with it at first sight, even though it was open to the weather; of course, Elizabeth knew it would be her favourite, too – and Sibylla's – which was why she'd been in such haste to secure it for herself. In Laura's mind only the Opel tonneau and the Clement Talbot remained in the running – apart from Giles's mundane but sensible choice of the Lanchester. If Sibylla hadn't been of the party, Laura would probably have agreed with Giles at once, but some strange perversity made her want to display her independence of mind to her cousin that day. An unspoken contest thus developed between the women, for Sibylla favoured the identical two choices, and, naturally, neither of them wanted to drive around Helston in the same make of car.

Sibylla, too, had a third possibility at the back of her mind. She agreed with Giles that the touring Mercedes was more of a horseless omnibus than a carriage, and yet the sight of her driving it, all snug and dry through Cornish mists and drizzle, would surely rub Petifer's nose in the distressing fact that he had chosen the wrong sort of bodywork for the local climate.

Giles knew the cousins well enough to realize that a direct question as to their preferences would be the most disastrous way to go about it. He listened to their *mmms* and *aaahs* at each of the showrooms, watched their eyes, noted whether they bit their lips with a little smile or with a mildly dubious frown . . . and only when he was quite sure of the way the currents were flowing did he dare dip his oar.

His strategy was first to get Sibylla to make up her mind about one or other of the cars – it mattered not which, as long as she left the Lanchester out of it. That would narrow the choice for Laura, making it a little bit easier for him to steer her toward the Lanchester. They were in the Opel showroom in Portman Square at the time, looking at the tonneau; Sibylla was clearly teetering on the edge of choosing it.

'Three children . . .' he reminded her gently, larding his voice with an anxious doubt.

'Oh, they can fit there, easily.' She waved a dismissive hand at the seating, which was, indeed, quite adequate.

'Three *growing* children,' he sighed. 'Martin and

Meredith flailing at each other with their fists every other mile?'

'I'll strap them down like petrol tins. Stop manufacturing objections, Giles. This is the one you really want for yourself, isn't it. That's why you're trying to put me off.' She turned to the salesman. 'Is that really your *best* price?'

Giles interrupted. 'She's been raced, hasn't she?' he said. He knew the answer already, for the man had told Elizabeth so on Saturday – understanding very well that it would get her blood galloping.

Now the poor fellow's eyes filled with alarm, for he judged Sibylla to be of quite a different type. 'Saints preserve us, no, sir!' he said in a shocked voice. 'Not this particular vehicle.'

'No, but this marque. She did more than sixty, I gather?' He tipped the man the merest wink.

He played along at once. 'Oh indeed, I believe it has, sir. Sure, isn't it part of Opel's excellence in engineering that, although the car isn't what you might call especially built for racing – as you can see, it's equipped with every luxury a mortal could ever want – it can nonetheless beat many racers into a cocked hat. I want to tell you that!'

Giles turned to Sibylla and said, 'I'm not sure you could handle a machine of such power, old thing.'

She looked daggers at him but did not disagree. Alarmed that he might have been too persuasive, he asked the man what she was like on corners, adding, 'I don't know if you're familiar with Cornwall, but our lanes were made for drunkards, not sober people like you and me.'

The man laughed and said Irish roads were no better and if he had the choice of any car to drive home in, the Opel was the man for him. Then, with a truly Irish disregard for gender, he added, 'She's pretty nippy round *any* sort of a corner whatever.'

Just in case Sibylla wasn't getting the point, Giles persisted: 'But wouldn't a longer car be better still? A mutual friend of ours has a very long car, a Mercedes Simplex open tourer – he seems to get round "pretty nippily," as you put it.'

The salesman could hardly have missed the look of distaste on Sibylla's face at the mention of this 'mutual friend.' Being Celtically quick on the uptake, he gave the leather upholstery of the Opel a confident pat and said: 'Well now, sir, I want to tell you that this fella would put the Simplex in the halfpenny place any day of the year, so she would.'

Giles sucked a tooth and drew an inward sigh, loaded with misgiving – but he felt no more words were necessary.

And so it proved. Ten minutes later Sibylla had paid her deposit and arranged for the vehicle to be delivered to Helston station in two weeks' time. The delighted salesman ushered them to the door, though Sibylla lingered for one final act of worship before her new deity. Halfway to the door Laura went back to share the moment with her. Giles took advantage of their absence to murmur to the man, 'If that car's only half as quick as yourself, she'll do very well.'

Laura did not overhear the remark but she guessed its drift well enough from the man's appreciative laugh. She let Sibylla climb back into the cab first and then tugged at Giles's sleeve, delaying him long enough to murmur, 'I never saw anything so blatant in my life. You needn't imagine you're going to manipulate *me* so easily!' Then, on a sudden brain-wave, she called up to the cab driver, 'Take us to Warren Street, please – near the Tottenham Court Road end.'

'Eh?' Giles grunted as he climbed aboard behind her.

'Aha!' She grinned at Sibylla, who was miles away –

three hundred and eight of them, to be exact – nipping round drunken corners, leaving Maurice Petifer gnashing his teeth, choking in her dust. 'You three weren't the only ones who went looking at cars last Saturday, were they, Sibylla! And I think I may have found the very one for us – all on my ownio.' She gave his arm an encouraging squeeze. 'Actually, with a little help from Blanche.'

'Enough said!' he grumbled. 'That darkness outside is not the evening drawing on, I have just realized, it is the storm clouds of defeat, already massing high in the sky.'

From Portman Square to Warren Street was a mere ten minutes. They paid off the cabbie when they arrived because the two women were intending to have a swift browse through Shoolbred's, the big departmental store in Tottenham Court Road – once they had put the trivial business of choosing an automobile behind them.

'*Voilà!*' Laura crowed, waving a hand at the showroom window.

'A Lanchester!' he exclaimed with delight. 'You minx!'

Laura peered more closely through the glass and saw that, indeed, where the little Renault had stood last Saturday there was now a brand new Lanchester, the exact twin of the one he had shown them earlier that morning in Marylebone Lane. The Panhard was still there, though – looking as grand as ever. She almost said, 'That wasn't there last Saturday!' – but changed it just in time to, 'I knew it wouldn't stand comparison, you see. See them side by side and there's no contest.'

Now full of doubt he followed the two women into the showroom. Until that moment he had felt sure she was opposing his choice merely to make a point – in other words, she agreed that the Lanchester was the car for them but she'd run the gamut first and make it look like *her* considered choice, too. But now, looking at the Panhard, he was less certain – not only of her true feeling but of his own.

The two cars that everyone talked about as the flowers of the field were Mercedes and Panhard. Laura had confronted him with the only car that could compete – in terms of esteem if not of speed – with Maurice Petifer's. Perhaps, after all, she was quite serious, and not merely making a point about her own dignity?

And perhaps, he thought, looking at the magnificent machine now before them, she was right! It would certainly take the shine off Petifer's petty triumph.

'You're pretty amazing,' he told her ruefully. 'I have to admit it.' He chuckled. 'I can just imagine Maurice Petifer's face when he sees what we've bought!' He gave a demonstrative wave at the Panhard.

'Giles!' she exclaimed crossly.

'What?'

'Well, of all the reasons for buying a car, that's the very weakest.'

'Quite, quite,' he said penitently. 'Anyway, it's not true. There are one or two things he could look down his nose at with the Panhard.'

'For instance?' she asked sharply.

'Well, the Mercedes has a steel chassis. The Panhard's is of wood.'

'Armoured wood, sir,' the salesman pointed out as he joined them smoothly. 'There's a lot more craftsmen around the country who can repair wood than can weld steel.'

Giles shook his head sadly, 'Not in Cornwall, I fear. You can hardly cross the road without bumping into a steel welder down there.'

The man cleared his throat but said nothing further on the point. Instead he drew their attention to the magnificent coachwork, which was entered from the rear of the vehicle, by opening double carriage doors between the back wheels.

'Now that *is* good,' Giles exclaimed with renewed enthusiasm, patting the seats, which ran in a backward-facing U around the other three sides of the passenger compartment. 'We could get a local carpenter to make up a sort of platform that would sit on top of the seats. When I'm using the car alone, I mean. It would be like a huge shelf. We could put stuff on the floor as well – so we'd get two storage areas for the price of one. Better even than the Lanchester!'

The salesman gave him a pained look. 'Do I understand that you might be using this limousine in the way of *trade*, sir?' he asked.

Giles explained that he owned several warehouses over an area of some twenty miles, all of which he visited regularly – and that it would be convenient to have some means of ferrying material between them at the same time.

This merely confirmed the fellow's worst fears. 'I'm not sure the Panhard Company would quite approve of using one of their limousines for such a purpose, sir,' he warned.

'Damn their impertinence!' Giles replied. 'You almost make me determined to buy the thing on the spot!'

'Giles, dear . . .' Laura plucked at his sleeve and again drew him aside.

'Where's Sibylla?' he asked.

'I've changed my mind,' she said. 'I don't think it's the right car for us after all. You were right – the Lanchester's more our mark, or' – she smiled and pronounced it the French way – 'our *marque!*'

'But damme, I'm not going to let a bunch of garlic-reeking Froggies tell me that my business isn't good enough for their *limu-zeen!* Who do they think they are!'

'It doesn't matter, darling. It's not what they think that matters – it's what we think. And I think you're right. The Lanchester is much more suited to our purpose.'

He put on his best disappointed face and stared grumpily at the Lanchester. 'Well,' he conceded reluctantly, 'I have to admit it is a more *sensible* car. But oh!' He gestured toward the other vehicle as if it would break his heart to turn it down now.

'Next year, perhaps,' she offered soothingly. 'When the Lanchester has earned its keep and raised our profits so high we can buy a couple of Panhards out of petty cash!'

He gave her a grateful smile and said, 'Without you, my dear, I'd just be a little boy going mad in a toyshop. Very well, then – if your mind is made up – the Lanchester it is!' Again he looked about the showroom. 'Where *is* Sibylla?'

'She just popped out for some fresh air, or so she said. Actually, I suspect she's beginning to think she ought to have bought the Panhard rather than the Opel! Go and tell her the good news. It'll buck her up to hear we aren't buying it, either.'

'You tell her. I'll settle with this chappie.'

'No. I need to wash my hands.'

He went out and found Sibylla standing a little way up the pavement, at the corner of Fitzroy Street. 'What now?' he inquired as he approached. 'Penny for 'em?'

'It's like that game,' she said, continuing to stare vacantly down the street toward Fitzroy Square.

'What game?'

'Stone, scissors, and paper. You're going to buy the Lanchester, aren't you? I know it.'

'Laura talked me into it,' he confessed lamely. 'Just when I'd set my heart on . . .'

The rest of his sentence was drowned in her laugh. 'I've just realized what you made me do.'

'I?' he asked in a wounded tone.

'The Opel's not the car for me at all. It's too . . . I mean I should have bought the Panhard.'

'Oh! For heaven's sake!' he exclaimed. 'You'd just drive around looking like a chauffeuse of an empty car – or you'd *need* a chauffeur, if you wanted to ride with your children. No, Sibylla – the Opel is absolutely *made* for you.'

'For me?' she asked blankly. 'What am I?'

'A free spirit. A wild, free spirit. Picture yourself on a summer's day, sitting behind the wheel with your hair streaming free in the wind – pushing the Opel up to sixty across Pendeen Sands! How can you *think* of getting any other car!' He put one arm round her and gave her a friendly hug. 'What are you staring at? I thought your Uncle Drogo's is round the corner.'

He knew he ought to let his arm drop; leaving it there, around her shoulder, was adding layers of significance to a passing gesture. He told his hand to let go but it refused.

'It is,' she said, leaning her head lightly on his shoulder. 'Oh, Giles! I feel so . . . I mean, why have I bought a car at all? Why am I in London? Why am I . . .?' She completed the question with a momentary press of her head.

'Everyone has days like that,' he said. 'Are you worried about whether you can afford the car? There's no need – you could buy a dozen and not worry.'

She shook her head and gave the briefest little laugh – too brief for him to know whether it was genuine or despairing. 'You are very good to me – and *for* me, too.'

'We're good for each other.'

She lifted her head away and stared at him in surprise. 'Yes!' she exclaimed. 'That's true, isn't it.'

Now he had to let his arm drop, or propriety would have forced her to remove it for him. 'What *were* you gazing at so intently?' he asked.

She pulled a rueful face. 'You'll be shocked.'

'I doubt it.'

'There's a house of doubtful repute down there. Aureole de Verity told us about it . . .'

'The devil she did! I don't wish Laura to discuss such things.'

Sibylla laughed harshly. 'But for me it's all right!'

'I didn't mean to imply that – and you know it. You're a free spirit, as I said . . .' He faltered and stared at her unhappily, aware where his unguarded words had led him.

'Yes, my lad!' she said grimly. 'Scratch the libertine and you find a prude. Scratch the liberal and you find – what?' She jabbed a finger at him in answer.

'I deserve that.' He hung his head.

'*Aaargh!*' She clenched her fists and shook them at the street lamp.

At that moment, as if it were a cue, the lamplighter cycled up, slowing to a snail's pace while he deftly hooked down the lever with his long pole, then picking up speed as he made for the next lamp. 'Sorry ducks!' he called back over his shoulder – having taken her cry of frustration as rage at his lateness.

'How dare he speak to you so insolently?' Giles exploded. But the sight of her laughing face melted his annoyance – though he had no idea why she was laughing. 'We ought to go back,' he said, making no move. Then, after a pause, during which her eyes fixed him with unnerving keenness, 'Why did you cry out like that, anyway? Was it something I said?'

She nodded. 'You are so uncannily like Adam in some ways. Most men, when they find themselves in the wrong – especially with a woman – try and bluster their way out of it. But he always just hung his head and gave a little grin and admitted he was wrong – if he agreed, I mean. And you're the same.'

He peered keenly into her face, now that he could see more than a twilight blur, and smiled. 'I can't decide from your tone whether you approve or not.'

'Nor can I,' she confessed. 'In one way it's admirable but in another it's just awful. Women are brought up to cope with almost anything but that. You know why that lamplighter was so insolent, don't you. You know what sort of woman he took me for.'

'Oh – back to that, are we?'

'Does it embarrass you?'

He shrugged, unwilling to admit that it did.

'You seemed sanguine enough at the Café Royal the other night. Is that because Elizabeth Troy led the way – and she's Jimmy's problem, not yours?'

He shrugged again. 'Something of the sort. Come on – or Laura will be wondering.'

'Wondering what?' She did not move.

'All sorts of things.' He touched her arm gently.

She took one last glance down the street as she readjusted the fur of her coat collar. 'Three,' she said. 'Oh no, there's two of them going in. So that's four.' She turned to Giles. 'Four men have gone into that house in the last – what? – it can't be more than ten minutes.' She gave a theatrical shiver and clutched the fur coat tightly to her neck. 'I can't imagine it.'

He offered her his arm. 'What did you mean about paper, stone, and scissors?' he asked as they set off on the stroll back to the showroom.

She chuckled drily. 'Not very apt, is it. I mean, you manoeuvred me into buying the Opel but you also manoeuvred Laura into buying the Lanchester. So we're not paper, wood, and stone after all, are we.'

'Oh well,' he said, 'as to that, you may be closer to the truth than you think. I know Laura only brought us here to delay the choice. I know she didn't expect to find the Lanchester here as well – I could see it by the shock in her eyes.'

'No. It was a little Renault when we were here on Saturday.'

'There you are, then. But even so, she came within a whisker of convincing me to buy the Panhard. If she'd been sincere herself, we'd certainly have bought it. So we might very well be wood, paper, and stone to each other after all. It just needs you to defeat me at something.'

They were almost back at the showroom by now. He was aware that she was dragging her feet and wondered if she realized it, too. On a sudden inspiration he said, 'D'you remember that time I kissed you?'

She stopped dead. 'Yes.' It was little more than a whisper.

'Have you ever thought about it since?'

She glanced rapidly all about them and dragged him into a darkened doorway, recessed a little beside the projection of the showroom. There, before he could protest or make his escape, she clasped his head between her hands and pulled his lips to hers.

Later he told himself that if she hadn't more or less forced him to it like that, he would have found some way to avoid what happened; but he only had to remember the warmth of her lips, the softness of her lips, the sweetness of their touch, the desperation of her kiss . . . and he knew that he would have traded the wonder and beauty of that moment against a guaranteed millennium in purgatory.

Next door, Laura gave up the struggle to open the lavatory window, just as, a few minutes earlier, she had given up the struggle to light the gas in the tiny little lavatory to which the maid had shown her. She stood at the darkened pane and stared. Half of her simply did not believe the plain evidence of her own eyes. But, strangely enough, the other half exulted in a new and curious sense of liberation.

Shock alone carried Laura through the next few hours. Shock enabled her to smile at the other two when they met again in the car showroom; shock helped her to walk arm-in-arm with Sibylla through the departments at Shoolbred's, enthusing over this, criticizing that; and shock allowed her to sit through dinner and the theatre that night – and to behave throughout as if nothing were amiss. True, Giles noticed that she seemed a little absent and he asked her if she was going down with Jimmy's cold (from which the man himself had now recovered sufficiently, at least, to be up and about again).

Then, somewhere around two o'clock that night, alone in her hotel bedroom (for although Giles snored lightly at her side, she had never felt more alone in her life), the numbness began to wear off. She became aware that she was suffering not one shock but several – or, perhaps, that it had several layers. At the most superficial level it was the actual image, blued and romanticized in the gaslight, of those two heads, her husband's and her cousin's, devouring each other with such ravenous passion. Had she kissed Maurice like that? Laura wondered. Surely not? Her kiss had been tender, compassionate, born of sorrow for his loss and pity for his terrible loneliness; it had not been an invitation to . . . anything further.

Perhaps Sibylla hadn't been lying after all when she said Giles had also come to the hospital that night and seen her and Maurice out on the lawn beneath the stars. So was this his idea of a just revenge? Never! The Giles she knew was simply not like that – which proved yet again that Sibylla must have been lying.

But why? To cover up this betrayal – in case she, Laura, ever found out what was going on? Her stomach fell hollow at the thought, for it implied that what she had stumbled on last night was no isolated incident but one of many – stretching back to at least that first night here in London, and probably much further. The viper!

It dawned on her, too, that she was more shocked at Sibylla than at Giles. Did that mean she no longer singled Giles out as someone special, the one and only man in her life? Did she now lump him in with all the others – for she certainly expected men in general to be faithless to their wives and to seize whatever opportunities were put in their way.

The words 'put in their way' lingered in her mind – begging the question as to who did the putting? Hussies, they were usually called . . . trollops, wantons, mantraps . . . they had a thousand names but none of them 'Sibylla' – until now. Whether or not last night saw the first act of infidelity between them, it had been Sibylla who dragged Giles into that darkened doorway, Sibylla who had thrown her arms around him, Sibylla who had pulled his head to hers and wakened his passions to a point beyond his control. Yes, she had done everything possible to put herself in his way. No death was too good for her; the Chamber of Horrors at Madame Tussaud's Waxworks provided the basis for several pleasing fantasies of revenge – which had started running through Laura's mind even in the immediate aftermath, even as she and her cousin held up lengths of dress fabric and furnishing material for each other to admire or reject, joking and laughing like the best of friends.

And that, she now saw, was why she felt so much more bitter about Sibylla's betrayal than her husband's – it was the loss of her friendship. Sibylla had been the best friend she'd ever had, and now it was over. Even if, in the fullness of time, they patched it up and forgave and forgot, it would never be the same between them, never – as Sibylla would say – never never *ever!* The echo of that moment of shining tenderness between them only increased the bitterness of her loss. Now she had no really close friend – no *bosom* friend – in all the world. How bleak the prospect that stretched before her!

Giles turned in his sleep. She, in her wakefulness, turned to him and studied his face, as much as she could see of it in the dim light that struggled feebly through the curtained windows. All the emotions she had invested in those dear features over the years – where were they now? She felt neither warmth nor coldness for him, merely an all-pervading . . . numbness. There was no other word. How could she feel such anger toward her cousin, who was no doubt blissfully asleep next door, and nothing for her husband, whose share of the blame was almost as great?

A disquieting answer occurred to her: She could *afford* her anger at Sibylla, for its only consequence was the loss of a friendship that had already suffered a mortal wound; but anger at Giles involved calculations that paid scant regard to questions of right and wrong and all those finer feelings. The marriage of emotions may wither, but the legal union remains. It was like stripping a house of all that made it a home: the carpets, the soft chairs, the cushions, beds, mattresses, the fires and fireplaces – leaving only the cold stone walls, the empty, echoing chambers, the memories and ghosts of departed joys and laughter. It was the difference between Chynoweth and Parc-an-Dour!

A terrible sense of desolation filled her as she realized she could not *afford* to show her anger to Giles – or, rather, she could not afford to show it to the man Giles would become if she withdrew her love and let him see how bitter his betrayal had made her. The Giles now sleeping at her side had married an unwilling and resentful girl, had courted her with kindness, brought her bouquet after bouquet of his own goodness, and finally captivated her so totally that – as Sibylla had once said – it was almost embarrassing to be near them at times. *That* Giles found it only too easy to let the powers that were his by law and custom rust in their locked and disused armoury.

It would be quite another matter if she were to withdraw her love and replace it by her anger. For she would then be turning a marriage based on affection and trust into one based on right and duty. She might as well shove the law books under his nose – with markers at all the appropriate pages!

And yet *he* was the one who had first removed that trust.

Her own little episode with Maurice didn't count. She had enough warmth and love in her – no, not love, but something close . . . devotion, perhaps – enough of it, anyway, to spare a little for Maurice without depriving Giles of the smallest share. And anyway,

Giles knew nothing about it. What the eye never saw, the heart never grieved.

There was a little, exhausted silence in her mind before she told herself that Giles might very well think the same of what he and Sibylla had done. She gazed at his face again and was suddenly overwhelmed with all the tenderness that, only moments earlier, she had failed to summon.

Angrily, she turned away. She did not *want* that gentleness to win her over now. She wanted to go on nursing her grievance, exploring the new sensations of pain and aversion . . . learning new things about herself – awkward, uncomfortable things that had become honeyed over in the bland cocoon of her marriage. And how could she do that if she kept seeing Giles's point of view and thinking, oh well, what was it really? Just a little kiss!

She wanted her rage. She wanted her bitterness – pure and unalloyed. Through them she had been granted a brief sighting of a Laura whose existence she had never suspected. She had seen a Laura who did not define herself by her marriage to Giles; a Laura who drew no strength from her kinship with Sibylla (nor their friendship, either); a Laura who did not even need her children in order to uphold her claim on a time and space in which to live.

And the Laura who *was* Giles's wife, who *was* both cousin and friend to Sibylla – and mother to five adorable anarchists – wanted to know more of that other self. After all, she might, in time, prove a better friend than ever Sibylla had been.

More reliable, anyway.

Not that that would be difficult . . .

Sleep came at last, leaving everything unresolved and offering no solutions of its own – as usual.

The shallow, restless sleep that had finally wakened Laura in the small hours was balanced by one so profound that she slept without further disturbance until seven. Then she came wide awake all at once, feeling so bright and refreshed that the best part of a minute went by before she realized she had no right to be cheerful at all. Her mind returned to the brief, life-shattering incident she had witnessed the previous evening and found, to her surprise, that it was no longer quite so life-shattering after all. She lay there, watching the first rays of an almost horizontal sun make patterns on the wallpaper behind her head, exploring this unexpected change.

It was not that she had grown miraculously more complaisant during the night; nor was it that she cared less about the betrayal. The parts of her that sustained and fed upon those emotions were as large as ever. But something new had joined them, she decided – something within herself. It looked forward, not back; it was indifferent to yesterday and preferred to sniff at the wind for harbingers of the morrow; its indifference extended to *all* her yesterdays, the good as well as the bad. It paid scant heed to Giles or Sibylla – and even less to anything they might do.

This last was borne out for her in the most immediate way, for she was fully clothed and half-way downstairs before she realized that nothing but a single, unlocked door now separated her husband and her cousin – and she didn't even falter in her stride. They could get up to whatever they liked, she told herself bitterly. She would not let it hinder her.

Yet she was canny enough to stop for a word with the porter. 'I didn't wake my husband,' she told him. 'I'm only going for a stroll in Green Park. Will you let him know, if you see him looking worried before I return? And if I'm not back by eight, I'll be taking breakfast with our friends at the other place.'

Only when she was out in the street, walking down St James's toward The Mall, did she realize that her words to the man had been full of overtones, to anyone with an inquiring mind. Why, for instance, did she not write a note now and have one of the chambermaids slip it under the door? Why should Giles look *worried*, anyway? Puzzled, yes – even bemused – but not worried, surely? Not over something so trivial. But, she thought comfortingly, perhaps the first thing hotel porters lost was that sort of inquiring mind. Their way of surviving.

And was this her way? Cultivating her own company . . . crying a plague on both their houses?

An omnibus went by, almost full, all going to St Pancras Without. Without what? London was always busy. The poor horse looked tired and worn already.

Actually, she wasn't just cultivating her own company, she was befriending that new Laura, whom she had only glimpsed last night – the self who owed nothing to Giles and drew no succour from her friendship with Sibylla. Laura Without!

At the bottom of St James's, she hesitated, being uncertain as to whether she could get to Green Park by turning right through Cleveland Place. She had just decided to go round the longer way, by The Mall, where she was quite certain of access, when she heard a halloo from behind. Turning, she saw Maurice Petifer striding down St James's, smiling broadly. 'Pardon me, young lady,' he said as he drew near, 'but you seem lost. May I be of assistance?'

'Yes!' She gave a little toss of her head. 'I'm looking for my Self – have you seen it lately?'

He stopped a few paces short and looked at her with his head on one side. 'That doesn't sound like you. That's the sort of joke Elizabeth might make.'

'Perhaps it's infectious. Perhaps that's what I've caught instead of Jimmy's chill. Actually I was wondering if one could get to Green Park that way?'

'On foot one can,' he told her. 'There's a little gate between Bridgewater House and the London Museum. I come this way each morning. D'you like fresh milk?' He offered her his arm and, thrusting his cane forward like a lance, escorted her across the road.

When they reached the far side she did not let him go. 'Isn't this nice,' she said.

'So far, anyway,' he agreed.

She poked her head forward and looked up at him. 'That's not like you, either. That's the sort of thing Jimmy would say.'

He laughed. 'Then it is infectious. In fact, they're a compelling couple, aren't they. Don't you agree? They've put their own stamp on this London jaunt. Even though you're staying in a different hotel you must feel it. I mean, wouldn't it be an entirely different visit if it was just the three of you?'

She shivered dramatically. 'I don't even want to contemplate such a possibility, Maurice!'

'Oh? What now? Trouble in paradise?'

They turned down into Stable Yard, making for the back of the London Museum.

'Talk about something else,' she said.

'Hmph!' he said heavily, pursing his lips and sinking his chin as if giving her injunction the gravest thought.

'Why d'you call it paradise?' she asked.

'Slip of the tongue.'

'Ah! You mean you're giving something away! Is that Elizabeth's name for our . . . *ménage-à-trois?*'

He stared in amazement at the phrase. 'D'you know what it really means – *ménage-à-trois?*' he asked.

She blushed. 'Well, I don't mean *that!*' She laughed awkwardly to prove it – and then added, 'Although, I don't know . . .' Then, more firmly, she repeated: 'No! I *don't* mean that.' Then she looked away and sighed. 'Oh God!'

He steered her up the side of the museum railings – only to discover that the gate he had mentioned was padlocked. However, he seemed to expect it, for he at once took out a silver toothpick on a chain and began to fiddle with the mechanism of the lock.

She watched him in astonishment awhile and then said, 'Here – you can't do that!'

'So I can't!' he replied as the padlock sprang open. He swung the gate wide and ushered her through with a courtly bow.

'Giles would have a fit if he could see us!' she murmured as she went past him into the park.

'He'd also have quite a long walk round,' Maurice pointed out as he swung the gate to behind them, snapping the padlock closed again.

'Did you know it would be locked?' she asked.

'Of course I did. I told you – I walk this way every morning.'

'But what if someone had caught us?'

'What if?' He laughed. 'Actually someone did the first day, one of the keepers. I told him it was all right, the duke had given me a key. Duke is the most powerful word in the English language. Ah! And here's the wood nymph with the milk! Good morning, Charlotte! You are looking radiant today. It must be all that healthy milk.'

The woman, who was in her early twenties and who did, indeed, look extremely bonny, rose from her milking stool and, carrying the pail safely out from under the cow, gave a low curtsey – far too low to be anything but ironic. The cow went on placidly chewing the cud.

Maurice winked at Laura and said confidentially,

'She drinks it *before* she waters it down, of course!'

Charlotte smiled at Laura as she handed her a cup of warm, fresh milk, dipped from the pail. 'It's only 'is 'umour, lady.' Under her breath – but intended to be heard – she added, 'And 'e's welcome to it.' She favoured him with a roguish grin as she handed him his cup.

Laura remembered the young females in Piccadilly that night, and what Elizabeth had said about their easy conversation with the gentlemen. It struck her now that it was not just women of that sort who enjoyed the privilege but many others of the labouring class, as well. Perhaps Miss Sweet? Certainly Miss Sweet!

The milk was good – slightly bitter, as it often is when still warm and frothy from the cow. Maurice gave Charlotte a shilling and told her to keep the change; the cheeky smile returned, hinting that she had never intended doing otherwise.

'That's an outrageous price to pay for two little cups of milk,' Laura admonished when they were out of the woman's hearing. 'It's a maid's wages for a whole day, d'you realize!'

'Ach!' he replied scornfully. 'You don't understand money, you and Giles. That girl's smile lifts my heart every morning. She's better than a whole flock of skylarks. What would that shilling do if I left it in my pocket? Wear a hole there, that's all.'

'A fool and his money are soon parted,' she observed.

'A fool and his money can teach the world to dance,' he countered. 'Take your pick.' He laughed. 'They're both equally untrue!' He stopped and turned to her then, serious again. 'You never used to be like that, Laura. You used to be so carefree yourself. Talking of which – you made a joke back there in St James's –

about looking for your *self*. I'm not so sure it was a joke now.'

'No.' She stared down at the grass, wishing he'd start walking again.

He waited for her to say more and then sighed. 'Ah well . . .'

She linked her arm with his and urged him gently forward.

'Where were we?' he asked. 'Oh yes! *Ménage-à-trois*. Perhaps we'd better not go back to that!'

'Call it a household-à-trois, then,' she said. 'Does Elizabeth call our household-à-trois a paradise?'

'If I said no, you wouldn't believe me.'

'And if you said yes, you'd be telling tales out of school.'

'There you are, then.' He gave her arm a brief squeeze.

'She probably meant you to pass it on,' Laura observed. 'She's like that, I'm afraid.'

'Aren't we all! I intended her to pass on what I told her about Sarie and Jannie.'

She remained silent.

'Why didn't you stop me when I told you?' he asked. His tone was mild – puzzled rather than accusing.

She shrugged. 'Maybe I wished I *had* heard it from you rather than from her. Would you find it hard to tell me about Sarie?'

'Ha!' He pulled his hand out of his pocket and revealed two slightly crushed chocolates. 'I lost those last night. D'you mind a bit of fluff?'

She picked off the worst of it and blew the rest away. 'Gritty praline!' she said. 'My favourite!'

He sucked all his teeth clean before he said, 'The hardest thing is not to idealize her. I've given up trying with Jannie because he was only two when he died. I've idealized him out of all real existence. That's why it's so good to see young Maurice and Meredith about the place – and hear them! But with Sarie . . . it's different. It's easier not to sanctify her.'

'Describe her. D'you mind? I mean, not if it's painful.'

'No,' he said dreamily. 'It's not painful.' He gave her arm a little shake. 'Relax! You're so tense as a trumpet, maid!'

'Sorry.' She forced her hand and arm to go limp. 'Now I'm so wet as a flounder, boy.'

He chuckled. 'That's just the sort of thing she would've said. Afrikaans, of course, not Cornish, but it's her sort of humour. In some ways you're very alike. In all sorts of ways, in fact – which is only to be expected, I suppose.'

'I meant describe her looks.'

They reached a fallen tree by the side of the Broad Walk; with a lift of the eyebrows he invited her to sit awhile. When she prepared to do so, he whipped out a clean handkerchief and spread it on the trunk where she sat. He, however, did not sit beside her but put one foot on the trunk, like a hunter with his trophy, and leaned on his cane, staring off into the distance, toward Hyde Park Corner, as he spoke.

'She was a little shorter than you, slender, but strong as an ox. She could lift me up in her arms and carry me. She was fair-haired, almost ash-blonde – like yours – which is uncommon among the Afrikanders. She looked more Nordic than Dutch.' Pauses began to grow between his words. 'High cheek bones . . . intense blue eyes . . . like blue glass, blue diamonds . . . and such a *spitfire!*'

The word brought Laura up with a jolt.

He laughed. 'Oh yes! Not *only* a spitfire, mind. She was so intense in everything she did. I never met anyone else with such a . . . such a *rage* for life. She wanted . . . everything. To know, to do, to feel, to taste, to touch, to experience . . . everything! There used to be a little travelling library that came round to all the *dorps* and she asked me if I thought it would be possible to read all the books in it! She was very difficult to live with because nothing ever satisfied her for long. She always wanted to change it. Everything always had to be different . . . different.' He stood erect again and waved his hands at the hopelessness of trying to convey a character so mercurial without seeming to grumble or criticize. 'Anyway, that was Sarie. And I'm sorry I didn't tell you directly.'

She rose and took his arm again. 'Well, for my part, I'm glad you waited until now, Maurice.'

'I didn't exactly *wait*,' he pointed out.

'I'm glad Destiny waited, then.'

'Oh, him!' he said disgustedly.

She laughed. 'Don't you believe in Destiny?'

'When I hear *he's* stalking the land, I go and oil my guns.'

'Well, I do,' she said firmly, giving his arm a *so-there!* shake. 'I believe it's Destiny we met this morning rather than yesterday or tomorrow. Can I ask you a question?'

'As long as it has nothing to do with the price of milk.'

'Oh Maurice!' She butted her head against his shoulder. 'I'd forgotten so much about you. Let's not go back for breakfast. Let's just wander off all day together and renew . . .' She did not complete the suggestion.

'Renew what?' he asked after a pause.

'Well, the old friendship at least. We could do that, surely?'

'All right,' he said simply.

'Which? Renew the friendship or just not go back for breakfast?'

He stopped and turned to her, forcing her to look at him. 'The question is,' he told her solemnly, 'can we do the one without also doing the other?'

And she knew he was not talking about such a trivial matter as where they should eat their breakfast.

Laura had obviously not noticed that the door was slightly ajar. Sibylla could hear everything as she lay in bed and listened to her dressing. She could tell her cousin's mood just from the way the clothes went on – crisply, irascibly, with no pause for preening or admiration. She could just picture Laura buttoning up her bodice, then gripping it firmly between the butt of her palm and the tips of her fingers and yanking it down. Then hook, hook, hook, hook, pat, prod, and tramp-tramp-tramp across the floor to her wardrobe to deal with the jacket. That was arm-thrust, arm-thrust, tug at the lining . . . ditto the other side, tummy in (the little, cross-tempered exhalation gave that one away), bottom button, next, next, damn! – then two more buttons followed by several exasperated noises when the hook at the collar refused to mate. Then it was just gloves . . . three choices there before she settled on the right ones . . . hat, hatpin, fox fur, and cape. Five steps to the door. And silence.

Or Giles giving a little groan and then silence.

Sibylla rose and tiptoed down the corridor, intending to do all her toilette and get dressed. Somewhere at the back of her mind was the thought that she ought to go out and find Laura, who was probably working up an appetite for breakfast in St James's Park; the two of them ought to have a serious talk. Somehow Laura had divined what had taken place in that stupid, mad moment with Giles in Warren Street yesterday; Sibylla had to make her understand that it meant nothing and would lead to nothing – and that she'd move out of Chynoweth the moment they all returned to Helston. But her spirit quailed at the prospect of such a distressing interview, and then a great lassitude overcame her and she went back to bed. What was a holiday for, after all.

Five minutes later Giles staggered from his bed and padded off down the corridor, too. After a couple more minutes he returned – and only then did he notice that his wife was no longer in the bed beside him.

'Laura?' he called softly.

Then, no doubt noticing that the connecting door was slightly ajar, he came and stood just the other side, murmuring again, 'Laura?'

After a pause he muttered, 'Oh, well . . .' and Sibylla heard him go back to bed.

'She's not in here,' she called out.

Meanwhile, things had been livening up in the vestibule below. The porter, realizing he might not have time later – and might miss the lady's husband altogether – decided to make sure of her message by writing it down and getting one of the chambermaids to slip it under the door. Giles, who had got out of bed again to see if the two cousins were playing a trick on him, spotted it on his way to Sibylla's room.

Thinking that the pusher of the note must be Laura – and that the two of them were, indeed, playing him some kind of jape – he flung open the door and frightened the poor maid out of her skin with his roar of 'Gotcha!'

Several apologies and a sixpenny tip later, he was knocking at the connecting door, saying, 'May I come in? Here's a devilish rum thing.'

'Very well.' Sibylla sank down in the bed and pulled the bedclothes tight up around her neck.

'She's gone out for a walk,' he said, still perusing the letter. 'Says she's going to have breakfast at Earl's. She didn't even write the note herself – just told the porter to let me know. That's not like her. It's all very odd.'

'Oh dear!' Sibylla sighed.

He tore his eye from the page and looked down at her. 'Why d'you say it like that? Don't you think it's odd?'

'I heard her get dressed, about twenty minutes ago. She sounded very . . . tetchy. Oh Giles, I'm awfully afraid she saw something last night – in Warren Street. Except how *could* she? We were well out of sight of the showroom.'

'Ah!' He cleared his throat awkwardly and explained why Laura might not have been actually in the showroom at just that moment.

'Damn!' Sibylla, feeling distinctly awkward stretched out flat like that, sat up and hugged her bedjacket around her. She bent her knees till they met her chin and let her head slump between them. 'She did see us then. There must have been a window in that side wall. I didn't spot it. She had no light on. Oh, my dear – I'm so sorry. It's all my fault.'

He slipped the letter in his dressing-gown pocket and sat tentatively on the outermost inch-and-a-half of her bed. 'I don't know how you can say that, old thing.' He reached across and patted her head, turning the gesture into a caress before he made to withdraw altogether.

But she reached up and clamped it there, against the back of her neck, saying, 'Because I dragged you into that doorway entirely against your will. Admit it! You were as surprised as could be.'

The tips of his fingers began a feather-light massage of the nape of her neck, which was pale and beautifully slender against the dark of her hair; in the deep shadows on either side he could just discern the fine lines of her collarbones. He tried to make out the soft curves of her breasts but it was too dark. 'The only thing I'll admit to,' he replied, 'is that I was too much of a coward to make the move myself.'

Her head shot up from its resting place on her bent knees, trapping his hand beneath the long, free mass of her hair. 'Why? I don't understand. Where does cowardice . . .'

'Oh, Sibylla, ever since you kissed me that time at Parc-an-Dour I . . . I haven't been able to get it out of my mind. I know it's wrong. I know I ought to have the self-discipline to forget it. No – I can't ever forget it. But the self-control to *do* nothing about it. I ought at least to have that much character. But I'm like a man caught in a quicksand. The more I struggle, the deeper I sink and the faster I am held in this . . . morass of my own feelings.'

She groped for his hand and placed it between her knees and chin – and gently massaged his knuckles with little movements of her jaw.

'So what d'you want to do next?' she asked.

He closed his eyes. 'You know what I want to do next.'

She stopped breathing, for she had meant, 'How do you want to extricate yourself?'

'Don't *you?*' he asked. He was shivering now though his hand felt hot and fevered.

She kissed it ardently. 'Yes,' she whispered.

As he got into bed beside her she added, 'But just this once, Giles, my dear. It must never happen again – certainly not after we get back to Cornwall. Promise?'

'Promise.' His hand curled round her head, pulling her face down to meet his.

'Never never never *ever?*'

'Mnmh!' His could not talk because his lips were full of hers.

The very act of *not* going back to Whittaker's for breakfast, and not letting the others know her whereabouts and plans, was one of such monumental independence for Laura that, for quite some time, she did not want to talk about it, or even think about it – as if, by some childish sort of magic, that would somehow diminish the enormity of it all. She held tight to Maurice's arm, for moral as well as actual support, and together they sauntered up Piccadilly looking for somewhere to eat breakfast. They almost decided on the Ritz but then Maurice suggested they should be more adventurous and go farther afield; after all, they were not exactly pressed for time.

As they left the Ritz behind them and crossed St James's they were spotted by Elizabeth Troy, who also relished a walk before breakfast, though not the sort of route march Maurice indulged in; she had, in fact, been hoping to catch him on his return from Green Park and enjoy his company for the last furlong or so. To have Laura's company as well was a double, if unexpected, pleasure. She lifted her hand, intending to wave and catch their attention, when it dawned on her that they were crossing the street rather than turning into it. Intrigued, she walked up to Piccadilly, thinking they probably intended turning in at Duke Street or cutting through the disused graveyard at St James's Church, either of which would bring them back into

Jermyn Street and Whittaker's Hotel. She was just in time to see them entering the Burlington Arcade – in other words, going in precisely the opposite direction. Smiling to herself, she turned and hastened back to Earl's to share this fascinating intelligence with Jimmy.

At the top end of the arcade Laura and Maurice turned right into Burlington Gardens, past the London University building and the West End branch of the Bank of England. 'And there's Savile Row, with all the best tailors,' he said. 'And the famous Albany.' He pointed out the modest entrance. 'Where all the rich bachelors live.'

'You could have chambers there,' she said, referring to his use of the word *rich*; but then she realized he might be thinking that she was referring to the word *bachelor*, forgetting Sarie and Jannie already.

'They call them sets, not chambers,' he told her as they wandered on into Vigo Street. 'I could, but I'd consider idleness to be a kind of living death. It's strange – when I left the Cape, after my luck with the diamonds, everyone patted me on the back and said now I could live the rest of my life in *idleness*. Why is idleness considered so desirable? D'you understand it?'

They had to step around a gang of labourers who were hauling large capstones up to the roof of the post office, on the corner with Regent Street. 'I'll bet those fellows do,' she replied.

'If I hadn't bumped into you today, I'd probably have gone back to Cornwall. All this traipsing round galleries and museums, and night after night of dining and theatre-going . . . it's not my style of thing at all. I keep wondering what sort of mess Peter Hosking and George Munroe are making, and whether my new cypresses are surviving these frosts we've been having.'

'Yes!' she interrupted. 'That was quite a plantation you made!' Why didn't he mention Miss Sweet, too?

'It'll be very decorative,' he replied defensively. 'I chose a wide variety of different greens. Also it'll give you wonderful shelter from the east wind . . .'

'I was thinking more of the ones you put up along the roadside,' she said archly.

'They'll shelter me from the north.'

'And from all visual connection with Parc-an-Dour!'

'So it will!' he said, as if that had never occurred to him. 'As a matter of fact, they were Miss Sweet's suggestion, when I was going through Leyland's catalogue. Talking of which – it's a jolly good thing you reminded me!'

He patted several pockets and drew a fat-looking letter from one, which he dashed back half a dozen paces to post. Laura just managed to glimpse Miss Sweet's name on the envelope.

'You write very large,' she said when he returned. 'Or copiously.'

'It's mostly patterns she asked me to get from Swan and Edgar.'

Laura wondered what a mere housekeeper would be wanting with patterns from a leading West End store but held her tongue.

Maurice obviously felt the disapproving weight of her silence. 'I wish you could learn to like her more,' he said as they set out to cross Regent Street. 'She thinks the world of you.'

Laura was so astonished that she halted in the middle of the crossing, and was regaled with some colourful suggestions from drivers in all four directions. 'She hardly knows me,' she objected.

'Oh absolutely,' he replied with laconic agreement. 'That's what I tell her.'

'Maurice!' She gave him a playful punch as they set

off again, making now toward Brewer Street. 'Seriously though, how can she possibly have such a high opinion of me?'

'It's your children. She judges you by them. She says that for general pleasantness and intelligence in conversation they're head and shoulders above any other children in Helston. D'you want me to go on – there's lots more!'

'She hardly knows them, either,' Laura objected – but her tone was not nearly so scornful as before.

'Oh, you'd be surprised. They pop over most days. They seem especially fascinated by the pigs. They like feeding the chickens, too, and seeing Molly milk the cows. Really, I suppose, they like the farm because dirt doesn't matter. Miss Sweet usually does her best to send them home clean and tidy. That's when they chatter away with her.'

Laura shuddered to think what intimate family affairs they might have revealed in their artless gossip – 'My daddy's got three teeth he can take out . . . my mummy's got hundreds and hundreds of perfume bottles . . .' and worse. 'I suppose she dredges them for all our secrets,' she said grimly.

'Blanche put her in her place, all right.'

Laura was glad to hear it. But then he explained: 'Culdrose Farm, Lizard Road, Helston, West Penwith, Cornwall, England, United Kingdom, Europe, Northern Hemisphere, the Earth, the Solar System, the Milky Way, the Universe!'

'Oh yes, that's Blanche all right!' She clutched his arm. 'Oh Maurice, I miss them suddenly. Blanche especially. I know a parent shouldn't have favourites, but there it is. They grow up so fast, don't they – they're someone different every month. I think I want to go back home, too. Tomorrow. We've got our car, so there's nothing more to stay for. Shall we go – you and I – even if the others don't?' She chuckled. 'That'd set the cat among the pigeons!'

'Your car,' he remarked. 'Tell me about that. You got the Lanchester in the end, I suppose?'

'I wanted the Panhard.'

'Oh? We didn't look at a Panhard.'

'No. Sibylla and I saw it . . . in . . . no I don't want to talk about it.'

He let the subject drop. They were approaching Little Pulteney Street, where Soho – or the gastronomic part of it – begins. Spices, curries, the obscure smells of Italian warehouses and of German *Delikatessen* assailed their nostrils, making them acutely aware of the appetite they had worked up by now; they were also the aromas of the Curnow family business, so they carried additional resonances for Laura.

'What about here?' Maurice waved a hand toward a bistro called *Au Boul' Mich'* in Wardour Street.

Laura peered in through the glass of the door and saw the menu chalked up in large letters over the counter. The first item was *omelette aux fines herbes*. 'Yes,' she replied without bothering to read further. They went in and took a table in the corner; the place was more than half full, mostly with office people on their way to work.

Unbidden, the waiter brought them two small glasses of cognac and coffee. Their shocked stares challenged each other to be the first to refuse the liquor. 'Cheers!' Maurice said at last, draining the glass in one.

'Cheers!' She followed suit. 'It's going to be that sort of day, I feel.'

The waiter returned with the bottle but they both declined a refill. 'I suppose I'll have to tell you,' she said glumly. 'Else it'll nag at me for ever. I can't get it out of my mind.'

He sipped his coffee – not taking his eyes off her – and waited.

'Can I ask you a question?' she began, looking nervously around to see whether those within earshot were eavesdropping.

He nodded.

'Remember that evening Trevanion got kicked . . . when we met up at the hospital . . . when you kissed me out on the . . .'

'Well!' he said. 'I was under the impression it was the other way round. Never mind.'

'All right. But what did you think I meant by it? Did you think I was . . .' She swallowed heavily. 'I mean, did you think I wanted . . .' She closed her eyes and murmured, 'Oh dear!'

'I never supposed you were suddenly overwhelmed by my charm and beauty.'

'No – be serious!'

'Very well. I thought you were moved by an extraordinary sympathy to do something that would otherwise never have crossed your mind.'

She opened her eyes and smiled at him, a smile overflowing with gratitude. 'Exactly!' she said. 'There – I knew it!'

'Why is it so important – I mean at this moment?'

'Because of what happened in Warren Street yesterday evening.'

'Is that where you saw the Panhard but bought the Lanchester?'

She nodded. 'Among a thousand other trivial events, yes. I mean, trivial compared with what *I* shall remember that day for – and remember it until my dying breath.'

And she went on to tell him what she had seen from the unlighted window in the car showroom.

His face betrayed no emotion whatever.

'Well?' she prompted.

'It could have as innocent an explanation as what happened outside the cottage hospital.'

She shook her head. 'There wasn't time. Anyway, what secret tragedy has Sibylla been hiding from us?'

'Perhaps the tragedy was Giles's, not hers?'

The waiter brought their omelettes, together with croissants and a bowl of soft, white butter, which Laura tasted from the tip of her knife with a gesture whose professionalism outweighed its impoliteness. 'Unsalted,' she said. 'Normandy?'

The waiter nodded and beamed at both of them – and thereafter treated them as honorary French.

When he had gone she said, 'What tragedy could Giles possibly have been concealing? It's absurd.'

He waited until he had finished his mouthful – taking care to make appreciative French-style gestures of approval at the chef. 'I was just thinking. You remember Sibylla interrupted us that night – otherwise you'd no doubt have explained at once that it was sympathy and tenderness alone that had moved you.'

'Oh, Maurice, don't!' she said petulantly.

'Don't what?'

'Go all supercilious like this.'

He stared at her briefly, intensely, and she realized that her justification for kissing him that night had wounded him. 'Anyway, what about Sibylla?' she went on.

'Even at the time it struck me as odd that Giles didn't come up to the hospital with her. They both returned home from Parc-an-Dour at the same time, I presume? She said they'd been there, inspecting Dancey's work, and she'd only just heard. Surely she'd never have come out without telling him – and surely then he'd have come, too?'

'But he didn't.'

'Didn't he? That's my point. What if he *did?* What if he heard us? We weren't exactly whispering. What if he came running along the hedge and saw you kissing me?'

She shook her head. 'That's exactly how I know he didn't.'

He grinned at her. 'But I saw you hesitate a moment.'

'Only because Sibylla tried to tease me by telling me he *did* see us. But you don't know Giles as well as I do. He couldn't possibly keep something like that bottled up, even for three hours, without saying anything – and certainly not without my being aware of it. How long has it been? Almost three weeks.'

He eyed her speculatively. 'I wonder how well you do know Giles. Would you, for instance, believe me if I told you he threatened to shoot me if he caught me so much as looking at you?'

Her laughter drowned the end of the question. But when she looked up and saw he was actually waiting for an answer she became serious at once and said, 'No!'

He nodded.

She persisted: 'I don't believe it.'

He continued to nod. 'On the eighteenth of July last – the evening of the auction.'

'But he took you out to dinner that evening. He was being the last word in Rational Man – free of primitive emotion and so forth.'

'Well, all I can say is that Rational Man has a pretty turn of phrase when it suits him. Giles's last words to me on that evening were, as close as I can recall them: "If you make the slightest move to take up your old relationship with Laura, I'll break every bone you possess, I'll flog the skin off your back, I'll break you in tiny pieces. They won't need a stretcher to carry you off on – they'll need a sack." You may laugh. You may think I'm inventing it. But I assure you those were his final words to me that night.'

'Giles?' She still couldn't believe it. She remembered how he had come smiling up to their bedroom and assured her how civilized he'd been . . . telling Maurice he was welcome as a neighbour – more or less putting him on trust to behave responsibly. 'D'you tell me that on your honour?' she asked.

He nodded.

But then if Giles could conceal something like that from her . . .

She was unwilling to complete the thought. Instead, she said, 'But why would he have said nothing about . . . the other matter? Going back to that evening by the hospital, now. Why would he have kept silent about that for the past three weeks?'

He gave her a trapped sort of look. 'I can think of several reasons,' he said, 'but are you sure you want to hear them?'

She smiled glumly. 'Whether I want to or not, I think I'd better, don't you? I hardly seem to know the man at all, it would appear.'

'Well . . .' He drew his words out reluctantly. 'Suppose that what you saw in Warren Street last night was not the first . . . I mean, it's such an *odd* place to snatch a kiss – *if* it was their first, don't you think?'

'Oh God, Maurice!' she murmured, closing her eyes and shaking her head in disbelief.

'I'm sorry. I should have kept my mouth shut.'

'No, no. You did absolutely right to point that out.'

'It was the first thing I thought of.'

'And you're right – it *is* an odd place, an impossible place, for that sort of thing to . . . begin. In other words, it means that obviously wasn't the beginning.' She opened her eyes again. 'I don't even want to go back to the hotel at all now.' Then a further thought struck her and she gave a hollow, almost sepulchral laugh. 'And I've left them virtually alone together! I might just as well have opened her door and pushed him into her room.'

Maurice looked at her accusingly. 'And you mean to say that thought hasn't occurred to you until this moment? Truly?'

She smiled, unable to sustain the pretence.

He went on remorselessly: 'Are you sure you didn't leave them like that precisely in order for it to happen?'

'How can you possibly say such a thing?' She stared at him, her eyes dark with shock.

'Very easily, Laura. I notice, for instance, that all the dreadful revelations of the last five minutes haven't made the smallest dent in your appetite.'

She glanced down at her plate and found it empty. She reached for the second croissant, being sure it was there – only to find she had devoured that, too. 'I had no idea . . .' she murmured.

'Now *there* I believe you!'

She frowned. 'Why are you being so . . . cold, Maurice?'

'Far from it, my dear. Analytical, perhaps – but one of us has to be.'

'I can't see why,' she grumbled.

'I'll tell you, then. Ever since last night – and certainly from the moment we met this morning . . .'

'By chance!' she put in quickly.

'You're still doing it!' He pointed briefly, accusingly, at her. 'You know jolly well I've been going for a stroll down that way every morning. Never mind – never mind!' he added when he saw her draw breath to object. 'The point I'm making is that you have embarked on a certain course of action and you're wriggling like an eel to disguise your real purposes from yourself.'

She suspected there was more than a grain of truth in his words, but she didn't wish to face it. 'What does it matter if I am?' she asked.

'It matters a great deal, Laura, because Giles, I suspect, knows precisely what *he* is doing. And why. And that puts you at an enormous disadvantage.' He smiled sympathetically. 'Doesn't it!'

Giles and Sibylla sat disconsolately on an Italianate marble bench in the North Court of the Victoria & Albert, pretending to inspect the electroplate copies of the armour in the Tower of London. In fact, Giles was genuinely inspecting them – for want of something to fill the rather oppressive silence. He was thinking of all the labour and skill – and money – that had gone into those copies. And for what? The resulting objects would be shut away in glass cases for ever, to be gawped at by visitors who, for a twopenny bus ride, could go and gawp at the originals. And what did it mean to them? One woman had just passed by, commenting to her companion, 'Weren't they titchy little fellows in them days!' The futility of all human endeavour had never seemed more obvious to him than at that moment.

'No chastity belts,' he muttered to Sibylla.

She remained silent.

'In fact, I'm beginning to wonder if there ever were such things,' he went on. 'Probably what happened, you know, was that bold Sir Harry Fitzknightley got a spanking new suit of armour made up for one of the crusades – something like this stuff here – and his wife said it wasn't fair that men got all the glamorous outfits, and he said he was off to defend Christendom, and what, pray, did she have to defend? And so she reminded him. And then, just for a joke, he got his armourer down in Savile Row to make up something appropriate – the first and only chastity belt! A joke!'

'Giles?'

'What?'

'Please stop talking about chastity belts.'

'Oh very well.'

'In our present awkward circumstances you know it is hardly the most tactful of subjects.'

'Yes. Sorry.' He sighed. 'I do think Elizabeth needn't have shown quite so much relish.'

'Ha!' Sibylla exclaimed, as if Giles had just made one of the greatest understatements she'd ever heard.

'She could simply have told us she saw them entering the Burlington Arcade. Thousands of people enter the Burlington Arcade every day. There's nothing at all . . . you know . . . in that. Maurice told me he wanted the new edition of *The Commercial Market Garden*. Perhaps they went to buy that.'

'If he'd wanted a book, they'd have gone to Hatchard's, which is on the opposite side of Piccadilly and farther along. Oh!' She closed her eyes and put her hand to her midriff. 'I feel sick.'

'We could go and have a cup of tea,' he suggested. 'It was unwise not to eat any breakfast, as I said at the time.'

She clamped her jaw tight and counted to ten. Then she said, 'I mean sick with dread. Not sick for want of food. How you can eat the way you did . . .'

'Why sick with *dread?*' he asked in surprise.

'Because she *knows*, Giles! Laura knows.'

'How can she? The porter saw her go out and he's sure she didn't return. Are you suggesting she shinned up a drainpipe? There's no other way. And in any case, Elizabeth saw them just over half an hour later coming back from Green Park along Piccadilly. She'd have have had to be a champion sprinter to spy on us *and* get round Green Park in that time – especially if she had to shin up a drainpipe, too.'

Much against her will Sibylla laughed, saying at the same time, 'It's not at all funny, Giles – except that the picture is so impossible.' Then, glum again, she continued, 'I don't know *how* she knows – I mean, obviously she left the hotel and obviously she didn't come back.'

'Well then!' he said cheerfully.

'Perhaps it was telepathy. I often know what she's thinking without her saying a word about it.' More softly, speaking half to herself, she added, 'I know I was thinking about her all the while we were . . . doing it.' There was an even quieter afterthought: 'And so were you.'

'Not in any very affectionate sense, I assure you,' he said grimly.

'I realize that! Your every thrust was like a vindictive . . . spiteful . . . like a shout of triumph in her face, almost.'

'Don't be so indelicate,' he said. 'It's unseemly.'

'Oh yes! You're happy enough to *do* it, Giles, but please don't let's talk about it. Fie! Well, I say shame on *you!* I wouldn't be surprised if you didn't actually *want* Laura to know. You probably even want her to watch us *doing it.*'

'Don't keep on using that vulgar expression.'

'I'll use one even more vulgar if you keep on.'

'Anyway, the idea's absurd. Why should I want such a thing?'

'So that you could shout "So there!" at her. You don't feel any love for me at all. You just want to use me as a vehicle to help you vent your anger and humiliation over her behaviour with Maurice Petifer.'

He absorbed this in silence. He let the silence extend until it had put enough distance between her anger and his reply. 'May I remind you that I kissed you *before* I saw her betraying me.'

She looked at him wearily and shook her head. 'If I thought you believed that rubbish – what you've just said, Giles – I really would despair of you.'

'But it's true! Can you deny it? I kissed you at Parc-an-Dour that afternoon . . .'

Her eyes searched his face, staring rapidly, first at one eye, then at the other. 'You don't honestly believe *that's* when it began, do you?' she asked. 'It goes back much farther than that – at least to the day of the auction. For all I know it goes back to the day of your wedding.'

He felt a great chill spreading inside him. Sibylla was right, of course. He nodded morosely as he thought back to the day of the auction. 'Bloody Pettifer!' he said. 'It all goes back to him. He didn't actually need to do a thing. He didn't need to smile at Laura – or even look at her. He just needed to *be* there! I mean, simply for us to *know* he was there – even if we never even saw him – it was enough to change our lives. To make us change. I sometimes look back on the way we were – this time last year, say, when we thought he was dead – I mean, I look back on the sort of people we were then and I see us as . . . sort of automata, almost. We were just going through the motions of living. I had Laura, she had me, we had our family, our house, our business . . . we got up each morning knowing exactly what needed to be done and we sallied forth and did it. Every day we made a little improvement. We increased our trade, got a broken slate mended, bought a new outfit, wrote half a dozen long-overdue letters . . . you know? We just . . . went on. We accepted yesterday's little improvements and added one or two more.' He stood abruptly and clawed at his collar, as if he were suddenly choking. 'God, weren't we arrogant!'

'Giles?' Sibylla rose, too, and plucked at his sleeve, worried at this sudden access of passion.

Their eyes were on a level. He stared into hers and said, 'Is this how murders begin?'

Her jaw fell open.

'Is that the logical end of all this – the things that have been happening to us – the changes that odious man has forced on us? Shall we spend the rest of today quietly plotting the perfect murder?'

'No.' She swallowed hard.

'Why not?' he asked, though she could tell from his tone that he was now merely debating the question. A moment earlier she was sure he had been actually promoting it.

'Because that would be his ultimate triumph – to take three sane and happy people and turn them into creatures so bereft of good sense and reason that they'd plot his murder. It would be the crowning of his mission.' She gave a little laugh – a genuine laugh, too. 'D'you know what, Giles? I feel suddenly hungry. There are refreshment rooms here, aren't there?'

He nodded. 'At the very heart of the museum. Say what you like about the English, they know how to put first things first. Actually, I'm a little peckish, too.'

'You!' She prodded a finger in his tummy. 'How you can put so much food away and keep such a trim figure, I don't know. It's not fair.'

The waitress brought them a pot of tea and a fine selection of treacled and honeyed buns. 'I feel as if an enormous weight has suddenly gone,' Sibylla said cheerfully as she made her selection. When the waitress had gone she added, 'It's the absence of guilt, of course. I don't feel guilty any more. I wonder why that is?'

'What did you mean when you talked about Petifer's mission?' Giles asked. 'You said that if he provoked us into murdering him, it would be the crowning of his mission.'

'Oh, that.' She wrestled with the dough, having nothing but a little fork to assist her. 'These buns are really only suitable for picnics, where you can wash your hands in a rock pool after. I say! Let's all go on a picnic when we get back to Cornwall, eh? The first fine day of spring. You always used to swim before Easter. Perhaps we can arrange an accidental drowning? When is Easter this year, anyway? I must look it up.' She glanced up and found him patiently awaiting her reply. 'Oh, because I believe the Fates make special arrangements for smug people like you and me and Laura. You said we were like automata. I think a better word is smug. I mean, we all thought we'd arrived at our final destinations in life, barring catastrophe. And all we had to do was keep the paint fresh and add the odd little improvement here and there. But we didn't have to fight for things any more. It was all just sparring – shadow boxing, don't they call it? Well Fate, as I say, has a special range of horseshoes to slip inside her gloves for folk like us. And the one she slipped in – in our case – is called Maurice Petifer. "Teach them a lesson, Maurice!" she told him. And by heavens, hasn't he just!'

Giles, though amused by her whimsy, was chagrined at the truth in the heart of it. 'You said it goes back to the very first day, the day of the auction. D'you know I threatened to kill him that night – twice! And invited him to dine with me at the Angel in between!'

She stared at him in amazement – for, of course, it

would never do to reveal that Maurice had already told her of it. 'You?'

He nodded.

'I can't believe it, Giles! You who have always maintained that wars between nations could be outlawed forever if only people would sit down and talk rationally over their differences . . .'

'I know, I know!' His hands warded off the accusation. 'I aimed a shotgun at him and told him the wounds would be consistent with the accident I would describe. I had him more than half-convinced I meant it, too! And then, as I say, we dined at the Angel – just to still the Helston gossips and keep the fight a private one – you see, he and I were able to cooperate perfectly over that! And then, when we parted at my gates, I told him . . . oh, I don't know what – I described five other deaths I had in store and told him his friends would need a sack to bring him home in . . .' He vanished in a reverie for a moment.

'Giles?' She touched his arm hesitantly. 'You're supposed to laugh when you say things like that.'

He managed a smile at least – and then looked quizzically at her again. 'When you said just now that we'd *arrived*, and only needed to give our lives a lick of paint, et cetera. Did you really mean that? In your case, I mean?'

Her eyebrows shot up. 'Why should my case be any different? I was every bit as self-satisfied as you and Laura. I had a bouquet of happy memories, three loving children, a fine house . . . I was comfortably off and happily in charge of my own affairs. What more could I want?'

'Well . . .' He was flustered at having to put it into words. 'There is also . . . I mean – what happened this morning . . .'

She grinned. 'Ah! So Laura *didn't* tell you! One up

to her. I owe her an apology. I felt quite sure she would tell you.'

He frowned with one eyebrow but said nothing.

'Suffice it to say that I had made adequate arrangements in that department of my life – at least, they were adequate for me.'

Still he stared at her.

'No, Giles, give up! I am certainly not going to tell you the name of the obliging gentleman.'

The news left him crestfallen, but she mistook his expression for one of criticism. 'Ah,' she said coldly. 'It's all very well for men, isn't it! There are girls on every street and houses *in* every street – for all I know. But let a respectable woman like me make a quiet and modest arrangement with a caring and considerate gentleman – hurting no one – and the sky might as well fall in! Well the reason I feel no guilt, dear Giles, is that I've had *lots* of practice.'

He closed his eyes and gripped his forehead in his hand, massaging it as if in pain. She continued to misinterpret him. 'If you can't accept me as I am,' she began . . .

He shook his head. 'It's not that, Sibylla.'

'What then?'

'I'm too ashamed to tell you.'

She sat there, with the wind taken out of her sails, not quite sure what to tell him. At last she said, rather tentatively, 'And if we can't be frank with each other . . . well, there's also no point in continuing.'

He stared at her bleakly. 'I'll tell you, then. When you said you've had lots of practice at feeling guiltless . . . can you guess what thought immediately ran through my mind?'

She shook her head.

'Then women simply do not think like men,' he said, as if the discovery depressed him enormously.

'The immediate thought that ran through my mind was: *Good! Perhaps we can do it again soon, then!* Now, I suppose, you'll never want to speak to me again.' Almost pleading with her, he added, 'Yet it was you who asked for absolute frankness between us, Sibylla.'

She gave him a reassuring smile. 'D'you really believe women don't think like men? Of course, *that* thought's been going through my mind as well.'

'Why didn't you say, then – when I asked you if you could guess?'

'Because I didn't imagine you meant something so obvious! However, I'm not going to think about it now. If it's going to happen, it's going to happen.' She grinned again. 'I'd much rather take up your other suggestion – how to murder Maurice Petifer and not get caught. Just as a game, you know.'

'All right,' he said. 'But not here. It's too oppressive. Let's go up and walk in Hyde Park. It looks as if the sun's come out.'

They finished their small but sticky repast. He slipped twopence under the plate as they left.

'You're in a generous mood,' Sibylla said, taking his arm.

'I wonder what Laura's doing now?' he replied. 'Is she with him still? Are they wandering around some other museum or art gallery, talking about us? Perhaps he's telling her that I threatened to kill him if he so much as touched her? And perhaps she's suggesting he might as well be hanged for a sheep as a lamb!'

He halted and clenched his eyes tight in pain, clasping her hand firmly against him in case she tried to take it away. 'Oh, Sibylla! Are we just going to go on like this – Laura and me – drifting apart? Why can I not speak to her? I can speak to you – why not to her?'

'People are looking at us, Giles,' she murmured.

'Bugger them!'

'Come on outside, my dear.' Firmly she guided him toward the entrance in Exhibition Road. As soon as they were outside she felt the tension relax in his arm, though he still kept up enough pressure to hold her there. 'It's a good question, Giles,' she went on – knowing she dare not let the moment pass. 'Why can't you talk to Laura?'

He stared up the rise toward the park gates; he seemed to be wondering if they'd ever make it. 'Because I fear what she might say,' he told her. 'She might tell me it's over. She might say she's going to leave me and live with him.'

'And lose her children?' Sibylla asked scornfully – before adding somewhat lamely, 'Not to mention losing you!'

'Hah!' He gave an ironic little laugh. 'Well fielded! Even worse, she might say she is *not* leaving me but I must understand that our marriage is now a mere matter of form and that her heart is engaged elsewhere, even if she doesn't . . .'

'Giles!' she exploded, shaking his arm and propelling him forward, up the hill. 'You're talking about Laura! Does any of that sound even remotely like her? I never heard such tosh!'

But he would not be jollied out of it. 'I don't know her any more, you see. When Petifer first came back to Cornwall, I felt sure she'd simply cut him dead – not out of her own feelings but out of consideration for me.'

'But the fact that she didn't only goes to show how unimportant it is to her – or was at that time. It's *you* who've made it important ever since. I've stood back in amazement sometimes, watching you doing things that almost drove her into his arms.'

'I know, I know! It's all my fault. I'm not saying that sarcastically. I truly mean it, every word. I know I've been my own worst enemy in everything I've done . . .'

'And Laura's worst enemy, too.'

He rallied at that, however. 'But she has been deceitful about it,' he said. 'For instance – something I never told you – but when the horse kicked Trevanion that day, it was because Petifer had been driving Jimmy Troy out in his new car – and he couldn't resist showing off how loudly he could make it backfire. That's what frightened the horse and made him kick out.'

'How d'you know this?'

'Because Hinks told me. He was there, actually in the stables, at the time. But what he also told me was that Laura gave him the strictest instructions never to mention that the cause of it all was Petifer's car. She told him to keep his name out of it at all costs. That was like a knife in my heart, Sibylla – when I heard that. Trevanion was at death's door for all she knew, yet all she could think of was to protect her darling Maurice!'

Sibylla made no reply to this intelligence.

After a while he became calmer again and said, 'Or d'you think I'm making a mountain out of a molehill?'

'We could,' she said slowly, 'tamper with his car in some way and then challenge him to a race.'

That evening everyone behaved as if it had been a perfectly normal day. They were all urbane and charming to each other at dinner. Laura gave a glowing account of the Covent Garden fruit and vegetable market and the colourful characters she and Maurice had encountered there; while Sibylla listed the wonders of the Victoria & Albert Museum as she and Giles had experienced them. Rather unwisely, as it turned out, she included the electrotype copies of the armour from the Tower of London. Jimmy, recalling a conversation he'd had with Giles the previous November, turned to him with a smile and said, 'No chastity belts, I guess?'

Elizabeth, shocked at his bluntness, asked what on earth he meant.

'Oh, just a little conversation this fellow and I had once,' he replied, grinning at Giles, who did his best to respond.

The others exchanged bewildered glances. But when Laura noticed that her cousin's expression was tinged with annoyance, too, she decided not to let the matter drop. 'See here, Jimmy, you can't just leave it at that,' she complained.

'It was a trivial, *trivial* conversation,' Sibylla put in belligerently, daring Jimmy to contradict her.

'Were you there?' Elizabeth asked, her surprise growing greater with each new revelation.

'Yes!' Sibylla insisted tetchily. 'We decided that there never was such a thing. It was all a joke. What happened was . . .' And she went on to give, almost word for word, the jocular gloss of events that Giles had spoken that morning. 'Anyway, that was Giles's opinion,' she concluded amid their laughter. 'Wasn't it?' She turned to him.

He smiled gratefully. 'I didn't think you were listening.'

'I wasn't,' Sibylla replied. 'It's all so tedious, anyway. Thank heavens we live in modern times.'

Laura looked at Jimmy, who winked back at her, as if to say, 'Now watch the fun!' He cleared his throat. 'Tell them what I said, too, Sibylla,' he exhorted. 'It maybe wasn't so funny as Giles's contribution, but it was wittier.'

Sibylla had no need to think, she fostered on Jimmy the thought that had run through her own mind while Giles had been annoying her at the museum that morning. 'It should be in your own words, Jimmy,' she told him calmly. 'They are always so *justes*. However, to the best of my recollection, you said that the full-length mirror is a far better guardian of the average wife's chastity than anything that blacksmith ever forged of fire and steel.'

'Jimmy!' Elizabeth exclaimed accusingly. 'How ungallant!'

'No no!' Sibylla leaped to his defence. 'He meant that, thanks largely to the widespread availability of full-length mirrors, modern *men* have a far better idea of how absurd they look in a state of nature than their forefathers obviously did in the days of Good King Hal. Isn't that what you meant, Jimmy?'

He bowed his head and applauded her silently, symbolically.

'*Touché*, Jimmy!' Giles mocked.

'*Le mot juste*,' he replied; a courteous dip of his head conceded that his tease had backfired for once.

Laura, aware that some obscure battle of wits was going on and that Sibylla had just won it, was miffed. 'I don't think either of you two men is right,' she said. 'You only consider it from the male point of view.'

'Aha!' Elizabeth rubbed her hands gleefully. 'I knew there'd be more to it!'

'We're all ears,' Jimmy told Laura.

'And thanks to your full-length mirror,' Sibylla put in swiftly, 'you're only too painfully aware of the fact!'

Laura took advantage of their laughter to think of something, for she had, of course, spoken off the top of her head, merely to avoid having to let Sibylla have the last word.

'Think of Penelope, while Ulysses was away,' she said. 'All those suitors for her favours, pestering her and pestering her – until in the end she says very well, but just let her finish weaving this length of cloth. And then for the next nine years – or however long it was – she has to spend all day at the loom and all night unpicking the day's work, just so that she never finishes it. What a life! What woman wouldn't leap with delight at the prospect of a steel belt all covered with spikes – or whatever they were!'

'I'd call it out of the frying pan into the fire,' Elizabeth said.

Laura, tired of being made to feel one down by two women who, she knew, had enjoyed fully adulterous liaisons, wanted to make her point. 'Some women would leap at it with delight, anyway,' she said.

'*Some* women,' Sibylla apparently agreed. 'But then *some* women bind their feet until they can't walk – or stretch their necks with gold rings until they'd die if you took the rings away – or stick plates in their lips until they can't talk. That's *some* women for you!'

'Some women,' Laura replied frostily, 'realize it is far more pleasurable to break the Seventh Commandment in their minds than in somebody else's bed!'

Maurice, dividing his attention evenly between the other two women, was surprised (though not greatly) to see how this assertion confounded them. Both flushed slightly; both drew breath to respond; and both faltered. Sibylla recovered her poise first. 'Actually,' she said, staring directly at Maurice, 'when it comes to breaking commandments in your head the Sixth has the others beat hands-down for sheer prolonged pleasure. One can spend all *day* at it!' She turned to Giles and added, 'Can't one!'

He smiled at Maurice to show it was a joke and said, 'Indeed one can.'

Maurice staightened his tie and, staring Sibylla out, echoed her earlier remark: 'Thank heavens, indeed, that we live in modern times!'

'Actually,' Jimmy said to Elizabeth that night as they were preparing for bed, 'we live in exciting times. Did you pick up one half of what was going on there tonight?'

She finished rubbing cream into her pores before she replied. 'I didn't even twig what you were saying. What was all that about chastity belts and mirrors?'

'Oh!' He waved his hand dismissively. 'Something Giles once said to me over the port. Sibylla certainly wasn't there. Everything she said was invented – but she was *good!* She sure can think on her feet. But it was pure invention.'

'Pure is not the word I'd use! However – what did Giles really say? When did this conversation take place, anyway? And apropos what? How do two men like you get onto the subject of chastity belts?'

'I'll give you one guess!'

'Oh that!' she exclaimed wearily. 'Petifer?'

He nodded.

'Dear, oh dear!' She rose and went across to their bed. 'Men make such a fuss about fidelity.'

He chuckled. 'Don't we just!'

'Laura's given Giles five. Why should he be so obsessive about the tail-enders?'

He lay down beside her and cleared his throat. 'Talking of which . . .'

'Yes,' she said.

'You did say you'd think about it after we came back from the tour.'

'Yes.'

'And we've been back six months and are well settled again.'

She smiled at him. 'Jimmy – I've said yes twice already. Do you want it in triplicate?'

At that same moment Laura, too, was removing the ravages of the day from her complexion. She and Giles were discussing the meal they had just eaten – in particular, whether the béarnaise had been quite sharp enough. Neither of them had referred to her day-long absence with Maurice, nor to his hours with Sibylla. As the small platitudes of daily life fell easily from their lips, she just sat there, thinking it the most extraordinary conversation they had ever held in all the fourteen and a half years they had been married. He *must* be wondering why she had simply walked out of the hotel that morning, leaving nothing but the briefest word with the porter (and that a lie, as it turned out); he *must* suspect, at the very least, that it had some connection with events in Warren Street the previous evening. Surely he would have to mention it soon? Or did he expect her to be the first to broach the subject?

Perhaps he did. He had always made such a point of stressing how free she was, how equal with him in all the most important aspects of their life together. Perhaps while the jealous husband chafed and raged down in his bowels, the rational man was calmly sitting there behind his eyes, insisting she had a perfect right *not* to tell him how she had spent her day. Also that he, consequently, had no right whatever to demand to know. If she wished to tell him, she would.

And did she wish to tell him? she wondered. She decided she did, indeed – but not directly, somehow; she wanted him to interrogate her, insist on being told, force it out of her – so that she could then fling it defiantly in his face. How could she nudge him to the point?

Her speculation as to what was going on in Giles's mind was not too wide of the mark, as it happened. There was, however, a further layer to it of which even he was only dimly aware. In one way, it suited his troubled conscience very well *not* to know what Laura and Petifer had done that day. Imagination offered a salve that detailed knowledge might remove. In the mists of his suspicion three points already stood out clearly: She had once whispered Petifer's name in her sleep; she had once tried to conceal his responsibility for Trevanion's injury; and she had once kissed the man. And now there was a fourth: She had stolen a day out of their marriage and spent it with him.

But suppose the mists were swept away and those four points stood revealed as *all* there was to it! Set against his own infidelities, it would be meagre indeed. Better then to leave them be – hinting at so much more. It did briefly occur to him that his unwillingness to sweep away his doubts about her was, in fact, the greatest infidelity of all; but he needed those doubts. They were his shield. And so his mind shied away from the monstrous implications of that notion.

'Maurice says he's pretty fed up with this London jaunt,' she said, taking the combs out of her hair and letting it fall.

Though he had actually lifted the blankets and had one foot in the bed, he let them drop and came over to take up her hairbrush. With long, gentle strokes he began to sweep it through her liberated tresses. 'Quite a while since I've done this,' he commented.

She moved her head slightly, this side and that, to show him where to go next.

'I feel pretty guilty, too,' he went on.

'Guilty?' Her raised eyebrows met his in the glass.

'About all this idleness. I'll bet he's thinking of muckspreading . . . harrowing . . . sowing spring greens . . . hoeing the violets. Just as I keep thinking of all the people in the trade I ought to be seeing while we're up here. And instead, here we are, him wandering round the West End and me haunting the museums!' As an afterthought he added, 'And failing to find an electrotype of a chastity belt!'

Oh no! she thought. *You don't slide into it that easily!* She also wondered why he failed to mention her presence in the wandering and Sibylla's in the haunting. 'As a matter of fact, I believe he'll go home to Culdrose before Saturday,' she said.

'And you? D'you want to go, too?' he asked. 'I could stay on a few days, see these people, and follow you early next week. Would that suit?' His tone was far too casual.

This determination to be reasonable infuriated her. Sometimes it was an admirable principle with him; at others – like now – it was a weapon, designed to provoke her into giving way to her feelings, so that she would seem the emotional, unreasonable one. It almost worked. A sudden anger, of quite unexpected force, very nearly overwhelmed her self-control; but she mastered it in time. 'Are we going to drive our new car down?' she asked, adopting the same casual tone. 'It would be quite an adventure.'

He chuckled. 'Sibylla could cancel her arrangements to have hers sent by train and we could make a race of it.'

That was the next turn of the screw, of course. When simple blandness failed to madden, throw in a dash of jocular childishness. It angered her again, but now she was more prepared. 'She couldn't drive all that way on her own,' she replied calmly.

'Petifer could go with her.'

She sighed. 'I was trying to be serious.'

'So was I. Actually, it would be an interesting challenge. Sibylla is so competitive . . .'

'Ssh! She'll hear you!'

'What if she does? She knows it well enough. It would be a titanic struggle between her competitive spirit and her notorious love for the man.' He giggled. He really was pulling out all the stops tonight.

Suddenly she snapped. She caught hold of his arm, pulled it round in front of her, and bit it hard, in the muscular part just below the elbow.

She expected him to bellow in pain, strike her, grip her jaws as one does a dog's and squeeze her bite open, catch hold of her hair and jerk her head back – all the things she would have done in the same circumstances. To her surprise he made no sound. He merely tensed the muscle of his arm until it felt as hard as steel buried in velvet; she could not even hear him breathe. She dared not bite harder for fear of breaking the skin.

Then the brush fell into her lap and his hand closed round her breast, caressing it through the silk of her nightdress. Then both hands were there. All at once she was filled with an amazing longing for him. Most amazing of all – her anger was in no way diminished; indeed, it had swelled to the very limits of her self-control. A moment ago she had wanted him to force her to say what she and Maurice had done that day; now she wanted him to take her by force.

'No!' She let go her bite and delivered the word in one long, ferocious whisper. She lashed out behind her with her fists, hitting his knees and the sides of his thighs.

He gave a growl such as she'd never heard before, certainly not from him, and dragged her backward off her stool. She clutched at him; two buttons flew off his nightshirt as she dragged it down off his shoulders. He hurled himself upon her and pinned her to the carpet. She flung her thighs around him, kicking at his backside with her heels and flailing his shoulders with her fists. There was a wild gleam in his eye and bubbles of spittle at the corners of his lips; from his throat came strange little animal noises, blending a snarl with a laugh and a gasp of pain. As a final, irrevocable act of defiance she closed her eyes and pretended he was Maurice. He certainly was not Giles, anyway.

It was very soon over, and then she was hugging him in angry joy, crying into his hair and neck, and kissing him with frustration and fury.

Next door, Sibylla took her hands off her ears and strained to listen. Hearing nothing, she put her head out above the blankets again. Still hearing nothing, she let out a sigh of relief and stretched out flat on her back, staring at the ceiling, forcing herself not to remember Giles, the weight of him, the heat of his breath. A few minutes later, unable to find ease, she turned on her side. Her cheek was immediately aware of every crease in the pillow. The tip of her exposed ear grew cold; she pulled the blanket over the side of her head – and rapidly became too hot. She turned over on the other side. That hip was a bit tender – for no reason she could remember.

At last she got out of bed and put on her dressing gown, thinking that if she couldn't sleep, she might as well get up, have a sip of milk, and write a postcard or three to friends.

First, though, she'd close the window.

She hadn't parted the curtains more than three or four inches before she saw him – Petifer – also in his dressing gown. He was standing at the window of his darkened room, pale and still in the light of the half-risen moon. And he was staring up at her.

Her immediate instinct was to withdraw at once and close her curtains again; but she resisted it. He had seen her, of course. He must have done. So if she withdrew, it would look as if she quite often came to her window to spy on him. She realized she might have many other reasons for coming to her window, but that was the one the conceited Petifer would settle on. Anything rather than give him that satisfaction!

With a flourish she drew her curtains wide and stood there in full view, staring down at him; he, for his part, continued to stare up at her – there could be no doubting it now.

Do you believe in telepathy, Maurice Petifer? she projected toward him. *Listen to this! You are destroying all our lives – whether you mean to or not. Just by being there you're wrecking our peace and turning us into mockeries of our real selves. Go away! If you can hear these words from my mind, turn about now and go back into the dark of your lair dawn there!*

He continued to stare at her, not moving a muscle; she could not even detect his breathing.

If you won't leave us alone, if you won't go of your own free will, she added, *we shall just have to find ways to make you.*

PART FOUR

Thoughts of a Housekeeper

Marriage is a bribe
to make a housekeeper
think she's a householder

Thornton Wilder

Maurice leaned on the gate and ran his eye over the neatly turned dungpile – which was, in effect, the entire area of the yard; the store bullocks had been put out in one of the lower fields, down by the shores of the Loe, whose waters helped to moderate the frosts and so promoted an early bite of green, even in mid-January. 'Well, boys, that's some pretty sight there,' he told George Munroe and Peter Hosking, whose unenviable task it had been to turn over every cubic foot of it during their master's absence 'up Lunnon.'

'Some louster that was, too, boss!' Hosking favoured his back with a gentle massage to show he had not recovered from it yet. 'I shouldn't want to do that twice in a year.'

'Let's hope it doesn't come to that,' Maurice replied enigmatically.

'That damn old straw is so long, see,' Munroe explained. 'That's wheat straw, that is. You lift one eevil-full and, dammee, you find you're still standing on half of 'n. That's when it do pain your arms, see.'

'Of course,' Maurice said. 'But the straw at the bottom must be well rotted by now, surely? You wouldn't hardly have that difficulty once you get down a foot or two.'

They assured him that was the case.

'I mean, down at the bottom,' he went on, 'you'd stick your eevil in, I expect, and 'twould fall into fletters at once. You'd have a job to lift it without it breaking up, I daresay?'

They hastened to assure him that was the case.

'I suppose you did go *right* to the bottom?' he asked casually.

They almost tumbled over each other to assure him that was the case.

'You exposed all the cobbles – bit by bit, as you worked your way across the yard?'

'Why dam'ee if I couldn't give each stone a face and a name, boss,' Hosking replied.

'Good!' He smiled at them benevolently. 'Excellent!'

They basked in his compliments and breathed easy again – until he added, 'Then perhaps you'll be so good as to inform me where you found the gate?'

They stared at him in bewilderment, and then Munroe said, 'Why, boss, we'm a-leaning on 'n now.'

Slowly Maurice shook his head; the lazy smile persisted. 'Not this gate, boy. The gate I'm talking about is that rusty old iron thing that used to lean foreanenst the hedge out along the lane.'

Munroe, the eternal optimist, drew breath to assure him the diddicoys who dealt in scrap iron up the top of Sithney Common Hill had made off with it, but he was stopped in mid-flight by a nudge from Hosking, the eternal pessimist.

'Backalong last fall,' Maurice continued, 'the day we ploughed up the five acres down there, I carried that gate back home here and buried it somewhere under the dung in this yard. Right under it – right down at the very bottom. So if you truly had exposed every cobble, you'd surely have come across it.' He laughed into their crestfallen faces and, patting them on the shoulders, said 'Come on, boys! Waistcoats off! There's a good hour 'till sundown. You've two hard days turning ahead of you now – and, what's worse, the old bugger his-self is here to watch over 'ee this time!'

That evening when supper was over and he and Miss Sweet were seated by the fire, she with some darning, he with his copy of *The Commercial Market Garden*, he recounted these events to her. She was delighted that their little ruse had worked.

'My dear soul, Mister,' she sighed when their laughter had run its course. 'I wouldn't be in their boots, not for the world, these next few weeks, and that's a fact.'

'It'll hardly take them that long to do the job properly,' he replied. 'It had better not, anyway.'

She shook her head. 'The loustering is the least of it,' she explained. 'Those two won't be able to show their noses out of doors without some smart edjack asking have they seen *an old gate* . . . would they know where he could lay his hands on *an old gate* . . . would they like to buy *an old gate* . . . what's the price of *old gates* up Culdrose? There won't be no end to it.'

'Well, it serves them right. They should jolly well do a job properly in the first place.'

She sighed and became serious again. 'The truth is, I should have kept a better eye on 'em while you was gone, and that's a fact.'

'Don't blame yourself, Miss Sweet. You've enough work managing the house without thinking you should be my acting-unpaid farm manager, too.'

'I could do it easy,' she assured him. 'I grew up on a farm. 'Twould be nothing to me. I could tell any of them poor fellows their jobs.'

He knew it was an offer – indeed, a bid – for the place, but he let it pass with the vague comment that there was 'time enough to be thinking of that.' She'd won the battle to be housekeeper – at a wage and a half – and that should content her awhile. He continued to smile at her, though, until she felt obliged to ask why.

'It just struck me how differently I treat you from the way I treat them. There must be scores of tricks like that, tricks one could play *inside* the house. Like . . . I don't know – deliberately placing lengths of cobweb in certain obscure corners and seeing if they're gone by evening . . . things like that.'

'You never did, did 'ee?' She laughed.

'No no! I'm only saying there must be tricks like that one *could* play. But the point I'm making is that it never crossed my mind to play them on *you*. Never even crossed my mind, you understand.'

She blinked rapidly several times and swallowed hard – then busied herself furiously with her needle. 'Well, I never felt like a servant under this roof, Mister. Never once did you make me feel that, and that's a fact.' She held her darning up to the light and deemed the sock fit for wear once more. 'Still,' she added, 'I mustn't be bothersome now. You got your book to read.'

'This?' He raised the volume in one hand and snapped it shut. 'I can read that later. Tell me what's been going on in Helston while I've been gone – apart from Munroe and Hosking not finding our old gate?'

'We-ell,' she said, ''tis hard to know where to begin, rightly. We had twenty murders, half the town burned down, and Jack Thomas lost two geese to a fox. Which shall I tell 'ee first?'

He chuckled. 'Whichever one is true.'

'Ah, well now,' she said, 'this old fox, see, he's been after they geese some time . . .' Then she joined his laughter and said, 'Nothing happened here while you was gone, Mister. What happened to you up Lunnon, then?'

He was just about to tell her when they were distracted by a distant booming noise. He frowned.

'Ship in distress? That sounded like a maroon. But it's a dead-calm night.'

They heard it again.

'That's out in the yard, that is,' she said.

They both rose and made for the door. The moment they opened it they heard a bellow – followed by the booming sound, which, they now realized, was a beast of some kind kicking at a door or stall. Maurice thought at once of the horses but Miss Sweet's indentification was more sure. 'That's Wellington's Bombardier the Fourth,' she said, naming the new bull. 'He don't sound too happy, neither.'

'Rats?' Maurice hazarded the guess as he went along the passage to the lobby.

Behind him she gave a little smile but said nothing.

As soon as he opened the door and smelled the keenness of the frost he had the first inkling of what the trouble might be. He said no more then but hastened into his boots and overcoat and, taking the lantern, which Miss Sweet had meanwhile kindled, hurried toward the cowshouse. As he suspected, Molly Hendren had left the cows in overnight, because a sharp frost cut their milk yield by more than the cost of the extra feed it required to keep them penned; and, as he also suspected, one of the cows was 'troublesome.'

The bull pen, for long unused, was built, as they say, foreanenst the cowshouse and thus shared its ventilation. So whatever come-all-you-young-sailors perfume the troublesome cow was giving out, it was drifting among the rafters and, though indetectible to the human nose, was sending poor Bombardier into a frenzy.

The cow in question was, in fact, the one he had named Sibylla, in a fit of pique just after the incident with the roof at Parc-an-Dour – because she was the stubbornest cow in the herd and had beautiful, gazelle-like eyes. She was a Jersey, with a fawn-coloured face and a coat so dark brown it was almost black. 'It would be you, wouldn't it!' he said grimly as he hung the lantern up fast to the beam and ran his hand along her spine toward her tail. She was hot and sweating. 'Poor old thing!' he murmured more sympathetically.

Her eyes were wide and her ears were up. He twisted her tail aside; she bore all the signs of a cow at the peak of her readiness. 'Can we risk leaving you till tomorrow?' he asked her. 'How d'you feel, yourself?'

She let out a great bellow in answer to one from Bombardier and locked herself rigid on all four legs.

'All right, Sibylla,' he told her. 'Us'll do what us can for 'ee, old girl.'

He went back to the house and opened the door just wide enough to stick in his head. 'Miss Sweet,' he called out. 'Would you get out your bike and go over to Frank Tresidder – tell him he's wanted here.'

'Coming!' she called from somewhere upstairs. He was rather surprised to hear the clump of heavy boots. He was even more surprised, a moment later, to see her dressed, not for cycling off the farm, but for yard work. 'You don't need no Frank Tresidder,' she told him scornfully. ''Tis that Sibylla, isn't it – she's all troublesome.'

'Well . . . yes,' he admitted reluctantly. 'But see here . . .'

'I knew it. She and the two heifers were bulling out in the field all afternoon. I told Frank but he said leave it go till tomorrow. 'Course, he never knew then that Molly'd leave them in all night. That's where the trouble's to. We shan't get a wink of sleep while they're so fretful.'

She was standing before the door now, waiting for him to open it fully. Again he tried to object: 'I hardly think it would be proper, Miss Sweet . . .'

But again she interrupted. 'Gusson, Mister!' she said scornfully. 'I've put cows to bulls scores of times – from the age of ten, I should think. And sows to boars. If you want to come back indoors and read your book, you can leave it all to me, if you mind to.'

He could see that she thought his discomfiture highly comical, and he could just imagine how the tale of it, suitably embroidered, would make the rounds of the district. Determined not to let that happen, he changed his attitude at once. 'Well,' he asked crisply, 'you're sure, now?'

'Sure enough to put up these old clothes,' she replied. 'And to light another lamp.'

He thought at first that this was some indelicately rural reference to making sure of a good view of the event; but then he realized she had thought even farther ahead than had he. 'Come-us on, then! The sooner we're back by a warm hearth, the happier I'll be.'

'I'll go down the cowshouse and bring her,' Miss Sweet said. 'You could bar the door to his stall, if you mind, till I've got her into court and the gate fast.'

'Then watch me win the world champion sprint for the six-yard dash! Very well, she'll hardly run away on you, I suppose.'

In fact, as far as Bombardier's character went, he had so far proved a rather docile bull, still young enough to be playful. But all Guernseys, male and female, were notoriously fickle in temperament. John Trenoweth, who had sold the bull to Maurice, told him of a farmer called Boase, over to Crowntown, who bought Wellington's Grenadier, a halfbrother to Bombardier, and who had led him out to drink at the pond every day for two years without a hint of trouble. 'Yet that old fellow turned on he one evening afore you could say ducks. Inside half a minute, boy, there wasn't nothing left but what you might feed to a cat! A Guernsey bull is a heller!'

So Maurice set his lantern on the ground outside the court, took up a good, stout pitchfork, opened the gate quietly, and tiptoed as silently as he could to the door of the stall – taking care to keep at least one of the escape holes firmly in the corner of his eye. There were five altogether, one at each corner and one in the middle of the long side. He did not breathe until his hand was on the doorbolt and discovered it to be already tight home. Then he could afford a little scornful smile at his caution, for Bombardier was making such a racket that an army could have marched up outside and still have taken him by surprise.

The sounds from the cowshouse next door were another matter however; the beast's ears were well tuned in that direction. A moment later, when Miss Sweet let the chain loose from round Sibylla's neck, he fell silent; the only sound then was his stertorous breathing.

'That's it, old fellow!' Maurice called out to him. 'You do know all the signs, don't 'ee! She's on her way to 'ee now. She'll give 'ee some fine old flagary in just a minute.'

The explosive snorts of the creature's respiration continued. There was no more bellowing but Maurice heard him pawing at the flagstones of his stall. 'Just a little more patience,' he advised. 'And you'll see the sweetest little Jersey cow you ever clapped eyes on.'

Sibylla came groggily out by the cowshouse door, slithering a little in the hard frost. Miss Sweet was at her heels, touching her gently, though needlessly, with her blackthorn stick. Bombardier gave out a sound that was the nearest thing to a growl Maurice had ever heard from a bovine throat. Sibylla's head jerked up and she started to trot precariously along the front of the cowshouse toward the sound; her bag, quarter-filled again with milk, swung wildly from side to side, threatening to unbalance her. Miss Sweet, perforce, had to trot to keep up. Tense as he was, Maurice could not help smiling at the sight and the all-too-obvious parallels it suggested.

Sibylla tried at first to squeeze in through one of the escape holes but a tap or two from Miss Sweet's blackthorn helped her discover the gate. 'Head her down to that near corner,' Maurice suggested.

'That's a good idea!' she exclaimed sarcastically, for she already had the cow there. 'What are you holding back the bull for, then?' She pulled the court gate to and shot the bolt, all the time maintaining a light tattoo with her stick on Sibylla's rump, in case she tried to pull her head out of the corner.

'Oh . . . sorry!' Maurice drew back the bolt and pulled the door wide open; a few thousandths of a second later – though it seemed an age – he skipped through the nearest escape hole, which was diagonally across the court from the gate. From deep inside the stygian dark of his stall Bombardier snorted . . . but that was all; nothing else happened.

Maurice walked around to the gate, keeping his eye on Miss Sweet all the way. She was leaning against it, her arms dangling loosely over the topmost bar, the stick gripped with firm yet casual assurance in her right hand. If she had not been in skirts, she would have been the very picture of a livestock farmer – the sort of countryman Maurice saw every week down in Helston market. With chagrin he realized it was the sort of picture he himself would never cut, no matter how long and hard he tried. You had to grow up on a farm, not next door to one, to stand with that nonchalant air and that quietly observant eye at a time like this. A pang of envy, bordering on anger, seized him at the unfairness of it all. This was his farm, his bull, his cow, and Miss Sweet was his servant – and yet she could stand there now, quite still, saying nothing, and nonetheless proclaiming in her very stance that she owned more of it than he ever could. He might own it as a business; she possessed it as a way of life.

'Come on, old fellow!' he shouted crossly. 'You're keeping your public waiting!'

Miss Sweet looked at him sharply; it was the sort of boisterous humour familiar to anyone who grew up on a farm, but hardly what she had expected to hear from a gentleman-farmer like Mister.

Bombardier's head loomed out of the black of his stall. The moon emerged from behind a thin veil of cloud; its light, now almost painfully bright, made their two lanterns seem pathetic indeed. The bull's hot breath shimmered like silvered smoke from the nostrils of a mythic beast.

'Oh, my gidge – that's some sight!' Miss Sweet said in an awestruck voice, little more than a whisper.

Sibylla appeared stricken with a bovine version of the same awe. The moment she caught sight of her deliverer she once again performed that curiously subtle manoeuvre by which every joint in her body seemed to lock tight, making her as rigid as a piece of sculpture. Her head went up and stayed there, slightly turned from the two onlookers; the one eye visible to them was so huge and so black that only the miniature reflection of the moon defined it.

As if he knew he was now the star of the show, Bombardier took two majestic steps out into the court. All the frenzy suggested by his bellowing was gone. He was a lord of creation, king of the castle, cock of the walk – a sultan in his hareem. More even than that, he was a god, calm, superb, and pitiless – a ton and more of muscle and bone, fashioned for this single purpose. There was no need for a preliminary. He leaped straight upon Sibylla's back, almost felling her to the ground.

'He'll kill those heifers when their time comes,' Maurice said. 'We shall have to make a stand for him.'

Miss Sweet nodded and said, 'Yes.' She was at a loss with her Mister now. Until he had shouted out to the bull about keeping his audience waiting, she had been ready to tease him a little – nothing forward, of course, just a gentle, rural leg-pull from a low-quarter woman to her high-quarter boss; but now she wasn't so sure. If he had remained the master and she the servant, with a proper distance between them which both acknowledged, then they could, by some strange paradox, be very free and easy with each other – teasing, joking, leg-pulling. They could be like carnivores in the zoo, happily roaring their empty threats at one another from the inviolate safety of their cages. But take those bars away, and their behaviour would at once have to become very circumspect indeed.

For his part Maurice was disappointed by her sudden reserve. When she had first offered her assistance for this simple agricultural operation, he had dreaded it; but then her robust cheerfulness had quite subdued his qualms. Now its withdrawal left him nonplussed. Hoping to revive it, he gave a little, nervous laugh and said, 'Hardly so well as the bull! You know that old joke, do you?'

She laughed nervously, too. 'The little boy who's late for school and says he had to take the cow to be served – and the teacher asks couldn't his father have done it?'

'That's the one!'

She laughed again, too heartily this time. Then a memory struck her. 'I'll tell you one that really happened, too. Old Joel Bennett, who used to live out Goonhilly – ever know him, did you?'

Maurice shook his head. 'I heard tell of him, all right.'

'Well, he's dead now, poor soul, but he took a cow to be served up Bochym Farm one day. That was Albert Cory's place then, except he died years before and his widow kept it going. Well, old Widow Cory, she made a bit of a name for herself. Her heels had feathers, if you follow me? And old Joel Bennett, he was standing there beside her – same as what we are now – looking on, like – and he thought he'd try his luck. So he sidles up to her, like this' – she sidled up to Maurice – 'and he gives her a little nudge, like this' – she nudged Maurice in the ribs – 'and he puts on a soppy old voice and says, "Yur! I'd just like to be doing that, Mrs Cory!" And old Widow Cory, she turns and looks at him, so sweet as a hallan apple, and she says, "Go on, then, Mr Bennett," she says. "'Tis your cow!" ' Miss Sweet laughed until she ran out of breath and then, giving the obligatory envoi to any Cornish joke, she repeated its salient line: ' "'Tis your cow!" That's what she said.'

Maurice gave the obligatory reprise of his laughter; at the same moment Bombardier fell off Sibylla and stood there, looking defeated, panting balefully and hanging his head. 'And that's all there is to it!' Maurice exclaimed.

After a brief silence Miss Sweet said, 'I hope you don't think I was too forward, like, Mister?' She was still standing where her tale had carried her, right up beside him.

'I was ahead of you by a nose, Miss Sweet,' he replied. 'Every inch of the way. No!' He waved a hand at Bombardier and Sibylla. 'Nature could teach us a lesson or two if only we'd learn from her. As I said just now – that's all there is to it. And yet just think what a fuss and dalver we humans make about it!'

He was so sure of his own meaning – namely, that he was weary of the world's turmoil on the subject – that the ambiguities in his remark passed clean over his head.

Not so poor Miss Sweet. 'Mister?' she asked.

'Mind you,' he went on, 'there's a heavy price to pay for all that speed and simplicity. It leaves neither time nor space for the finer feelings. Look at the world from Bombardier's point of view and you'd hardly want to trade boots for hooves! It's just self, self, and self with him. He walked out of his stall like a god. Did you see him?'

'Surely!' The awesome memory stirred her again.

'We imagine we're his superiors, me who bought him for cash and you who can drive him with your stick. But that's not how he sees it. In his mind, he's the god-king and we're his slaves. And haven't we proved it to him this night? All he needed do was bellow out his wrath and – lo and behold! – we propitiate him with the gift of a female!'

'What's the price you talked about?' Miss Sweet asked, still not understanding his point at all.

'That!' He waved a hand at Sibylla, who was waiting calmly for act two. 'Look at her, poor thing! She's not a fellow creature to old Bombardier. He has no fellow feeling for her at all. Did he greet her? Did he go up to her head and sniff hallo? Give her a little lick of affection? Not a bit of it! That's the price, I was talking about. He pays it as much as she – not that either of them knows it, of course.'

Now poor Miss Sweet was completely at a loss. 'So should we learn from nature, like you said, or not?' she asked.

'You put your finger on the heart of the matter, Miss

Sweet,' he replied. 'As always! It's a question we must each answer for ourselves, of course. But, speaking for my own part, I do honestly think we ought to be able to find some acceptable middle way for dealing with . . .' He waved a hand at Bombardier and Sibylla for want of a polite word. 'There must be something in between our soul-destroying, life-sapping fear and the brute simplicities of these two creatures. Don't you agree?'

For one brief second a little window opened in her mind. And through it drifted his words, mellifluous, full of pleasant echoes, penetrating the mists of her upbringing and speaking directly to her mind – and body, and soul. And while that moment lasted she understood him perfectly – which was why she said, 'With all my heart, Mister.'

The fervour of her answer puzzled him. He looked at her, and she at him. Her brief flame of comprehension flickered and died. In her eyes he saw nothing but a *desire* to understand. He realized then that his words had not outlined a programme – not even for himself. They had merely described an impossible dream.

There was an almighty grunt from the court as Bombardier lunged at Sibylla for act two.

It was a difficult choice for Laura. The children were excited about the new piglets, which they had discovered at the actual moment of farrowing in a scrubby corner of the wetland down by the Loe. This had given them a proprietorial claim on the litter; they saw themselves, if not quite as parents, at least as godparents – despite Aunt Sibylla's jibe that if there was no God, there could hardly be god-parents and they ought to nail their colours to the mast and call themselves 'huxley-parents'. But, whatever name one might choose to describe their status, a visit to Culdrose Farm by their mother (or Aunt Laura, in the case of the Johnson three) for the express purpose of being introduced to *their* litter would confirm it. They arranged it for Saturday afternoon – Saturday being the only half-day their various schools enjoyed in common.

The children had carte blanche to play around the farm, of course; but Laura felt she could hardly turn up and wander around uninvited. On most other days that would have presented no difficulty; she would have found Maurice about the yard or in one of the fields and, naturally, he would have given her the run of the place. But on this particular Saturday – the first in February – the Cury Hunt traditionally met at Culdrose and hunted over Goonhilly Downs. So he, being a keen follower of the hounds, was miles from the farm all day. And the prospect of even *seeming* to ask permission of Miss Sweet was not one that appealed to Laura.

However, the combined willpower of all eight youngsters – now including Phillippa, who had lately graduated from mere walking and talking to running and screaming – was invincible. Laura swallowed her misgivings and, feeling rather like a Pied Piper in reverse, followed them up the well-trodden path that led straight across the fields from Chynoweth to the farmyard. Only toward the end did she insist on a small detour that would bring them past the farmhouse itself.

And there, to her great relief, Miss Sweet spared her the indignity by throwing up a window and calling out, 'Come to see the piglets, have you? Go on down, then –

they've been a-squealing for you all since dawn this morning.'

Laura called out her thanks and on they went. That's all there was to it! She felt so grateful to the woman that if they'd met face-to-face, she'd have hugged her. It began to dawn on Laura that perhaps her behaviour toward Miss Sweet had not been the brightest – not just over today's little dilemma but over the 'problem' she posed in general.

What problem?

Until now the answer would have been so obvious it would have been absurd to clothe it in words. Miss Sweet was the third daughter of an indifferent tenant farmer. She had no schooling to speak of. She'd had several offers of marriage from men of her own sort – labourers and small farmers – and she'd rejected them all; therefore she must have had a plan for her life, one that would carry her out of that humble sphere into something more exalted. And you only had to look at what she'd done since to see what that plan was.

She hadn't applied to Culdrose Farm directly, of course – that would have been far too blatant, even though the farm was short of a good housemaid and she'd certainly have gained the place. But a direct approach wouldn't have suited her at all. When her plans were fulfilled, people would look back to see how she'd managed it and, if they then remembered she'd once walked bold as brass up to Culdrose and asked for work, it would look very bad for her. So instead she'd gone to Liston House, knowing very well that, although the Troys had no position to offer, they were close friends to Maurice Petifer. There she'd spread the charm like treacle syrup and captivated Jimmy Troy, whose democratic American eye was purblind to the nuances of English Society. Otherwise he'd have known that Miss Sweet was too good for the position of maid at Culdrose but not quite good enough for that of housekeeper – at least, not to a gentleman-farmer like Maurice Petifer; the highest she could have aimed in the normal course of events would have been housekeeper to a doctor or a clergyman . . . perfectly respectable people but on the fringe of good Society rather than actually in it. However, thanks to her astuteness, the first approach had come not from her to Culdrose but from Culdrose to her.

After that it had been plain sailing. Anyone who kept half an ear open to the affairs of the district (and Miss Sweet seemed to have a dozen ears, all wide open and each as acute as a cat's) knew that Ma Harvey wouldn't be parted for long from her dear old mistress – in short, that the position of housekeeper would soon fall vacant at the farm. But the master stroke had been to persuade Maurice Petifer, the master, that she could combine the work she was already doing as housemaid with what Ma Harvey had done. And since Ma Harvey's work had been mostly confined to cosseting an elderly and infirm lady, the combining was easy enough, especially as she still had a daily maid and a living-out cook to perform most of the actual labour. The fact that Miss Sweet had, at one stroke, eliminated the only other living-in position at the farm was made to seem like an accidental result of the new arrangements, rather than the principal reason for proposing it. So clever!

Now all she need do was lie back (probably quite literally) and let nature take its course. Many a chill union had been forged in the heat of such dangerous arrangements.

Naturally, Laura had never thought out her objections in this coldly systematic way, otherwise she would have been forced to admit, not merely that she had no real evidence for any of it (apart from the chain of circumstances – and they could just as easily be explained in ways that were entirely creditable to Miss Sweet), but also that it was hardly any business of hers in the first place! And that, in turn, would have brought her right to the nub of the matter. Plainly put, she was jealous!

In some part of her being she had never let go of Maurice. Her marriage, her children, her love for Giles, which, despite recent knocks, was still strong – all combined to suppress that remnant of the love which had once claimed every atom of her soul. But they could not kill it off. And when she saw another woman there in Maurice's life – true, only his housekeeper as yet, but a woman free to marry him if she could move him (or seduce him) into that state – then reason fled.

However, the fact remained that Laura never had spelled out her objections in that coldly reasoned way; and so these further, mellowing insights were denied her, too. Nonetheless, just as she had a strong intuition about her dislike of Miss Sweet, so, in this sudden access of gratitude toward the woman, she felt some vague intimation of that new mellowness, as well. Also, of course, she could not help recalling Maurice's assurance that Miss Sweet 'thought the world' of her. It is difficult for one woman to hate another when she hears that the reciprocal sentiment lies so powerfully in the opposite direction!

These notions, though Laura glimpsed them but briefly and dimly, tugged her feelings this way and that as she let the children lead her down the side of the house and through the gate into the yard. The first thing Henry pointed out was the rusty old gate that had been the subject of so many jokes at the expense of poor Munroe and Hosking; it was now tied to the railings round the bullock yard, ready to be used again in next year's challenge. The two labourers themselves were now loading up the cart with the rather pungent fruits of their double labour – the best-turned dungpile in Cornwall – prior to spreading it over the fields.

Gillian next tugged her across to the bull pen, where Wellington's Bombardier IV stood placidly chewing the cud. 'He weighs two tons,' she said in an awestruck murmur. Laura doubted it but said nothing.

'He's got no milk,' Blanche said.

'And bull beef tastes all *yech!*' Agnes put in.

'And bull beef tastes all *rank!*' Blanche went on primly. 'He's not much use, is he!'

Laura saw the older children exchange amused glances. It made her wonder how much of the Great Secret they had picked up in their wanderings round the farm. Probably more than they realized – or more than they could have put into words, anyway. She remembered that when Sarah Laity had told her the facts of life – on a Sunday School outing to St Ives, where the artists painted ladies with no clothes on – it had not come as an amazing revelation but more like finding the last few bits of a picture puzzle. That was back in 'eighty-five, so she'd have been . . . Her fingers went pit-a-pat against her thigh but they could work out the sum 85 – 69 no nearer than 15 or 16 or 17. Anyway, it had happened in her mid-teens. But she'd realized that she already knew most of it, without actually being able to put it into words.

A bit like her confused feelings toward Miss Sweet, come to think of it!

'He's there to protect the cows and their little calves,' she told her daughter. 'Look at those wicked horns and that great strong neck! Even a lion or a tiger would think twice before challenging a fellow like that.'

'But lions and tigers can't swim,' Blanche objected.

It was a moment or two before Laura supplied the missing links in the chain of her argument – which Meredith then usurped by saying that tigers could swim.

The pair of them settled into a private duel as the whole gaggle wandered on toward the pigsties. Laura hesitated briefly at the spot where she had stood and watched Maurice release the two youngest boys last fall – a memory that still had power to move her.

'Come on, Aunt Laura!' Martin called out irritably.

She came out of her reverie and hastened to join them. 'So all you mean is that they can swim a river,' Blanche was saying. 'That's very different from swimming between India and Loe Bar.'

Under Maurice's system of farming the sows roamed free in the scrub down by the Loe shore, being brought up to the farm only for service by the boar or to farrow and suckle their young; now and then, as with this particular litter, a sow would farrow ahead of her expected time and Hosking and Munroe would have to bring the piglets up in sacks. As soon as her young were weaned the sow went back to the great outdoors; but the weaners remained inside for two or three months while they were reared to bacon weight before being sent for slaughter.

A young pig's day is divided between fighting, squealing, guzzling, and sleeping; no wonder, Laura had often thought, the children felt a greater affinity for them than for all the other farmyard animals put together! The piggery had a feeding passage all along the back of the individual sties. As the party from Chynoweth spread out along it, those pigs that were fighting stopped, the sleepers awoke, and the squealers fell silent; there were no eaters, since every last morsel of bran had long since been fought over, and squealed over, and finally consumed. Heads went up everywhere; pointed ears added a blood-pink or mud-black palisade to the walls dividing the more distant sties; nearer to the intruders, where more of each sty was visible, it was a sea of bright eyes, disconcertingly human in their intelligence.

'Now which is your lot?' Laura asked. She was surprised at how clean the place smelled. It was rank, of course (as Blanche would no doubt say), but not offensive; the same could not be said of the stench outside, which had been dreadful.

'Here! Here!' They led her up to the last sty but one.

As they passed the sties filled with older weaners, Laura was again reminded of the behaviour of children; the creatures were both sly and playful at the same time. They would pretend to take fright and bolt (though they never ran more than a couple of paces); then they'd stand there grinning at you, just as children do when they shout, 'Caught you! I was only pretending!' Or – still grinning – they would squeal in a fright they quite obviously did not feel, challenging one another with their eyes to see who could scream the loudest and make the grown-ups angriest. Like children, too, they soon tired of their sport and returned to the boundless anarchy of their normal routine.

There were eight piglets in the children's special litter, so naturally they were named: Henry, Gillian, Maurice, Blanche, Phillippa, Martin, Agnes, and Meredith; naturally, too, the baby female called 'Pigling Henry' was not the largest of them, nor was the little male called 'Pigling Phillippa' the smallest. That would have been too easy for the children; apart from anything else, it would have removed all chance for the sort of argument that now broke out among them in response to Laura's apparently harmless question: 'Which of them is which?'

She just stood there, wishing she hadn't opened her mouth, watching the litter fight for the best teats, and trying to decide whether they reminded her more of babies or of rats. It was ended by a cry of outrage from Blanche: 'Where's Pigling Blanche? Where's *my* pig?'

Laura, who thought she had counted eight when they had all been one squirming mass of black-spotted pink flesh, re-counted and found that there were, indeed, only seven. 'Perhaps she's gone outside.'

'He!' Blanche insisted. 'Blanche is a him.'

'Perhaps he's gone outside for a breath of fresh air, then. Let's go and see, shall we.'

The suggestion kept her quiet at least until the two of them reached the door into the yard again; the others stayed behind to admire their pigling namesakes.

Out in the fresh air – or what would have been fresh air if the wind had been anything but southerly – Laura saw Miss Sweet hastening toward them.

'The minute you'd gone by, I remembered,' she shouted from some way off. Then, moderating her voice as the distance between them narrowed. 'I thought the first thing Blanche is going to notice is that her pig is gone. Did she? I'll lay she did.'

'Indeed,' Laura assured her. She was quite close now.

'Well, don't be jealous, my lover.' She squatted down and took Blanche's hands between hers. 'I've got him all wrapped up nice and safe for you up home in my kitchen. He was feeling some poorly last night, so I fetched him up and dosed him with physic and – we-ell! You wouldn't hardly know him for the same little widden now.' A heavenward sweep of her eyes as she rose to full height again alerted Laura to the fact that the creature up in the kitchen was not 'the same little widden' that Blanche had adopted. Some agricultural tragedy must have intervened. 'Shall us go and see him?' Miss Sweet held out a hand to the little girl.

Together they tramped back to the farmhouse, skirting the puddles and leaping the little mounds of spilled dung from the laden cart, which was now making its third trip of the day out to the fields. All the way Miss Sweet explained to Blanche that baby pigs weren't very gentle to each other and if one of them was a weak little widden, the others would be unkind to it and never let it suck the best teat nor get in the middle where it was warmest. So the poor little cooze would never thrive. She blamed herself, she said, for not rescuing little Pigling Blanche earlier, but last night the cruelty of the others really had been too much for the dear little fellow, so she'd brought him up and given him a good drench of lung tonic and rubbed neatsfoot oil into his skin, and the improvement on him was a joy to see. 'He's just *splitting* along now, my lover!' she concluded – again giving Laura a significant lift of the eyebrows.

They wiped their boots as best they could and went into the kitchen. It was a flagstone floor all the way, with fresh sand strewn daily. Laura saw at once that though the piglet in the tea chest by the fire was beyond doubt a widden, it was from an older litter than the one the children had adopted. Blanche realized it, too – Laura could tell by the look in her eyes. Soothing words and reassurances rose to her throat but something made her withhold them for the moment. She watched in fascination as her daughter progressed from the simple discovery to a much subtler adjustment: She decided not merely to accept the lie but to participate in it – to join the conspiracy.

It must have been a wonderful feeling of power for her – that moment when she held the adults' deception in the palm of her hand, saw it for what it was, weighed it, and decided to accept it as her own. It was one more stepping stone on that long journey from childhood to maturity, a rare one, in that it was so compact and so visible. 'His condition has greatly ameliorated,' she said, stooping to pet the new Pigling Blanche.

'She's been reading Macaulay,' Laura offered by way of apology.

'Pick him up if you mind to,' Miss Sweet said. 'Wrap him in that old bit of shawl and you can carry him out in the yard. But I wouldn't put him back along of the rest yet awhile.'

Blanche did as she was bid. Standing there, holding the little creature in its shawl, she must have had a mental picture of what she looked like for she said, 'Pig and pepper!' as she went back out into the yard again.

'She's a little Alice-in-wonderland, all right,' Laura murmured fondly, watching her cuddle and rock the little creature as if it were her favourite doll.

'She *knew* it wasn't the same widden as yesterday,' Miss Sweet observed. 'She was just being kind to me.'

'Yes, what happened to the real one?' Laura asked.

'The sow ate him,' was the laconic reply. 'They always do that if one of them dies. I calculate she smothered him by accident. Then she ate him. But there's some things about a farmyard as children shouldn't be asked to understand too young. Draw up a chair, Mrs Curnow, if you mind to. They'll be a half-hour yet afore they tire of their play.'

Laura seated herself at the plain deal table while the other brewed a pot of tea. She glanced around at the kitchen, which was spotless. 'You must be on your feet from dawn to dusk – and beyond,' she remarked.

''Tis the cook's half day,' Miss Sweet replied. 'And Lizzie Waring, the daily maid – say what you mind about the Warings but she's some hard worker – she's shining the upstairs windows now. Without those two,

I should be run off my feet, like you say. As it is, I calculate there's just enough work left over to keep me out of mischief.' She smiled as she brought the pot to the table. 'Just let that stand a minute. Can I tempt you with a bite of fuggan, Mrs Curnow? Fresh baked this morning.'

Laura said that would be very nice. 'You find it works very well with all the servants living out?' she asked. 'You wouldn't prefer them under the roof – where you can keep a watchful eye on them?'

Miss Sweet took down an old biscuit tin, dating from the diamond jubilee; it gave Laura a small shock to see the old queen's face. Two years dead, yet how swiftly she had faded from the scene! 'That was my first thought, of course,' Miss Sweet replied. 'If Mister fell ill, God forbid, there should be one to fetch the doctor and one to tend him meanwhile. But the telephone has taken care of that. Now Lizzie brings all the news from up the Wendron-Street end of town and Mrs Cowles tells us all the goings on down St John's. So I'm well content.'

'You mean you'd rather have the news coming into the house openly than going out of it secretly! Yes, there's a great deal of wisdom in that, Miss Sweet. And what sort of news do they bring?'

Miss Sweet cut a generous slice of fuggan and bore it deftly on the knife blade to her visitor's plate. 'Nothing much,' she admitted. 'Small change, mostly. Who's got drunk. Who's in trouble. Who's been served a paternity summons. Who's got the bailiffs in.'

'Small change to us,' Laura observed. 'But large disasters to the people themselves.'

'Yes!' Miss Sweet sighed. 'I suppose, when you wash off the high colours, we're not all that different from the litter that squeezes out the widden.' She glanced through the window at Blanche and said,

'She's a-singing of him to sleep, bless her! That'll surely ameliorate his condition! She's a little never-come-twice and no mistake.'

'Once is enough, believe me!' Laura assured her.

Miss Sweet, reverting to their earlier topic, said, 'Mrs Cowles was telling us yesterday that Billy Dancey was down the Blue Anchor last Monday and got that merry on their best ale, he walked into a broom closet thinking 'twas the way out. She says you hardly ever see that fellow now but he's "pisky-laden with ale," as they call it.'

Laura nodded glumly. 'He's certainly deteriorated greatly this past year or so.'

'I should say Mrs Johnson has the patience of a saint to go on employing him up there to Parc-an-Dour. There's many would have shown him the toe of a boot backalong last fall, when the roof blew off.'

Laura nodded vaguely but thought it better to say nothing.

'There, that's drawn now surely.' Miss Sweet started to pour out the tea; she was a milk-in-last hostess, Laura noticed with approval. 'Or,' the woman went on casually as she handed Laura her cup, 'maybe she still blames Mister for what happened that night?'

Looking back on the conversation later, Laura realized that was where she ought to have changed the subject – in a gentle, kindly manner, to be sure, but firmly nonetheless. Instead she said, 'Mr Petifer was the first to blame himself.'

'He would, wouldn't he – being the sort of man he is.' Miss Sweet helped herself to two heaped spoons of sugar, cut a morsel of fuggan off her own slice, and popped it in her mouth. 'He's a first-cousin to a saint,' she added.

Laura smiled at this piece of hoopla. 'It must be pleasant to work for a master of whom you have such a high opinion,' she remarked.

Miss Sweet turned and stared out of the window for quite a while, until Laura began to wonder if she had even heard her last remark. At length, still not taking her eyes off the grey outside world, she said, 'I shouldn't talk about him, I know. A housekeeper talking about her master with the neighbour's wife – it's not right. But there's no one else, see? And I'm that 'mazed with all the goings on.' She turned to Laura then, fixing her with great, searching eyes – two troubled pools of blue.

The woman's words slipped beneath Laura's guard, wringing from her the reply, 'I don't know why you should feel I might be able to help, Miss Sweet, but – well, I'm willing to listen at least.'

Miss Sweet cut another morsel of the cake but then merely toyed with it. 'The worst thing about living so close to a body – in one way – and yet not being so close to him at all – in another way – if you follow my meaning, Mrs Curnow – the worst thing is when you can see so clearly what he's all troubled about but you daren't say a word because it's not your place like.'

After a pause Laura said, 'By "troubled" you mean what? Dejected . . . something like that?'

The housekeeper nodded.

'And what has caused Mr Petifer to feel so dejected?'

Miss Sweet drew a deep breath and said, 'Your cousin, Mrs Curnow – and that's the plain truth of the matter. When the price of cattle cake rises, he remarks, "Oh, Mrs Johnson *will* be pleased." And when we get more return for our milk, it's, "Oh my, Mrs Johnson won't be happy to hear that!" The poor man is never free of her, see? Up here.' She tapped her forehead. 'She's like some burden he can't leave down.'

Laura thought of several possible responses but in

the end all she said was, 'You haven't noticed any change in him since he returned from London, then?'

'How?' Miss Sweet asked.

'They had quite a set-to one evening – when we were all out together. If we hadn't known them so well, we'd have been quite alarmed. Then Mr Troy played a little jape on them – tricking them both to share a cab for the ride home – just the two of them. And they turned the tables on him by going off for an hour-long ride together. After that we thought they were a little less . . . how shall I put it? A little less *spiky* with each other. But you haven't noticed such a change?'

Miss Sweet shook her head. 'Every little stroke of fortune, good or bad, he says Mrs Johnson'll be happy or Mrs Johnson'll be ramping mad over that. He looks out the window at those new trees and says, "Another five years and she won't be able to see us at all." And that's since he came back from London, that is. I don't think it can be right for a man to set his clock by a neighbour-woman's moods like that. How is she so maggotty with him, anyway? He was gone fifteen long years. 'Tisn't natural for a woman to harbour maggots like that, all that time.'

Throughout this exchange Laura felt a growing irritation at the endless references to Sibylla; surely, she felt, Maurice's proximity to her, Laura, should play *some* part in his distress, too? Only the reflection that, even if that were the case, Miss Sweet would hardly tell her so, saved her from bursting out with an ill-tempered remark. All she said was, 'I don't know what may have happened between them to set her so violently against him. That may sound odd, but I assure you it's true. However, I think Mr Petifer himself *does* know. And then there is the undeniable fact that nobody compelled him to buy Culdrose.'

Miss Sweet looked at her askance, as if to imply,

D'you really believe what you're saying?

'Nobody did compel him,' Laura was forced to repeat.

The woman shook her head. 'That's not how men's minds think, alas,' she said. 'Trevor Hosking – Peter's cousin who works here – he lost his life down Greatwork because he was certain-sure he could run half a mile over open slopes in the pitch dark. And he was sober, too – that wasn't liquor talking. Willie Angove, down Snell's Joinery, when they got in that new planing machine – the gaffer told him the touch of it at top speed was like fine velvet, yet 'twould take the flesh off your hand before you could count to two. And that's how Willie Angove lost the tips to three fingers! Danger to a man is like a troublesome cow to a bull. She could be out of sight, three fields away, but there's no restraining him.'

Laura counted one, two, three fields between Culdrose and Parc-an-Dour; did the woman's mind work quite so literally? Probably not, she decided. 'What d'you think should be done about it?' she asked.

Miss Sweet gave a hopeless shrug, implying that her answers to the problem were no answers at all. 'Either Mister should go away – sell up here and buy a good farm somewhere else – or *someone*' – she studiously avoided her visitor's eye – 'should strive Mrs Johnson down into a better humour toward him. Or,' she added glumly, 'the sky should rain gold sovereigns and no one need never work no more.'

It rained heavily around sunset, when the Cury gave up the chase for the day. Maurice came home drenched but happy – a mood that was crowned by the aroma of fresh-baking Cornish pasty, which greeted him the moment he opened the farmhouse door. He struggled with the bootjack and his sodden boots for the best part of a minute, until Miss Sweet took pity on him and, throwing a piece of oilcloth over his right boot, raised it between her knees to ease it off in the old-fashioned way. She was wearing high-buttoned boots herself, so the uncovering of her lower calves by this manoeuvre did not trespass beyond the bounds of decorum. Even so, it was a greater intimacy of contact between them than had ever occurred before and it gave him a moment or two of disquiet.

The left boot, though it felt no tighter to him, proved far more difficult for some reason and she had to lift it higher, between the upper portions of her nether limbs, and enlist his aid with a well-placed foot in her 'lower back' (as he tried valiantly to think of it).

'I'm sorry to put you to this indignity, Miss Sweet,' he said awkwardly as they strained at the apparently unyielding leather.

'My dear soul, Mister!' she exclaimed. 'I should just like a farthing for every time I've done this. I should be a rich woman by now.'

It came off in a rush and she fell in a disordered heap of frills and laughter. She was so artless and so light-hearted he felt ashamed of his thoughts and feelings on seeing a mere inch of her actual flesh – and then only for an instant during the final collapse. The inch in question was at the very top of her left calf, behind and below her knee. In itself, it was unremarkable – except that his eye had expected to find it encased in hose of thick lisle or some equally serviceable material. But bare flesh it was – peeping out between the top of her boot and the lower end of her . . . ethereals (for want of a better word). The very top of her boot was secured with a lacing of bright scarlet; and the termination of her . . . what *could* one call them? . . . her inexpressibles, was decorated with a frill of black and white broderie. Thus, as many an indifferent picture in a gallery is rescued by its frame, so, too, for Maurice, an inch-wide band of Miss Sweet's skin was transformed into a vision of incandescent temptation.

Indeed, it combined with his memory of the taut, squirming muscles of her lower back and of the nutcracker grip of the upper portions of her nether limbs and heaped him with guilt and confusion. Yet Miss Sweet herself, bless her, was sublimely indifferent to the havoc she was causing him. She prattled gaily on about the hunt, asking which coverts they had drawn, and where they had found, and what line the foxes had owned, and whether the hounds had rioted after hares, and all the other mishaps that can beset even the best of hunts . . . while he laboured manfully to respond to her questions and *only* to her questions.

Respite came at last. He stretched his liberated feet toward the hearth and watched them steam in the red glow of the fire, while she brought in the big, galvanized bath that hung on a nail against the scullery wall. She wedged its rim beneath the huge brass tap beside the kitchen range, which was soon gushing with piping hot water. At last she left him to cool it to his taste and soak away the aches and bruises of his day in the saddle. As he sank among the suds and felt the heat close around him, pushing its fiery needles into every pore, he thought there could surely be no more contented man in all the world. For one long, luxurious minute he emptied his mind of all its preoccupations and abandoned his senses to that most sybaritic and hedonistic of pleasures – the almost-too-hot bath.

Then he remembered Miss Sweet and the incident with the boots.

Then he tried hard not to remember Miss Sweet and the incident with the boots.

Was there a little noise out in the passage? He had heard Miss Sweet go into the back yard for a scuttle of coal and then carry it through to the drawing room. After that . . . silence. He strained an ear but heard nothing beyond the steady patter of rain on the window panes and the singing of the newly cold water in the back boiler – heating itself for Miss Sweet's bath, which she took every night before retiring. He tried not to think of Miss Sweet lying in this bath, her body exactly where his was lying now.

It astonished him – this sudden change in his attitude toward her. During all the months they had lived beneath the same roof he had never been plagued with thoughts like these – not about her, anyway. That is not to say he had been completely unaware of her charms; far from it. He was a healthy young man and she an attractive young woman. But, despite his calloused hands and the fact that he could show a clean pair of heels to any of his labourers at all the jobs about the farm, he had also undergone the ordeal known as 'becoming a gentleman.' At sixteen, before that ordeal began, he had hungered for every young female old enough to be in long skirts (and day-dreamed his way beyond those garments, too). Now, at more than twice that age, he would hold in the deepest contempt any man who took advantage of a servant's dependence and he hoped the honour of any unmarried female, servant or lady, would be safer with him on a desert island than if she were there alone. (On the other hand, the honour of a married lady or a widow was more in their keeping than his, for, though a gentleman, he was, indeed, a gentleman of his time.)

Thus on two counts he had managed to live a life of almost total propriety with his nubile young housekeeper, never mind what the gossips of West Penwith might make of their situation. True, there had been the occasional, rather jocular lapse, as on the night they had assisted Bombardier and Sibylla in the perpetuation of their lines – but those had been of a pardonable nature, as one might pardon a safety valve on a steam engine for venting off a little superheated steam. The same might be said of the occasional and very fleeting thoughts that had crossed his mind at the sight of the morning sun on Miss Sweet's cheek or the dance of the evening firelight in her eyes; a gentleman could experience the same passing thoughts a dozen times a day – at the sight of a few pretty tresses during a dull sermon in church, for instance, or the touch of a shop girl's hand as she returned his change. It meant nothing. It was the body's way of sneering, 'Ha-ha – still alive, see!' It was also a gentleman's way of coping with that sneer.

It helped greatly, of course – in Maurice's particular circumstances – that Miss Sweet herself was so loftily unconcerned with all that sort of thing. The fact that this evening's little display of skin and clench of limb was so incidental and artless made it possible for him to accept and cope with it. For, had there been the slightest suggestion of design or purpose behind it, he doubted all his gentlemanly resolution would be stout enough to withstand the ardour she had inadvertently aroused in him. Thus, by her very inadvertence, she had appointed him the guardian of her continued innocence – without which childlike trust his determination might easily have crumbled.

'Mister,' she called softly from somewhere out in the passage, 'you got five minutes afore that pasty do spoil.'

He rose at last from the water and, thanking heavens (and two inches of solid oak door) that Miss Sweet could not see what condition she had brought him to, threw open the firebox of the range and towelled himself vigorously by the glow of its coals. His clothes were hanging on the brass-railed mantel, warm as hot towels at the barber's. He put them up one by one, luxuriating afresh at the touch of each new garment, then stuck his feet into his carpet slippers to slip-slop over to open the door and tell Miss Sweet she could come and rescue his supper.

He was still several paces from the door, with his fingers reaching for the handle, when he noticed a most singular thing: The key was missing from its hole and, what was more, the little wooden escutcheon that would normally hang down and seal it in those circumstances was stuck out to one side – wedged with what appeared to be a small spill of paper. But before he could examine it closer, Miss Sweet threw open the door and bustled officiously in, saying, 'Ready or no, Mister, I shan't let that pasty go to ruin.'

She closed the door behind her, masking his view for a moment. When she walked past him to get to her oven, he saw that the escutcheon was hanging down normally and the spill of paper, or whatever it had been, was gone. A moment later, however, the ambrosial aroma of fresh-baked pasty drove all other thoughts from his mind; he actually felt the saliva start like a freshet beneath his tongue, almost floating it off the floor of his mouth. There was a smaller pasty for her. She put them on two plates and opened the drawer to get knives and forks as usual; but he told her to put them back as far as he was concerned. Today he'd eat his pasty 'fitty like' – in the hand, which is the true Cornish way.

Tactfully she decided to do the same, since to use the utensils would suggest she knew better than he did. 'That's a real farmhouse spread,' she said approvingly as she set down two pewter tankards and a flagon of Rosewarne's best export ale. 'You want pepper, do you? Mrs Cowles put plenty in.'

'I want nothing better, Miss Sweet, than the sight of you sitting there, eating away and not fussing around me like a headless chicken.' He lifted the pasty in his hands and sank his teeth into the very point of it. Though he bit off no more than a corner of the pastry, he opened a vent through which rose a steamy bouquet of succulent fragrances – of beef and turnip and potato baked to the very point of perfection. It rose like a culinary anthem around his intoxicated head. 'Oh, Miss Sweet!' he sighed in a trance of admiration, 'I have dreamed of this moment all day. The French may keep their *haute cuisine* and the rest of the world go empty-bellied for all I care – but a true Cornish pasty cooked by a doxy Cornish maid will content me till the Loe runs dry.'

Miss Sweet blushed prettily and, taking a ladylike bite, allowed that it hadn't spoiled as much as she'd feared.

'And what sort of a day has it been here?' he asked when two or three more bites had taken the sharpest edge off his hunger. 'I see Hosking and Munroe made a good start on the muckspreading. If Mrs Johnson were living at Parc-an-Dour, we'd have had complaints today!'

He noticed a small frown pass over her brow at this last remark, which struck him as odd; her face was usually quite impassive whenever he mentioned either Sibylla or her cousin.

'Mrs Curnow came over to see the new piglets today,' she told him.

He stopped eating in mid-bite, and then started again, just as abruptly. 'Did Blanche notice the switch?' he inquired.

She told him what had happened but said nothing more about Laura Curnow. At length he was forced to raise the topic himself. 'How did she seem to you?' he asked. 'She has tended to appear slightly . . . aloof in the past, hasn't she?'

A distinct worry wrinkled Miss Sweet's brow; unlike the earlier frown it did not fade away. 'She's . . .' she began. 'I mean, she seemed . . .' Again she faltered. Then, after a moment's effort, she shook her head and murmured, 'No, it's not my place to say it.'

He wagged a jocular finger at her. 'It's your place to do what I tell you, young lady! Speak when you're spoken to. Answer questions when asked. So?'

Miss Sweet smiled dutifully but soon became solemn again. 'I don't know as you'd be so grateful for my opinion, Mister, when you hear what it is.'

'Nonetheless . . .?' he prompted.

'Well . . .' She drew in a deep breath and squared herself to say it. 'I felt *sorry* for the poor soul. There now! Call that presumption, if you will, but I felt so sorry after she'd gone, I near broke down and wept.'

'Good heavens!' Maurice was so startled he laid down the remaining third of his pasty. 'What did she say? What did she tell you?'

Miss Sweet shook her head sadly. 'It was more what she *didn't* say, and what she didn't tell. It was that look in her eyes, poor body!'

'But what on earth were you discussing – to bring on such a . . .' He shrugged, unable to encompass it with a word.

Miss Sweet sighed. 'That's where it's hard to explain to a man, see. We never spoke what you might call hurrisome or deep. 'Twas all on the rearing of children and the difficulty of finding good domestic help . . . and what a blessing 'tis to have the old telephone, and, oh . . . gossip and that. Billy Dancey always being drunk, and such-like cooze. Nothing different from what any two women might coursey on about over a dish o' tay and a slice o' fuggan. But the look in her eyes! I always thought she was such a high-quarter lady, the sort of woman I'd give body and soul to be like. But now I'm not so sure.'

'Why not?' Maurice was aware that the intensity of his interest unnerved her, so, although his appetite had all but vanished, he forced himself to take another bite of his pasty and ask the question as casually as he could.

Miss Sweet heaved the deepest sigh of the evening. 'She was . . . lost! That's the only word I can think of for to describe it. She ask me my opinion on this or that and she'd nod away like she thought I was reading out the Holy Bible or something. She behaved to me like I thought I should behave to her! There now – I can't put it plainer. And the look in her eyes – all . . . they were all . . .' She shook her head, somehow managing to imply, not that the words eluded her, but that those which did occur were too ghastly to speak aloud.

He shuddered now at the baleful light in Miss Sweet's eyes – which, he presumed, was but a pale reflection of the emotion she had observed in Laura's.

'Did you and she pass comment about me, when you were up Lunnon?' she asked suddenly, catching him off guard.

His face betrayed him, so he was forced to allow it. 'I probably did say something in passing.'

'What?' she asked, maintaining a neat balance between diffidence and sharpness.

'Oh . . . just that *I* had noticed she was rather cool toward you and that *I* thought your feelings might be hurt by it – but that you were too good a housekeeper to show it openly. Sentiments to that effect, anyway.'

Miss Sweet's smile was a tantalizing mixture of the jesting, the provocative, and the distrustful. 'How, I wonder, did such a topic arise between you? Not that it's my place to ask, mind.'

'No, that's right,' he said, as if suddenly recalled to himself.

'I'm just here to *answer* questions, howsomever personal to me, and never show my feelings *openly*, howsomever hard that is.' Her lip trembled and she took a huge bit of her pasty, which she then munched with vicious concentration, studiously avoiding his eye.

His spirit sank to watch her. Why was everything falling apart tonight? That delicate web of understandings which had enabled them to live in such proximity without harbouring unseemly emotions or giving way to unbecoming feelings of any kind – where was it now, when they most needed it? Fleetingly he wondered if, by some strange telepathy, there were any connection between this outburst and his own earlier loss of control, though he had masked it so scrupulously from her. But there was no time to pursue the thought. He had to deal with her distress before it hardened and set between them like concrete.

'Curse me for a clumsy, unfeeling oaf, Miss Sweet,' he said humbly. 'You deserve a far better master than I shall ever be, I fear. But were I to give you the honest answer to your question, I think you would be as distressed to hear it as you thought I would be to hear yours just now.'

Her smile was pure gold; he felt as if the sun had come out from behind a cloud. 'And were you so distressed, Mister?' she asked. 'I fancy not.'

He shook his head. 'I was not.'

'Well,' she went on, 'you now have me put to a disadvantage. I daren't wag a finger at my *master*, see, and tell him what *his* duty is – like my *master* did to me!' Her smile brimmed over into pure mischief. 'I shall have to trust that office to my *master's* own conscience, I dare say.'

He reached across and squeezed her hand briefly, saying, 'You'll do, Miss Sweet. I can't deny you the request – but I still fear you'll dislike what you hear. The how and the wherefore of it – how Mrs Curnow and I came to be discussing you at all – is that she drew my attention, as tactfully as she could, mind, to certain scurrilous talk going around Helston – idle gossip concerning the fact that you and I are alone with each other's company in this house every night.'

Miss Sweet's expression was such a blank he felt compelled to enlarge on what he'd said. 'I'm sure the question occurred to you backalong last fall, when Ma Harvey left for good and the . . . er, situation first arose. I thought of raising it with you then, you know. But – cowardice, I suppose . . . squeamishness – something like that . . . anyway, I didn't say anything. I contented myself with the thought that you were the better judge in the matter. I mean, the possibility of nasty gossip – to put it no higher – must have occurred to you, and . . . oh, dammit! To be honest, I was a selfish brute. I felt happier not living here all alone – and I put my own gratification above all thought of your reputation!'

'Gusson! We could have made Lizzie Waring live in, too,' Miss Sweet pointed out. 'We still could, if it really does bother you. She's keen enough, I'm sure.'

Even as he had stumbled through his 'explanation,' he'd been painfully aware how thin it sounded; her remark gave it a merciful death. He popped the last corner of piecrust into his mouth and chewed it mechanically. 'Why didn't we do that, then?' he asked morosely.

'I know why *I* didn't,' she said lightly, pushing his tankard toward him and placing her own, which was empty, on her plate.

He raised an eyebrow at her.

She smiled almost sadly in response and, emitting an explosive little sigh, said, 'I did it to help *you*, Mister. Because it would give folk something else to think about – stop them talking about you and her all the blessed time.'

Her brief, almost casual confession left him stunned. It took some time for all its implications to sink in. At length he said, 'But . . . good heavens, Miss Sweet. That was a terrible thing to do – for you, I mean. A terrible sacrifice for you to make.'

She rose with that same enigmatic smile and cleared their plates, not for one moment taking her eyes off his. 'Sacrifice!' she echoed fondly – and, he thought, a little scornfully, too – as she walked over to the sink.

It made him feel he hardly knew the meaning of the word.

Pigling Blanche came home with Blanche; it saved a lot of argument. Laura's only small victory was to ban the creature from the main house at Chynoweth; a farmhouse kitchen was one thing, she said, but the kitchen of a private house was quite another. Yesterday, it struck her, she would have said 'respectable' house. So Pigling Blanche went out to the stables. He (fortunately the changeling-widden was of the same gender as the one lately devoured by his own mother) was the first thing Giles saw on his return home that evening.

'I expected Petifer to be raising vegetables for me,'

he pretended to complain. 'Now we're raising livestock for him.'

'Somehow,' Laura replied, 'I suspect that widden's career as "livestock" came to an abrupt end around the middle of this afternoon. I don't know how long pigs can live in a land without pork butchers, but I can see us fifteen years hence saying that now Blanche is married she really ought to take that creature off our hands.'

'Blanche married?' he echoed, giving her an ironic pat on the back. 'Ever the optimist! What happened around the middle of this afternoon, anyway? Why was she no longer content to leave her little namesake with his siblings?'

Laura explained. 'The extraordinary thing,' she concluded, 'is that Blanche realized at once that the new widden wasn't hers. Talk of brain cogs clicking and whirring! You could almost see hers doing it: Shall I have a lovely big howl and make them feel awful for trying to pull the wool over my eyes? Or shall I pretend not to notice and extract some nice juicy concession out of them?'

'Which she has done!'

'Which, indeed, she has done. It was a real growing-up sort of moment for her. The curious thing is, *we* know the new Pigling Blanche is not the same as the old one. Blanche herself knows it, too. And yet none of us can ever mention the fact! There's a sort of conspiracy to maintain the fiction between us.'

After a pause he said, 'Yes. That's very grown-up, isn't it!'

Their eyes met, faltered, and looked away.

'Where's Sibylla?' he asked.

Later, when Laura was inventing a new bedtime story for the brood, or the 'Eightsome Reel,' as Giles sometimes called them, Sibylla came down to the drawing room; like Giles she was already dressed for dinner. She picked up *The Tatler* and skimmed three pages before she realized she'd read it days earlier. 'There's a terrible amount of inbreeding going on,' she muttered as she threw it away and looked about for some other magazine.

Giles raised his face from the *Financial Times*. 'Is that an agricultural observation or a social comment?' he asked.

'It's a comment on *The Tatler*, anyway,' she replied. 'The same faces week after week. The same dresses. The same hair styles. The same pearls. The same *teeth*. Only the names get changed. It must be inbreeding. What else could explain it?'

He laid his paper aside. 'Laura will be some time yet, I expect,' he said.

She looked at him sharply. 'What's that supposed to mean?'

He shrugged. 'Nothing.'

'Nothing and everything!' She gave out a brief, almost explosive sigh and said, in the tones of someone making a rapid confession: 'I've dismissed Dancey and I've asked Harry Sampson to send a good ganger and half a dozen men to finish the job off.'

'Half a dozen?' he echoed in surprise.

'Yes!' she snapped.

'I see.' He glanced toward his paper, regretting now that he had cast it aside so demonstratively.

'Well, this can't go on, Giles. My nerves are just . . . *frazzled!* We said it would stop as soon as we got back to Cornwall.'

'We?'

'You didn't object when I said it.'

He grinned. 'I thought I had a better ally in you. The real you.'

She looked as if she were about to argue for a

moment but then collapsed upon herself. Eyes lowered, she said, 'That's why I have to finish the work at Parc-an-Dour this week – and move back there next.'

Her morose spirit infected him. He lowered his head and massaged the bridge of his nose between thumb and forefinger.

'Laura took the brood over to Culdrose this afternoon,' she told him. 'Or they took her.'

He nodded. 'Petifer was away all day.'

'That's what was so extraordinary.'

He looked at her askance, thinking she was making a cruel jibe.

'I mean, I thought she couldn't stand the sight of Miss Sweet. But apparently that's all changed.' She picked up *The Tatler* and immediately threw it down again. 'Any danger of a drink round here?' she asked, adding, 'As Paddy Doyle always says.'

He chuckled faintly and rose to mix her a cocktail. 'How do *you* feel about that woman?' he asked.

'She's as common as dirt, but I think she deserves a medal.'

'Really? I have the feeling this isn't going to taste the same without ice. I shall have to start bringing some home from the store each day.'

'Having to serve up meals for that man morning-noon-and-night! Having to watch him eat! And to scrape his slops into the bucket! To empty his bathwater!'

'All right, Sibylla!' He pretended her words were a gale against which he had to struggle.

'Make his bed! Sort through his . . . *linen – eurgh!*'

'I'm sorry I asked. We'll just have to pretend there's ice in that.' He handed her his version of a Manhattan and sat beside her, about two feet away – which she at once enlarged to three.

'I sometimes wonder if we are entirely sane,' he said

mildly. He sipped his glass and gave a sad, slow shake of his head – though whether at their possible insanity or at his cocktail's lack of resemblance to what they'd enjoyed at the Café Royal she could not tell.

'I don't have the slightest doubt,' she asserted. 'I'm quite sure we're both absolutely mad. That's why I *have* to get away from here, back to Parc-an-Dour.'

'I'm not talking just about that. Our *melting moments* are merely one small symptom of . . . this whole business.' He turned and stared at her. 'D'you know – I can't even remember what I was *like* this time last year. Can you? I wish . . .' He paused and squeezed the bridge of his nose again. 'I wish I'd kept a journal or something. A book of my thoughts. So I could go back and read it now and see how I've changed.'

He shot her a look of such mute despair that all her petulance deserted her. She would happily have squabbled with him and sniped at all his pretensions until her cousin came down to dinner; but now, in that brief glance of his, she felt he was nearing the end of his tether.

It shocked her. Giles had always seemed so . . . *big*, somehow. Not in stature, to be sure, but in spirit. Emotionally he had had the broadest back of any man she ever knew – or such would have been her opinion . . . last year! Suddenly she saw what he meant. She realized, too, that she had been relying on that broad back, that vast reserve of genial steadiness within him – the certainty that, whatever else happened, Giles would be the last to crack. She had been relying on him as a kind of pugilist's punchbag for her own emotional sport – so that she could lash out at him, indulge her resentment, gratify every ill-humoured whim, and all the time feel safe in the knowledge that he could take it and feel no pain.

'I can remember you then, Giles,' she murmured.

She bit the fingertip of her cotton glove and stretched it an inch or so, letting go with a ping! Then, turning to him, 'When you use the word *insane* . . .'

'Yes?' His expression was pathetically hopeful.

'I know what you mean. Not, you know, gah-gah.' She pulled a comic face in an attempt to lighten their mood. 'In fact, I don't think many insane people are what you'd call gah-gah, either. Adam told me about his old tutor, Doctor Maindy . . .'

'I remember old Maindy,' Giles broke in. 'Poor old boy went off his chump. They kept him in that private home over to Hayle.'

'Yes, well, when Adam went to see him once he said they spent half an hour in conversation and you'd never guess he was anything but his old, wise self. They talked about politics, gardening, agriculture, new discoveries in natural science, volcanoes . . . everything under the sun. The only odd thing was that he wouldn't allow the curtains to be drawn back. They talked by lamplight, though it was midday. But that's not mad, is it. You'd call it eccentric at most. I mean, there are plenty of people around like that. In fact, Adam was mentally composing a petition to have the poor old boy released. But on the way out he noticed that a small square of tinplate had been nailed over the keyhole. And then, before he left, the attendants told him all about it. The old buffer, it seemed, had an absolutely morbid fear he was being spied on all the time. Sometimes it got so bad he made them erect a tent in the room, because he thought *they* – these nebulous creatures who were sent to spy on him – had drilled holes in the ceiling. Yet there he was – perfectly sane on any other topic you cared to raise with him!' She remembered a little afterthought: 'And the odd thing was, Adam said that when Doctor Maindy first became their tutor, he hung up over his desk a picture of an eye. Not a diagrammatic eye. He said it looked like an eye torn from a creature in an abattoir. Catholic, of course – you know how they love religious blood and gore. And underneath it, in letters of fire, were the words, *Thou, O God, Seest All!*'

Giles raised his fist and shook it at the ceiling. 'Oh God, Thou surely hast a lot to answer for on Judgement Day!'

Sibylla laughed with delight and pointed an accusing finger at him. 'Now *that's* exactly what you'd have said this time last year!'

His smile soon faded. 'You mean you, too, have noticed a difference in me?'

She gave a vague shrug, implying she'd accept the notion for the sake of argument. 'Tell me how you see it, Giles. Where d'you think the biggest change has been?'

He stared into his glass awhile and then put it down on the arm of the sofa. 'That is almost undrinkable,' he said.

'Go on,' she urged.

He drew a deep breath and began. 'You've hit the nail on the head when you say that insanity can affect just one small part of the mind. I go to work every day. I make rational decisions. I face the hurly-burly of business with at least as much shrewdness as I was ever blessed with. I attend meetings of the Ratepayers' Association, the Town Council, the club committee . . . blah-blah-blah. I'm sure no one out there suspects there's a single screw out of place.' He tapped the side of his head. 'Yet inside here I'm beginning to feel – and increasingly so – that I'm getting away with it! *I* know I'm not quite sane, but I'm successfully hiding it from all of them!' He laughed, more with despair than with humour, and turned to her. 'Does none of this ring a bell with you? I mean, do you see your behaviour now, in nineteen-oh-three, as a direct and predictable development of what you did in oh-two?'

She hesitated. The big change, this year, was, of course, her adultery with him (ugly word, but there it was). She hesitated because she still could not be absolutely certain Laura had kept her secret, concerning Daniel Jago.

He misinterpreted her silence as a reluctance to speak of herself until he had put more of his own cards on the table. 'Actually,' he went on, 'this isn't an insanity of the mind so much as an insanity of the conscience. It's shaken me, I don't mind telling you – the things that have happened to my conscience since Maurice Petifer turned up again. Let's stop talking vaguely about this year, last year. Let's give the thing its proper starting date: Friday, July the eighteenth last.'

'The auction?'

He nodded. 'Sometimes I've only just managed to stop myself from wishing I could believe in God again. It would be so easy, wouldn't it! Just follow the code and there are the pearly gates! I thought a rational morality would have much better answers, but so far it's let me down every step of the way.'

Sibylla decided to let silence be her prompt this time.

'Laura said a funny thing this evening,' he went on. And he repeated, as near as he could recall it, their conversation about Blanche and how she had decided to take part in the conspiracy over Pigling Blanche. 'And it will hold, you see,' he concluded, 'that particular conspiracy, because no one has an interest in breaking it. And now I begin to think that this wonderful, strong, rational, morality by which I had lived until last July was of the same order: It was a pure fiction, but it worked because we all had an interest in keeping it going. But put that a different way: It will work only as long as none of us has an interest in breaking it! That's not nearly so impressive, is it! My whole scheme of things turns out to be no stronger than a gossamer web – which may seem powerful enough when tested by nothing more vigorous than a fly, but to you and me it's no more than a ticklish nuisance as we lightly brush it aside. That's the real test!'

'Giles, how bleak!' Sibylla exclaimed.

'Isn't it! But isn't it also true? Aren't we all doing things, and thinking things, and saying things we wouldn't have *dreamed* of before last July? And *planning* things, too! Yet couldn't we still justify them in the same old rational way? Reason!' he blurted out scornfully. 'It just slips and slides whichever way we wish it to go.'

She stared morosely into her glass.

He smiled. 'You don't have to drink it, just because I mixed it for you. I'm not touching mine.' He moved his glass firmly onto the whatnot to prove it.

She tossed her drink back in one gulp and breathed out its fiery afterburn. 'Do you love me, Giles?' she asked.

He swallowed hard, as if she had punched him, and then said, 'Yes.'

His lack of decoration to this simple reply surprised her; she caught a fleeting expression in his eye which showed it surprised him a little, too.

'Now justify that!' he challenged himself ironically.

'All right.' Her tone implied she could accept it equally as a game or as a serious discussion.

He sank so deep in contemplation she thought he was going to refuse, either to play or to discuss. But then he gave a laugh of self-contempt and said, 'God,

I've just remembered something! Last June! The night of the Troys' coming-home ball at Liston House. You weren't there? No, of course – you came home to the good news a bit later. But in the carriage on the way into Helston – of course, we knew nothing about Maurice Petifer's return then. He was there already, waiting for us, and our carriage – like some doomed Ship of Fools in a medieval morality play – sailing blithely on. And d'you know what I said? I must have had a premonition or something.'

'What? Something about Maurice Petifer?'

He laughed sourly. 'Judge for yourself! I said I thought any robust marriage should be able to weather a little mild adultery without too much strain!'

'Oh, Giles – you didn't!' Trancelike, she raised her empty glass and tried to drink from it.

'I know!' He took it from her nerveless hand and went over to the tantalus. 'A simple dry sherry, eh? Poor Laura! She thought I was trying to tell her gently that I was indulging in some minor affaire.'

'Oh really?' Sibylla mimed surprise. 'Now I, in her shoes, would have assumed the opposite – that you were granting me that indulgence! But that's just my . . .'

'That was her next thought.'

His interruption ran parallel with her own conclusion, so she could not halt herself or take it back: ' . . . just my guilty conscience!'

'But you wouldn't have had a guilty conscience, had you been in *her* shoes, would you!' He handed her the sherry.

He was teasing her merely for the flaw in her logic – having no idea of her past adulteries. So he was greatly surprised to see her blush. 'I was muddling up me-now with me-then,' she explained lamely. Then, returning to the attack: 'Anyway, you haven't justified your assertion that you . . . made just now.'

'D'you really want me to?' he asked. 'Or is it one of those Pigling Blanche sort of conspiracies where you know, I know, but neither of us says a word?'

'I'd just like to hear you try,' she said, almost with a sneer in her voice.

'Very well.' He dipped his head gravely. 'The Giles Curnow who was so cavalier about adultery – in that carriage on the way to Liston House last June – would have been far more cynical about it than I can be today. He knew everything, of course. He had the most granite-solid marriage in the world – otherwise how could he joke about it like that! His code of morality didn't depend on some Stern Papa-in-the-Sky, nor on what some bearded loonie once brought down from a mountain, carved on bits of stone. His code was *rational!* He was fireproof, insured to the gills . . . monarch of the glen. Funnily enough, it would have been the easiest thing in the world for *him* to have a little adulterous affaire – which, of course, is why he never did!'

She frowned in bewilderment.

'Why bother with the easy things?' he explained. 'He'd have justified it in purely animal terms – or what the philosophers grandly call *utilitarian*. Towns must have sewers; the sanitary arrangements adequate to Robinson Crusoe cannot simply be multiplied up ten thousand times. You see the parallel, I hope?'

Her eyes narrowed. 'You mean your adultery – or rather, the adultery you'd have been able to justify then – would have taken place in a . . . a disorderly house? My God, Giles! Is that how you see *me* – as a kind of common . . .'

'No, Sibylla! For heaven's sake, dear girl – that is my entire point! The sort of affaire I so flippantly dismissed that fateful evening had nothing to do with *love*. But whatever you call this . . . this *thing* between us – give me an untainted word, please! Whatever you call it, it exists entirely thanks to *love*. It doesn't matter to me now if we *never* go to bed together again (which the utilitarian would say is the whole point of the thing) – it wouldn't matter to me, I say. You can go and live in Parc-an-Dour . . . you can go and live in Timbuctoo! The love I feel for you would not be diminished by one jot or one tittle!'

She closed her eyes and bowed her head. 'Oh, Giles!' she murmured.

'Quite!' he said bitterly. 'I warned you.'

'But . . .' Her face was quite haggard when she turned to him again.

'What about Laura?'

'Are you asking me – or the utilitarian?'

'Oh, damn your utilitarian? Damn and blast him to hell!'

'Many a true word . . .' he said dourly. 'I have no answer. I love Laura more desperately than ever. In fact, desperately is quite the wrong word. I never loved her desperately before this. Comfortably, yes. Solidly. Placidly. Serenely . . . and now that's all gone. I love you *and* I love her – and there's no possibility of explaining it to her. I think she feels the same about me and Maurice – and she can't explain that to me, either. But she doesn't need to explain it – because I already know it! And I don't need to explain it – because *she* already knows it! So we're both caught up in this conspiracy, you see? That's why she told me about Blanche and the new widden, the way she did. How have we arrived at this . . . awful . . .' He gave up the search for a word dire enough for their predicament.

'Bloody Maurice Petifer!' she said bitterly, sipping her sherry for the first time.

But he shook his head. 'I've tried that, Sibylla.'

She looked at her glass, frowned, and looked at him.

'No,' he said. 'Blaming Petifer. I tried that. It's no good.'

'Another of those things that's just too easy, I suppose!'

They heard Laura coming down the stairs at that moment. Giles half rose to go back to his paper and then thought better of it. When she appeared, however, he got up and poured her a sherry. 'I tried to concoct a Manhattan,' he said, 'but it's awful without ice.'

'You could get ice from the water butt outside that window,' she told him. 'It must be five below.'

'I never thought of it. Too late now.' He handed her the sherry and poured one for himself. 'Sibylla says Parc-an-Dour will be finished inside a week,' he added.

Laura turned to her cousin. 'Did you light a fire under Dancey, then?'

Sibylla smiled. 'I have *fired* him altogether, as Jimmy Troy would say.'

'Given him the boot?'

Sibylla nodded. 'And asked Sampson to send up a small army. I want to move in again next week.'

Laura laughed. 'Just because you're getting your car!'

Sibylla's face fell; she turned guiltily to Giles. 'I forgot to tell you. Daniels, that young porter up at the railway station, cycled out to Parc-an-Dour this afternoon while Laura was with the children over at Culdrose. He says our cars have arrived – my Opel, your Lanchester, and the Troys' Thorneycroft, too.'

'Mercedes send telegrams,' Laura observed tartly. 'We get a porter on a bicycle!'

Sibylla was still looking guiltily at Giles. 'Sorry!' she said.

'You forgot?' Laura asked skeptically. 'What on earth could you have talked about more important than that?'

'Utilitarianism!' Sibylla waved a hand toward Giles.

'Mea culpa,' he acknowledged.

Laura sat in his chair. 'Oh! The best moment of the day!' she murmured, closing her eyes and raising her face as if to the sun.

Sibylla saw Giles looking at her and knew he had spoken the truth when he claimed to love her still; whether his other claim, that he also loved her, Sibylla, was also true, she was more dubious. It was such an easy thing for a man to say. 'Have you changed your opinion of Miss Sweet, then?' she asked boldly.

'What opinion of Miss Sweet?' Laura murmured.

'What opinion of Miss Sweet!' Sibylla's echo was full of scorn. 'You know very well you wouldn't have given her the time of day not so long ago. And now you're over there, sitting in your boots in her kitchen, sipping her tea, and guzzling her fuggan! I've heard all about it.'

Giles began to laugh, but Laura was not amused. 'If you want a true utilitarian,' she asserted, 'it's Miss Sweet. I only hope Maurice has the sense to marry her one day.'

For some reason this response roused Sibylla to fury; but then, the more she thought about it, the more amusing the idea became. So the breath she had drawn to give vent to her rage came out in the form of laughter, though equally harsh. 'It would just about serve him right!' she said gleefully.

'Why?' her cousin asked.

'Because it would. That's all. Can we go in and eat? I'm starving to death. I shouldn't have had this sherry on an empty tummy.' She smiled to herself and added, 'Or *belly*, as I'm sure the *utilitarian* Miss Sweet would call it. Oh yes! She and bloody Maurice Petifer absolutely deserve each other.'

On that same Saturday, while Laura had been eating Miss Sweet's fuggan and Sibylla had been giving Billy Dancey the boot, Elizabeth and Jimmy Troy had slipped up to the station and collected their Thorneycroft; they drove it to church in style the following morning and *only*, as Elizabeth bravely expressed it, suffered two punctures – one in each direction. As the distance involved was less than half a mile, others were of the opinion that the Almighty was intending them to read something into these mishaps.

Sibylla and the Curnows had to wait until Monday morning before they could collect theirs, since the railways did only perishable-goods business on the Sabbath. They arrived around mid-morning to find Maurice Petifer already there, looking very *automobilist* in a white trench coat, goggles, and peaked cap. 'I thought you'd never get here!' he called out when their gig was still halfway up the station approach.

'We wouldn't, had we but known,' Sibylla muttered darkly.

'Now now!' Laura chided. 'Remember what the man from the Automobile Association said – we motorists must stick together.'

'Oh, please darling!' Sibylla exaggerated her distress theatrically. 'I've only just had breakfast. The very idea of "sticking together" with *that* specimen of pond life is . . . *eurgh!*'

'We have company.' Giles drew their attention to the far end of the station courtyard, where two worthies of the town constabulary, Sergeant Drew and Constable Eddy, were staring innocently at the sky. 'I'm not going to tolerate this,' he added, giving the reins a shake.

Maurice, standing by the gate onto the platform, turned to see why he was driving past.

'Be with you in a moment, young fellow,' Giles called out to him.

'Now do be careful, darling,' Laura cautioned.

'They are within their rights, after all,' Sibylla put in.

'Rights!' Giles echoed in disgust. 'What about the rights of property? What about the right of respectable, law-abiding citizens to go about their peaceable purposes?'

'What kind of citizens?' Laura asked.

'Well – some laws are just too idiotic to obey. As Elizabeth Troy says, we do them more honour in the breach than in the observance.'

'Well, don't tell Drew that,' Sibylla warned. 'He has a rather more simpleminded approach.'

'Morning Drew, morning Eddy!' Giles called out with bluff heartiness as they drew level. Then, following their skyward gaze, he added, 'Cloud shaped like a poacher, eh? I spotted it myself and thought the same thing.'

The sergeant grunted. 'More the shape of a man with a red flag, in my opinion, Mr Curnow, sir.' Then, sweeping his gaze around the forecourt, he added, 'The only one in sight, too.'

Giles's lips narrowed to a dangerous line. 'Now see here, Sarn't Drew,' he said in a direct, man-to-man fashion, 'aren't we in some danger of forgetting what you chaps are really for?'

'Danger?' the sergeant replied coolly. 'I don't think so, sir. Red flags is the usual sign of danger – and, like what I said, I don't see none o' them hereabout.'

'Hang your red flags, man!'

'From a pole, sir, of wood or other serviceable material, not exceeding six foot in length . . .'

'The civil police were formed,' Giles went on doggedly, 'to maintain civil order – after the army bungled the job. You're there to prevent the civil power from being subverted by riot and insurrection. D'you understand? You are *our* fist against *them* – the forces of disorder. I'll wager there are half a dozen crimes against property and person being plotted in Helston this very moment. And where are you? Hanging about the station and making an idiotic fuss about red flags. That law has been repealed – or will be very shortly. Now surely you have more serious crimes to pursue? So I'll trouble you to cut along now, like the good chaps you are!'

The sergeant clasped his hands behind him and stared somewhere over Giles's shoulder. 'I don't know anything about all that, sir . . .'

'You do, because I've just told you.'

'I'm just a simple country bobby who goes by the law. I apprehend them as breaks it.'

Giles, realizing he was going to get nowhere with the fellow, started to turn the horse about. 'I shall have a very strong word with the chief constable about all this, next time I dine with him at the club.' As he drove away he had one more over-the-shoulder try: 'It's also very foolish to bite the hand that feeds you like this. The police are detested by the criminal classes – for the very good reason that you harass them without mercy. But if you make yourselves detested by the law-abiding classes, too, you won't have a friend left in the land!'

The sergeant calmly took out his notebook and wrote something in it.

'Giles,' Laura said as they went back to where Maurice was still waiting. 'D'you know who you're beginning to sound like?'

'Who?' he asked crossly.

'My father!'

He stared at her in horror; then his jaw fell wide open. 'Lord, old girl!' he exclaimed. 'D'you know – you're absolutely right!' He took out his handkerchief and passed it across his brow.

'What are we going to do?' Sibylla asked. 'We haven't brought any red flags . . .'

'We haven't *got* any red flags to bring,' Giles interrupted. 'And as long as I live and breathe, we shan't get any, either. We shall just drive away so slowly that even the good sergeant won't dare estimate it above one mile an hour.'

'And if he follows us?'

'I shall ask him to make a note of the precise time we leave the station here, and the precise time when we get down to the main road, and the precise time when we enter Clodgey Lane . . . and so on, all the way home. No one travelling that slowly has ever been fined for not having a flagman. By Jupiter – what is this fair land of ours coming to!'

They arrived back at the gate into the station.

'Trouble with the constabulary?' Maurice opened the gig door and held out his hand for Sibylla to lean on.

Laura usurped the offer and bore him away a pace or two, leaving Giles to help Sibylla. 'Don't provoke her,' she warned under her breath.

'I've already had my name taken,' Maurice said cheerfully.

'I just resent paying fines for breaking idiotic laws,' Giles explained.

'Oh, I shan't pay any fine,' Maurice told him. 'Mrs Drew thinks we produce the best milk in the district. She and Molly Hendren are thick as thieves. Well . . . not the best simile, in the circumstances, perhaps! Poor Drew's life wouldn't be worth living if he pressed charges. Mind you, he doesn't realize it yet – or I doubt if he'd be up here, wasting his time.'

'Well, in that case I shall *insist* on being charged,' Sibylla said as she swept grandly past him. 'If he doesn't do it, I shall report myself. Oh – just look at that!'

Her eye had caught sight of her Opel, gleaming in the pale, silvery sun of that February morning. 'There now!' she exclaimed. 'Is that or is that not a car to be proud of? A car, did I say? Why, it's a veritable equipage!'

'I rather expected them to be kept under tarpaulins,' Giles grumbled, eyeing their own, rather mundane Lanchester.

'I'm to blame for that,' Maurice admitted. 'I had the covers removed. I thought you'd prefer *this* to be your first sight.' He smiled at Sibylla as if to say, 'And wasn't I right!'

She said angrily, 'And I suppose you've filled them with petroleum spirit and run the engines over, too!'

He hung his head like a naughty schoolboy – and grinned at her.

Old Chigwidden, the senior porter, came down the platform and beckoned them to follow him along the boardwalk that bisected the lines and made a crossing of the shunting yard a relatively easy affair. They followed in his wake and then fanned out as they approached the cinder hard-standing where their cars were waiting.

'I gave them a little polish, too,' Maurice admitted. He grinned again at Sibylla and added, 'See – self-accusation, now! You appear to have started a fashion.'

She turned on Laura and asked her what was so amusing.

Laura glanced at Giles, who touched Sibylla on the arm and said, 'Remember poor old Doctor Maindy, my dear. How near the surface madness lies!'

Maurice and Laura exchanged puzzled glances at this, sharing a bewilderment that merely increased when they saw Sibylla struggling heroically to contain her vexation.

'Er . . . what now?' Giles asked uncertainly. 'You've had them both running, you say?'

Maurice nodded. 'Yours has dual ignition. You might just be lucky and start her by fiddling with the trembler-coil switch. If she stopped just three degrees off top-dead-centre, you know.'

'Of course!' Giles exclaimed. 'How could I forget?' He pulled a face of blank incomprehension at Laura, who said, 'Never mind, dear – Blanche will no doubt explain it to you when we get home. She won't understand it, either, mind – but that has never yet stopped her from explaining anything.'

Giles continued to stare unhappily at his new toy. 'I've read every motoring magazine I could get my hands on for the past six months,' he said morosely. He lifted the bonnet and stared at the works, continuing his complaint all the while: 'I've studied Rankine's *Encyclopaedia* from cover to cover. I never go on to a new page until I'm sure I understand the present one. And I *do* understand it, I assure you. I could sit down and draw you a trembler coil now. Yet here I am, standing in front of the blighter itself, and I can't even tell you which of all those . . . *things* it is! There's bags of knowledge stuffed away up here – and it's all somehow related to this beast here – but there's some vital connection missing. Is that the trembler coil?'

'Bullseye, old boy!' Maurice said. 'So now at least one vital connection is no longer missing!'

'And all I do is this?' Giles reached forward and moved the switch on the side of the coil to *Start*.

A sluggish groan rose to a purposeful whir and a moment later the engine leaped to life. 'I see!' he said thoughtfully, flicking the switch back to *Run*.

Laura laughed and punched him on the arm. 'Talk about beast!' she said. '*You're* the beast! Pretending to know nothing! You knew jolly well all along exactly what to do.'

He winked at her and said, just above the throb of the motor, 'Ignorance is bliss, love.'

It was such an unexpected moment of intimacy between them that it took her unawares, making her catch her breath and blink rather rapidly. She felt suddenly warmer toward him than she had for weeks, ever since their return from London. She grasped him by the arm she had punched and pretended to rub it better. 'Race Sibylla home!' she suggested. 'I'll bet this thing can beat that old Opel any day.' She let him go and jumped up into the passenger seat. 'In the right hands,' she added. Then, feigning surprise, 'Come on, cousin dear – haven't you got yours going yet?'

'I would if I knew how,' Sibylla answered crossly.

Maurice licked his lips and spoke to her cautiously, as a menagerie keeper to an escaped lioness: 'Turn the petroleum-spirit tap to on. Activate the electrical circuit. Engage the crank-handle and grasp it firmly in the right hand making sure that the thumb is on the same side as the fingers . . .'

'Oh, ha-ha, Mr Petifer!' she said even more crossly as she turned to Giles. 'Are you going to relapse into ignorance again?'

Giles looked inquiringly at Maurice, who resumed his diffident instruction: '. . . and swing it firmly and deliberately, up to half a dozen revolutions before resting again.'

Her chin went up; her lips almost vanished. 'You imagine I can't do any of that, I suppose?' she snapped. 'Well, let me just show you!'

She stared at her vehicle and, for a moment, was almost overwhelmed at the hopelessness of it all. What the hell had Petifer said? Petroleum-spirit tap! That was first, anyway.

'Tap,' she murmured, searching the floor around the driver's seat and all along the dash. 'Tap.'

Giles, taking pity on her, put his hands to the bonnet catches. But she leaped at him and barged him aside.

'You'll get your gloves all oily,' he warned.

'Yes, I *will* get my gloves all oily,' she affirmed, unhooking the catches and lifting the bonnet herself.

But she didn't, in fact, because Maurice had spent twenty minutes cleaning and polishing every inch of the car, earlier that morning.

'Tap!' she exclaimed triumphantly, pouncing on what certainly seemed to be such an article. She gave it a quarter-turn, from horizontal to vertical, and glanced at Maurice for confirmation – remembering to glance away fiercely before he gave it. However, she had the comfort of catching it out of the corner of her eye.

'Make the electrical circuit,' she murmured.

That was easy, in fact, for she'd noticed the switch on the dash in her earlier hunt. She turned it on. Nothing happened but she remembered not to look at Maurice for confirmation this time. Then, trusting to luck, she went round to the front of the car, grasped the crank-handle, fiddled with it (as she remembered the salesman doing) until it engaged, and vented all her anger on it in one powerful turn.

The engine, being still warm, burst into life at once and she dropped the handle as if it had scalded her. She was so delighted at her triumph she almost gave Petifer a hug. At the last minute she managed to transform it into a punch on his shoulder. 'So there!' she crowed.

'Now there'll be no holding you,' he replied sadly.

His sadness was a remnant of a more powerful feeling that had overcome him, fleetingly, while he watched her rise to her own challenge. *What a truly wonderful woman she'd make*, he had thought, *if only she weren't Sibylla!*

Sheer nonsense, of course, but he was still trying to reach the nugget of sense which, he felt sure, lay at the heart of it. 'And now,' he said, turning to the Curnows, 'for a *real* trial of strength!'

'Oh no!' Laura exclaimed in alarm, quite forgetting her own earlier ebullience. 'No racing now. We can go and race on Pendeen Sands one fine day, if you want. But no racing here, please!'

'Oh, I wasn't talking about that,' he assured her. 'I said a *real* trial of strength – by which I mean: Is Sergeant Drew's love of law and order *outside* the home greater than his liking for peace and harmony *inside* it!'

In a careless moment Maurice had allowed his name to go forward for the committee of the Rescue House, a charitable home for reformed unfortunates at Constantine, a few miles southwest of Falmouth. He couldn't think why, now – except that Jane Scawen, who had founded the home many years earlier, had such compelling eyes and such a winning smile; her description of the death of a friend of hers had been particularly telling – a respectable tradesman's daughter who became an unfortunate, was rescued by marriage ('to a man worth his weight in gold, Mr Petifer,') but, being unable to believe that Society had accepted her back into its ranks, suffered years of mental anguish and finally took poison. However, away from Mrs Scawen's persuasive eyes, smile, and tongue, he had to allow that it was not a subject that either interested or appealed to him. He suspected that Mrs Scawen knew as much and had, indeed, focussed her attention upon him for that very reason – his conscience would ensure he came up with the cash.

The trustees of the Rescue House were not the kind who met once a month to guzzle tea and digestive biscuits, praise samples of embroidery, and issue certificates of diligence; they met twice a year to hand over the large sums of money they had raised toward the running of the place. 'And I expect more than a single cheque every six months, Mr Petifer,' she had said with waggish sternness. 'I want the subscription list that supports it. I want to know that every respectable person in the district has *actively* thought about and contributed to this most deserving cause – especially the gentlemen, who have the most to answer for . . . and,' she had added delicately, 'the most to give, by happy coincidence.' And to avoid overlapping of effort, she had also furnished him with a map of his collecting district, his 'tax farm,' as she called it.

'A tax farmer for taxed-out tarts,' was the joke among the heartier members of the Cury Hunt. It was another 'happy coincidence' that Maurice's district covered the Hunt's country to the very last field – and that Mrs Scawen had waited until a month or two after his joining, to assure herself he was a popular member.

Miss Sweet, bless her, had volunteered at once to share some of his burden. She, too, had no particular interest in the subject. The only view she offered was that 'men are so silly – some of 'em, anyway,' a view he did not press her to elaborate. In fact, ever since the episode with the wet riding boots, he had steered almost painfully clear of any reference, however shallow, to the natural relations between men and women. Since that fateful evening he had been plagued, he would almost say obsessed, by thoughts of her in that relationship.

The horseplay with the boots was nothing – a bit of country rough-and-tumble that could have been laughed off and forgotten. The flash of her bare calf, or four square inches thereof, voluptuously framed between scarlet-laced boots and frilly broderie, would have lingered a few days longer, but he was not the sort of obsessive character who could take such molehills and from them fashion a continental divide. At least, he would not have considered himself obsessive until now. But now he could not seem to banish from his mind the picture of that escutcheon wedged up by a spill of paper.

It was one of those seemingly trivial discoveries that can nonetheless change one's whole perception of a person. The more he considered its implications, the more he realized that Miss Sweet was not at all the sort of woman she claimed to be – especially when he recalled the smoothly efficient manner in which she had removed the evidence before he could confirm it.

From the moment she had arrived on the scene at Culdrose, she had carried herself about the place with blithe disregard for their difference in gender. Her behaviour was conventional in the profoundest sense of the word – that is, there were obviously no strong feelings behind it at all. She was modest simply because that had been her upbringing – not because she sensed danger in *not* being modest, not because the thought of being immodest carried a little frisson of excitement, which she therefore had to fight with an enforced display of virtue. It came naturally and easily to her because she was so charmingly untouched by incandescent thoughts and feelings of any kind. She was a child still, with a child's delightful innocence.

Such, at least, had been the impression she gave. Even the earthy jokes about bulls in service and the horseplay with the boots could be seen as a charming part of that same innocence, for it implied that a young woman like her could *know* the facts of life and yet remain blissfully untouched by their power.

A scrap of a butcher's bill – rolled into a spill to prevent a short length of carved wood from doing its job – had changed all that. For the job of that escutcheon (apart from stopping draughts and whistlings through an untenanted doorlock) was to deny access to the prurient eye. And a prurient eye implies a prurient eyer. Time and again he remembered himself rising from the bathtub in the state of moderate excitement to which his thoughts of Miss Sweet had raised him. He tried to picture that scene as viewed from the keyhole and to imagine the wanton thoughts it might have stirred in a breast now revealed as far from innocent.

He did not, in fact, have to try too hard, for on that very same evening, when he had bade Miss Sweet good night and she had retired to the kitchen to take her customary bath, he had crept back downstairs to conduct the reverse experiment for himself. But as his fingers reached forward to ease up the escutcheon on his side of the door, he realized he had forgotten to do the trick with the spill of paper on the other side. Relief flooded through him. His thoughtlessness had saved him from a most shameful act of betrayal.

He had been about to return to his room when, on

the merest insouciant whim, he had flipped the escutcheon to one side anyway. And there in the palm of his hand, etched in gold, was a keyhole-shaped sliver of light! So once again Miss Sweet had propped it open – this time with herself in the bath.

Unthinkingly he had stooped to peep, only managing to hold himself back at the very last moment. For he realized that if he did go through with it, his serenely untroubled relations with Miss Sweet would be changed forever. Never mind the *implication* of the propped-up escutcheon on the far side of the door . . . in the fullness of time it could be accommodated – one of those petty mysteries of life that must have an innocent explanation, even if one cannot quite think what it might be. Like the theft by the Jackdaw of Rheims. Yes, it could be accommodated, and their pleasant, harmonious intercourse would resume its own serene progress. But one glimpse of her through that keyhole would shatter the serenity for ever.

So he had returned to his bed without putting his eye to that invitingly opened chink. And he had risen an hour early the following morning, to go down to the Loe and plunge himself into its freezing waters – staying immersed long enough to feel reborn, purified, and fit for every challenge his base nature could throw his way.

It had not helped one bit! What his anatomical eye had so nobly forborne to witness his mental eye furnished in distressing colour and detail. Miss Sweet moved about the house in her sober, almost puritan dress; that shameless inner eye stripped her to her scarlet-laced boots and her broderie frills. Within days he was at his wits' end.

Or rather, to be frank, he was at the keyhole again, having realized that, on the scale of moral turpitude, the real Miss Sweet in all her fleshly nudity enjoyed an artistic licence denied to the scantily clad nakedness of that imaginary Miss Sweet who would otherwise fill the vacuum in his mind's eye. And then a rather extraordinary thing had happened.

After about a week of playing Peeping Tom he discovered that the sight of Miss Sweet in a state of nature no longer roused him to any great degree – no more than the sound of her laughter heard from another room or the touch of her fingers when she tut-tutted over his cravat and straightened it for him before he went out in the morning. The sight of her nakedness was pleasing, of course, but no more so than when she was fully clothed; she was, quite simply, a pleasing woman to behold, no matter what the circumstances. He was so relieved at this discovery that he had to restrain himself from bursting in upon her, crying, 'It's all right, Miss Sweet! Everything's fine! I no longer . . .'

And there the imaginary conversation died in his throat. He no longer what? Felt attracted to her? No, that certainly wasn't true. He was no longer obsessed by her? Even that wasn't true – though it was a start. He was no longer obsessed by her-as-an-object-of-desire, a mere *thing*, to be peeped at lasciviously through chinks in doors.

He realized that, during those six or seven days when he *had* gloated over her, merely as an object of desire, he had only been able to do so at the expense of everything else; he had, perforce, to forget what a wonderful companion she was, how sound her opinions could be, how competent a cook, how capable a housekeeper . . . and all those other qualities that had so enhanced his life at Culdrose since her coming. He had reduced her to a kind of superior marionette, a naked horse on which to hang his own base hungers. What had happened, after a week of this gloating, was that his appreciation of all her other wonderful qualities had finally burst through his shame. That was the good news – but how could he throw wide the door and explain something so complex in one rush of breathless excitement?

But . . . to every reaction an equal and opposite reaction! Behind his euphoria lay an even subtler realization. He could not blink the fact that whenever he took his twice-weekly bath, Miss Sweet made some little occasion to wedge up the inside escutcheon – and deftly removed the evidence later, as she had done that first time. Also, when she took her nightly bath, she did the very same thing. She wedged up the escutcheon so that *he* might watch *her*. So she knew he was out there – or, at least, she had to make that assumption as she soaped and rinsed and towelled her body. And, although she never made the slightest movement that could be called lewd or provocative, she moved with a certain grace and finesse that suggested (to put it no higher) she knew full well his gaze was upon her.

Therefore, to pursue this argument to its distressing conclusion, her character of utter, childlike innocence, which she continued to maintain through all their daily intercourse, was nothing but a charade!

Now indeed he felt he was perched on the edge of a sleeping volcano – one from whose depths came almost imperceptible rumblings, portents of some mighty cataclysm that was yet to engulf them both. And the more 'serene' and 'natural' her behaviour toward him appeared, the more brittle seemed the crust over that heaving, restless core.

'And yet life goes on!' he told himself hopefully. 'Nothing untoward has happened thus far.' But that was no comfort. *Life* furnished a thousand chances for the crust to break and for the lava to come flooding out. He imagined one or other of them falling ill . . .

long, dark hours of anxiety at the bedside . . . slow recovery . . . intimate words, intimate gestures . . . all leading to intimate actions. Or it did not have to be near tragedy; full-blown farce could serve as well. He could lose his balance against the door one night at the keyhole . . . go tumbling head over heels into the kitchen. That would put paid to all pretence! She'd either have to get back on her high horse and behave like a nun thereafter or nail her colours to the mast and sink to the floor, murmuring, 'Maurice, my lover, why did you wait so long?'

These rather childish fantasies revealed one further aspect of the whole affair: Maurice Petifer, the 'master,' was waiting for Miss Sweet, the 'servant,' to act!

He realized it had been so from the very beginning. If she had shown signs of wantonness back in those early weeks, he would most likely have accepted her happily enough in the additional role of mistress. But her cherubic innocence had killed off the very idea – and he had accepted *that* cheerfully enough, too. And even now that it had been revealed as a sham – and even though she knew that he knew all about it – he was still waiting for her to make the first move!

It ran so contrary to all his ideas on the sexes, on the properly unequal roles of men and women in accomplishing their most fraught and difficult union, that it left him feeling stunned. More than stunned: trapped. 'Will you come into my parlour, said the spider to the fly!' Uneasy thoughts of spiders and their mates occurred to him, too. He decided he would have to *do* something soon; but no very clear solution occurred to him.

And meanwhile, life had to go on – even the sham, even the life that might turn to tragedy or farce at any moment and remove the decision from his hands for good. And among the many things that had to go on was the collection of subscriptions to Mrs Scawen's Rescue House.

'I'll go and get Mrs Curnow's if you mind,' Miss Sweet told him when the subject came up one lunchtime toward the end of February. 'I'll go and do it this very afternoon. She's making a collection of Cornish receipts for pasties and cakes and things, and I jotted down a few I know. So I can do that, same time.'

Maurice said he thought that was an excellent idea. His feverish imagination had furnished him with a thousand ways in which the whole delicate web might start to unravel – the web that linked his life to Miss Sweet's and to Laura's and Giles's, and even, in a negative way, to Sibylla Johnson's, too. Even so, the idea that it might begin with the simple act of telephoning a neighbour to ask if it would be convenient to call by with a few cookery receipts would never have crossed his mind.

The children's main path between Chynoweth and Culdrose was now so squelchy with mud that, as with the carriageways of old, it had spawned a number of competing byways, meandering more or less in parallel with it. Miss Sweet made her pick of the best as she wound her way across the fields to visit Laura Curnow. Precisely why she had chosen this particular afternoon to pay her call she could not say – but that applied to most of her actions nowadays, or at least to the things she *chose* to do.

Like letting Maurice (she always called him that to herself) . . . like letting him watch her in the bath, for instance; she didn't really know why she did that. It started as an act of devilry, just for something to do, to chase away the monotony. Then it became a habit. Perhaps if she told herself why she did it, in so many words, she'd see it was so ridiculous she'd laugh herself to shame. So she just went on doing it and never inquiring too deep about why.

She was certain he was out there, watching her most nights, because you could feel things like that, a man's eyes on you like that. You could feel it on your skin, like prickles. She'd expected something to come of it before now. She couldn't say what – her dismissal, a polite ticking off, a hurrisome offer . . . something, anyway. But nothing had.

She used to lob pebbles in a pond when she was a little girl. Once, very early on, she'd killed a fish, a good big one. Pure fluke, of course. Then, in six more years, just chucking a few in every day, passing to and from school, she'd never hit anything. Yet she never gave up. Even now, when she passed that pond, though it was seldom enough these days, she'd still lob in one or two for luck. For luck, see! That was it. You did things for luck, to make ripples where your life got too still. That was reason enough, surely? Things didn't always need to be part of some grand plan where they all fitted together.

She envied people who thought like that – turning everything into one great scheme. Maurice, for instance. He wanted everything to be part of the same plan – his life. The Grand Design, he called it, which he pretended was a joke, but it wasn't. He hated loose ends. That's why she liked him. Not because he was rich and knew a lot (and was also good and kind and et cetera) but because you knew where you were with him. He'd either worry and worry away at things until he made them fit, or he'd drop them altogether. Like his garden. It was all complete in his head before he planted a single shrub; in fact, he *hadn't* planted a single shrub yet – only the trees – but he could tell you where everything went, down to the last little quickset.

She hated people like herself. 'If I had to live with you,' she often said to herself, 'you'd drive me mad.' If *she* ever built a garden, it'd be in a hundred little fits and starts all over the place, and maybe they'd join up and maybe they wouldn't. And this bit would suggest one way to go and that bit another, and sometimes she'd let them fight it out, and others she'd tear it all up and start again. She'd enjoy it while she was doing it but she'd hate the result – because there never would be a result, just a lot of vague hopes and one-fine-days.

That was her and Maurice, all right – vague hopes and one-fine-days! But *he* wouldn't see it like that. The poor man must have sweated blood trying to think *why* she let him watch her through that keyhole! That's why she'd had to make it plain – by using the paper spills – that she was *permitting* him look at her, deliberate-like, no accident. Poor fellow! What *would* he make of it? He'd explain it this way and explain it that way until he'd worked up some great confloption of ideas about her – and no loose ends!

Poor dear cooze!

Would she marry him if he asked? Or be his missy and just sleep in his bed if that was all he wanted? She often wondered. What she'd really like was if some old witch somewhere could let her have a potion to put Maurice in her power for a day or two. Like that mesmerist last Harvest Fair who stitched up George Mollard's lips with cobbler's thread and he never bled nor felt a thing, nor never remembered it after, neither. Then she could try him out, like, and see if he was fitty to her. And then she could pass the fluence over his eyes, and he'd wake up to his old self again and never know what they'd done. But then *she'd* have her answers. She certainly wouldn't marry him – nor any other man, neither – till he'd proved he could fix a babby inside her. It was hard to make high-quarter people see the sense of that, though. Maybe *that* was why she left the keyhole open!

She knew he'd have a fit if he could rest his ear to her scalp and listen to her thoughts like you can to messages on the telegraph poles! He thought she was the crop of the bunch, just because she could housekeep so proud. Little did he know! Housekeeping was work, and everyone was different at work from the way they really were at home. Work gave a body no *choice*. And there's no point having loose ends where you hadn't a choice. That was just slovenly.

Anyway, it would all come out in the wash, as they say. Man proposes, God disposes. In the midst of life we are in death. And – to be practical – how much is Laura Curnow going to give to the lucky unfortunates?

She was near the boundary between the two properties now. The Curnows had got their odd-job-man to construct a simple wooden stile for the children – a hefty oak plank set at right angles through the fence and fixed on two stout uprights. Then, for four feet on either side, the wire fence had been replaced by solid wood siding. That may have been all right for the children, but it forced a lady to lift her skirts up to her knees. (All right for young couranting couples, too!) Miss Sweet hopped up onto the plank and then, before performing this delicate manoeuvre, made a slow, careful scan of the Curnows' garden ahead of her.

Seeing nothing, she started to hitch up the hem of her skirt, but was halted by the crack of a twig underfoot – under someone's or something's foot. One of the children playing a game with her, she decided – at least, that was the most likely. They were always ambushing each other here because the undergrowth was so thick, even in winter. On that chance, anyway, she dropped her hem, set both feet back on the ground, and crouched down behind the siding. A moment later she remembered to snatch off her hat – an absurd concoction of pheasants' feathers she'd found in the attic. She'd only brought it along because Laura Curnow was very clever at that sort of thing and might be able to suggest some way of rescuing it and making it half-way wearable.

'Sibylla? Is that you?' It was a vehement whisper but Miss Sweet was sure the speaker was a man – indeed, she was sure he was Mr Giles Curnow, himself.

'Bloody thorns! Bloody branches . . .' That was certainly Mrs Johnson!

'Ssh!'

'What *is* all this about, Giles?' So there – it was him.'

'Please! Keep your voice down.'

'I thought I saw a movement over there.' She made some small effort to lower her voice. Miss Sweet guessed they were side-by-side now.

'Only a pheasant,' he replied.

'Are you sure?'

'Of course I'm sure. I saw it. D'you want me to go and make it squawk for you or something?'

Miss Sweet's belly turned over; for a lunatic second she wondered if she could do a convincing pheasant squawk now and save him the trouble. Then Mrs Johnson, Lord love her, said, 'No. What's it matter anyway? Why all this secrecy? Why send . . .?'

'We've got to talk, Sibylla.'

'Well, dear boy, if that's all you want, you may come up to Parc-an-Dour and talk your head off.'

'Parc-an-Dour's full of servants. Chynoweth's full of servants. The whole damned world is full of inquisitive eyes and ears. D'you realize that? There's absolutely nowhere we can go this side of Truro where at least one of us wouldn't be recognized. Anyway, come on – we're wasting time.'

'Come on where? I'm not going another step through this bloody jungle. Talk about going off your chump!'

'The children have built a den a little bit farther down. We can go there and talk in safety.'

'Talk! Ho-ho-ho! I know the sort of "conversation" *you're* after. I'm going home.'

'No, please, Sibylla!'

'Giles! If you think I'm going to take my clothes off on a freezing cold afternoon like this, and lie on rotting carpets and upholstery salvaged from the Pengiggan Omnibus . . . then you really are going off your chump. Now let me go!'

'Please, Sibylla? I promise you I mean only talk.'

'I shall start shouting in a moment.'

'Please?'

There was what seemed like an eternity of silence. Miss Sweet hardly dared breathe.

'Talk . . . about what?' Sibylla asked reluctantly.

'Us. The future. Arrangements. I can't forget you, Sibylla. I can't get you out of my mind.'

'For heaven's sake, Giles!' She drew his name out contemptuously – even with a hint of venom.

'Well, I can't,' he asserted miserably.

'Well, you'll just have to, dear boy. We should never have started in the first place – and you may defend him all you want, but I still blame that bloody Maurice Petifer for all this. For everything.'

'Oh yes!' Now he was contemptuous of her. 'The price of kangaroo meat falls in Australia – and, of course, Maurice Petifer's to blame! You're a fine one to talk about me being off *my* chump! Anyway, bugger Maurice Petifer! I didn't come out here to . . .'

'It never should have started – as I was saying. And

we ought to have stopped the minute we came back from London. Let me tell you – I wept tears of pure joy, I went down on my knees and thanked God, the day I moved back into my own home! It was over at last!' A hard edge crept into her voice. 'And it's going to *stay* over, too. You're never going to get me into bed with you again.'

After a pause he said, 'So there's someone else.'

'And if you make the slightest attempt to revive . . . you know what' – her voice grew harder with each word – 'I'll confess the whole thing to Laura and leave you to stew in your own juice. No, she won't stew you – by God, she'd *roast* you alive!'

'There *is* someone else,' he said. Miss Sweet thought she had never heard a voice so bitter. Then he came out with it: 'Daniel Jago!'

Absolute silence! Even the birds in the trees seemed to fall in a hush. Miss Sweet searched frantically, but in vain, for some small chink or knothole in the siding; she was desperate to see the expression on Mrs Johnson's face.

'I thought as much!' he sneered.

She broke her silence at last – in a flat, wan voice: 'So Laura told you after all!'

'Nope!' He was triumphant now. '*You* did.'

She must have looked at him contemptuously for his next words reversed his earlier emphasis: 'You *did!* By your blushes . . . your hesitations . . . your too-too casual references to the fellow. And . . .' But he fell silent at that.

'Well go on!' she challenged.

'It's enough, I think.'

'No – let's have it all. I'm not sure we're ever going to speak to each other again after this, so you'd better get it all off your chest.'

'Very well, if you insist. Your children give you

away, too. Jagos all, to the roots of their hair!'

'And that's it, is it? No more pearls? You're quite finished?' The words were very clipped.

He had clearly not expected her to respond in this icy fashion, for he now tried to soothe and cajole: 'Sibylla! I don't mind . . . honestly. You're the last person in the world I'd . . .'

'Oh, I'm *so* glad you don't mind, Giles,' she went on relentlessly. 'Retrospective approval is better than nothing, I suppose, but it makes me wish I'd sought your consent, *as well as Adam's*, all those years ago.'

Miss Sweet wriggled with an excitement she could barely contain. Mrs Johnson was suddenly promoted to one of her heroines. Say what you mind about high-quarter folk, but they knew some *plenteous* words when their gander was up! Mr Curnow swallowed so you could hear it yards away. 'Oh . . . God!' he moaned.

'Too late!' she sneered.

He gave an ironic little laugh and when he spoke next his tone was much calmer; Miss Sweet, who knew him only by his outward appearance, gained the impression of a man who could master any of his feelings very swiftly. 'It was all so simple – in my own mind – before I sent to ask you to meet me here. Listen, Sibylla, my darling – let me try again. There is no *need* for all this . . . this *feast* of emotions. We're behaving like those absurd Russians in that play we saw. Let's just be ordinary, quiet, decent Britons, coming to sensible arrangements with one another and *not* getting hot under the collar and . . . simply enjoying life and each other's company in our quiet Cornish way.'

To Miss Sweet's surprise, Mrs Johnson said nothing to this; actually, she had to admit it to herself, it didn't sound too bad an idea. And Mr Giles was a proper handsome man . . .

'You are the devil incarnate, Giles Curnow,' Mrs Johnson told him, but Miss Sweet could tell that her mood was now yielding to his.

She felt acutely disappointed. Her newly promoted heroine was behaving like an ordinary woman, doing what Miss Sweet herself would have done in the same shoes. An heroine should never go all flopsy like that but stay true to her ideals and throw herself off a cliff in a flash of lightning in the end, if need be.

'Can we at least talk about it?' he suggested gently.

'Well . . . now I'm here . . . I suppose . . . How far is this den, anyway? I'm freezing to death in this breeze. Why didn't Petifer plant those trees of his five years ago? Useless bloody things!'

'Bloody Petifer again!' he said with a laugh, in which she now joined.

By the tone of their voices they had plainly turned to go. Their conversation continued as they moved onward, down the slope, still sticking to the thickest part of the woodland belt. The last words Miss Sweet heard were from Mrs Johnson: 'But if you have any hope that I'm going to rut away with you under hedges and ditches – or even in children's dens – you may forget it at once.' There was further banter but only its tone carried as far as the stile.

She waited until the behaviour of the birds all around confirmed that they had truly gone; then she rose, stretched her cramped limbs, and climbed awkwardly over the stile to resume her interrupted journey.

'Well, fancy that!' she said aloud, and then put the palm of her hand to her lips and gazed around with her wide, guilty eyes.

No harm done, thank the Lord. But . . . Mr Giles

and Mrs Johnson, eh! What a turn up! Who would have thought it! And Mrs Johnson and that Daniel Jago, too! *And* by her husband's leave! Because he couldn't fix a babby in her himself, no doubt. So there! Didn't that just show the sense of *her* way – fix the babby first, then call the banns. So much to remember! She only hoped she wasn't too mazed to recollect it all.

And poor Laura Curnow, too, and Mrs Johnson her cousin, and them such fast friends! It just showed you couldn't trust anyone. Still, the immediate thing was – it would be best if Laura Curnow never got to find out about it. A thing like that might make her feel a bit more freer, like, in her own mind, concerning Maurice!

And that would be one loose end too many – even for a secret anarchist like Miss Sweet.

Laura saw Miss Sweet strolling across the grass, deep in thought; she herself was already dressed for the outdoors and had only been waiting for this moment. She opened the french windows and stepped out. The woman did not notice her until they almost met, one at each end of the steps between terrace and lawn. 'Stay there,' Laura said. 'I thought we might smell the air, as they say.' She trotted lightly down the broad steps. 'That must have been some rare old conundrum you were pondering.'

Miss Sweet's mouth went dry. 'Oh . . . yes,' she replied vaguely.

'Just down to the Loe and back,' Laura went on. 'D'you mind awfully? I've had this stuffed-up feeling in my head all day.'

'No, of course not.' Miss Sweet brightened. A walk to the Loe wasn't dangerous. They could stroll directly down to the water and back without going nearer than two or three hundred yards to the children's den. 'I could just do with a stretch, myself,' she added as she placed herself on Laura's right, which would force her to turn mainly away from the direction of the den.

'I . . . er, like your hat, Miss Sweet,' Laura said.

'Whoops!' The woman put her hand to it, as if a sudden gust of wind had blown – but the only sudden gust around them was of her laughter. 'I look like some real Betty Toddy! That's one of Mrs Mullard's old lids, that is. It must be fifty years old, I should think. I only brought it to see if you might suggest some way to improve it?'

'I think I'd begin with a box of matches,' Laura warned.

Miss Sweet laughed. 'Well, 'twill serve to keep the cold at bay for now, if nothing else.'

'Although . . . I don't know.' Laura eyed it speculatively.

They had reached the lower end of the lawn, where a short flight of steps led down into the sunken garden, half way to the Loe. The den was in the belt of woodland, some quarter of a mile or so away to their left. If only she could keep this hat conversation going until they reached the wild garden below, Miss Sweet realized, the danger would be past. 'I thought, you see, if I cut the brim back a bit this side . . .' She took it off to show Laura what she meant (and to keep her faced away from the den). 'And put a bit of ribbon binding round it in some handsome colour like, I don't know, yellow or something . . .' She raised her eyebrows hopefully. 'It's a handsome hat, else. I mean, it's well furbished.'

'Well furbished with feathers, certainly!' Laura

commented. 'There's enough to start a taxidermist's here. The Victorians never knew when to stop, did they! If you took them all out except these three biggest . . . what's your sewing like, by the way?'

'I don't rightly know.' Miss Sweet saw with relief that they were now more than half way to the wild garden.

'Did you do the buttonholes on that cape?'

Miss Sweet squinted down at the needlework and allowed, with modest pride, that it was hers.

'Oh, then you'll manage very well. Your idea with the ribbons isn't at all bad. But not yellow – a good, rich gold, I'd say – to go with those three feathers. And try and get it broad, about three inches, and work it into a gorgeous rosette, here, with two long ribbons down the back – with vee-shaped vents at the bottom. Hanging down to here.' Her fingers brushed the lower end of Miss Sweet's shoulder blade. 'It would have a splendid effect.'

Miss Sweet could not help darting a glance toward the woodland that concealed the den. Only a glance, but it induced Laura to look that way, too – and then she was reminded of something. 'Actually, Miss Sweet,' she said, still staring toward the den, 'd'you mind awfully if we make a little detour? Just into the woods over there?' She pointed directly toward the dreaded spot.

Miss Sweet made a few uncertain noises.

'You've heard, I suppose, that the children have constructed a den somewhere in there?'

She admitted she'd heard tell of it.

'I don't suppose you know exactly where it is?' Laura went on. 'What worries me, you see, is I'm sure Henry and Martin sneak away there to smoke cigarettes – and perhaps some of the younger ones, too. I just thought, while there's no one about, I'd go and root around the place. *Would* you mind awfully?'

''Course not, Mrs Curnow,' she replied brightly. 'But I'll tell you what – we're so good as down by the Loe now. We could go along the shore a bit and up that other path. The children made another path up through the trees there.' She smiled hopefully.

Laura fell in with the idea at once, remarking that it would be nice to take a circular walk rather than to go and come by the same path. Miss Sweet was reassured at this, for she had half-suspected that Laura knew something of what might be going on in the den and was playing an elaborate game to get her there as a witness, all 'accidental' like.

Much relieved, she continued their stroll, returning once again to the utterly absorbing topic of how to rescue a hat twice her age – and twice Laura's age, for all they knew. Soon they left the sunken garden behind them and went down by a series of broad stone shelves to the scrubby wetland along the edge of the Loe. There they stood awhile in restful silence, staring across at the farther shore, half a mile away – the renowned Penrose Walks, whose sheer rock walls were crowned with ancient woodlands. Now the scene was all dark and brooding with the watery sun sinking in the sky beyond.

'This side is Cornwall, all right,' Laura commented, 'but that shore always reminds me of some remote upland tarn in Switzerland. Cornwall is full of magical little places like this. We are so lucky.'

Miss Sweet felt some comment was due from her. 'There's scats of flies down here in summer,' she said.

'Yes!' Laura agreed and then burst into laughter. Suddenly she linked arms with Miss Sweet – taking her greatly by surprise – and said, 'You're an absolute tonic, my dear! D'you know that?' She glanced down at their linked arms and asked, 'D'you mind?'

'No,' Miss Sweet replied, and then added, ''Tis a bit of a surprise, like, I suppose. To me.'

'Yes,' Laura said, 'I suppose it is.' But she didn't explain.

They turned and wandered along the shore, taking a gravel path that Giles had created when they first moved into Chynoweth. Each year he sprinkled it with chlorate, which poisoned the path for six months and then, as it leached away into the soil, transformed itself by some chemical magic into fertilizer, promoting a luxuriant growth on either side. The most luxuriant growth of all, in this wet soil, was the salley – a pale, lanky willow that could flourish even when three parts drowned. Now more than ten feet tall, they had been lightly culled to form picturesque clusters on either side of the path, which meandered this way and that under their short, skeletal tunnels.

'I'm always reminded of a military wedding along this path,' Laura mused aloud. 'The way the officers hold up their swords, you know?'

Miss Sweet sang gently: 'Here comes the bride, big, fat, and wide . . .' And then she froze.

From her position she could see farther down the winding path at that particular point than could Laura, but in another few paces her advantage would vanish and Laura would see it, too. And what she would see was Giles Curnow and Sibylla Johnson, standing in a bower of 'officers holding up their swords,' kissing away like bride and groom.

'Ooh!' she screamed at the top of her voice, falling heavily against Laura and almost toppling her – but also pushing her still farther away from the dangerous half of the path. 'My ankle!'

Out of the corner of her eye, even as she stumbled, she had the satisfaction of seeing the guilty pair start up and leap apart.

'Oh, my dear!' Laura gripped her arm tightly, filled with concern.

Miss Sweet gave a gasp or two and hopped on her supposedly good leg, carrying herself a pace or so back along the path – and thus facing Laura away from the scene of the crime. The criminals, she was relieved to see, were running away as fast as Mrs Johnson's skirts allowed. Miss Sweet continued to hop for a little but allowed a smile to stretch her lips, hinting that things might not be as bad as they had first seemed.

Gingerly she placed her foot to the ground, tested it, relaxed, tested it harder, smiled yet more broadly, and then put all her weight upon it. 'Whew!' she fanned her face. 'Only just saved myself,' she exclaimed. 'Thank the Lord you were there to stop me, Mrs Curnow, else I should have glorified meself in mud!'

'We both nearly glorified ourselves in mud, Miss Sweet. Are you sure it's all right now?'

Miss Sweet took a couple of steps along the path, which she now saw was deserted once more. 'Certain sure,' she said, lifting her skirt and flexing the ankle. 'That's good leather,' she said admiringly.

'Scarlet laces!' Laura exclaimed. Then, full of contrition, 'Oh, do forgive me! Such a personal remark! But I was so surprised.' She waved a hand vaguely at the rest of the woman's clothing. 'You always dress so soberly. Well, if you're sure there's no harm done . . . shall we continue?' Not really waiting for a reply, she took Miss Sweet's arm again and resumed their stroll. 'You're a *bundle* of surprises, you know,' she said. 'I only wish I'd been more neighbourly when you first moved into Culdrose. Or became housekeeper, I mean.'

After an awkward pause Miss Sweet said, 'I still don't understand why now, if I may be so bold, Mrs Curnow. I mean, nothing has really changed, has it?'

Laura, who desperately wanted to unburden herself to *someone*, almost yielded to the temptation. But a cooler instinct warned her that too much effusion at this stage would only frighten Miss Sweet off. And the times were too pressing, she felt, to permit mistakes of that kind. 'Nothing really,' she admitted, forcing herself to speak lightly, as if thoughtlessly. 'Except that if one wants to make up for past wrongs, well, there's no time like the present, is there. Tell me – are you happy at Culdrose? Is it an easy house to run? I should have asked you that six months ago.'

'Well . . .' Miss Sweet wasn't quite sure how to reply – whether to play for sympathy or admiration. 'It's a great hake of a place, to be sure. But, on the other hand, bachelor's measure never was high, nor yet farmer's neither. So put the two in one and I don't suppose it's too hard a place to manage.'

'Of course, you're from a farm youself, aren't you. You like the life on the land?'

'I'd sooner be a farmer than a farmer's wife, and that's a fact.'

Laura gave her arm a confidential squeeze. 'And that could happen soon enough, I dare say? There's many a young farmer's mother hereabout must have said to herself that if you can keep a great "hake" of a place like Culdrose up the standards of a gentleman like Mr Petifer, you're worth a line all to yourself in her list.'

'I never thought of that.'

Laura leaned forward and smiled accusingly. 'Truly?'

Miss Sweet shook her head. 'Truly. I should never be such a dawbrain as to let myself fret over things like that. That's how most girls ruin their own lives, or so I believe.'

Laura, who had not taken her eyes off the woman,

shook her head in amazement. 'Well, I never!' she murmured. But she believed her entirely, all the same.

'Mister's different. He can schemey everything out like that. He could schemey his way into the deepest, darkest pit in Cornwall, I always say.'

'To his face?'

'No!' Miss Sweet laughed 'He wouldn't listen to me anyway.'

Laura decided to risk it after all – or a little bit of it, at least. She drew a deep breath and said, 'I suppose you know there are those in the neighbourhood who would almost die of astonishment to hear you saying all this?' she remarked. 'When Lizzie Waring wasn't required to live in at Culdrose, the populace was almost calling the banns for you and Mr Petifer.'

'The same folk as think that piskeys turn the milk all sour,' Miss Sweet remarked indulgently.

'Well . . .' Laura spoke dubiously. 'I have to admit that even I . . .' She laughed to show how absurd she thought it now. Then she said, 'But you honestly mean to say it has never crossed your mind?'

Miss Sweet gave an awkward little sniff. 'High-quarter folk like you don't think the same as low-quarter folk like us.'

'You're not low-quarter folk,' Laura said scornfully – almost as if Miss Sweet were putting on airs.

'Middle-quarter folk, then. I mean you go for betrothals, stuff in the papers, rings, parties . . . all that.'

'Whereas you . . .?' Laura could not see her point at all. 'Surely you get engaged before getting married?'

'Well,' she replied in the most matter-of-fact tone, 'being engaged, like . . . I mean, if *I* was to get engaged, that'd be the time between when I was sure I was quickened with a babby and when I stood before the Lord's table and said, "I do." And that's three weeks with banns or one with special licence. It's hardly worth calling "engaged," see. We call it "spoken for," really. But I don't think I should care too much if I never married. I never knew a happy marriage yet – but *I'm* happy enough single. I know that.'

This abrupt assertion brought Laura up short; she had a fleeting intimation she was not the only one who was trying to probe the other's feelings and attitudes – also that Miss Sweet was getting the better end of the stick so far. She stared in consternation at the ground, wondering what tack to try next; certainly not the question of unhappy marriages!

She stared in even greater consternation at the ground when she realized what her eyes were seeing: footprints!

Footprints that, even as she watched, were slowly filling with an ooze of water!

She darted a glance at Miss Sweet, merely to see if she had noticed it, too – and saw there a look of such emphatic guilt that she let go of her arm at once and, taking a pace or two back, stared at her aghast.

The thoughts flew and multiplied too fast for words; everything was clear in a flash.

She pointed at Miss Sweet's ankle. 'That . . .' She faltered and then pointed vaguely back along the path behind them. 'Back there . . . that was . . .' The accusation petered out as her eyes dropped again to the footprints, now seeking their line. They led along the path toward the boundary with Culdrose.

'I suppose it was Mr Petifer you saw,' she said slowly. 'But who . . .'

'No!' Miss Sweet blurted out – and instantly regretted it. The man could only be either Maurice Petifer or Mr Curnow himself. She should have refused to say anything as to who it had been. Too late now.

'You're very quick to defend him!' Laura challenged. 'And you were quick to see him, too.'

Miss Sweet merely shook her head this time. 'I've got to be getting back,' she said. 'I'll come for the money again, tomorrow.'

Laura's attitude changed completely. Solemnly she took Miss Sweet's arm again and turned them round, facing the way they came. 'It's all right, my dear,' she said in a resigned, almost weary voice. 'In fact, it's not as great a shock to me as you might suppose – except that, no matter how strong one's suspicions may be, it's always a shock to have them confirmed, isn't it. I know very well who you saw, so I won't embarrass you to name them for me. And I think we'll leave them to enjoy' – she hesitated delicately before saying it – '*that* half of the garden.'

'I'm sorry, Mrs Curnow,' Miss Sweet said, almost in tears.

'There, there, dear!' Laura forced a little joviality into her tone. 'One adapts horribly quickly. I suppose ninety-nine hundredths of the process was already done without my knowing it. It's a squalid business and I don't see why you, of all people, should sully yourself in it. You're quite right – there's no such thing as a happy marriage. And you are, indeed, far better off staying single.'

Miss Sweet was quite sure she had never met a nobler woman than Laura Curnow. She suddenly towered over her cousin. Such resignation! Such courage! She was quite obviously heartbroken at what had happened yet here she was, taking it all on herself. She could not possibly let her suffer so much alone. 'He said he loved you, too,' she blurted out, praying to be forgiven the lie.

'What d'you mean?' Laura asked sharply.

'That's what he said,' Miss Sweet repeated lamely.

'When? Good heavens! D'you mean to say you and he have been discussing our marriage?'

'No! That's how I was late, see.' And she went on to explain how she had come to overhear the two lovers near the stile. 'He said he loved you, too,' she added. 'More even than he loves her, Mrs Johnson, but he couldn't forget her, either.'

'And what did *she* say?' Laura challenged, still only half believing the entire story.

Miss Sweet's invention failed her. 'She said she was going to confess it all to you and leave Mr Curnow to stew in his own juice. And then she changed her mind, like, and she said no, you wouldn't exactly *stew* Mr Curnow, you'd *roast* him alive.'

It was so exactly like Sibylla that Laura burst out laughing – and believed Miss Sweet completely now.

Miss Sweet looked at her in amazement and said, 'I'll give you those old kitchen receipts another time, too.'

Laura saw the connection with the mention of stewing and roasting and laughed even louder – until she realized it was becoming hysterical. Then she took a firm grip on herself once more. 'I'm sorry, Miss Sweet, you must think me quite heartless. I don't think it's funny at all – but then it's either laugh or cry, isn't it.'

This time Miss Sweet took her by the arm and once more they resumed their homeward walk. 'What'll you do now?' she asked.

Laura swallowed and said, 'Talk – if you'll listen. Will you?'

'Don't have a lot of choice, do I,' she answered laconically. Then she added an incongruous, 'Gladly.'

'I'll take your word for it,' Laura said drily. 'It's an extraordinary thing, you know, but that little detail you let slip – about Giles telling my cousin he loves me more than her – changes the whole thing. I'm still confused, of course, so don't mind me if I say black one minute and white the next. I'm just talking off the tip of my tongue. Rambling, you could say. But when I saw those footprints back there and then looked at you and saw the horror in your expression – everything sort of fell into place at once. D'you know the picture it made? The picture I saw immediately in my mind?'

Miss Sweet shook her head. It was hard to realize that less than an hour ago she'd set out to collect a subscription and hand over a few kitchen receipts!

'I saw the two of them living up there at Parc-an-Dour. And me on my own here with five children at Chynoweth.'

'That's better than drowning at sea,' Miss Sweet offered hopefully.

Laura laughed again. 'True enough. But, as I *don't* face the immediate prospect of drowning at sea but *do* face that of losing my husband, that is little real comfort.'

'It's only a saying,' Miss Sweet pointed out.

'Ah! That's a different matter, of course. Anyway, as I was trying to explain, your bit of eavesdropping has changed the picture entirely. You did honestly overhear him say that, didn't you? You're not just saying it to comfort me? It's much too serious for that.'

'Cross my heart and hope to die,' Miss Sweet intoned, cutting her throat with the tip of her gloved finger.

'Good. What it means, you see, is that the husband I thought was dying to get away from me has turned into a much commoner creature.'

'What?'

'A husband who wants to keep his cake and eat it.'

'Ah,' Miss Sweet said vaguely, not seeing much practical difference for she wouldn't give tuppence for a husband of either kind. 'Bit like beef and mutton,' she commented.

'*Exactly* like beef and mutton,' Laura said savagely. 'And as an experienced cook yourself, I'm sure you'll also agree with me that it's very important to know which – whether you intend to stew them, or roast them alive!'

Watching her face as she spoke, Miss Sweet thought she'd rather be falling headlong down Cornwall's deepest abandoned mineshaft at that particular moment than be standing on firm ground in Giles Curnow's boots.

They carried the last of the dung out to the fields that day. Maurice finished up early and came in to take his bath ahead of his usual time. 'Don't come too close,' he warned Miss Sweet. 'I really need it today.' She was still in her visiting clothes and had obviously only just arrived back from Chynoweth. 'You were gone some time,' he commented as he slipped the bath in under the tap and turned it on.

Huge gouts of steam enveloped them. 'Oh, that's going to be good!' he said. 'I say – you remember those foaming powders the children gave me after Christmas? Do we have any left?'

She went to the cupboard and brought out the last three, which she offered him for choice: pine, bay rum, and eucalyptus. 'Put them all in,' he said. 'Let there be foam up to the window sills!'

Smiling, she opened all three packets and, holding two in one hand, one in the other, tipped them all in together. A moment later the pair of them felt almost drunk on the mixed aromas.

'Foam to the window sills' was not much of an exaggeration. They watched in amazement as it grew and spilled over the side and lapped across the flagstones, where, however, the sand pricked the bubbles fairly smartly.

'You want for me to return and scrub your back, do you?' she asked casually.

He turned sharply and looked at her; rather more lazily she looked up at him. Their eyes dwelled in each other's for a moment; she did not actually say that it was time to end the keyhole nonsense, but she might just as well have done. 'I'd welcome that very much, Miss Sweet,' he said gravely. 'There's a bit just below here that I can never reach.'

'I know,' she said as she left him.

He diluted the bath with cold and climbed in. She returned without bidding the moment he was seated. But instead of coming directly to him she walked a couple of paces beyond, where she opened the door of the fire and threw something into it. In the last second, before it ignited in a silent flare of yellow, he realized it was a small spill of paper. She closed the door, dusted her hands a time or two, and then advanced upon him with a smile. Her sleeves were already rolled up. Smiling, too, he handed her the sponge. She drew up a little three-legged stool and seated herself just slightly more behind than beside him.

'You were some time over to Chynoweth,' he repeated. 'How much did she cough up?'

She dipped the sponge in the water behind him and, raising it to the level of his neck, squeezed it slowly until it had disgorged every last drop. Liquid fire ran in rivulets down his back; he let out one long, ecstatic moan. 'Ten pound,' she said.

'What?' He forgot his ecstasy and turned – painfully – to stare at her in amazement. 'Ten pounds?'

She nodded demurely and dipped the sponge once more. 'You aren't relaxing,' she chided.

'Sorry.' He made an effort to obey. 'I expected five at the most. Ten pounds – good heavens! They must have done well for themselves this year, the Curnows.'

She squeezed the sponge over his left shoulder blade this time; again he luxuriated in its cascade of rapturous warmth. 'I wouldn't hardly say that,' she replied.

He turned and frowned uncertainly at her. 'What happened, Miss Sweet?' he asked.

She smiled wanly back at him. 'What *didn't* happen, Mister? That's what I should like to know.'

'I suppose you did *see* Mrs . . . oh yes, obviously you must have – for her to give you ten quid.'

'There'll be murders done over there before this night is out.'

'I think you'd better tell me,' he said quietly. Then he grinned. 'But please don't stop with the sponge.'

The bath was barely lukewarm by the time she'd finished, and Maurice's hands were all puckered and wrinkled with the waterlogging. There was also very little foam left – but enough scum by now to preserve modesty between them.

He was still thoughtful after he'd changed up and returned for his supper – a chicken casserole that Mrs Cowles had put in the slow oven just after lunch. 'Perhaps I'd better pop over there and see what's what,' he said. 'After we've supped, of course. Oh, that smells good!'

'Hardly so good as *you!*' she teased. 'Your smell's so sweet as a French lady's boudoir.'

'I wouldn't know,' he said airily. 'I'm happy to inform you I've never been in a French lady's boudoir. I suppose you're popping in and out of them all the time!'

'You've got a proper 'ansum back,' she said. 'I

forgot to tell you that at the time.'

He laughed as he sat down to a full plate. 'Well, Miss Sweet, that puts my face in its proper place, I suppose!' He took an ample mouthful. 'And it tastes even better than it smells.'

She looked confused, sorrowful even, for she had meant her remark as a compliment, not as a joke. He saw her disappointment and softened. 'You've got a lovely nature, and that's far more important. Don't you think I ought to pop over to Chynoweth – see the lie of the land?'

But she saw a chance too good to miss. 'That puts *my* face in its place, too, I suppose!' She pouted.

'You have a lovely face as well as a lovely nature,' he assured her, speaking deliberately as if soothing a petulant child. 'And a lovely back. And a lovely top. And a lovely . . . well, ahem, I don't know about the soles of your feet. So that'll just have to wait.'

'Yes, it will,' she said firmly, trying to suppress a giggle.

'Perhaps you could go up to Parc-an-Dour first?' he suggested, turning serious once more.

'That might be the best way,' she agreed, taking up his mood at last.

He wondered what, of all the nonsense he had spoken, had satisfied her enough to allow her to drop her jokingly aggressive banter. After the tale she had just told him, he felt he now understood Laura and Sibylla to the very last atom; but Miss Sweet had somehow become a deeper enigma than ever. 'What's your opinion of them?' he asked. 'Those two ladies? Forget they're my friends, if you can. Cross your heart and tell me your honest opinion.'

She stared at him uncertainly, biting one edge of her lip.

'Unless you'd rather not,' he allowed. 'May I?' he

picked up a chicken drumstick in his fingers but raised it no more than a provisional quarter of an inch.

'Of course,' she said, picking up her own. 'Eat it fitty-like, 'tis the only way.' She took a bite and chewed thoughtfully. When she had swallowed it, she said, 'That Mrs Johnson, she blames you for everything.' She swallowed heavily again, though this time there was nothing in her mouth; she seemed oddly desperate to say what was on her mind – and yet fearful of it, too.

'Well,' he said reasonably – and to give her time to collect herself, 'she has a point, hasn't she? I presume they lived in perfect harmony until I turned up from the dead last year. And, of course, I simply had to go and buy the property that lay right between Parc-an-Dour and Chynoweth! I'd say she has quite a point.'

'How?' Miss Sweet challenged pugnaciously.

'Obvious,' he said.

'I can't see that. For the life of me, I can't. You bought Culdrose, right? How does that force-put Mrs Johnson to turn all cuddlesome with Mr Curnow? They were neighbours long before . . .'

'Very directly.' He gave her a wan smile. 'I think I know the very morning on which it began. It all started when we were in London after Christmas, you said?'

'That's what it did sound like from what she said.'

Maurice told her then what he had merely glossed over before – his meeting with Laura on her way to Green Park and their spending the day together. 'It was quite innocent on our part,' he concluded. 'But on theirs – I'm not so sure.'

Miss Sweet chewed over another morsel before she said, 'Of course, Mr Curnow never knew it was innocent on your part – unless you went and told him?'

Maurice shook his head. 'We never exchanged a single solitary word on the subject, but I assure you it was innocent, nonetheless. Indeed, if I ever had any romantic feelings left for Laura Curnow, that was the day I lost them for good.'

This information was highly interesting to Miss Sweet. Her eyebrows shot up and she cocked her head on one side. 'How – quarrel with her, did you?'

He shook his head. 'I discovered I could no longer see her as an *object* of romance. D'you know what I mean? Love . . . desire . . . all those powerful feelings – they turn their subjects into objects, don't they. I discovered a new Laura Curnow that day – a complete woman, no longer a simple *object* of my longing. It has happened to me again, since then, too – not with her, of course. I mean, it's not the sort of thing that can happen twice with the same woman. It happened to me with *another* woman. D'you know what I'm referring to?' He turned slowly and stared at the keyhole before looking once more at her.

'No!' she said swiftly, her eyes filling with alarm.

'Well, I'll tell you all about it, one day,' he promised, as if closing the subject.

But she immediately gave away the fact that she understood, or at least had a jolly good inkling as to what he meant, by saying, 'Well – that leaves Mrs Sibylla Johnson, then!'

'Yes, tell me about her,' he urged.

All her earlier reluctance returned, coupled with the urge to speak, to unburden herself, no matter what it cost. 'It's my opinion,' she said slowly, 'that Mrs Sibylla Johnson is the cause of all our woes.'

'Come!' he chided. 'You are much too harsh.'

Miss Sweet closed her eyes and went on. 'Because she loves you, Mister. She loves you so deep, it hurts. And she can't abide it.'

She went on repeating these assertions until it dawned on her that he was not offering her any contradiction. She opened her eyes and looked at him then. He was just sitting there, staring into the wreckage of his casserole. 'My God!' he whispered.

'There!' she said bleakly, more to herself than him.

'How long have you known that?' he asked, still numb with shock.

'From the first day I seen her – I mean *saw* her.' There was a pause before she added, 'And you.'

'Me?' he exclaimed. 'But I can't bear the woman. No, that's not true! But I certainly don't . . . I don't carry her name engraved on my heart – the way you're suggesting.'

'As to that,' she said wearily, 'I couldn't say. It's as hard to tell when a man loves a woman as 'tis easy to tell when he hungers for her.'

'And do I hunger for her?' he asked challengingly.

She shook her head.

'Well, that's a relief, anyway!'

Miss Sweet sniffed coldly. 'You couldn't say as Bombardier *hungered* for that other Sibylla, either. He never knew which cow it was when he could smell her on the air. But she hungered for him, all right. And then he had no choice but to obey.' She stared at him glumly and added the words, 'Poor feller!'

He knew she was no longer talking about old Bombardier.

Miss Sweet stacked the plates in the drying rack and set the cloths to dry before the range. She wrapped up well for the brief walk up the road to Parc-an-Dour. The night was damp rather than cold, but with that maritime sort of wetness which crept into one's bones and felt almost colder than the genuine thing. All the way she worried about Maurice's statement that *he* was responsible for the upheavals of these past six months. It was so clear to her that the worm in the bud was Mrs Johnson, and she racked her brains for ways of making it equally obvious to him.

After she left Culdrose, Maurice rattled round like the only pea in the pod and then, for want of anything better, took up the storm lantern and went out to do a round of the livestock. Wellington's Bombardier IV, who had served three virgin heifers that week, using the new supporting stand, stood complacently in his stall, sniffing fastidiously at his ration of hay. When he saw that the master was intending to stop – instead of giving his usual glance-in-passing – his head went hopefully up and his eye burned a little brighter.

'No such luck, old fellow!' Maurice apologized, reaching in with his stick to scratch the beast across its haunches. 'You like that, too – don't you! Eh? Almost as good? Eh?'

Bombardier surrendered to an orgy of scratching.

'I'll tell you a thing I saw in the Cape once,' Maurice went on. 'A farmer there nailed the head of a yard brush against the wall, just the height of a bull's head. That old boy groomed himself all day there, happy as a sandboy. I'd forgotten that. I think we'll do that for you tomorrow. What d'you say? Would you like that? I think you would.' He sighed. 'And I wish you could do something for me, too. I wish you could tell me if Miss Sweet is right. Is it general with us but particular with them? And can the female who is possessed by the particular need always overpower the male whose needs are merely general? What d'you say to that, eh? It's the central problem of life so don't rush your answers.'

He had stopped his playful scratching. Bombardier gave a low bellow of complaint.

'Who cares?' Maurice said – as if interpreting the cry. 'Perhaps you're right there, boy! That's the central answer of life: Who cares!'

He gave the creature a loving tap or two and wandered off down the side of the court, intending to go through the dutch barn to visit the piggery. Two sows were about due to farrow.

She was facing away from him and standing so still he did not see her until he almost bumped into her. 'Laura?' he said. 'Lord, but you gave me a start! What are you doing out here?' He touched her arm hesitantly. 'And why haven't you put up a coat?'

In a flat, remote voice he would never have recognized, she said, 'Want to buy a good home? Partly wrecked.'

He put down his lantern and stick and, taking off his overcoat, draped it round her shoulders. 'You're frozen,' he said.

She turned and fell into his arms; she was, indeed, like a large block of ice against him.

'Come away indoors,' he urged. 'Come by the fire.' He tried to move aside, to assist her to walk.

'Oh, Maurice, I've ruined everything,' she said.

'Nonsense,' he murmured, hugging her head against his chest. His hand, when it brushed her cheek, came away wet and he realized she must have been weeping for some time. 'What's the matter?' he asked gently. 'What's happened?'

'Can I sleep here tonight?'

After a pause he said solemnly, 'No. You'll have to come up to the house for that.'

She punched him, laughed, and then burst into real tears, floods of tears. He simply stood there, offering what comfort he could, holding her tight in his arms, combing his fingers through her hair . . .

And all the while he tested his earlier boast to Miss

Sweet – and found to his surprise that it was true! Not just mostly true but entirely so. The love he once felt for Laura Nisbet – a love powerful enough to drive him half a world away – had gone. Laura Curnow managed to stir none of it; yet she was a dearer *person* and a warmer friend, perhaps for that very reason.

'Come on,' he urged when the storm had passed. 'Miss Sweet has gone a-visiting. We'll get you looking presentable again before she comes back.'

He almost had to push her the first few paces, but as her joints flexed and the blood began to flow again, she stepped out with some small vigour of her own.

'Is she out collecting more money?' she asked. 'How she works and works! You ought to marry that young woman, Maurice. You're a fool if you don't.'

'Well, I shall have to consult old Bombardier about that,' he replied evenly. They were passing the court as he spoke. 'He understands all that sort of thing far better than I.' Then, in a more serious tone, he said, 'I gather I'm to thank you for making a most generous donation?'

'Did I?' she asked vaguely.

'Ten quid,' he reminded her.

'I don't recall.' Suddenly her whole body went stiff. 'I should have made it ten thousand!' she said savagely. 'That *would* have hurt!'

'We could have started a home for the lunatic rich as well, then,' he remarked lightly.

The tension left her and she burst into laughter, though still not too far from tears. 'Oh Maurice – you are impossible!'

'I hope so, love.'

'You deflate everything.' After a pause she went on, 'I suppose Miss Sweet told you all about our little dramas over there? Are you sure she's not in the house?'

They were approaching the back steps now. He risked telling her: 'She's gone up to Parc-an-Dour to see if Sibylla is still alive. She implied you were intent on cracking a few skulls.'

Laura hesitated, one foot on the bottom step. 'It might have been cheaper at that,' she said grimly.

'What did you do instead?' He maintained a steady pressure on her elbow, edging her up toward the door.

'Smashed everything,' she replied, almost gaily, as she tripped up the steps and let herself in.

'Except skulls?' He twitched his coat from her as she continued up the passage toward the kitchen door.

'Oh Maurice, what a haven this is!' She paused in the doorway, staring in at the kitchen, luxuriating in its warmth. The soft lamplight, bright after their walk through the dark, laid its golden radiance on her and, just for a moment, an earlier Maurice Petifer, still dying somewhere deep within him, sighed his heart toward her. 'I can just imagine you coming home to this each evening,' she added. 'Kings are not so lucky.'

He hung up his coat and ushered her inside to his chair by the range. 'Shall I heat up some milk?' he asked. 'Would you like something a little stronger in it? Miss Sweet has been brewing some mead but I don't think it's ready yet.'

'What an extraordinary young woman she is!'

'Yes, don't say it again, Laura. I've run out of jokes and might have to start taking you seriously.'

'I do mean it seriously, my dear.' She reached her hands gratefully toward the fire.

It would be the answer to all your problems! he thought. He almost said it aloud, too. Who ever imagined it was men who ran the world!

Miss Sweet herself returned at that moment, bustling in by the back door and crying, 'Oh, thank the Lord you're here, Mister!' even before she saw him.

'Why?' he asked, going to help her out of her overcoat.

'Well, when I saw your lantern and stick just lying on the ground by the dutch barn . . .'

'That was my fault, Miss Sweet,' Laura called from the kitchen.

Miss Sweet's eyebrows shot up as she turned to Maurice. He conveyed by a shrug that he knew very little and said, 'I found Mrs Curnow standing out there – where you saw the lantern. She was very cold.'

She stared at him a further second or two, not, he realized, in hope of gaining further information but to prepare all the required emotions – sympathy, concern, affectionate curiosity . . . the whole arsenal. 'She wants to stay the night,' he added.

Miss Sweet's expression hardened and she shook her head vigorously, but then the smiles returned and the melting light in the eyes – and into the kitchen she sailed. 'My dear Mrs Curnow! You must have caught your death out there on a night like this! And *he's* sat you before a fire that wouldn't warm a dorymouse!' She seized up the poker and riddled the coals to a furious radiance. 'Men! And he hasn't offered you a sup to drink, either, I'll warrant. I've a bit of mead put by that's just about ready. Would you care for a sup of that?'

Laura smiled at her and said, 'The honeymoon ale. That's why they call it *honey*moon, you know.' She smiled teasingly at Maurice. 'Why didn't you tell me you had some mead in the house?'

Miss Sweet misinterpreted the smile and changed her mind at once. 'Perhaps it isn't quite ready yet awhile,' she said. 'But you can have a drop of hot milk and whisky. That's even better now I think of it – oh, I'm all of a dalver, still! If Mister could just make himself useful and fetch the whisky from the parlour?' She smiled a thin smile at Maurice, who escaped gratefully to do as he was bid.

He was just relocking the tantalus when Miss Sweet came bustling in, closing the door behind her. 'I haven't got but two seconds,' she said urgently. 'I told her I forgot I had the key. Now listen! Mrs Johnson has gone! Nobody knows where, though they say she must be bound for Falmouth and you-know-who! Chynoweth looks like a storm passed through it – which I suppose it did. Mister Giles has gone looking for her. Come-us on now, we must get back to the kitchen.'

They returned just in time for her to snatch the saucepan of milk off the top of the stove, which was now cherry-red. Laura, sunk in some half-smiling reverie, had not even noticed.

'I reckon that's warm enough now,' Miss Sweet commented. 'Mister could just squeeze in there and shut down the fire a bit?' She poured out half a mug of scalding milk, added some cold, and topped it off with a good slug of whisky. 'You want a bit, do you, Mister?' she asked.

'Just the hot milk, thanks,' he said. Then, turning to Laura, 'They say Sibylla has vanished off the face of the earth.'

Laura laughed unkindly. 'Too much to hope for. No, she's gone to her *other* paramour, down Falmouth.'

'And Giles has gone after her?'

She shook her head. 'I don't think Giles knows about Daniel Jago.'

Maurice and Miss Sweet exchanged puzzled glances at this. Surely Laura couldn't have forgotten what she'd been told that very afternoon? Miss Sweet drew breath to remind her but Maurice silenced her with a tense shake of his head. It was all done inside a couple of seconds. Laura was still speaking: 'I mean, he can't have known Jago as a direct rival. He surely couldn't have taken up with her if he had.' She frowned at Maurice and added, 'Could he?'

She was asking him as a man. What she really wanted to know was whether *men* could do such a thing. How could he deny it? 'The general versus the particular,' he murmured.

She frowned as if the words rang a distant bell somewhere in her mind; then she gave up the search for a connection. 'Perhaps he did know about old Jago. It's grown into such a web of deceit and secrets, I no longer remember who knows what about who.' She raised both hands to her forehead. 'I no longer even know . . . my own . . . I mean, what I . . .' She stared in consternation at Miss Sweet. 'Did we walk down by the Loe this afternoon?'

'Here, wrap your hands about that, Mrs Curnow, and take a good sip.' Miss Sweet placed the glass between Laura's two hands. 'This afternoon it was,' she added as an afterthought.

'And was it only this afternoon?' Mechanically she took a sip, and then woke up as the spirit warmed her palate. 'Giles thinks she's gone to the Troys.'

Miss Sweet glanced anxiously at Maurice. 'Maybe *you'd* best go over Falmouth, then,' she suggested. 'She's taken her car, we know that much. She could be anywhere by now – lying in a ditch or anything.'

Maurice realized her chief purpose was to get him out of the house, away from Laura Curnow while she was in this unpredictable mood. She wanted to work on poor Laura, restore some of her backbone, and send her off home before he returned from his – probably fruitless – search. 'Falmouth it is,' he said.

He stooped and gave Laura a brief kiss on the cheek. 'Don't worry,' he murmured. 'I just know Sibylla won't have come to any harm. I think the worst is over.'

'You haven't seen Chynoweth!' she exclaimed. Then, more gently, 'Thank you . . . for everything. You know.'

'I know.'

Miss Sweet followed him out to help him into his motoring outfit. 'She'll be gone when you get back,' she said.

'I realize that.'

'And you can give me a kiss on the cheek, too, if you're still dishing them out.'

He obeyed but at the last moment she turned her mouth to intercept his. Their kiss was no more than a brush of lips on lips. She pushed him away fussily, as if he had pressed an unwelcome attention on her, and made several unnecessary adjustments to his lapels and epaulettes and cap as he backed smiling out of the door.

The smile lingered as he crossed the yard toward the garage door; his mind was already leaping ahead along the Falmouth road – Tresilian, Manhay, Laity Moor, Halfway House . . .

Then the smile vanished, his pace faltered, his blood froze. A vast hollow opened up in his stomach as he realized that, of course, Sibylla had *not* gone to Falmouth at all! Everyone would follow her there; she knew that very well. So she'd go in precisely the opposite direction . . .

And Maurice alone knew where.

There was just the smallest chance that Sibylla had, after all, gone to the Troys. It would be absurd, Maurice realized, for him to drive like the furies for twenty-two miles when twenty of them might be taking him steadily away from her. So, as Liston House lay on his best route through Helston, he decided to cry-in in the passing. Sergeant Drew, lurking in the shadows outside the gents' WC at the top of Church Street, hoping to entrap some of the town's budding Oscar Wildes, thought he had a little bonus for his notebook when he heard the automobile approach and saw no flag-bearing flunkey ahead of it. But when he recognized Maurice Petifer's Mercedes, he recalled his wife's cold shoulder and tucked the book away. Then, making a virtue of necessity, he gave Maurice a smart salute as he passed by. Maurice was merely amazed to see that the rest of the world was going about its usual business all around him, quite mindless of the dramas taking place in the town that evening.

The carriage drive at Liston House was deserted, so Giles was either parked round the back or had already come and gone. Too late he saw the Lanchester drawn up in the shadows beyond a rather straggly rhododendron. Giles came out beneath the front portico at that moment, dressed to go. Maurice braked and throttled down to idle. 'Is she here?' he asked.

'I should have shot you that night and have done with it,' Giles snarled at him as he strode on by, making for his car. 'There's not a jury in England would have hanged me for it.'

Maurice looked at Jimmy Troy, who had come out beneath the portico, too. Jimmy merely shrugged a kind of apology.

'I take it Sibylla isn't here?' Maurice asked.

'We haven't seen her at all,' he confirmed.

Maurice, seeing that Giles had pushed his car out onto the drive ahead and was now trying to start it, began to reverse. Jimmy ran after him. 'We're both so very sorry all this has happened,' he told Maurice.

'It had to be,' Maurice replied. 'It'll settle down now.'

Only when he was halfway along Cross Street, heading for St John's, did the oddity of Troy's remark strike him. The words had been ambiguous, denoting either sympathy or guilt; but the tone of voice – now that Maurice heard it re-echoing in his mind's ear – had been unequivocally of guilt. But why should the Troys feel guilty? It seemed to be everyone's first thought tonight: *This is all my fault!* Even Giles Curnow's taunt had hinted at a *kind* of guilt, macabre though it was in the form he had given it.

Perhaps they were right, too – all of them: It was nobody's fault – and everybody's.

The car laboured all the way down into bottom gear going up Sithney Common Hill. He wondered if he had enough petrol; it was too dark to see out onto the running board, where the spare tins were normally strapped. When he reached the summit and could afford to take his foot off the accelerator, he tried to feel for them with his toe, but ended up almost in the ditch.

He switched off and coasted on the long downhill run past Antron to Stop Gate – now a mere name for a place where there had once been a real gate and a real toll keeper. When he let in the clutch, the engine only just managed to restart; the damp night air must have affected the electrical wiring. He could not afford to coast again. The problem over his fuel reserves nagged him afresh up the next long hill into Breage, where he turned off the main Penzance road to call at the forge beside the church; the blacksmith there had lately started selling tins of petrol.

Fortunately the man was still at work, shoeing a percheron. By the light of the forge Maurice saw that the Mercedes had, in fact, two spare tins already strapped to the running board – and he knew his tanks were pretty nearly full. He was about to press on, with no more than a wave to the smith, when it occurred to him that Sibylla might not have the same degree of reserves, so he stopped after all.

The last horseshoe was just coming up to red hot. The farmer, pumping away at the bellows, gave the hearth a few extra-vigorous puffs to hasten the work along. The sparks were like a fireworks display in miniature but Maurice almost had a fit when he realized they were expiring among the petrol tins, which were stacked not six feet from the roaring flames.

'D'you always keep those tins there?' he asked the smith.

The man looked to see what he was talking about, then laughed and said at least they'd never freeze.

Maurice, who had intended waiting patiently, could bear it no more. He served himself with a couple of tins and left a florin on the anvil, though the price was only tenpence a tin. 'Have two quarts of beer on me, lads,' he said.

The two of them thanked him effusively and said he was a toff. 'Not at all,' he replied. 'They may be your last.'

Out on the open road again, up the shallow slope past Penhale to Ashton Toll Gate (another relic of a vanished age), he reflected that, but for his fear of death-by-inferno, he would now, in all probability, be standing in that forge, holding the horse's head, talking sweet nothings into its ear or discussing the price of turnips and the prospects of a break in the weather – trying to pretend that this was one day like any other.

And he would have done so, not to deceive *them*, not to make it seem to the world that nothing at all was amiss, but to hide from himself – to avoid facing the awkward question that even now he was struggling not to pose. But at that hurdle his defences fell and he confronted the awkwardness head-on: Why was he following Sibylla at all? What had her guilt and her distress to do with him? And behind all that was the memory of what had happened last time he had taken it upon himself to come to her aid unasked!

If everybody was now going to claim the ultimate responsibility for this state of affairs – even Jimmy Troy, for heaven's sake! – then, really, no one was to blame, at least not in an individual sense. So the answers to his questions were not to be found by pursuing the question of blame.

He had an uncomfortable memory – a little flash or hint of a memory – of Miss Sweet's ridiculous assertion that Sibylla loved him. He pushed it away so quickly that the implacable little censor who sat in his skull (and who cared nothing for the comfort and well-being of Maurice Petifer) knew at once that the answer lay there. Or thither. Like a silver minnow in a murky pond, it darted from him, glinting and invisible by turns, while the censor goaded him to follow. Thither. The half-glimpsed landscapes of Germoe Cross and Falmouth Packet and Rosudgeon coalesced in his now fevered mind with that abstract hunt for purpose in this whole madcap venture.

It did not matter whether the assertion itself were true or false, he realized when he had run it down at last. The very possibility that Sibylla *might* love him was sufficient in itself; indeed, that possibility was the only justification for following her like this. For if the

Recording Angel could drop into the passenger seat at that moment and prove to him – forward, back, and sideways – that Sibylla did, indeed, love him (or that she most assuredly did not), it would transform the entire nature of his journey. He would at once become a mere neighbour on an errand of mercy – to a badly deluded woman, in one case, or to a woman in the throes of some unknown distress, in the other.

But take away either of those happy certainties, and there rose up before him a spectre of an entirely different kind, dark enough to obliterate any plea that he was merely playing the Good Neighbour. It was the spectre of unfinished business. If she loved him now, if her well-bannered hatred for him down the years had been nothing but a mask for her inability to cope with that love, then a contract existed between them. And – in some obscure way he could never even begin to understand – it must be honoured tonight.

He came out of his trance half-way up Market Jew Street, Penzance – having no memory whatever of having passed through Marazion, or Long Rock, or any of the hamlets in between. The same happy uncertainty did not apply to the way ahead; he knew to the last inch of the final yard where this journey had to end.

He found her Opel abandoned, one wheel in the ditch, a quarter of a mile beyond the First and Last, which, being a mere half mile from Land's End, prided itself on being the last public house in the land – or the first, if, improbably, you had just landed from America. He took out his pocket knife and cut a withy from the hedge. He trimmed it clean, dipped the tank – and found it empty.

He switched off his own car and unstrapped three of his spare petrol tins. The filler was awkwardly placed and he had to roll up his road map of Cornwall to make a funnel. Then he hunted for her starting handle. The engine would probably be too damp to start but at least he could put it in reverse and wind it back onto the highway. The handle, however, was nowhere to be found. He had a brief picture of her starting the car and then hurling the thing aside. It seemed all too probable. He tried his own starting handle, but it seemed that Mercedes and Opel spoke different languages.

In the end he pulled her out with a towing rope. He lighted two small paraffin lanterns he kept for such emergencies as this, one of which he placed behind his car, the other before hers. His last act was to spread an old horse rug over his own engine to keep it warm and ward off the damp. Then he set off for Land's End, or, rather, along the path to Sennen Cove, making for a small hollow in the cliffs about a quarter of a mile northeast of that most westerly headland.

The moon dipped out from behind a cloud the moment he left the highway, almost as if it had been waiting its cue. Dry, sedgy grass and thick tufts of sea pink, some of them yards across, turned to silver underfoot. One kind of visual magic – murky, subdued, and dimly glimpsed – yielded to another in which everything was either silver or black. Silver billows pranced inshore over water that was black and quiet as velvet. Silver clouds drifted southwest behind him, leaving the sky ahead as black as midnight.

He glanced at his watch, now silver gilt in the black shadow of his hand. It was no more than nine o'clock, though he had expected to find it well past eleven.

What did it matter, anyway? On this night of his life, if on no other, time must be stretched to fit the event.

Rabbits by the thousand scutted away before him and crept back to forage behind, frightening none but each other with their panicky stamping. Among them the sheep grazed placidly on. If he were right about Sibylla, she had come this way more than fifteen minutes ago.

He called her name, loud and clear – loud enough to startle the sheep at last – as he drew near the little hollow above the cove. Nothing moved but the sheep and the rabbits; several fields inland a screech owl cried, imposing a brief hush of dread upon its world.

'Sibylla?' he called out again as he approached the two sentinel chimneys of rock between whose shafts the footpath led.

Again she made no response; he did not doubt for a moment she was there, though – nor that she could hear his call.

As the path led through the giant outcrops it descended sharply over two natural steps and then skirted in a wide semicircle to the right, around a steep, grassy slope – at the foot of which an unguarded eighty-foot cliff fell sheer to the boulders and the sea below. Sibylla hit him with the rock the moment his head appeared in the gap.

His legs buckled beneath him and he fell without a sound to the first step, rolled onto the second, and, having nothing to stop him, continued to roll on down the grassy slope to the edge of the cliff.

'No!' Sibylla screamed and, hurling the rock from her, stumbled and rolled and lurched after him and, by grabbing at his overcoat, finally stopped him a mere yard from disaster. 'Maurice? I'm sorry!' she shouted. 'I'm sorry! . . . Maurice?'

He was terrifyingly still.

She clung to his coat, panting with more than mere breathlessness. 'Maurice?' she tried again.

Still there was silence.

Changing her grip to the other hand she squirmed awkwardly around in the forlorn hope of discovering someone or something to help. She stared hardest at the two tall stones, sentinels of this deserted killing ground, almost as if she expected to see herself – her self of two minutes ago – standing there still; if she had, she would have shouted, 'This is all *your* fault!'

'How near am I to the edge?' Maurice's voice, amazingly calm and clear, came out of the dark behind her.

In her excitement she almost let go of him as she wriggled back round to face him again.

'Am I as near as it looks?' he continued.

'Yes. Maurice – I'm sorry . . .'

'Shut up!' he said. 'Just listen. I'm going to try and roll myself back uphill. I'm not even sure it's possible – it's not a thing I've practised much lately, I'm afraid . . .'

'Oh Maurice!' She began to laugh quietly, but hysterically, crying at the same time.

'What I want to try and do is move my head uphill by more than my feet move downhill. D'you follow? Are you even listening?'

'Yes!' she assured him, taking a grip on herself and changing hands once again.

'I'll need your help,' he went on. 'Can you edge down just a little bit further and grab hold of my collar? Or my scarf? Or anything you like up this end? Or, rather *down* this end, the way I'm presently situated.'

She did as he asked though she almost fainted from her terror; she was a good three feet farther away from that fatal drop than he, but she could see, superimposed on the distant waves – the *vertically* distant waves – individual blades of grass she could have touched. That's all there was between them and a plunge to certain death.

He made his first move, catching her unawares – so that the grip of her arm actually prevented his head from moving uphill. His feet, however, made a very successful move toward the cliff edge.

'Sorry! Sorry!' she shrieked.

His almost supernaturally quiet voice again had a calming effect: 'I think there must be a small stream somewhere near my knees. It is very wet and slippery there. Can you pull? Just keep pulling steadily.'

This time he warned her of his move, and this time he managed it. His feet moved nine inches nearer the cliff edge but his head was twelve inches farther away.

'Don't relax,' he warned as he moved again.

And once again he won more ground than he lost.

'One more and I think I'll be able to do it by ordinary wriggling – which is child's play for us snakes in the grass, as you know.'

'Maurice!' she shouted into his face. 'How can you possibly make jokes about it?'

'Come on!' he urged.

Together they made one supreme, exhausting effort – and he at last achieved a position that offered him some small hope of getting out of this nightmare unaided, for he was now so close to Sibylla that she had little leverage left.

'You can swing round where you are now,' he told her. 'And crawl away a bit.'

'I'm not going to let go of you,' she said at once.

'You're going to have to, old girl. You're in my way.'

'But you could slip back down again. Where are your feet? Are they on the grass still?'

'They're all right. If you don't move out of my way . . .'

'They're not on the grass, are they! They're over the edge of the cliff. Oh my God – this is all my fault!'

'Sibylla! I'm just about sick of people telling me that this evening. Now just get out of my way, will you?'

She did not move. Their eyes were only inches apart, upside-down to each other.

'If you don't . . .' he threatened.

'What?' she asked scornfully.

'Look, I'll prove I can move on my own. Just relax a little.'

The moment she obeyed he edged himself upward until his eyes were level with her lips. Then he kissed her on the tip of her nose.

Her lips shouted, 'Stop that!' into his eyes.

Without a word he edged himself up another few inches – far enough to kiss her upside-down lips.

'Mnmh . . . mnmh!' she protested in disgust.

Then her chin.

'This is going to get better and better, Sibylla!' he warned. 'My feet are on solid ground now.'

'All right! All right!' she shouted into his neck. 'You've proved your point. I'll move. You're an impossible bloody man!'

He rested flat on the sloping grass while she struggled round and, with a movement that would have been graceful enough in water but which was merely comic at that angle on grass, skeetered herself up ahead of him to safety; he was reminded of some silver-coloured pupating grub trying to wriggle out of its cocoon.

Rather than suffer the same indignity in her eyes he took the riskier course of rising on elbows and knees and crawling up the first few feet – then he risked using fingertips and feet – and finally he rose to his feet alone, giving just the occasional prod of one hand or the other to keep his balance forward.

When he gained the path he saw she was back where she had hit him, sitting on the top step beside the uphill sentinel. As he strolled toward her he favoured the spot behind his ear where the stone had caught him. Considering the strength of the blow it was remarkably free of cuts or abrasions; indeed, it was hardly even tender. He decided it was probably his fall on the stone steps and the confusion of rolling over and over in the sodden grass that had left him so winded and confused. He was almost certain he had not actually lost consciousness. But by harry, it had been a close-run thing!

'Want to try it again?' he asked. 'Try and do better? We can call that a practice one if you like.'

She burst into tears.

He dropped awkwardly to his knees at her side and put his arms around her at the shoulders. 'Sibylla,' he murmured. 'If we make the same mistake all over again, it'll haunt us for *another* sixteen years!'

She stopped sobbing but continued to cry gently as she looked up at him and asked what he meant.

'You know what I mean. If we'd been able to laugh at ourselves last time, everything would have been different. Perhaps we could have tried again and . . .'

'You humiliated me.' Her grief turned swiftly back to anger at the memory of that day.

'I know I did. I can't tell you how many times I've taken back that moment – in my imagination – and played it differently.'

'You ruined my life for two years. Two years when you're eighteen is a lot longer . . .'

'What about that, then?' He waved a hand toward the cliff edge. 'You almost ruined mine for good.'

Still she did not laugh, or even smile. 'What you said

that day was absolutely unforgivable.'

'I know. I know. How many ways can I say sorry? Young people blurt out such things. Young, inexperienced, immature people don't know better. Is there never to be a moratorium?'

'Propelling pencil!' she spat at him.

He winced and let go of her, flopping exhausted in the grass at her side. Then, from the depths of his exhaustion, he chuckled. 'It's that silver tongue of mine, you see. I'll never learn. I had it even then. It gets me into endless trouble.'

'Oh . . . you!' she flew at him in a fury, hurling herself on top of him and lashing out with her fists.

After a brief, unequal struggle, he held her in a bear hug, still on top of him but with her arms pinned uselessly to her sides. She tried to pinch him but too many layers of clothing intervened. She collapsed then and, for all of two seconds, remained absolutely still, not even breathing. Then she turned and kissed him on the neck. 'It's not true, anyway,' she whispered seductively.

He cleared his throat and said airily, 'I suppose I'll have to take your word for that.'

She put out the tip of her tongue and touched the lobe of his ear. 'You don't *have* to,' she pointed out.

Some thirty minutes later, both rather stunned at the way things had turned out, they sat in the private bar at the First and Last, sponged clean of the worst of the mud. They huddled over the fire and steeled themselves for the return journey with the help of a hot rum toddy. 'Do we announce our engagement at once?' he asked. 'While everyone is still reeling from the shock. Or wait a while? Or . . .' Other possibilities escaped him.

She sipped her toddy and, staring into the flames, murmured, 'Engagement? What engagement?'

'Well . . .' He gave a baffled laugh and moved a hand vaguely in the direction of the cliffs. 'I thought . . . after all that . . .'

'D'you *want* to marry me?' she asked curiously.

He hesitated. 'I do if you do,' he allowed.

'D'you love me?'

'I could in time . . . in rather a short time, I feel.' He laughed with much of his earlier spirit. 'I mean, just *look* at the progress we've made today!'

But she was not to be cajoled out of her curiosity. '*Why* would you consider marrying me?' she insisted.

'I feel I sort of owe it to you.'

'Duty, in other words!'

'Words of your choice, not mine.'

'Either way, it's a very priggish sentiment. And the last thing anyone on earth would call you is a prig.' Her eyes narrowed and she peered at him even more closely. 'What's your real game, Maurice Petifer?'

He stirred uneasily. 'Nothing. I don't have a "real game".'

'Oh yes you do. I'm tempted to say yes, go on, announce our engagement tonight – the moment we get back. Because I'm sure you'd never go through with it – the actual marriage, I mean.'

'I wouldn't go back on my word,' he assured her.

'No, that's the one thing that's holding me back – the thought that you might just be foolish enough to try to live by that principle. But you're not running to me with this absurd offer of marriage, you're running *from* . . . something.'

'What?'

'I don't know – but I think *you* do.'

He felt a sudden eagerness to change the subject. 'Do *you* love *me*, Sibylla?' he asked.

Her expression remained impassive.

'At least you don't explode at the very suggestion,'

he observed. 'Why don't you answer?'

'Because you didn't really answer *me* when I asked the same . . .'

'I did.'

She shook her head. 'That's what you're running from.'

He laughed scornfully. 'By offering you marriage, I suppose! I don't understand. You're saying – or hinting – that I love you but can't admit it. I'm running away from it. And my *method* of running away is to offer to marry you! Is that a fair summary?' He banged his fist against his forehead suddenly. 'God, listen to me! Are we in a court of law?'

'Not yet!'

He looked sharply at her and saw her smile at last, though feebly. 'You think it would come to that?'

'As night follows day.'

'Why?'

'Because I know myself too well, my darling. I cannot bear the shackles of love. I never could. Back in your courting days I used to despise Laura for loving you so much. I felt *so-o-o* superior, ha ha! That day I took you from her, on that walk along the cliffs to Sennen Cove, and seduced you . . .'

He gulped. '*You* seduced *me?*'

'You wouldn't have got below my collarbones if I hadn't intended it.'

'But why?'

'To show my contempt for Laura. To hurt her in a way no one was ever going to hurt me. And then, halfway through, I suddenly realized it wasn't true. I, too, was in love with you.' She gave a brief, despairing laugh. 'I loved you with all the passion I so despised in my dear little cousin . . .'

'But she's older than you,' he objected.

She snorted contemptuously. '*I* never thought so!'

'And is that why you . . .' He hesitated.

She supplied the word. 'Froze? Became a frigid woman? Not big enough for a propelling pencil? Yes. And that's why I always will be frigid with any man I love – truly love – as desperately as I discovered I loved you that day.'

'And ever since.'

'And on occasions since. I loathe its bondage far more profoundly than I enjoy the thought of surrendering to it. *I will not be possessed!*'

'Except by loathing.'

She shrugged.

'You were hardly frigid out there just now,' he taunted shyly.

She smiled with warmth at last and raised a hand to cup her ear. 'Do I hear the distant tinkle of a penny dropping somewhere?'

He considered the question and then nodded. 'And that's your last word? Regardless of whether or not I love you?'

'But you don't.'

'How d'you know?'

The smile was unwavering. 'Put your hand on your heart, look me straight in the eye, and swear to me you do.'

When he did not answer, she reached out and gave his arm a squeeze. 'Go on! Or don't you know what it is to be in love? Why don't you throw yourself on my mercy? Why aren't you pleading with me? Promising me anything? Putting your heart in my hands? Why don't you make yourself as vulnerable to me as you've never been vulnerable before – never, never, never, ever? Why this strange silence, Maurice?'

He drew the deep breath her mocking outburst had postponed, and let it out in one long sigh.

'See what I mean?' she taunted.

'I don't see anything any more. I'm just a simple farmer.'

A softer light stole into her eyes and her smile became genuinely warm. 'Hold fast to that,' she advised.

He drew out his watch – no longer silver-gilt but gold once more. 'We'd better be heading back. I'll have to tow you all the way if she won't start.' He remained seated, however.

An instinct warned her they could not part on this note of high honesty; it was too naked, too brutal. Now she must muffle it, cloak it in some more conventional sentiment. Not necessarily a lie but – if a truth – a rather shallow, comforting one. 'Why *did* you offer to marry me?' she asked. 'Did you imagine that was the only way you could go on having me? Surely you know I'm a very easy woman to have!' Her lip trembled and her voice cracked. 'I thought everyone in the world knew that by now.'

He leaned forward and kissed her on the lips. 'Don't,' he begged.

She put her head beside his and flung her one free arm around him, holding him there. 'Oh, Maurice, what am I going to do?'

'Marry Daniel Jago,' he said.

She pulled away and stared at him in surprise; that was one bit of advice she had certainly not expected. 'Honestly?'

'Why not?'

'You don't think people would laugh at me?'

He put the tip of his nose gently to hers and rubbed it. 'I shall, of course – I promise. But all *sensible* people will applaud you.'

She kissed him one last time then, tenderly and without passion.

On their way back to try and start her car she said,

'I'm glad you withdrew your offer, Maurice, because – let me freely admit it now – it's the most tempting one I've ever had. Lately, anyway. You're a very nice man. But we'd never do as husband and wife – we'd kill each other within a year.'

'One way or another,' he agreed. Then he laughed. 'Come to think of it – we had some jolly fine practice at both ways tonight!'

Laura did not leave Culdrose until she was quite certain that her portrayal of a severely disoriented woman (and the onetime love of 'Mister's' life) had alarmed Miss Sweet enough to make her stop her drifting and start treating life with some purpose. It had been a long, tiring day – with so much that could have gone quite horribly wrong – and it was not yet over. Indeed, the hardest part was probably yet to come.

Although it was bright moonlight she decided not to return by the familiar path, trodden by the children across the fields and over the stile; it held too many resonances for her now. Instead she went the longer way round, by the road – which was how she happened to see Giles returning home – or his car, anyway. As she came out of Culdrose and onto the highway, she saw its lights coming up Meneage Street and then cutting a quick lighthouse-swathe across the landscape as it swung in at Chynoweth gates.

He had come *up* Meneage Street, from the centre of Helston – which was annoying because it allowed her to draw no hard and fast conclusions. He had almost certainly gone over to Falmouth; at least, he had certainly been away from Chynoweth too long to have spent all evening with the Troys, and he could have searched every street in town, twice and on foot, in that length of time. So – assume he had gone over to Falmouth.

But had he found Sibylla there? That was also impossible for Laura to tell. She could not even say whether, having found her there, he had brought her back or left her with her *other* . . . what was the male equivalent of a mistress? Sleeping partner? She shuddered at her cousin's duplicity – but shied away from the fact that her own earlier approval of Sibylla's adultery (when it had concerned only Adam, to be sure) had not left her much moral ground to stand on.

She shook her head angrily and told herself to stick to the point – which was: Had Giles found her and brought her back to Helston?

If he had, there was one certainty in the whole affair: He would *not* have brought her back to Chynoweth! Laura's little tantrum earlier in the evening would have made copper-bottom sure of that. He had also not brought her back to Parc-an-Dour, or he would have approached Chynoweth's gates from the direction of Clodgey Lane. But he could have left her to spend the night at the Troys', perhaps?

Unlikely.

They were all a bit weary of the Troys since Christmas – weary of being no more than sport to them. They hadn't fallen out, of course, but they didn't share quite so many of their trials and tribulations as formerly they had. It was therefore equally unlikely that Giles would have called on them merely to say he'd found Sibylla at Daniel Jago's and all was well; he'd leave that sort of news until morning.

So it was beginning to look most likely that he'd drawn a blank in Falmouth and had gone back to Liston House to see if she had turned up there during his absence; she might simply have driven around in circles until her terror of Laura wore off.

In short, Sibylla wasn't at home, she wasn't in Falmouth, and she probably wasn't with the Troys. Where had she vanished to, then? What was more – where had Maurice gone in search of her? Also to Falmouth? There was nowhere else, surely. Or, if there was, he of all people would be least likely to know it. They were hardly even on screaming terms these days.

Worry began to gnaw at her and when she reached Chynoweth gates she paused, knowing she really ought to turn back and see whether or not Sibylla had sneaked home without any of them realizing it. They needn't meet. In fact, Sibylla needn't even know she was there. She could just peep into the garage and see if the Opel was back. The dog might bark a little but it knew her and would stop when she got near; the household would assume it was a fox or something.

She had retraced her steps no more than a quarter of a mile when she heard two cars coming down Clodgey Lane, and saw two pairs of headlights startling the rooks from the trees. A moment later one of them turned in at Parc-an-Dour, accompanied by the unmistakable *parp!* of the Mercedes hooter – and then came the equally unmistakable whine of the Mercedes itself, continuing its journey to Culdrose. She waited until the motor died to silence before she resumed her walk. As she turned in at her own front gate the clock on the workhouse tower chimed half-past eleven.

It was still only Thursday! What a momentous day it had been – and it was not over yet!

As she stepped out down the drive, now being sure that Giles had not brought Sibylla home with him as part of some lunatic act of defiance, she realized that one set of uncertainties had been replaced by another.

Where on earth had Maurice tracked Sibylla down? How had he persuaded her not only to come home but to allow him to escort her? And that cheery toot on his hooter . . . it had been like shouting, 'See you soon!' over three parishes. No remotely plausible resolution of these conundrums occurred to her. Tomorrow looked as if it was going to be *another* exciting day!

When she drew near the house she heard the sound of hammering. She guessed what it was, of course, but she had to walk round onto the lower lawn to make sure. Giles had flattened some old tea chests and was tacking them to cover the broken glass in the french windows.

What a futile exercise! He could simply lock the inner door. There was nothing left in the room worth stealing.

She stood there in the dark awhile, watching him – until it dawned on her that he was not trying to secure the house at all. He was merely killing time, waiting for her to return. If she had stayed the night at Culdrose, as she had pretended she wanted to do, he would be cleaning up all night.

What with the slogans on the sides of the tea chests, he looked so like a piece of merchandise that she found herself considering him in that impersonal light. Was he the sort of thing she'd buy and take home? Slightly shop-soiled but still in good working order. Only one left.

Well, that was true, all right! She felt a sudden flaring of anger that they would never again be able to share that absolute trust and assurance they had known until . . . she was going to say, 'until he started cheating with Sibylla,' but she realized, of course, that it went back quite a few months before that!

If *absolute* trust between them had died, it was when Maurice Petifer returned from the Cape. Even worse, that death had more to do with the equivocations of her own heart than with anything Maurice had done. Or anything Giles had done at *that* time. She groped around for her anger but found it had gone.

She became aware that Giles had stopped hammering. Indeed, he had stopped moving altogether. She grew alarmed. From the way he was standing, clutching his waistcoat like that, she thought he might be having an attack. She was just about to burst in upon him when she saw that in his other hand he was holding their wedding photo. Not the big one, of course – no one would ever hold that again! This was the one in the little silver frame, which had simply bounced off into the general rubble when she toppled the china cabinet.

He was staring at it and weeping.

Suddenly she began weeping, too.

She wasn't going to let him see her like that – not for a while yet, anyway – so she waited until he slipped the frame into his inside pocket and then tiptoed off the terrace and went round to let herself in by the front door.

As she passed through the hall she looked up, by habit, toward the door that led to the nursery and the children's rooms. A movement on the half-way landing caught her attention. 'Which one of you is that?' she said into the shadows.

She put a foot on the lowest step to show she was serious. A moment later Blanche emerged into the light. 'What a mess the sitting room is in,' she said.

'Why aren't you in bed, little lady?'

'I was.'

'And why aren't you asleep?'

'I was that, too. What happened?'

'A storm, dear. It doesn't matter – it's over now.

We'll clear it up in the morning. D'you want to come and give me a hug?'

Blanche almost fell down the steps in her eagerness. In her hand she clutched the most malevolent-looking rag doll Laura had ever seen. He had one right eye, one left ear, and one arm and one leg, equally balanced – or unbalanced, depending on how you looked at it. To make matters worse, it appeared that the creature had actually been made with these mutilations from the very beginning. Blanche held him out to receive Mummy's first hug.

Laura tried not to flinch. 'I don't think we've been introduced, darling,' she said.

'He's from *my* Rescue House for cripples,' Blanche told her. 'I'm going to collect subscriptions for them like Miss Sweet.'

Miss Sweet had obviously told the children a white lie or two about the Rescue House, bless her.

'Oh, well that's all right, dear.' Laura found it quite easy to give the thing a hug in those circumstances. 'And now you.'

She scooped the little girl up in her arms and carried her toward the drawing room door, where, all this while, she had heard Giles picking up debris and dropping it into undamaged tea chests. It seemed important that his first sight of her should be with one of their children in her arm.

He had his back to the door, and a particularly heavy decanting of broken glass masked the sound of its opening. He did not turn round until Blanche exclaimed, 'What a storm!'

'Oh,' he said. 'Hallo.' His face was a mask.

'No, don't put your feet down, dear,' Laura said to the squirming Blanche. 'You'll get cut by the glass. I'll put you back on the stairs.'

She turned and carried her back to the foot of the

stairs. 'D'you mind if I don't come up and tuck you in, darling? It's not fair to leave Daddy to pick up all the pieces by himself.'

'Why can't the maids do it?'

'Because, darling, these particular pieces we have to pick up. No one else can do it.'

From immediately behind her Giles added, 'But we will do it, darling – no matter how long it takes.'

Blanche, sensing a rare chance to get away with murder, said, 'Can I take Peebee up to bed with me?'

Laura looked at the disgusting doll and said, 'Of course you can, dear. Run along now and leave Daddy and me to . . .' She turned and smiled at Giles. ' . . . pick up the pieces.'

He held out his hand and led her back into the wreckage of the drawing room. There he shut the door and took her in his arms.

They were so lost in that dear embrace they did not hear the incredulous Blanche dash (admittedly barefoot) through the kitchen and out across the yard to the stables. There she picked up P.B. and told him the amazing, marvellous, unbelievable news.

Maurice completed his round of the livestock before he went up to the house. The moment he opened the back door, he heard the familiar sound of swilling water and knew Miss Sweet was taking her nightly bath. Quietly he eased off his boots and, wriggling his feet into his slippers, started tiptoeing up the passage toward the stairs. He was too exhausted to face her tonight. He was too exhausted even to stoop for a token moment of keyhole-homage to her outward beauty; he just blew her a kiss through two inches of oak as he stole quietly by.

He was too exhausted to see that she had put his stool ready for him tonight – indeed, had done so the moment she saw him coming up from the cowshouse, not two minutes ago. If leaving the escutcheon trigged up wasn't enough, and burning the spill in front of his eyes wasn't enough, and scrubbing his back wasn't enough, he could hardly ignore the stool.

He didn't. He fell headlong over it – fortunately without doing either himself or the stool any permanent damage. He sat in the strewn sand, rubbing his arm and groaning.

'Mister?' she called out.

'No!' he shouted back. 'He's gone up the wooden hill. There's no one here but us mice.'

'I'll give you mice!' she laughed. 'Come in here and scrub my back. I want for you to tell me everything.'

He sank his head between his knees and groaned.

'Mister?' Her tone was more peremptory now.

'Coming,' he sighed as he picked himself up and dusted the worst of the sand from his clothes. 'Is the door locked?' he asked as he paused before it.

'Just laugh at the locksmith if it is!' she called out.

He opened the door, closed it behind him, and, being too shy to look at her immediately, kept his gaze averted as he pulled up a chair and placed it slightly behind her, at one side of the bath. When he did at last look, he found her lying full length in soapy water, no better than translucent, and with only the occasional random bubble clinging haphazardly to her fingers or the side of the bath. She was grinning like a gamine. Shimmering just below the surface he could glimpse her breasts, her nipples, her navel, and the dark delta beneath it.

'But there's no foam!' he blurted out in horror.

'Nor there isn't,' she said darkly. '*Someone* went and used it all up. And I just wonder why! You haven't rolled up your sleeves.'

While he was complying she sat up suddenly – so suddenly that when he turned to look at her she was bent forward over her knees, showing him nothing but her long, slender back and the pinned-up glory of her hair.

'Shall I let in a little more hot?' he asked.

'In a minute. My back's getting cold.'

He picked up the sponge and squeezed it out over her spine as she had done to him earlier – it seemed impossible that had been a mere six hours ago. She gasped and squirmed, which he found arousing. He filled the sponge again, squeezed again, filled again, squeezed again . . . as fast as he could, to keep up the momentum and to hear the sounds of her pleasure.

Then suddenly his mood changed and he stopped.

She was about to turn round and complain when she felt him pick up the soap. He worked up a good lather on his hand and began to massage it into her skin; but before she could surrender to this new pleasure he said, 'This is all wrong, Miss Sweet.'

'It takes two to make a wrong of this kind, Mister,' she replied. 'And I don't feel it so.'

'No. I mean there are things I ought to tell you *before* anything like this takes place between us. For instance, I think I ought to tell you I've been in love with you – without exactly knowing it – for quite some time.'

She swallowed heavily. 'How could a body not know a thing like that?' she asked.

'All right, I *did* know it, but I didn't want to admit it because . . . I don't know. It would have changed too many things between us – good things. Things I really appreciated and enjoyed.' He laughed awkwardly. 'D'you realize we've done everything in exactly the wrong order – exactly the reverse order from normal? For six months we've lived like Darby and Joan – sitting together each evening, me with my book, you with your sewing, happy as two old turtle doves. Well, we're not supposed to do that for another forty years!'

She raised her head and looked at him slyly under her arm. 'At least we'll know what to do when we get there!'

'But the problem, you see, is *now*,' he told her. 'I don't rightly know what to do now.'

She lay back full length in the bath again, not hugging the bottom so much this time – more floating on the surface, a soft, voluptuous, floating flower of a woman. 'Gusson!' she said scornfully. 'You surely don't expect me to believe *that!*'

THE END